A Million Regrets

By Lori Meis

Here's to good books! from [drawing] Loved meeting you both!

To my mom
and all of my friends
who took the time to read and reread this
manuscript

This book would not be possible without your
support.

My sincere gratitude goes out to
Judy Beal
Donna Davis
Debbie Spence
Deb Nikkel
Deanne Martin
Julie Schomacker

KENNEDY ANDREWS, 50, died Monday, June 9, 2014, as the result of an automobile accident. She was born February 29, 1964, at Hill Town, Kansas, the daughter of Judith and Harland Andrews. She was a 1982 graduate of Hill Town High School and studied journalism at Kansas State University where she graduated with honors. She later earned a Master's degree in economics and accounting from the University of Texas. She was a financial consultant for Carey, Wiley & Associates, Valley View. Kennedy is survived by her fiancé, Greg Parker of Valley View; her brother, Lane of Wellsville, Maine; and several nieces and nephews.

Brenda

Dropping the mail on the coffee table had become an all too familiar habit. Lately nothing good ever came out of the mailbox – bill, bill, bill, junk mail, bill, bill, overdue bill, junk mail. The stack was piling up at an alarming rate. Tomorrow, she told herself, tomorrow I will sort through the stack and deal with it one item at a time. So far tomorrow never came.

Her work came in spurts. However, the bills still came every month – the rent, of course, the car payment, water, electricity, and that awful credit card. Blah, blah, blah. Brenda dropped into her comfort zone, her favorite overstuffed chair, and clicked on the television. As she mindlessly scanned the channels she tried to remember if there was ever a time when there was more money coming in than going out.

Back in college things had seemed easy. Student loans covered the basics, a part-time job at the student union covered the extras. At the time money seemed tight but there was always enough to go around. Maybe she should have stayed in college a bit longer. A degree – a degree in anything might be nice, not to mention helpful in finding gainful employment. But at the time, traveling across the country with friends and singing for her supper in local coffee houses held more appeal than 7 a.m. classes and biology tests.

Now, almost 30 years later, those friends had scattered. Most were married, many had children and all those promises to keep in touch and had dissipated. She wound up back in her home town of Rossford, in suburban Toledo, working for slightly over minimum wage at a discount retail outlet. No complaints about the job really. It was simple work and populated by many people she knew and loved to visit with. The money wasn't great but her needs were minimal. A bed, a shower and some sort of transportation. She filled her free time by checking out mountains of books from the local library and working the daily crossword puzzle in the newspaper someone always left behind at the local diner.

Gone were the regrets about not looking harder for love. Gone were the regrets about the children and pets she had hoped would fill her two-story picket-fence-lined home on the east coast waterfront. There was more to life than a soulmate and a houseful of snot-nosed rebellious kids, she rationalized. On the flip side, financial security would have been a definite plus to the whole lifetime commitment scene.

Brenda let her eyelids close as she slipped into a fantasy of wealth, fame and blissful happiness. The TV droned on while she drifted off to sleep. It must have been hours that seemed like only minutes when she awoke to an obnoxious banging on her front door.

"Brenda!" a kid's voice yelled through the open screen in the front door. "We got your mail again. Grams sent me over."

Shaking off the dizziness that swirled from the abrupt interruption to sleep, Brenda hopped up and met the young child at the door. Teddy and his sister Jane lived in the other side of her duplex with their grandma. Pleasant kids, but someone else's kids. She loved them like family, but from a distance. Children, she had discovered, were usually a pain in the behind.

"Thanks, Teddy," she managed to say as she took the stack of letters from the small child's hand and tossed him one of thw Tootsie rolls she kept in the candy dish by the door. The top envelope on the stack was that crazy credit card bill whose balance never seemed to get lower. Of course that is what happens when you make a $50 payment and then charge $100 at the market. Oh well. She added the half a dozen envelopes to the coffee table, not taking even a second to notice what other "goodies" the mailman had delivered to apartment B rather than her apartment A.

'Tomorrow,' she thought and she moped into the kitchen to scrounge up a sandwich. Who knew how long it would be until she found the bright spot in the amassing pile of depressing mail. It was a letter, or rather an invitation, from an old college friend, Kennedy Andrews. An invitation that would be life changing. Too bad it would have to wait until tomorrow. Whenever tomorrow came.

Sitting in the drive-through line at Spindelli's, Brenda contemplated her order. Cheesy corn? Or just an iced tea – with lemon and extra ice? Maybe both. It was, after all, pay day and who couldn't use a refreshing iced tea indulgence? It was only a few bucks. And besides, the extra job she had picked up to put a little away for a vacation hadn't made it into savings yet. Why not? She placed her order and pulled forward to wait.

Checking the clock on the dashboard she noted it had just been about two minutes. Quite reasonable. The order taker was pleasant and appeared to be accurate as she repeated her order through the adequate speaker system. So far Spindelli's was doing well.

Scanning the newspaper one day she had noticed a tiny advertisement at the bottom of the obituary section. "Make money while you wait!" the ad said. "Become a secret shopper. Earn coupons, food and money doing what you always do and going where you already go!" A web site was printed in red ink under the supersized and italicized word "MONEY." She could take or leave the coupons and free food would obviously save her money, but the word MONEY resonated through her mind. She had books to return to the library anyway so she made a mental note to at least explore the web site when she was at the library.

As it turned out, the premise was quite simple. Local businesses paid an outside resource a small bit of money each month to be represented by a secret shopper warehouse of sorts. The web site in turn advertised for individuals to visit these places to observe and note the service and efficiency of the business. The "shoppers" simply filled out a survey after the visit and submitted it on-line. Within a few days the secret shopper was sent a nominal payment.

Usually the payment was a free entrée at the establishment or a 20% discount on your next visit. But some of the surveys were worth money - $5 or $10 in most cases. And all you had to do was visit the business and fill out a five- to ten-question survey about their service and quality of their goods. Easy!

Searching through the on-line list of options she was pleased to see Spindelli's on the list. The web site promised a $5 pay out for visiting the fast-food chain and giving her opinion.

At last she approached the window, counted and handed the money to the window attendant. Without making eye contact the attendant intercepted the bills and asked her if she wanted any sauce. Sauce? I got cheesy corn and an iced tea. Hmmm...duly noted. Moments later Brenda reached through her car window and took the sack, setting it on the front seat before turning to reach for her tea. This time the window attendant did make a small attempt at eye contact but continued to talk through her headset to a customer several cars back while she handed the tea and a straw across the threshold. 'This is not turning out so well for Spindelli's,' Brenda thought briefly. Was the service always like this? She hadn't noticed before.

Finally with her order in tact she reached forward to set the tea in the cup holder. As she pulled away from the drive-through window, she discovered two seconds too late that the lid was not secure and bathed herself in an icy cold tea disaster.

Hmmmpf! She would get the last laugh, though, when she filled out her survey. No concept that barbecue sauce was not needed with corn. No communication with the customer. Loose lid. This would be the easiest $5 she had ever made. So she got a little damp. She would dry. Good thing she only spent $6.29!!!

Back home, relaxed and with a full tummy, Brenda decided this was the night to tackle the mail. Carting the kitchen trash can into the living room she began to sort. Anything slick and shiny was easy – automatically deemed spam and tossed. That narrowed things down. Maybe she could do the rest later. No. It couldn't be delayed any more. Fifteen minutes and a dull headache later she had narrowed the pile into two stacks – things that needed to be paid today and things that could wait until next week.

She made a mental note to dust off her bicycle in an effort to save a little gas money, turn off the air conditioner at night and open the windows to save on the utility bill and cut up the charge card first thing in the morning.

Feeling slightly more resolved after having mastered the stash of unopened correspondence, although realizing she was no closer to having any bills paid, Brenda stood to return the kitchen trash can to its rightful place. That's when she saw it. A slightly oversized cream-colored linen envelope addressed to her in perfect penmanship. There was no return address. What in the world? The postmark was May 2nd. Last week.

Slowly she turned the envelope over in her hands. Probably a graduation announcement. Another one. She started to throw it in the trash. After all, there was no extra money for graduation gifts right now. Still, something pushed her curiosity forward and she reached for her letter opener and broke the seal.

It was indeed an invitation. But not for a graduation. A wedding. Kennedy Andrews. One of her college friends from so many years ago. The invitation still carried her maiden name. Could she still be single at 50? Of course, she could. After all she herself had never married.

The delicate scripted ink gave the specifics. Kennedy Andrews and her fiancée Greg Parker, requested her presence at their wedding ceremony at 2 p.m. Saturday, June 14, 2014, at the Valley View Country Club in Kansas. Kansas? Kennedy had migrated back to Kansas? Brenda was sure she remembered her old friend had big dreams of being a national television news anchor. She chuckled out loud as she realized there were television news broadcasts every day in Kansas. She had really thought her freshman in college roommate would be living among the bright lights of New York City or Los Angeles. Certainly not Kansas.

There was more. A handwritten note was included between the see through slips of tissue that often accompany a formal invitation. The note was brief but personal, hoping she would be able to make the trip, so much to catch up on, regrets for not keeping in touch. There was to be a gathering for old dear friends the day before the wedding. There were directions for the restaurant where the reunion would be held.

Also included among the wrappings were two first-class airline tickets to Mid-Continent Airport in Wichita. Unbelievable.

Of course, there was no way Brenda could go. She would never get caught up on her bills if she took four or five days off work. She could not afford the hotel for one thing. And there would be other hidden expenses – taxis, eating out. Still. Kennedy had sent two airline tickets. And first class! That had not been cheap. And she would love to see her friend. It had been so long and Brenda had no excuse for not staying in touch all those years.

She dropped the envelope and its contents in the stack to be dealt with next week. She would think of some plausible excuse not to go. Somehow she would find a way to politely decline the generous invitation.

With a heavy heart she headed off to her bedroom dropping the kitchen trash can off on the way. Tumbling onto her bed and settling herself onto a stack of pillows, Brenda picked up the John Grisham book she had been trying to finish all week. She soon became absorbed in the words – her go-to strategy for dealing with stressful situations.

Jack

"Deuce!" Again.

Ben had lost track. Was this the eighth time the score had been tied? Or the ninth? The scorching heat was draining his brain. But it didn't matter — one tie or 100 — he had to close this match with two consecutive points sooner than later. He needed water.

From high in the stands, Jack watched with labored intensity. He always told his kids it wasn't about winning, but about how you play the game. He supposed somewhere deep down he still believed that. Surely he did. But with the match on the line and his son behind the service line, he was rethinking the value of winning. Come on, Ben. Nail this guy! You're better than him.

After a disappointing double fault, followed by seven grueling rallies, Ben at last walked off the court a victor and doused himself with his water bottle.

Filled with pride, Jack stood and made his way through the crowd to the sideline. Ben was just a freshman but had taken to tennis at a young age and now at 15 was a fierce competitor for his team at Sunny Springs High School. At this point in the season, just two matches from state play-offs, he was undefeated in #1 singles. Not bad for a freshman.

Not that long ago Jack had wondered if Ben would ever enjoy sports. As a five-year-old he had loathed soccer. His family watched with horror when he ran the other direction each time the ball came within 10 feet of his expensive new tennis shoes. A few years later he showed more interest in the nachos at the concession stand than his responsibilities as a right fielder. While watching major league baseball on TV with Jack, Ben had always wanted to be the "squatter" and throw hand signals back and forth with the pitcher. However, in real life the ball traveled a little too fast from the pitcher's hand to make that as enjoyable as it looked from the comfort of the sofa.

And then there was swimming. Not a bad sport as long as your head didn't have to go under water. Basketball? Not tall enough. Football? No thanks.

Ben did have a strong affinity for dodge ball, though. Plus he was good. And without a single lesson he was a natural at golf. But in the tiny northern Nebraska town of Sunny Springs, dodge ball and golf didn't make the cut of competitive high school sports. And so tennis it was. And Ben was the master.

Picking up the twins after school was one of Jack's favorite things to do. Both girls had made the adjustment from elementary school to middle school with amazing simplicity. God couldn't have crafted his precious girls with more contrast in both their appearances and personalities and yet they both had a love for learning. He had heard from other parents this was not a blessing to be taken lightly. He was lucky they took school seriously since not all kids did.

As he sat in the rusty but trusty old pickup truck that had once belonged to his father, Jack again marveled at the diversity between his girls. He spotted Beatrice – or Bea as everyone called her – immediately as she bounded out the double doors of the building. She sported her pink backpack on one shoulder and carried a few school books in her arms. Her straight blond ponytail bounced along behind her as she and a cluster of friends gathered near the table and chairs on the school's grassy front lawn. A quick glance toward Jack's once-red truck, told Bea that Betsy wasn't out of the building yet. That bought her some time to socialize.

Early on in their seventh grade year the girls had explained to their dad over dinner that it was no longer cool for a parent to hover on the grounds and "act like a parent." Whatever that meant. Bea, being the more social of the two, had gone into great detail about the depth of her love for him but explicitly pointed out that she wasn't in grade school anymore. She and Betsy were, after all, just inches away from being teenagers. Just about a month away in fact.

Jack listened with the patience of Job not reminding Bea that he was already halfway through Ben's teenage years and his job as a mailman in their small town had brought him into contact with hundreds of other teenagers over the years. He was well aware of the transition period in a child's life when the child/parent relationship shifted from bosom buddies to an odd anomaly where parents suddenly know nothing about anything and are relegated to a mere taxi

service. Sometimes an unappreciated taxi
service at that.

And so they came to an agreement.
Unless he had to step in to keep them safe,
Jack would stay on the periphery, provide
chauffer services when necessary and reserve
hugs, kisses and prolonged conversations
with his teenagers to a time when their
friends were not present. Although Bea and
Betsy thought this was their idea, Jack had
to smile internally knowing this is how it
should be.

No matter how hard it is to watch your
babies grow up, it is necessary to give them
wings. After all, what if they all wanted to
live at home until they were 50? No, no, no.
He looked forward to the time when Ben would
carve the Thanksgiving turkey at his own
house and clean up the mess after he left to
go home. And wouldn't it be great to show up
at Bea's house and find the Christmas tree
already decorated and the stockings already
dangling from the mantle? Ever since she was
a tot Betsy had said she wanted to have a
dozen kids of her own. Someday he imagined
those grandkids would be mowing his lawn and
taking his trash to the curb. He knew beyond
a shadow of a doubt if we waited long enough
this middle years transition would pass and
dad would be cool once again.

Speaking of Betsy, where was she? He
spotted Bea again out of the corner of his
eye. She had migrated across the school yard
with another group of friends and was
laughing heartily with a group of other boys
and girls. The clock on the dashboard said
school had been out for almost 15 minutes.
He started to reach for the truck's door

handle to check with the office when he noticed a young adult, too young it seemed to be a teacher, approach the truck.

"Excuse me," she said. "Are you Mr. Redman?"

"Yes, I am," Jack said cautiously.

"I am Miss Evans, Betsy's art teacher."

"It's nice to meet you, Miss Evans," Jack said with sincerity. "Betsy speaks of you often."

"Really?" the young woman replied. "We teachers often get the impression the children forget our names when that last bell rings at the end of the day."

A smile followed her comment. It was warm and her sentiment genuine, but Jack couldn't help worry if something was wrong. Plus with her close proximity at the window he suddenly felt the garlic in his sandwich from lunch was sending danger signals. Where was that mint they always give you at Sonic? You never ate it at the time but could never find it when you needed it.

"Is something wrong, Miss Evans?" he asked, retreating a smidgeon. "Is Betsy in some sort of trouble?"

"Oh no. On the contrary, Mr. Redman. Betsy will be right out. She wanted to finish her portrait project and she is up in the room putting away her supplies. Time got away from us. I told her I would let you know she was running late. Plus I wanted to let you know she has an incredible talent for art - especially drawing. You must surely know that already."

"Yes," Jack said. "She loves to draw. The refrigerator has been filled with her work since she was old enough to hold a crayon."

"Then you must know her work is exceptional. Few seventh graders are this dedicated to the specifics and proportions of creating a portrait. I wanted to show you this myself because she has told me it will hold significance for you. I was afraid it would get wrinkled in her backpack before you saw it. She really has a talent, Mr. Redman."

"Thank you. And it's Jack. You can call me Jack."

The teacher's smile deepened and she reached through the open truck window and handed him a paper. Noticing it had been torn from a spiral sketch book, the pencil drawing looked like it had been drawn by a high school student. It was the face and shoulders of a woman. Jack's jaw dropped wide open. It was an almost perfect replica of his mother – Betsy's beloved grandmother who had taught her appreciation for art.

Blinking to regain his composure, Jack glanced back at the art teacher. But she was already moving back toward the building.

"Have a good evening, Jack. Betsy will be right down." And she was gone from sight.

Still awed by the artwork in his hands, Jack quickly scanned the open space between the truck and the building looking for Bea. Both girls knew there was an unwritten rule about him picking them up from school. The first one out was free to visit with friends until her sister came out. They were to keep a watchful eye on the old truck and once one girl reached the vehicle the other had about 30 seconds to hop in also. Most days it worked with military precision. He knew Betsy would be out soon but where was Bea? The normally welcoming grassy school yard was almost always filled with small groups of chattering children. But now it was 100% empty. Not one student anywhere. He choked back panic.

Now Jack did reach through the dilapidated truck's window to unlatch the driver's side door from the outside. Within seconds he had bolted to the front of the building. Had she stepped inside? Through the plate glass windows he could see she was not there. Like a cheetah he sprinted around the side of the four-story brick building.

Relief washed over him like a tidal wave the second he saw her. Standing there talking to a lone child – a boy. Squinting into the sun with her books and backpack at her feet she was listening intently to every word the boy was saying. Who knows WHAT he was saying. At this point Jack didn't care. She was safe.

No words were exchanged between father and daughter, but Bea knew none were necessary. The look on her dad's face said so many things. For starters it said "Where have you been?" followed by "Get your behind in the truck."

As the three of them piled in Jack let out a sigh of contentment. Being a parent was one of the hardest things on earth. Being a single dad with full custody of three teenagers was one step short of impossible. But, as he reminded himself many many times, there was not enough money in the world to convince him to give it up. He was born to be a father and he relished every minute of it – the good, the bad and the ugly.

The brief drive home across town was soothing. Betsy had popped in a Tanya Tucker CD and the country singer's Lizzie and the Rainman lyrics spilled out the open windows.

In the otherwise solitude of the drive Jack wondered what would be the one thing Bea found to be her passion. Ben had tennis. Betsy had art. What did Bea have? Boys? Let's hope it is not that for several years. Like 20. She played volleyball, made the basketball team, enjoyed school in general and had a bevy of friends. However, Jack saw her real talent as singing. She was magic at remembering the lyrics to any song she heard and made the rest of the family jealous with her ability to match perfect pitch. But despite much prompting, taking a vocal music course never made her radar screen.

Oh well. Someday she would find her niche he knew. She *is* only 12 he remembered as he rolled into the driveway of his rural Nebraska home and cut the ignition.

Ben was already home when Jack and the girls traipsed through the door. Jack's hope that Ben had started dinner were dashed when they found him draped loosely in the recliner attached to his phone like a lifeline.

The familiar aromas of pork chops or chicken thighs searing on the grill were noticeably absent. Salad greens and the homegrown tomatoes still on the counter from last night's harvest had not magically sliced and diced themselves into a bowl either.

It wasn't entirely Ben's fault. After all, teenagers were predestined to ignore household chores and thrive on the latest technology while procrastinating research papers and Algebra homework, right? Right. Well so it seemed. And he did have a busy schedule, that kid. Forgivable. Tousling his hair as he made his way into the kitchen, Jack issued his first warning of the evening to Ben about homework.

"I am going to want to see that math stuff before dinner, OK?"

A barely audible grunt was the returned response.

The girls had disappeared into their room – no doubt to check their e-mail – and Jack sighed as he slipped out of his shoes and started the salad. Grabbing the knife and cutting board he noticed the small stack of mail on the counter. Bonus! So Ben had at least brought in the mail.

Mail was kind of a funny thing in the Redman household. As a letter carrier, Jack's family was quick to point out how he could go almost a week without checking his own mailbox. And he never had a stamp when he needed one. When his parents were alive his excuse for never getting birthday cards there on time was he didn't have a stamp. Ironic he realized, but did doctors mill their own medication at home? Did ministers recite Bible verses 24 hours a day? Did Rachel Ray come home and fix dinner after work? OK, maybe Rachel did.

Thumbing through the stack he discovered something unusual – a cream-colored envelope with beautiful scripted handwriting caught his attention. A thank you note? No, he hadn't specifically given anything to be thanked for lately. An invitation? Maybe. Not so carefully he released the contents from the envelope and examined what he found.

It appeared an old high school friend, Kennedy Andrews, was getting married. They had once sung in a competition choir together. High school. That had been many years and several addresses ago. How in the world did she find him?

Jack remembered Kennedy well. She was a personality plus, always quick with a joke, a pun and a healthy dose of sarcasm. She was several years older than he and had always treated him as her little brother. Choir practices were filled with spunk and positive energy when she was there. After she moved on and went to college it was never quite the same. Although they shared a love for music, they also shared a love for life and seeking the positive no matter the situation.

He wondered what had become of her over the years. She had dreamed of making it big as a writer. Wanted to see the ocean, travel the world. But the wedding was in Kansas. Not very coastal, not very worldly, but definitely a good place to call home.

Pulling himself back to the current situation, Jack leafed through the contents of the envelope. In addition to the printed invitation was a handwritten note, a map leading to a pre-wedding gathering of friends and – what? Two first-class airline tickets to Wichita. Kennedy's note mentioned how much she looked forward to catching up on both the old and the new and meeting his wife. Well, that is something that wouldn't happen. Jack's wife was long gone. But he would love to reunite with his old friend and introduce her to his children. He would let the girls have the first class seats and he would book two coach spots for Ben and himself. He made a mental note to ask for the time off and went back to the salad.

"Bea! Betsy! Come set the table! Ben, how's that math coming along?"

Nothing. No response. Teenagers. Gotta love 'em.

Mary Jane

Mike. Check. Mark. Check. Max. Check. Maddie? Where was that girl?

"MADELINE MARCELLA MENDENHALL??? Where are you?" Mary Jane yelled in the general direction of the front door. She really should have given that child a shorter name.

The van was loaded with the other three children, four packed school lunches, three backpacks, a stack of library books to return, the monthly bills on the way to the post office and the family pet – an oversized beagle named Tex. But no Little Miss Maddie. To get that girl through kindergarten it might take an act of Congress. She loved school, that wasn't the problem, but she had apparently inherited the running late gene from her grandmother.

Mike, her oldest and a junior in high school, slipped out of the shotgun seat and raced back into the house to oust his baby sister from whatever mischief she was probably up to. Even a casual observer would notice this was a fairly regular routine. No Maddie. Mike exits van. Mike enters the house. Five minutes pass. Miss Maddie makes an appearance, usually tossed over Mike's shoulder.

Today, on the other hand, was slightly different. Mike returned and Maddie followed close behind. Ready for school. Oops. Not quite. A pair of mismatched high heels graced her feet where her tennis shoes should be and the equivalent of what looked like three tubes of lipstick graced her face – and some of it actually made it to her lips.

"What do you want me to do about *that*?" Mike groused as he crawled back into the front seat and raised an eyebrow at his mom.

With a heavy sigh Mary Jane tossed him the van keys.

"Drop the boys off at school and I will take care of Maddie. I'll walk her to school this morning," she said with a half-smile and hopped down to fix her daughter's well-intentioned fashion faux pas, closely followed by Tex.

Mary Jane's four kids were the love of her life. She couldn't imagine life without them. However, she was eternally grateful they were now all in school. Those few hours of daily respite were sacred. Managing their schedules, packing their lunches, doing their laundry, sharing their joys and even listening to their woes was all she had ever wanted out of life. She had it all and then some. The house was the essence of the perfect suburban Tennessee comfort spot. The five bedrooms, four bathrooms and beautiful landscaped yards were something she didn't take lightly. Not to mention the lovely underground swimming pool that was the envy of her neighborhood friends. The house was embellished with beautiful paintings, plush carpeting and extravagant furniture. A state-of-the-art sound system was wired throughout the home and the children's rooms looked like miniature toy stores.

Her husband worked fiendishly so the family could afford more lavish extras than she ever thought she would own in a lifetime. Because of his dedication to his work and the late hours he worked every week day and often into the weekend, Mary Jane was able to stay home and raise the children. Less than a week after she had discovered she was pregnant with Mike, Andy had insisted she quit her good-paying nursing job and devote her time to taking care of the house and the baby. And later the three more babies as the family expanded.

Of course they did not live in this house then, but Andy had always taken care of Mary Jane and provided the best money could buy. In return she cooked, cleaned, attended PTA meetings, volunteered at church, carted children – both hers and the neighbors' - to a myriad of sports activities, piano lessons and most recently Maddie's ballet classes. Most of the time she did it without Andy. He was constantly busy, even when he was home there was always a phone call to return, an e-mail to send or a client to entertain. It seemed lately the only time they spent together was when she escorted him to a black tie event for the business or they had his associates and their wives over for dinner.

Still, taking care of their home and their children was what she valued more than anything else in the world. There would be time to spend with Andy later. Always later. She appreciated all he provided for her and the children. Never mind that she was unhappy. Maybe she hadn't even realized that herself yet.

Yes, everyone who came into contact with the Mendenhall family – Mary Jane, Andy, Mike, Mark, Max, Maddie and Tex – would believe beyond a shadow of a doubt that life was pretty close to perfect. And it was. Until one day it wasn't.

    "Mommy," Maddie had asked one day, "Do you ever kiss other daddies?"

    Where did that come from, Mary Jane wondered. Seemingly out of the blue her precious daughter had asked the most ridiculous of questions. This was her dear, sweet, innocent five-year-old who must surely have inadvertently watched something on TV that wasn't on the parent approved list.

    "No baby girl. Of course not. Where would you ever get an idea like that?"

    "Well," Maddie continued. "I just was thinking about it real much because sometimes Daddy kisses Jenny Henderson's mom."

    And then just as quickly as the words had slipped out of her daughter's mouth, the little girl disappeared into another room and out of sight. Mary Jane's knees buckled and she had to reach out to steady herself on the dining room table. Jenny Henderson's mom? Cyndi? That was her neighbor. They played cards together every Tuesday night and occasionally had lunch together at the country club after a tennis match. No. What in the world had her daughter seen? Whatever it was it could not have been Andy kissing Cyndi Henderson.

    With that matter settled in her head, Mary Jane inhaled deeply and pried herself away from the table. She would definitely take this up with Andy tonight. Definitely.

He would no doubt laugh about the innocence and misunderstandings of childhood and all would be right again in her world. Unless, of course, it was true. What would he say then? What would she say then? No, she would not discuss it with Andy. Ever.

Weeks passed and the childlike conversation with Maddie was all but forgotten. Life went on like normal. Thanksgiving came and went. Family and friends gathered to celebrate and the rush and excitement of the holidays filled the Mendenhall home with joy, dotted with homemade cookies, gift exchanges and holiday parties. Even Cyndi Henderson stopped by with a bottle of wine a few days after Christmas to offer the family best wishes for the new year. Nothing was out of the ordinary.

Mark's orchestra program at middle school was a tremendous success and he was asked to perform with Knoxville's adult symphony for two performances in the spring. Even Max's role as Joseph in his fifth grade Christmas pageant made him a celebrity for a few weeks, both at school and at home. It was a shame Andy hadn't been able to attend either event. The holidays were always a busy time in retail and this year had been no exception.

And so, even with that foreshadowing conversation months ago, it was still a total blow to her system when she returned from the supermarket one January afternoon and discovered Andy was already home from work. And he was not alone. Sitting cross-legged on the island in the middle of the kitchen – HER kitchen - with a glass of wine in her hand was Angie Newburg, her husband's secretary.

Outwardly she was able to repress her shock. Of course Andy was able to explain it all. The office heater had been on the fritz. There were reports to file and phone calls to make. These things absolutely could not be put off so they had no choice but to come here and work from home. Her home. But last she knew Andy and his secretary did not drink alcohol while they worked. Something was definitely missing from this story. Mary Jane's shock turned to anger and then to something close to hatred when she began to see through the mumbo jumbo.

No reason for alarm she quietly told her instincts. It was blustery cold outside and working without heat would be next to impossible so she did the only thing she knew how to do – invited Angie to stay for dinner.

As winter turned into spring Mary Jane had come to accept her husband was philandering with a variety of women. All the late nights he worked, the kids' activities he missed, the lack of interest in anything at home except eating and sleeping. Even that conversation so long ago with little Maddie should have been signs. She had talked herself into and out of confronting him about it and was currently in the "if I don't say anything to him it isn't real" stage. After all, what difference did it make because there was no way she could leave him. Where would she go with four kids? It wasn't about losing the money and the house – all the luxuries she had become accustomed to.

She was a smart woman with a nursing degree. She would have to renew her license but eventually she would land on her feet. What on earth would she tell the children? Your dad is a jerk so we are leaving everything you have ever known? Your dad is in the middle of a mid-life crisis and he has hurt my feelings? Or simply, this marriage isn't working so we are moving out. No, there was no way out. She was committed – no matter how ugly she felt and how betrayed she had been. After all, she was almost 40. Even if he lived to be 80, it was just another 40 years. The first 40 had been remarkably good so she would just have to suck it up and stick it out for the next 40. In her mind there was no other option.

Even though all the outward markers seemed to duplicate themselves day after day – getting the kids to school, attending all of their functions, cleaning and cooking for the family and even celebrating special occasions with her husband – Mary Jane was dying on the inside. Her perfect world as she knew it was a sham. How could Andy get up every day, kiss her good morning, shower, eat breakfast, head out to work, do who knows what with who knows who and come home from work day in and day out pretending all was well and all the promises they made to each other nearly 20 years ago were all neatly tucked into place? Was she just to blindly accept that he could live this life and another secret one simultaneously?

They had never spoken of his indiscretions. It was bad enough knowing what he was doing. She didn't want to hear about it, too. She had silently gone through the stages of grief – denial, anger, bargaining and depression but she knew she would never truly come to acceptance.

And so she turned to her own vice.

It started at the pace of a snail. In her moments of clarity she considered her new habit just borrowing a few minutes from her otherwise daily responsibilities and a few dollars from their joint checking account. It was a way to relax. After she had shuttled the kids to their three different schools and returned home to clean away the breakfast mess, she would let herself get absorbed in an on-line game she had seen the kids play on their phones and tablets.

It was a simple game of shapes, colors and patterns – mind numbingly simple and yet quite addictive. At the end of each game if she had a poor score she had to try again, just one more time, to try and improve her score. And if she had a great score she played one more time, just one more time, she told herself, because she was on a roll. And if she ran out of lives? You could get more for 99 cents it seemed. No harm done. She worked hard and she rarely indulged in things for herself. Who would object to spending a dollar on herself? The peace that came with the distraction of the computer game was certainly worth 99 cents. Thoughts of Andy and the flavor of the day were crowded from her memory when she escaped into her computer game world.

She was a little surprised, however, when she checked the bank statement at the end of the month and discovered she had "indulged herself" 57 times. Still. Sixty dollars wasn't an alarming amount. After all, she paid that much to get her hair done and even more than that when she bought something for the kids. She would just be more careful. She didn't want to explain it to Andy. These days she was finding it harder and harder to want to discuss anything with Andy. Even the events of his day. Ugggg…especially the events of his day.

And then there were other games. She loved to play cards and she discovered you could play poker on-line and even earn money. Well, that was easy. She would just earn back the $57 she had squandered on the other game. If only it worked that way. But she had never been addicted to anything before and the logic escaped her. Spend a little, win a little. It all comes out even she thought. And it did. Sometimes. But more often than not she came up on the losing side. This only served to motivate Mary Jane more. She was on a mission to break even. Maybe even earn a little extra to pad the family income. She hadn't contributed anything financially since Mike was born and that was 16 years ago.

She still managed to put a warm homemade dinner on the table each night, keep up with her volunteer commitments, make exquisite desserts for the church bake sale and keep up normal appearances with her neighbors and her friends at the country club. However, she found more and more excuses to steal moments of solitude with her tablet, gambling at all hours of the day. One night she even snuck into the bathroom after the children were asleep and played until her eyes could not stay open a split-second longer.

She won some and lost some but losing just made her gamble larger amounts to try to make it up. The money didn't seem to faze her. It was all about the challenge. After all there was more than enough money in the account to run the household. She was the one who paid the bills so no one would notice the balance fluctuations. At this point she wasn't even keeping track of wins and losses.

All she was processing was that while she was gambling the images of Andy and his "friends" were blocked from her thoughts.

The first reality check came when she opened a letter from the bank and discovered their account was overdrawn. How did that happen, she wondered. Had Andy purchased something and forgotten to write it down? She even wondered briefly if her account had been hacked. It wasn't until she had called the bank and discovered the amounts of cash coming out to support her on-line gambling were hundreds of dollars more than the dollars going in.

Oh well. Easy mistake, she told herself. She made a transfer from savings and vowed to be more careful.

But it wasn't that easy. Things were never as simple as they appeared on the surface.

Within a few weeks her life started to unravel. Steve McCrary, one of the bank's vice presidents was apparently a big fan of racquetball and had been playing frequently with Andy at the club. During a friendly sporting contest it was brought to Andy's attention that their checking account had been overdrawn multiple times over the last month.

That's when things really began to disintegrate. In 19 years of marriage she and Andy had never had a serious disagreement. She trusted him to go about his day and provide for the family and he trusted her without question to run the household. But tonight all the truths that had been assumed had been shattered.

It was a fight that would have made the Hatfields and McCoys look like bosom buddies. He was angry and he let it show with spiteful and hateful words she didn't know he was capable of uttering. For her part she remained silent. Fighting of any kind, with words or actions, wasn't a part of her skill set. She had never needed them and when she wanted to fight back the words wouldn't come. What could she say anyway? She was guilty and he was right.

It wasn't until he had pummeled her with malicious insults for an hour, screamed about how she had embarrassed him, ruined his reputation as a businessman and stormed out of the house in a rage that she let herself breathe. _He_ was angry with _her_? After his lying, conniving, cheating habits and he was angry with _her_? She was so upset that tears wouldn't come. Hours passed. In total darkness she sat on the floor with her back pressed against the bedroom wall willing herself to be strong. Eventually the dark ebbed away and dawn approached. She forced herself to shower and headed downstairs to fry bacon so the children wouldn't be late for school.

It was easy to explain why Andy wasn't home that morning because he was frequently gone for days at a time on business. Once again, on the surface everything seemed perfectly normal. But once again Mary Jane was dying on the inside. She hadn't let herself question where he might be staying. She really didn't care. There was nothing more he could do to hurt her now. For a long time she had felt nothing but apathy for the man who had fathered her four children, given her countless monetary allowances and provided for her over the years. But today she could care less if he was dead or alive.

Two days later when he did return home after work and joined the family for dinner it was as if nothing had happened. The children told him about their days at school, Mike talked incessantly about a girl he liked on the cheerleading squad and Andy ribbed Max about his homework. Like a fly on the wall, Mary Jane watched this man interact with the children who loved him so much and forced herself to bring the fork to her mouth over and over to keep up the facade all was right in the world.

When the supper dishes were done and the following day's sack lunches were made she had little choice but to interact with

Andy for the first time since he had discovered her gambling secret. The only thing different this time was that he spoke in hushed tones. The anger was still there bubbling barely under the surface and it punctuated his words but he was not screaming. He spoke matter of factly just like they were conducting a business transaction. First, he told her, he would be paying the bills from this point forward. She would have a small allowance each week to take care of the food purchases. All other expenses would be cleared through him. He was not interested in divorce he droned on. He wouldn't do that to the children. But he was so disappointed in her and she could no longer be trusted. After all he had done for her, she thought he was saying, there was no excuse for her behavior. At some point the words were just syllables bouncing off the walls. She got the idea and didn't need to hear the details.

Of course he didn't want a divorce. Which of his concubines would cook his meals, raise his kids, wash and fold his underwear?

In retrospect she should have packed her bags and left that night. After all, the gambling was her way of coping with the trust he had broken between them months before. It was the only time she could escape the awful thoughts that crept into her mind about who he was with and what he was doing while they were apart and she was maintaining this perfect life that he was not willing to give up. She should have left. She should have told him what she felt. What she knew. What others had told her about his "business" dealings when she started asking questions. But she didn't. She stood mute and listened. Nothing had really changed. Nothing. Except that she could no longer rely on gambling to escape the wicked thoughts that haunted her. She had no idea how she would survive the next 40 years but somehow she would. Wild horses wouldn't keep her from her children and to ensure that didn't happen she would have to continue to play the dutiful wife.

The next morning was when she got the invitation to the wedding. Kennedy Andrews had been her babysitter all those years ago when she had lived in Kansas. What a great piece of good news. Kennedy had met the man of her dreams. In her present state of mind a wedding was about as appealing as pulling her fingernails off one at a time, but she could also really use some time away. It was surprising that Kennedy had thought fondly enough of her to invite her to the wedding and even more surprising to see she had included two first-class airline tickets into Wichita. She would definitely attend. It was six weeks away but she was more than confident she and Andy would not be on speaking terms by then. She would go and take her mother. That was settled. At last she had something to look forward to. For the first time in months the world looked a little brighter.

Father Paul

The pews of the ancient church were no more comfortable today than they had been 50 years ago when he spent hours kneeling in prayer as a young boy. At that time he was asking God to lead him into the vocation of priesthood. Today he was asking God to watch over his mother as she battled all the tragedies that come with ailing health. The difference, however, was his body had aged considerably and his knees were much worse for the wear.

At last giving up on his knees, Paul let his body relax into the pew and buried his face in his hands. As an ordained Catholic priest he had come to see God's beauty first hand in everything – the birth of a child, the marriage of a Christian couple and even the death of a parent who was at last released from earthly pain and suffering. But there was no greater physical beauty in his eyes than the purity and sanctity of the church.

Lifting his head he slowly let the sights and scents of the old building envelop him in memories. The saints embedded in the stained glass windows seemed to stand at attention as if to say "Welcome home, Paul." The scent of pine wood cleaner mingled with hints of incense from this morning's Mass calmed him and gave him the peace he always found when indeed he did "come home" to the church.

For years he had stood at this very altar and offered Christ's body and blood to hundreds of followers who believed Jesus was the way to heavenly salvation. He was a part of the lives of the people he touched and they were a part of him as well. They invited him into their homes for meals and fellowship and stood by his side minute by minute and hour after hour when he had suffered a heart attack 20 years ago and his chances of survival were grim. In many ways the people of St. Fidelis Catholic Church were his family.

Today Father Paul was known to most as just Paul Odell or just Paul. For as long as he could remember he had wanted to serve the Lord as a parish priest. Sitting at the knee of his grandmother even before he could walk and talk, Paul knew the importance of God. He absorbed it from the faith of his deeply spiritual family. As he grew in size and stature he learned to value prayer and service to others as much as food and shelter. High school and college, he knew, were just necessary components to the greater good he was to someday be.

Now as he sat in the same pew as those he had served, he was just Paul. Circumstances had dictated another life for him and while he was not sad any more, his body was tired and it sometimes seemed his spirit was broken.

In the coolness of the air conditioned chapel he closed his eyes and got lost in what changed his course.

Actually he didn't remember all the details of the day that was the beginning of the end and he probably never would. Friends told him he had collapsed on the sidewalk while strolling with his beloved dog Spice. Without symptoms or warning, an otherwise healthy Father Paul Odell had suffered a massive heart attack at the age of 39. No one could explain, not even the medical team who nursed him through it, why a relatively young man who grew his own healthy vegetables, lived on lean meat and few desserts and walked twice a day would almost die of a heart attack. And the fact that he was able to survive it was almost as much of a mystery. Only God knew why he wasn't ready to receive Paul into heaven yet.

His recovery was long and tedious. All six of his brothers flew in from around the country to take turns staying by his side and his mother never left it. He cruised in and out of consciousness for weeks and later attributed his recovery to the constant prayers from the parishioners.

At last he was able to leave the hospital – all patched up with an almost new heart, a regimen of medication and a list of things not to do for the next few weeks. To Paul it seemed an impossible task. He needed to get back into the fold, throw himself back into the life he loved. His family always told him they had never seen him sit still for more than five minutes. Now he had been in a hospital bed for weeks and he was crawling out of his skin.

Gradually he was able to get back to the only thing he ever knew. Although he had to admit he did tire faster and the work of a parish priest was not a nine to five job. People needed him to tend to the sick in the middle of the night, marry their children on the weekends, lead meetings and hold prayer vigils at all hours of the day. He did not have time to be sick.

All of that seemed like a blur now. But he did remember what happened next. It was a Wednesday. Snow covered the ground and was still coming down in sheets when the rectory doorbell rang with a vengeance. Opening the door he found two members of the parish council and the bishop of the diocese standing on the stoop covered in white flakes.

Apparently it wasn't a social call. Bishop O'Connor accepted the steaming coffee and settled onto a kitchen chair. He cut right to the chase. The community had come to the bishop out of concern for Paul. They were worried about the grueling schedule and about Paul's health. While they loved and adored their spiritual leader, Father Paul Odell, they could see that the needs of the large and growing church family was too much for him. He needed help. Five Masses a weekend and all the other responsibilities of the job were too much for one man who was recovering from such a grave situation. Could an associate priest step in to help, they asked. Or perhaps an apprentice could be assigned to help Paul for a month or maybe two. And the bishop listened with care and concern for his friend, Father Paul.

Paul's spiritual side was deeply touched that the church community was behind him and had prayed so diligently for his recovery. And even beyond that they had petitioned his boss to get him some help with the responsibilities of the day-to-day chores of running his "business." But the human side of him felt a bit betrayed. Why hadn't they come to him and asked if there was anything they could do to help. And anyway, he didn't need help. He was fine. Wasn't he? Were things slipping through his fingers? Was he neglecting things without noticing?

He suddenly realized the bishop was still talking.

"Paul, we would love to send someone out here to help you but there just aren't enough of us to go around. We are stretched tightly as it is…"

"John," Paul interrupted, "things are fine here. I may move a little slower than I did a few months ago, but God will provide and we can manage."

There was a pregnant pause. Neither man was eager to break the silence.

"We would like you to consider retirement," he heard the bishop say.

It was almost as if he was having an out-of-body experience, viewing this conversation as a third party. Surely this couldn't be real. Retire? At 40? What would he do? Water the plants at the priest's retirement center all day?

"Just think about it, Paul," he remembered his friend and boss had said. "I will be in touch in the next few days."

The two parishioners from the parish council looked dumbstruck. It was clear this was not their intention when they reached out to a higher power. Paul was certain of that. They wanted to offer him help and instead got him a death sentence – or as Bishop O'Connor put it – an early retirement package.

The next three days passed in a fog. He was not ready to retire. He might be a little tired. He might need to take a little more time off to recover, but he certainly did not intend to give up what he cherished because of a little heart surgery.

But when the call came in from the bishop, he was insistent that Paul resign his post as the priest at St. Fidelis as soon as he could gather his belongings and say good bye to his church family.

"We have a comfortable spot for you at the Good Shepherd Villa. Don't worry, Paul, there is always so much to do. You will not be bored and you will spread light and joy to all your comrades who live there, too. It is a good place to be."

A good place to be? Maybe if he was 70. This conversation with his superior was permanently inked into his brain.

"Oh and Paul," the bishop interjected, "We will send someone out to take care of your church. I'll be in contact by the end of the week and you can show him the ropes before you leave."

Unbelievable.

"You're a good man, Paul," John O'Connor said and he meant it. Then the line went dead.

When the chips were down Paul did what most people did. He turned to his family. Usually priests didn't make decisions quickly. Everything was tempered with meditation and prayer. But at this point Paul was disappointed to discover he was too angry to pray. He couldn't remember a time he had been truly angry with God since his father had died when he was just five. A tragic car accident had taken something from him that even at that age he knew he could never get back. Even then, however, Paul relied on God for strength and comfort and had been able to work through those feelings and come to trust again in the power of God. Now he had to trust Him again and see this must be for his own good. As for now? He was still hopping angry.

By the end of the month he had wrapped up things at church, introduced the new young priest to his people in faith and told the bishop he needed a few months to rest and regroup before moving into the villa.

Packed into his rental car with a few suitcases and his faithful dog Sugar 'N Spice (who only knew his name as Spice), Father Paul made the long journey across Kansas and into Arkansas to stay with his brother Edward and his wife for a few weeks. As he drove he tried to reflect on his relatively short life and the turn it was inevitably taking.

The more miles he put between St. Fidelis and his temporary new home, the more he realized there must be more to the story. The bishop had made it clear there was no way he could spare another priest to help out while Paul got stronger because there were simply not enough young men in the profession to go around. And yet young Father Ted had been dispatched almost immediately to fill his shoes.

It couldn't be the lack of staff, then. He knew Bishop John O'Connor well. He was not prone to lie. But he had to be withholding something. In his present state of mind another phone call into John's office would not do. He would figure it out even though it might take weeks. Right now the only thing he knew for sure was he was definitely not ready to hang up his stole for a housecoat and slippers.

Time with family was always a welcome distraction and the days and weeks he spent with Edward and Annie were filled with great conversation, fabulous meals and buckets of quality coffee. Not having to set an alarm, no schedule to follow and the presence of his three nieces constantly badgering him to tell them a joke or sing them a song was priceless. Still it was not the life for him. He thrived on a strict schedule and being needed rather than being pampered, as lovely as it was.

Nights were the hardest. After the others had drifted off to bed Paul found himself wandering down the street to take long walks through the cemetery. He knew no one buried there but was able to disengage from his own worries by aimlessly walking the graveled pathways between the headstones and envisioning the lives of those who had already gone to heaven.

What were their stories? What demons did they struggle with? Did they ever find answers? Why were some lives so short and others so long? That was a question he was often asked over the years and honestly one that was difficult to answer. No one knew the wondrous ways in which the Master worked, but to a grieving family it was beyond comprehension. Scripture was there for support but there seemed to be no conclusive reason that one survived cancer while another did not.

One night as he walked through the exquisitely manicured yard of the cemetery he discovered a swing. It was a simple swing suspended above the ground by two fraying but still sturdy ropes. The bench of the seat was a simple wooden plank that was badly weathered. Lowering himself onto the swing, he closed his eyes and rested. Maybe the bishop was right. He needed more rest.

A few minutes later he opened his eyes and let them refocus. This was the precise moment Paul uncovered the real story to his dismissal from active duty. As he sat in the swing he noticed that a sitting position lowered his line of vision by four feet or so. He saw the cemetery differently. Instead of the view from above where a person could see hundreds of headstones in all directions, from the swing he could only see one clearly. Rachel Tomlinson. Wife. Mother. Sister. Friend. 1897 - 1969.

While standing, Rachel's "statistics" were next to invisible among the many others who shared her final resting place. But as he sat, her life came into perfect view. A new perspective.

So, he asked himself, what was the perspective of the bishop? From his own point of view he had been dismissed and replaced by a rookie because of his health. But from John O'Connor's perspective? It wasn't about stretching the diocese too thin. He had proved that by filling his spot with Father Ted so quickly. Paul had become a liability. What if something happened to Paul while ministering at St. Fidelis? If he wasn't strong enough to do the work and he died in the line of duty that would reflect poorly on John's leadership. It could be perceived John had not taken care of his flock as he was called to do by his superiors and ultimately by God.

He would become a statistic just like Rachel Tomlinson and Bishop John could not let that happen on his watch.

Of course this was just speculation on Paul's part but he simply wouldn't go out this way. He could not sit around and weed the watermelon patch, take his turn cooking and cleaning the kitchen, and sit for hours in the infirmary and pray with the dying. He knew these were necessary functions of a home for retired priests. And someday he might have been ready for them. But not now. He was too young for it now and despite some health setbacks he was not ready to give up on serving God in an active role.

He made his way across the grassy patches and through the cemetery gate confident in his rather hasty decision. There were plenty of other ways to serve the Lord and at 40 he wasn't ready to retire. He would leave the priesthood.

Turning the doorknob as he let himself back into his brother's house he noticed his hands were shaking. He made a mental note to pray for the repose of Rachel Tomlinson's soul and drifted off into peaceful sleep for the first time in weeks.

Now as he sat in the pew at St. Fidelis, back home in Kansas, almost 20 years to the day from the time he made that critical and unpopular decision, he knew that God indeed had a plan for his life and he was living it. One more time before he left the old church he loved so much he asked for God's blessing for his mother that she might take comfort in His grace and accept His will as she slowly endured her last days on earth. As he always did when he absorbed himself in prayer he felt a peace that nothing other than time in prayer could fill.

Telling his brother Edward that he was resigning as a priest was perhaps harder than telling the bishop. It was, he understood, difficult to understand. His brothers Peter, David, Jake, Joe and especially Father Aaron were also slow to comprehend. His mother, however, was his rock.

"What God has planned for you can never be decided by anyone other than your God," she had said. "Trust in Him and know that He will guide you.

And so, with just a little cash, a handful of civilian clothes and a dog, Father Paul set out to find a new life – the life of just plain Paul.

Actually, his new life had chosen him. After all, his skill set was limited to running a church. He made schedules, refined budgets, ran meetings and taught classes, but his favorite role was creating and developing a community garden that not only supported the rectory but helped members learn to become self-sufficient by growing their own food.

Gardening and teaching. Teaching others to garden. Perfect! Except for one thing. It wouldn't pay the bills. He didn't need much, but he did need shelter.

Soon Paul found work at a tiny farm off the interstate and was offered a small stipend and a place to sleep in the Miller's barn. The family welcomed Spice as well and came to love him almost as much as Paul himself.

The work was hard and the hours were long but that is all he knew. Some years later when the time came that he could afford to find his own place Paul moved just down the road and purchased a small aging farmhouse with a very little plot of land to start his own community garden. He became a full-time employee at the Miller's farm and taught others to garden in his spare time.

Once again he had found his niche. But this time he was no longer Father Paul. His new friends and church family in Arkansas knew nothing of his old life and knew him only as Paul. Just Paul.

As life would have it, however, twists and turns were part of the game. Paul was called back to Kansas by the family and they all sat with their mother in her final days. Fortunately her suffering was short and everyone was comforted by her abundant love for Jesus and her absolute faith that she would meet Him upon her death and be reunited with her husband.

Knowing her death was imminent should have made it easier for the boys but the emptiness of knowing both of their parents were gone left a deep feeling of isolation in them all. As they departed for different parts of the country a few days later, they promised to keep in touch more often.

So a bit of good news was welcome. When Paul returned home there was a pile of mail so high it took both hands to carry it in. And among the bills, junk mail and sympathy cards he discovered an invitation.

He smiled at the memory of Kennedy Andrews. They had met when he was the chaplain at Kansas State University, his first parish assignment. She was a student studying journalism and an avid volunteer at the college campus church. She kept everyone is stitches of laughter. He remembered how she loved to sing and that she had been a key player in organizing a folk choir at the small campus church.

And now she was getting married. Odd, he thought. She still used her maiden name and she must be close to 50. She had never married? Oh well, no matter, but it struck him as strange that someone with so much positive energy and such a great sense of humor would have to wait so long to find true love. Well, what did he know about that after all? He had **never** found it.

Two first-class airline tickets were enclosed and a sweet handwritten note thanking him for the positive influence he had made in her life and for his dedication to helping others. She was hoping he could make it to her wedding and would love to catch up after all these years. Boy, would she be surprised.

Into every life a little rain must fall, but moments like this were the sunshine that was always close behind. Six weeks from now he would travel back to Kansas AGAIN to celebrate with his old friend.

Sadie

Being a waitress was not for her. Really she knew this BEFORE she took the job, but she loosely figured if every customer left a $1 tip and every table served four people and you waited on six tables at a time you could make $24 every 30 minutes or so, right? I mean, how long could it take people to eat a hamburger? That was $48 an hour and that was darned good money!

Math may have been her strong suit in school but apparently logic was not. Sadie was now realizing, after three days on the job, that not everyone left a dollar. In fact some bozos didn't leave any tip. And not all tables for four seated four people. And, of course, no one came in, ate and left in 30 minutes. Even in this greasy diner.

Oh but the perks of the job were marvelous. People snapped their fingers at you. And those were the polite ones. Customers even got mad when every drop of coffee didn't hit their cup. The law of averages says sometimes you are going to miss. It's not like you spilled coffee on **them**. I mean really people. I am doing the best I can here. And the leg muscles. My goodness was she sore.

The first night when she counted her tips she had $18.13. And that included the quarter she must have dropped in her shoe. No wonder her feet hurt, too. That first shift was just four hours long but it was the longest four hours of her life and she had tipped out at just over $4.50 an hour. Something was going to have to change. Of course she would get a paycheck, too, at the

end of the week, but that first four-hour
shift would only net about $8. She never
made it until the end of the week.

Sitting at her friend's kitchen table
Sadie pored over the newspaper want ads
again and again. This would be so much
easier if she wanted to work, she thought.
The best job she ever had was as a
receptionist at a large accounting firm. The
hours were good, the pay was solid and she
loved dressing up and feeling important.
However, her tenure there ended abruptly
when she slept with the boss and outlined
the sordid details about it to a co-worker
who happened to be the best friend of the
guy's wife. In hindsight she should have
handled that a little differently.

Being a single mom was tough in the
best of situations and being an unemployed
single mom was the worst feeling on earth.
For the last three months she and her seven-
year-old son Ronnie had been staying with
her best friend Ami. She and Ami met in high
school while standing in line at enrollment.
During the course of idle chit chat they
discovered they shared a love for roller
blading and sushi. From that point forward
they had been as thick as thieves.
Through the ups and downs of Ami's
tumultuous relationship with her high school
boyfriends and Sadie's pregnancy at the age

of 17 the girls had been there for one another. Ami had pointed out to Sadie her life might be a little easier financially if she would press for child support from Ronnie's father. The problem there was Sadie did not know exactly who that was.

But now the girls were young women — Ami married to a wonderful man who sold advertising for a cable company and cherished the ground Ami walked on and Sadie with a seven-year-old son, no job and no support system.

Sadie's mom had died the day after her eleventh birthday from a quick spreading cancer. Her father had not handled the loss well and ran off shortly afterwards leaving an aunt to get Sadie through high school. Last she heard her father was in the Dominican Republic working as a bartender. It was unforgivable to Sadie that he had left her behind when she was hurting so much and she had little if any respect for him.

Her aunt provided all the basics for Sadie but had her own life to live and was not terribly excited about suddenly being saddled with a child. So Sadie turned to boys for comfort and there were plenty willing to console her. When she found out she was pregnant she took solace in knowing she would finally have someone to love again. As she would discover, it wasn't that simple.

For a time after the baby was born she stayed with her aunt and eventually was able to get a job in a day care center where Ronnie could come along. But the days began early. When she couldn't always get there at 5:45 because it was difficult to manage a baby on her own, she was fired. She was able to get another day care job but they weren't licensed for babies so Ronnie had to be left with a neighbor. There were too many days the neighbor couldn't watch him or one of her own children was ill and she didn't want Ronnie exposed to whatever was going around. Naturally this didn't make her a reliable employee. She was fired.

For about three years she bounced from job to job – usually quitting because she didn't like the management or she thought they asked too much of her considering what they were willing to pay employees with just a high school diploma.

At last she found the receptionist job. It turns out Ami had a friend who would put in a good word for her. They had an on-site day care so Ronnie could once again go to work with her. Everything was looking up. Sadie worked for Seachrest & Waverly Accounting for over two years – only missing one day of work. She had a perfect performance record with the company and was making excellent pay given her lack of education and spotty work resume. She couldn't afford Gucci purses or lavish trips to the spa, but Ronnie was in kindergarten now and she could afford to rent a modest two-bedroom apartment and pay a sitter to watch him until she got home from work.

Her downfall was that poor decision to extend the happy hour after the office Christmas party in the arms of her boss. That was definitely a turning point.

Since then jobs had come and gone. Some she liked, most she hated, but she was always able to scrape together just enough money to pay the rent and buy food. When she couldn't afford gas she walked. When it was too cold or too rainy to walk, she called in sick. And so the cycle continued.

Ami and Randy had offered several times to let her and Ronnie stay with them until she could really land on her feet. It may have been because Ami was tired of answering the phone at midnight with a sniveling Sadie relaying her sad experience in the world of the employed – or unemployed as the case might be. The Smith home had an extra bedroom and bathroom in the basement with its own entrance. They would just have to share the kitchen and both Ami and Randy loved little Ronnie. Sadie had refused their offer a number of times. It didn't seem fair for Ami to be responsible for her bad decisions. But desperate times called for desperate measures and here they were.

It was at the end of another workless day that Sadie found a pleasant surprise in the mailbox among the rest of the day's correspondence. It was pleasant because it was in a silky cream-colored envelope that resembled neither a bill nor an advertisement and it was addressed to her. Squinting against the brutal glare of the sun she struggled to read the return address which was hand-scripted on the back flap of the over-sized envelope. Kennedy Andrews. Kansas. Who was Kennedy Andrews?

Dropping into a deck chair on the patio, she carefully released the seal and allowed the envelope's contents to fall out onto the table. It was a wedding invitation to a clearly large ordeal clear back in Kansas. And from someone she didn't even know. She flipped the envelope over again and checked once more to be sure it was really addressed to her. Had she accidentally opened Ami and Randy's mail?

It was, in fact, addressed to Sadie Louise Nichols, but there was more. A letter was enclosed, handwritten in the same neat writing as the envelope. The message was brief but definitely cleared up the identity of the sender. Apparently her mother and Kennedy and been best friends in grade school and into middle school. They had rarely seen each other in person in the years since their teens. The letter said Kennedy and her mother Angie had kept in touch long after high school over the phone and through letters and e-mail. Kennedy said Angie loved being a mother. She always spoke highly of Sadie and the two often talked about Angie's hopes and dreams for her baby girl.

Apparently when Angie discovered her cancer was terminal she had pleaded with Kennedy to make a place in her heart for Sadie and watch over her after Angie was no longer physically able.

Hmmmmmpppffff, Sadie thought. Where was this Kennedy in all those dark moments since her mother's death? No contact in all these years and now come celebrate her wedding? No thank you, she thought. But she read on.

Kennedy, it seemed, had great intentions and kept Sadie in her thoughts, even praying for her well-being every night.

She regretted not making contact sooner, but was never sure how to approach a stranger. What would she say? Hello, you don't know me but your mom and I played hopscotch together in second grade so now I am her replacement? The time never seemed appropriate and the right words never formed.

As odd as the whole thing seemed, Sadie felt her eyes well with salty tears as she thought of her mother asking her friend to watch over her daughter knowing she wouldn't always be able to.

The letter closed with a request that Sadie would accept the invitation and fly to Kansas for the wedding with the hope they could meet and at last build a relationship in honor of her late mother. Two first-class airline tickets were enclosed along with a map of the venue and assurances that all her travel and lodging expenses would be covered. It was signed, "With care, Kennedy."

Of course it was ridiculous to consider the possibility of traveling so far to an event she could care less about to meet a person who she didn't know. But still. The possibility of meeting a friend of her mother had piqued her curiosity.

Sadie closed her eyes and sat at the table soaking up the last of the day's sun rays imagining what Kennedy might be like. Would she share her mother's sense of humor? She must be rich to be able to be so generous. The rich part was nothing like her mother but the generous part was. Maybe she wanted something from Sadie. Could it be a selfish invitation? Or maybe this Kennedy just wanted to ease her feelings of guilt for not keeping in touch as her mother had perhaps intended she would.

Whatever the reason, Kennedy had wasted several hundred dollars on air fare because Sadie was never going to trek across the country to meet a stranger – especially a stranger who would be so busy on her wedding day that she would never know if Sadie was among the revelers or not.

And yet as she fell into bed that evening, the thoughts of this odd letter and the randomness of its arrival filled her head. Vowing to never give it another thought Sadie rolled over and closed her eyes. Unfortunately sleep did not come until hours later.

J.T.

Although J.T. had always been athletic, he had compassion for those who weren't. He thought of it like school in a way. In his own elementary experience he loathed social studies. The essays about the culture of a teacher-assigned country that culminated in dressing up in character and reading an all too often encyclopedia-plagiarized version of a research paper brought back brought awful memories. Then there were the paper mache volcanoes that may or may not erupt on cue once they were delivered to the front of the class. And later, in high school, the endless drivel of dates and people to memorize and regurgitate on short answer tests. Intolerable! And yet, a game of pick up basketball at recess or challenging himself to exceed the goals of the Presidential Fitness Award each year were highlights he still remembered as if they were yesterday.

But then there was Sophie - a political science genius even in second grade. She knew every word of the U.S. Constitution, had an exit plan for ending the Cold War and by middle school wrote a student council acceptance speech that would rival the words of many presidents. Last he heard Sophie was serving in the U.S. Senate with aspirations of becoming a Supreme Court justice. However, even if the building was on fire, she couldn't run fast enough to save her life.

Everyone was hard-wired differently, he knew that for sure. And like his teachers who successfully guided him through fifth grade social studies, coddled him through U.S. history and somehow passed him through world geography, he considered his job vital in helping the Sophies of the world develop their physical strengths. He was a very smart guy, but just had no real interest in the academic lingo that went hand in hand with formal education.

He had been mercilessly teased by both friends and family for ditching college for a career as a physical trainer. Even his own brother, with his high stress career as a financial advisor to the rich and famous, had called him a chump for taking the easy way out. But J.T. made no apologies. He believed in the work he did. That was that.

Time marched on, however, and J.T. had moved past those days of teaching and coaching at the local Y and later at a posh country club in the suburbs of Atlanta. Five years into his career an opportunity to travel and promote a healthy lifestyle was something he couldn't turn down. His life had taken a turn for the better financially and now he traveled all across the United States as a motivational speaker. Representing a pharmaceutical company selling dietary supplements, J.T. was the face – and abs and pecs – of Universal Energy Products. His shirtless body was plastered on billboards in every state and even overseas. In the exercise industry he was a legend and suddenly, almost overnight, he had more women than he knew what to do with.

Now 10 years later, J.T. O'Malley also found himself swimming in more money than he could spend. He had married a beautiful swimsuit model shortly after moving to St. Louis, but his constant travel and intense dedication to fine tuning every inch of his muscular body put a strain on their short and constantly turbulent marriage. After a year they separated and a few months later the divorce was final leaving him hurt, angry and yet more determined than ever to be the best-looking man in America.

The events of the last few years had unfortunately changed his life plan. What was it they said? The best laid plans were meant to be broken? At the top of his game and happier than he thought possible – smothered in mountains of excess cash, fast cars and female companionship, J.T.'s life had changed irrevocably at the base of a pine tree amid a pile of snow and ice. A holiday ski trip with his cousins and a few high school buddies had gone sour when his skis flew out from under him and plunged him into near death. He was fortunate he knew to come away with just broken bones, narrowly escaping paralysis. But his career in the field of exercise was halted abruptly. No warning. No backup plan. Just over.

Both wrists had been fractured, a rib had punctured a lung and he had dislocated a hip. His left kneecap had been shattered which left him walking with a cane. The doctors had worked miracles on his torn up body but even the hundreds of hours of physical therapy would not make it possible for him to be the master of physical fitness. Ever again. Life as he had planned it was forever over.

J.T. wasn't prone to wallow in self-pity under normal circumstances. However, in many ways the accident left him feeling worthless and unattractive. For so long his identity had been tied to what he looked like rather than what he was really like that he had a hard time separating the two. He felt used up and empty - like he had come home to retire until it was time to die. Often it was a struggle just to get out of bed.

But thanks to a few friends who stuck to him like glue and carried him emotionally when he didn't seem capable of doing it himself, J.T. was moving forward again, albeit at a snail's pace. Upward and onward was his new mantra.

Determined to be self-supportive and make a contribution to society he had taken a temporary position with a direct sales company. Just a few months and you can work your way into management he had been told. Your people skills will carry you through and the money you can earn is endless his co-workers said. On paper it was a dream job. The only problem was that other than paying the bills, J.T. wasn't interested in making money any more. He was interested in playing tennis and golf and softball. Skiing had sort of lost its appeal, however.

So now he was relegated to an office job. Others had been correct when they told him it was easy to work into management. And he even enjoyed many of the daily tasks involved with the job. There was a competitive edge to the work which was the only real carryover from his previous career. The only rub? He had never been embarrassed to explain his career choice to people before but it was a little hard to admit to strangers he now spent 40-50 hours a week selling - soap.

Technically, he reasoned, he himself did not sell soap. He just supervised a team of about 600 other people who did. He was the marketing/team building link in the chain and the job had served him well.

Today J.T. was pushing it to get to his meeting on time. He only had to walk down the hall, but that last-minute phone call had him scrambling to gather his materials and get to the conference room ahead of the others. This bi-monthly meeting with the sales reps was a highlight. As he activated the projector, adjusted the screen and popped the jump drive into his computer, he felt oddly at ease. The meeting would lead with recognition, follow through with sales tips featuring the latest products and end with a challenge to boost sales and provide a vehicle for the next meeting's recognition. He was able to motivate, teach, challenge and raise his team's bonus pay all in the span of an hour. All things considered, it was pretty easy work. Over time he was sure he could consider this as meaningful as what he planned to do with his life until age forced him into retirement. Couldn't he?

"Hey J.T., got a minute?" Rachel called out as he headed back to his office.

"Sure. How can I help you?" he countered.

"Well, some of us were talking and we'd like to stage a fundraiser for Karen's family. What do you think?"

One of his representatives had stumbled on a streak of bad luck which culminated with a fire at her parents' home leaving them temporarily homeless. Fortunately no one had been hurt, but the financial loss was significant.

"Absolutely," J.T. said. "Do you have something in mind?"

"Not really. Can we get together and brainstorm?"

J.T. paused and scanned his electronic planner on his phone.

"Sure. Can you meet at 2 tomorrow?"

"Well," Rachel hesitated. "I was hoping for sooner. How about dinner tonight?"

"Tonight?" J.T. scratched his temple and tried to let go of a fleeting thought. Was this about a fundraiser for Karen? Or was Rachel angling for something else? A date? No. No. Surely not. Since his accident he had lost his confidence in wooing women and certainly that any woman would want to pursue him. He did not feel the slightest bit attractive. Hard to imagine that not that long ago he could – and often did – spend the night with most any woman in the world with little more effort than a smile and a wink. But still, just in case…

"I can't do dinner, but I have an hour for coffee," he offered. "Meet you at The Grille in 30 minutes?"

Rachel agreed and they parted ways.

When he returned to the office he saw the mail had been delivered and there was a healthy stack in the center of his work space where his computer normally sat. He filed the top two envelopes in the in box to be dealt with in the morning and focused on the third envelope. It was a mess. Originally it appeared the cream-colored envelope had been sent to his old address in Atlanta. He hadn't lived there for over five years. Then the letter, which looked to be personal-related rather than business due to its hand-scripted address, had been forwarded to his brother's address in Oklahoma where he had his mail sent during his seven-week hospital stay. From there it had been stamped several times by the post office with "return to sender – address unknown." It must have gotten lost between St. Louis and Kansas City, averting his current forwarding address card. At any rate, a different loose scroll had penciled his work address with bold printed letters above that read: ATTENTION: J.T. O'MALLEY.

What in the world? This letter had been all over the place and yet here it was at its final location. He was tired and he needed to get over to The Grille to meet Rachel, but this one was something that called out to be opened sooner than later. A glance at the return address brought a smile to his face. Kennedy Andrews. His high school sweetheart. After all these years, though. Amazing. Not just that she had found him, but that she still remembered him. Mentally doing the math it had been more than 30 years since he had seen or even heard from her. Indeed a breath of fresh air.

But there was no time. He wanted to savor this letter, or whatever it was that was inside the envelope. It, or rather she, deserved more than a passing glance. He tossed it into his briefcase and locked the door behind him.

A wedding invitation. His heart flipped. Is it possible that she is inviting me, her first love, to her wedding? If the shoe was on the other foot he was not sure he would do the same. And yet, curiosity kept him from tossing the invitation into the trashcan. Memories flooded his brain as he relaxed against the soft cushion of the sofa and gently eased into a reclining position.

He skimmed the cursory information – date and time of the wedding, reception and dance to follow, blah, blah, blah. He held the envelope against his chest and let himself slip into the 80s. Huge teased out hair for the girls, feathered duck tails for the guys. Khakis and polo shirts were the standard dress and letter jackets and class rings were the symbols of the times.

Cramming for tests. Late night diners and part-time jobs. First kisses. Fast cars. Prom. After prom. Lots of firsts that night.

Enough. There were other things in the envelope, too. A map of the venue, two first-class airline tickets dated just two weeks from now. That's a little short notice, but this letter had been traveling for weeks before it found him so that was understood. And there was a hand-written note that tumbled through his fingers and onto the floor. Picking it up, he read:

> My dearest J.T.,
> I hope this letter finds you well. Many years have passed since we have spoken but you should know that I have thought of you often. The moments we spent together will forever be a part of me that no one can take away.
> As I plan for my wedding with the man who will be my forever it is hard to separate memories of the first man who taught me to love. I hope you and your wife will be able to join us at this celebration. I want Greg to meet you and am anxious to hear how life has treated you all of these years. I have invited a few others to join us the night before the wedding at The Salted Olive, a favorite hang out here in Wichita, so that those people so precious from my past can meet those who are so special in my future.

It was signed "As always, Kennedy."

Wow. He was speechless. How could he go? How could he not?

He wasn't anxious to show up crippled – his body a shell of the young man she knew when they danced all night and stayed up until dawn on their last date. Yet he was proud of his life and the work he had done for others. There was no reason to shy away from that. Still he couldn't shake the feelings of wanting to be the big man on campus in front of the new guy. Ridiculous. It had been over 30 years. And she had sent a kind note inviting him back home. She wasn't interested in his bruised ego. She was interested in J.T., her friend, her high school sweetheart, her first intimate relationship. He laughed at the "you and your wife" line. That was another one of his best laid plans that hadn't come to fruition. Oh well. For the most part life was good.

He left the invitation on the coffee table and drifted into a restless sleep. Who sent airline tickets with a wedding invitation anyway? Who was she? A movie star? A musician? She really could play the piano he remembered. Surely not or he would have heard about that by now. Well, in two weeks he would know for sure.

Jeff

He loved to travel. Well, perhaps it was more accurate to say he loved to see the world. He was not a huge fan of airplanes and excessive travel by car gave him a headache. Perhaps a cruise ship would be his preferred method of transportation, although that was a bit impractical for day to day mobility.

Over the last eight months Jeff Moore had touched down in 38 states and had experienced every imaginable method of moving from city to city and state to state – plane, bus, taxi, subway, several times on a river boat or ferry and most frequently by rental car. Now he was three states away from being home at last to his family and friends.

As a high school math teacher he rarely had a chance to get away and see the ocean or mountains. His nights and weekends were consumed with grading papers, writing tests and completing office paperwork. For years he had longed to take his family across the country to see the Great Lakes of the Midwest, the majestic homes and culture of the South, the incredible scenery of the coastlines plus everything in between. At last he was seeing all of that and more, but his family was absent from the experience. He could only share it through the weekly post cards and pictures he had texted to his wife to share with his five children – Abigail, Angie, Ava, Adalyn and little Abe.

As Vermont's candidate for National Teacher of the Year he (and his family) had been shocked to learn that he had been selected by a panel of teachers and administrators from across the country to represent the nation as the 2014 National Educator of the Year. The application process had hinted of extended travel for a year and mentioned a paid leave of absence from his teaching assignment if he was selected, but never in his wildest dreams would he have thought he would be a finalist, not to mention the winner.

So for close to a year he had traveled from one state to another talking to teachers and administrators – sharing his story of working with children and preparing them for the world beyond the classroom. He spoke to civic groups, school staff meetings and parent nights but his favorite was when he got to sit and collaborate with other teachers who specialized in teaching kindergarten through second grade. Those who taught kids to read and write were a special breed in his opinion. He was fascinated by their stories. Without the foundation these teachers gave students, his job would not be possible. While his mission was supposed to be to share his story of how he inspired high schoolers in Vermont to attain their goals, he found he had learned far more than he had shared.

Through all of the things he had seen and learned there was no replacement for the time he was missing with his family. He had seen them just twice in the last eight months and it was taking a toll on his mental health. Tonight he just didn't have the strength to eat another dinner alone. He was hungry, but a warm shower and a soft bed sounded much better than a little food. So he put the car in gear and eased onto the freeway headed back to the hotel one more time.

As he drove, his mind wandered once again to his family. His wife Jenny was the love of his life. They had met at church camp almost 20 years ago. She was the recreation director overseeing all art, music and athletic adventures and he had landed the spiritual director position at the last minute. His job was to lead the campers in prayer before meals and activities and oversee the nightly campfire devotions.

He was not initially thrilled with the assignment because he had hoped to spend the summer backpacking across Europe with some college buddies. However, one of the guys had to cancel due to a family emergency and another broke his ankle two weeks before they were set to leave. So they had no choice but to cancel the trip and Jeff's parents had pushed him to apply for the church camp position rather than lay around and do nothing all summer. He procrastinated until it looked like all the positions would be filled but unbelievably was offered the job with two days until the first round of about 150 third, fourth and fifth graders arrived. The tiny camp in rural Kansas was just 10 miles from his parents' home. Inwardly kicking and screaming he haphazardly shoved a few t-shirts and several changes of socks and underwear into a duffel bag and arrived just in time certain to have the worst summer ever. Only it wasn't. Not even close.

Jenny was taking a year off from her small New York college the following year to serve an internship in youth ministry. That assignment, which would start a few weeks after summer camp closed its doors, is what brought her to Kansas where she met Jeff. At first she found him to be cantankerous, self-centered and a bit rebellious and wondered how this creature had ever found his way to church camp. It was hard not to like him, though. She watched from a distance as he blended in with the children over the weeks and months they were teamed together teaching by example that God was the center of his life.

Romance was never a part of the plan. She had ambition and dreams to return to the coast where she would lead a youth ministry program and he had a far less formulated plan to graduate from college and find a job that would support his love to drive fancy cars and play golf at the country club. The two couldn't be more different.

As he drove, Jeff reminisced over his first thoughts of Jenny. Efficient, but quiet and no-nonsense were the first things that came to mind. She gave the impression she was in charge and that all rules would be followed to the nth degree of the law. Uggggg. Just what he wanted when he didn't even want to be there in the first place. He had made up his mind to stay as far away from her as possible. She represented everything he WASN'T looking for this summer – rigidity and boredom.

But as with most things in life, your own plans do not directly follow God's plans. And it must have been God himself who brought these two seemingly opposite souls together because for his part, Jeff wasn't even the slightest bit interested in sharing even a meal with the Little Miss Perfect everyone knew as Jennifer Conwell. And from what he could gather, she was equally uninterested in him.

In a monotonous fog, he drove on, smiling at the thought of their first disagreement – more of an all-out fight actually. The night had been full of fun and excitement around the campfire with everyone enjoying the evening – high on the sugar from the toasted marshmallows and while laughter filled the air the campers shared memories of the last few weeks as they began to talk about keeping in touch after the summer was over.

Then, out of nowhere, a pack of wild coyotes changed the scenario. Jenny noticed them first and began to slowly alert the campers to danger, almost inaudibly by instructing them to make a single file line and move slowly back to the dormitory buildings. While she kept herself between the wild animals and the children, the other adults began to see what was happening and assisted in the process of herding the children without rapid movements. Crisis averted it seemed. But back in the main gathering room chaos had broken out. Some were thrilled at the danger they had almost encountered and others were petrified, crying and begging to call home. No amount of quiet rule-following strategies from the well-meaning Jenny Conwell could ease the situation into a tolerable moment. The children were definitely in control and the adults were useless to intervene.

At last there was a loud whistle that silenced the room. All eyes turned to Jeff who had thought just far enough ahead to get everyone's attention but not far enough ahead to decide what to do next. Several hundred eyes were fixated on him now, however, and he had to come up with something and fast.

Food. Now it was almost laughable that his best idea was to feed them 15 minutes before bedtime, but it was the best he could do in a pinch. Signaling the other counselors to follow him, Jeff bolted to the kitchen and grabbed all the ice cream they had and began passing it out as children scampered to tables and waited rather impatiently to be handed spoons. Four or five little grubby hands forced their spoons into each tub of ice cream and the children ate until they were green around the gills. However, they were quiet and comforted.

But the crises wasn't over it seemed. Little Miss Goodie-Two-Shoes signaled for Jeff to meet her outside. It was too much to hope for, of course, that she would thank him for consoling the campers, but he was completely unprepared for the wrath of Jennifer Conwell that night.

While she insulted his intelligence, his common sense, his ability to think on his feet and even the smirk on his face, his tolerance for her Hitler-like rules was beyond a breaking point. Jeff fired back – at an equally abrasive decibel level – citing every repulsive thing he thought she had done since they had been thrown into this situation together a few months ago. Fortunately there was no swearing, but their behavior was definitely not fitting for two responsible adults, not to mention two counselors at a church camp.

At last the door to the building opened and closed with a bang, stopping the heated confrontation. As Jenny and Jeff turned to see the cook staring at them in disbelief, they also noticed all one hundred plus campers gaping at them through the large window panes – eyes wide in wonder and mouths dropped open wide. Fight over. Conversation done. But not forgotten.

Jeff stomped off to the east and Jenny stomped off to the west. He knew he should apologize but not now. Not tonight. Not tomorrow. He was so angry. How dare she call him out for just trying to help in an unplanned situation. Her rules were perfect for maintaining order under normal conditions, but tonight was not normal and he would not apologize for trying to protect and comfort those who God had placed in his care. Not tonight. Not tomorrow. Not ever.

Jeff signaled and eased the rental car onto the exit ramp and onto the main avenue just a few miles from his hotel. He hadn't thought about that night for ages. And what happened next changed the course of his life forever.

Rolling down the window now for a little fresh air and inhaling the pleasant scent of the rain falling lightly on the windshield, he let his mind wander to the rest of the story. He recalled pacing in front of the building trying to calm his

anger when he finally decided to walk it off
and broke into a comfortable jog as he ran
across the campus of the campground. He
hadn't gotten far when he heard what sounded
like a struggle. Could it be that one of the
campers had been left behind outside?

Slowing his pace he could tell it was
near the pool. Someone was in the water.
Who, though? Realizing he, too, could be in
danger he approached the pool with caution
and was shocked to find none other than the
intolerable Jenny Conwell fully clothed and
thrashing around in the deep end of the
camp's swimming pool.

'What an idiot!' he thought as he
approached, being fully ready to lash into
her again about her ridiculous rules and
regulations. After all, one of the first and
foremost rules of the camp was you NEVER
went swimming alone. Her tone rang through
his ears as he could hear her tell the
children, 'Two by two, always more than just
you.'

Now, however, he realized she was not
out for a late night swim. She was in
trouble. She was drowning.

Tonight as he drove – just a bit
further to the hotel parking lot – sweat
beaded on his forehead as he remembered what
happened next. Without even stopping to
remove his shoes he dove straight into the
water and yanked her swiftly out of the
chilly pool. He held her tightly while she
caught her breath and regained her sense of
herself. To his surprise she did not pull
away. She did not pelt him with insults. In
fact, quite the opposite, she let her body
melt into his…and wept.

As the evening turned to late night and then to early morning she told him how she had been walking with such haste in her anger that she didn't even think about the pool. In the dark she had stumbled and fallen into it, then panicked and her mouth and nose had filled with water. She was sure she would have died, she told him, if he hadn't seen her.

Who would have thought, he chided her, that the activities director couldn't swim. It was true, she had told him. She had never learned to swim and had a healthy fear of any body of water bigger than a bathtub. Sympathy for her very real fear softened his heart and all was forgotten. As they talked she opened up to him like she had never done with anyone before him. She told him how frightened she was that she would fail or disappoint her family. She told him how she was never confident in anything athletic and she rationalized that is why she treated him with disdain.

As Jeff continued to drive he recalled every detail of that night's conversation. As he held her and soothed her until just minutes before the sun came up, he realized this woman who he thought was tough as nails was sweet and sensitive and vulnerable. And it was all of those things that would eventually make her the best wife in the world and the mother and role model to his children. Oh how he loved her. God had blessed him far more than he deserved.

Perhaps it was the distraction of his thoughts, or that he was so very tired or perhaps even the rain that caused his car to slam into the other car that night just before he reached the hotel parking lot. The officers told Jenny that he had likely died instantly and felt no pain. They thought, of course, those would be words of comfort to the strong woman who stood before them. But there were no words that could comfort her that night while she stood stiffly in the hotel lobby wondering how in the world she would tell Abigail, Angie, Ava, Adalyn and little Abe their dad would never be coming home from his trip.

The days turned into weeks and Jenny followed every protocol for a grieving widow with minute attention to detail. She planned the funeral, purchased the headstone and accepted gifts of food and memorials with grace and deep and sincere appreciation. But mostly she was a pillar of strength for the children at every turn. However there was one thing she could not do. She could not look at the mail. The letters and cards of condolence were just too much.

And so the invitation from Kennedy and Greg in its creamy linen envelope laid on the kitchen counter, unopened, among the seemingly hundreds of other envelopes that she couldn't bring herself to process. As each day passed it grew closer to the wedding day and Jenny didn't even know they had been invited. So it didn't seem likely that Jenny Moore would make it to the wedding celebration of Kennedy Andrews, her husband's next-door-neighbor when he was a teenager growing up near a little suburb of Wichita, Kansas, so many years ago.

A Change of Plans

Kennedy caught herself smiling as she dusted the crumbs of bread off the counter and began to add hot, sudsy water into the sink. What a great evening of food and friendship. Her only regret was that it was over. She never tired of entertaining friends and co-workers here at her cabin on the lake.

The spacious kitchen and open dining area were perfect for hosting friends. Tonight several from her old neighborhood had gathered around her piano to sing a few old show tunes before a light dinner. However, the minutes had turned into hours of singing, laughter and impromptu harmonizing. One of the best ways to spend free time, Kennedy thought. Tonight music had taken precedence over the food and it wasn't until after nine that the group finally settled into the dining room to enjoy some soup and homemade bread topped off by peach cobbler.

The cabin was an impulse buy - something Kennedy did not normally do. Normally her life - both at work and at play - was scheduled down to the minute. Her life was full and her responsibilities were many so life had dictated a strict schedule as a necessity. Her career operated around a mostly nine to five timetable with no weekends, holidays or late nights. She was lucky, she knew, to pull a lucrative salary without having to burn the midnight oil. However, she was active at her church, involved in a number of service organizations and truly enjoyed entertaining her friends. So to squeeze it all in she relied on a regimented schedule. If something wasn't on her schedule it didn't happen. The word "impulse" was not in her vocabulary.

Similarly, any purchase over $10 was something she agonized over for days. It wasn't because there wasn't money. She had worked hard to achieve and eventually exceed her financial goals. At this point in her life, approaching 50, she had accumulated more than she needed or could possibly spend on herself. Perhaps it was that philosophy of saving before splurging that had allowed her to become so financially comfortable. However, her resistance to splurge had inadvertently pre-programmed her brain to hesitate before making major purchases.

So what was different on that brisk October afternoon two years ago that led her to sign away an enormous chunk of change for this home? She had asked herself that question many times. It was so unlike her. While walking her dog along the trail by the lake that day she happened upon the four-bedroom cabin nestled among the pine trees. She was intrigued by the view it must have from the large windows that peeked out over the trees along the trail. Almost blocked from view was a tiny red handmade sign reading "FOR SALE BY OWNER."

She and her dog Mattie had walked this trail hundreds of times and had never noticed the spacious log home. It seemed to fit in so well with its surroundings that it was all but invisible. That day, however, the cabin had a vacant feel that caught her attention. She was drawn to its appeal somehow which was odd since she had never even noticed its existence before. Suddenly she wanted to walk through the door and turn on all the lights. Quickly grabbing her phone from her pocket she dialed the number and made an appointment to see the inside.

Within a week the paperwork was signed and the keys were hers. She still wondered sometimes, when she lay awake and couldn't sleep, how a girl like her who never did anything crazy like this ended up the home owner of this gorgeous space in just a matter of days. Regardless of how it happened, there was never a moment she was sorry for her decision. It was a perfect fit.

She learned from the phone call that the cabin had had only one other owner - a retired couple, John and Sharon Edwards, who built the house five years ago as a second home. Unfortunately, just days after the construction was completed John had died of a massive heart attack. Sharon couldn't bring herself to move in. Their daughter had stayed there one winter while she was writing a book and she had occasionally rented it to groups of vacationers. But the upkeep was becoming too much for her and she had decided to sell.

Now the couple's son had been charged with finding a new owner. The price was more than reasonable. The Edwards' were not looking to make money on the sale, they just wanted to find a new owner and erase the headaches of maintaining a second home.

For Kennedy it was love at first sight. As she had predicted, a great room with high ceilings and an over-sized fireplace filled the space that overlooked the walking trail and a good portion of the lake. A huge kitchen with a charming island spilled over into a relaxed dining area that opened onto a large deck with yet another spectacular view of Cherry Lake. A master bedroom and bath completed the first floor and there were two other bedrooms upstairs that shared a bathroom.

A smaller area across the hall served as the fourth bedroom. This room, perhaps, was the selling point. It wasn't an enclosed room like the others, but rather an open area at the top of the stairs that shared the slope of the cabin's ceiling forming a peak in the middle of the room. The walls had a natural wood paneling that gave the room the feel of a ski lodge. She envisioned the room filled with an overstuffed chair, dozens of pillows and floor to ceiling bookshelves along one wall. There would be no television in this room she quickly decided, just a stereo. Or maybe a piano. But oh my goodness! How would they ever get her piano up the narrow stairs. This room would definitely be her retreat area, but the piano would have to stay on the lower level.

Since she had moved back to Kansas and begun her tenure with Carey, Wiley & Associates she had been renting a two-bedroom apartment near the high school. The apartment was more than adequate for her but it had never felt like home - more like a place to sleep and occasionally fix dinner. Since she wasn't consciously looking for a place to move, the log cabin was a luscious serendipity at this point in her life.

The scent of turkey ruminated through the kitchen and out onto the balcony. Soaking up the aroma with a deep intake of fall air, Kennedy closed her eyes and settled deeper into her deck chair to count her blessings. This time 10 years ago she would have never dreamed her life could be this perfect. Several failed relationships, a number of job changes and even several changes of residence had left her in a much better position in life.

Even the fact a turkey was roasting in her kitchen was a bit of a shock to the system. Not that long ago, she had been a self-proclaimed non-cook. It wasn't that she couldn't cook. She could manage anything from a box, a bag or a jar she liked to say. And she could even follow a recipe. She knew how to execute all the appropriate kitchen vocabulary – like sautee, poach and even fricasee – but as a child and teenager she had never taken much interest in donning an apron.

Other things drew her in, like her internship at the local newspaper where she proofread copy after school and typed obituaries in the evening. On weekends she spent her waking hours manning the high school football and basketball score line until midnight or later. Her friends were the reporters, the subscription telemarketing team and the vending machine. Cooking didn't make the cut.

For fun she honed her musical skills – singing in church choirs for as long as she could remember. Others had compared her voice to that of Karen Carpenter. She didn't see it, but felt blessed to have a natural alto vocal range which made singing in barbershop quartets fun because she almost always got to sing the melody. Kennedy couldn't imagine her life without music. She eventually took a few piano lessons and toyed at song writing, but found over the years that she much preferred singing with friends to the tunes others had perfected.

In school she worked hard to double up on math classes – which sometimes came with two hours of homework a night. She organized and carried out numerous student council projects and in her spare time took classes in political science at the local junior college to get a jump on her journalism degree. The incidentals of high school, like the homecoming bonfire and most of the school dances, were for others. Her ultimate goal was to graduate from high school and college as fast as they would let her and start running up the corporate ladder to become a national television news anchor. Everything else was a blur. Eye on the prize.

But that was ancient history. So she had never learned to dump and pour at will and create a concoction equal to that of her mom and grandma, but instead had survived since college with take out and frozen dinners. Once she had even made a New Year's resolution to become a gourmet chef. When that hadn't materialized her next year's resolution was to teach herself Spanish. Not tremendously successful at that either, the third year her resolution was: Teach self to cook in Spanish.

Needless to say, she was the butt of countless cooking jokes among her friends and family. When she had to take food to a social function she would put together a beautiful tray of pickles, olives and gourmet cheese. It was always a hit and so she continued her survival tactics with take out and frozen dinners accentuated with an occasional crock pot chili. On rare occasions she would buy and clean an elaborate array of fresh veggies that she tossed together for a salad when she had an instant pang of guilt for not eating healthy.

Now, however, things were different. She was engaged to be married. At the age of 50 she had finally decided to quit fighting her stubborn independent streak and settle into a life of peace and solitude in her country cabin on the lake with a life companion. Work was solid, comfortable and dependable. Her friends were all happy in love and her family was scattered all over the country. And like they say, when you least expect it? Expect it.

Girl meets boy.
Boy likes girl.
Girl likes boy.
The two live happily ever after.
Perhaps it was time to learn to cook.
In just a few hours Greg and his father would arrive to celebrate their engagement and begin the planning for the upcoming June wedding. And with a multitude of elbow grease and a little luck, they would all enjoy a pleasant dinner first.

Greg

Ironically, Kennedy and Greg met in a culinary class at the community center. She had been drug there, kicking and screaming, by a few of her well-meaning friends and he had been sent there by his aunt who had begun to finally accept that he would forever be a bachelor. But even under these circumstances, it took more than a cooking class to bring them together.

Clustered on one side of the room Kennedy and her co-workers Chris and Kelly lamented over the stench of the raw fish set out at their work station. Meanwhile, across the room, Greg and his girlfriend of the week contemplated ways to stash the fish in the garbage container and steal away with the chocolate raspberry sauce bubbling on a nearby burner awaiting the final course. They might have pulled it off if not for the fear of getting caught.

The evening continued in that same manner. Kennedy and her cohorts reluctantly but meticulously following directions while holding their noses and Greg and "the girlfriend" clowning around and sabotaging the instructor's efforts at every turn. Eventually the entrees were complete and set out on display for the others in the class to view and sample. Everyone laughed at how they all used the same recipe and identical ingredients but the final results showed stark differences.

As for the Team Andrews fish dish, it looked beautiful! The creamy sauce and the asparagus spears on the side of the platter gave the appearance of a master chef. While some of the others had lumps in their sauce, the fish looked to be chopped or in one case shredded and one group even forgot about the asparagus all together. Then there was the plate from the cocky guy across the room and the platinum blond attached to his side like a parasite. Their sauce was a murky brown, their fish appeared to be charred and the asparagus smelled of vinegar.

But when it came to the tasting? What a surprise. The beautiful sauce on Kennedy's fish was the envy of the class. Maybe this cooking thing wasn't so bad, she thought. By all appearances it looked to have stolen the blue ribbon. However, even a nibble was more than the palate could take. It was far too salty. What was a "pinch" anyway? Who measured things by pinches?

Moving around to sample the other dishes made the group feel somewhat better. Most were nothing to write home about either. Too cold. Too sticky. Too spicy. No flavor. But the last one – Greg's fish – was extraordinary.

Not on purpose. He didn't know what he was doing either. But the unintentional char to the fish gave it a refreshing crunch. Their darker brown sauce had a mysterious color according to the ingredients they were given, but it was good. Maybe it was because they were drinking wine between each sampling to allegedly clear their palates or perhaps more realistically to tolerate the taste of a room full of creations made by a class of non-cooks. At any rate, Greg's fish was tasty, extremely so. And the vinegar-y asparagus? It had a mild pickle-ish flavor.

Surprisingly appealing. And definitely something to remember.

At last dessert was served – a safety net to the night since it was prepared by the instructor as a reward for their hard work. A soft and squishy chocolate brownie sort of thing layered with the raspberry sauce and a dollop of homemade sorbet.

The class dispersed with much laughter and promises to do this again although Kennedy was relatively sure most of them had no desire to actually pay money to destroy what could have been a great meal at a five-star restaurant. Personally she had a great time, but it was because of the camaraderie of her co-workers rather than the opportunity to demonstrate her ineptness in the kitchen. With witnesses.

She was still smiling at the thought of his incredible and her inedible salmon when she reached her car and noticed the driver's side front tire was flat as a pancake. No need to get mad, she thought. A not-so-perfect ending to a not-so-perfect night. Chris and Kelly had already left the parking lot and she knew no one else here. At this time of night and in these shoes she wasn't prepared to walk home. Flipping out her phone to call a taxi, she noticed the crusty fish guy approaching her as he walked to his own car.

After a few funny cracks about how they both needed to amp up their culinary skills, she noticed not only could he cook, at least a little bit, but that he was funny and not at all cocky like she had mistakenly assumed earlier in the evening. In her present state of mind she didn't have the energy to notice he was also extremely attractive. But she did notice the clingy blond had mysteriously disappeared.

"Do you need a lift?" Greg offered, noticing she wasn't opening her car door.

"Oh, uh, no. No thank you," Kennedy said. She couldn't jump into a car with a total stranger, no matter how frustrating it was to be stranded in a parking lot miles from home.

"I just seem to have a flat tire. I'll call a cab and deal with it in the morning."

"No, no. I can change your tire," he offered. "I may not be able to tell a salmon filet from a hamburger patty, but this I can do."

So 20 minutes later she had a new friend and a reasonable mode of transportation to limp home. He had told her the spare tire wasn't much better than her flat. Since she was close to home she would be OK for tonight, but he advised her not to put more than 10 miles on it.

Grateful for the help and eager to get home, take off her shoes and shake the ick out of this evening she didn't balk when he offered to follow her home (in the name of tire safety).

Was it a pick up line? Maybe. But she was exhausted. And after all she wasn't inviting him in, just accepting his generosity for the sake of her safety. He refused money for changing her tire so if it made him feel better to see her home, so be it.

As she pulled into her apartment's parking lot 10 minutes later she rolled down

her window to wave him on. He waved in
return and headed on down the street.

"By the way," she said out the open
window, "your dinner was very good." But he
was gone. The words lost in the wind.

Kennedy

Fresh out of college Kennedy had taken the first job offer that came her way. It had been too long spending money she barely had and she was ready to start making more than she needed. Even $20 more than she needed sounded like euphoria.

The time she spent attending college at Kansas State had been the best years of her life. Not that her childhood wasn't wonderful. Her parents were as close as you get to picture perfect. Nightly family dinners were an expectation and sharing household chores with her brother was not fun but character building and now that she was older she appreciated the solid family values of be nice and work hard.

But college was a new adventure. Exciting. Different. Crazy. Learning to live with a roommate might take top billing when it came to getting used to something new.

Among other things, Kennedy discovered she really had to study. Hard. These professors weren't interested in passing out A's because you were a sweet girl from a nice family. To the university you were a number – 4129432664. In high school she knew if she needed help with a class it was as easy as dropping by the classroom for 10 minutes after school. At K-State she was a tiny fish in a big ocean. To get help from a teacher you had to make an appointment. And as luck would have it she always had a question when the professor was only available before a 7:30 a.m. class across campus in blinding snow or torrential rain. Yes, college was a whole new world.

Arguably the thing she learned most while in college happened outside the realm of academics. And it had to do with finances. For example, if you rack up a big phone bill and can't pay it in full by the end of the month, the company disconnects your phone. No questions asked and they were not sympathetic to excuses. Or if you are flat broke and your parents send you a weekly allowance check on Wednesday, you spend it by Friday, you will be very hungry by Sunday.

Budgeting had not been necessary for the first 18 years of her life and suddenly it wasn't just important, it was everything. Unfortunately it wasn't as easy as taking a class or watching a video. It was a trial and error process and she made many mistakes.

So accepting the job at a Topeka television station as a copy editor sounded like receiving the Nobel Peace Prize. A real job in a real studio in a real apartment with a real income. She had made it.

The first month was fascinating. She was excited to get to work in the morning and not overly anxious to leave at night. She was actually getting a paycheck to do something she loved. Well, editing copy wasn't her first love in the journalism spectrum. She wanted to be an anchor. But those jobs weren't handed out to the new kids on the block. She was prepared to pay her dues. So she spent her days like a sponge, soaking up every tidbit of wisdom she could from the veterans. She brought them coffee and ran their errands. She watched live air time with intensity and memorized the anchors' mannerisms. She learned more about technology in that first 30 days than she had in the whole rest of her lifetime. She even broke her own promise to herself and reasoned that she would be willing to take a weather girl position if it meant live air time on a major network.

Someday, she told herself, I, too, will be on air, just like my idol Barbara Walters.

However, that first month of editing copy became months and months and eventually turned into almost two years of editing copy. The chances of advancement at that particular station were slim to none. It didn't take long to discover someone would have to die before a position came open and even then she was not the first in line. It was time to move on.

And move on she did. First to Kansas City, then to a Chicago suburb and finally got her big break in Houston. It was a step under the weather girl – she had the market reports. But she was live on the air for seven minutes a day. The rest of her time was spent as an off-air reporter. Basically she did the research and the "real" reporter got the air time.

She soon discovered the research was more fun, and a lot less stress, than the live air minutes. The income was modest and she was able to take care of herself and put a little away for a rainy day. Moving on from Houston she landed a prime time reporting job in upstate New York thinking at last she had found her niche. And yet to her disappointment, after a short time she found journalism depressing.

Approaching her 30th birthday she realized she could not spend the rest of her life digging up dirt on politicians, covering homicides and being on site at fatality accidents. It was time for a change.

Now, 20 years later, she found herself managing a large accounting firm in the city and bringing home far more money than she needed. But old habits die hard and it was tough for her to spend it, especially on herself.

She had spent years building solid accounts and adding businesses to her portfolio of clients. The work was easy for her – she had always loved playing with numbers, manipulating the what ifs of investing and diversifying but most of all she loved the people. Spending time helping others was what she loved best. Perhaps she should have been a nurse. But oh the blood. Or a teacher. But the student apathy her teacher friends talked about would be her undoing. Pharmacist? Too much memorization. Lawyer? Not into other people's problems. Social worker? No way! And so accounting it was and accounting was a perfect fit. At last her life was complete.

Perhaps her only regret was that she wasn't closer to her family. Her parents had died years ago and her brother and his kids lived in the northern tip of Maine where he was a thriving pediatrician in bustling community. Their lives crossed twice a year for holidays and they corresponded through e-mail and an occasional letter with pictures of the kids. But Maine was hours away and so very cold. She had never expected to land in Kansas permanently but here she was – happy as a duck in a puddle. Well, at least content.

***

On a rare occasion, work called Kennedy out on an evening or weekend. She pretty much had banker's hours when it came to how she earned her salary. Several times a year there was a social function that drew her and some of her colleagues out for an evening of public relations for the firm. Tonight was no exception. Little black dress, tiny purse just barely big enough to hold a driver's license, and, of course, painfully uncomfortable shoes.

She might even find herself enjoying the evening out if it weren't for the shoes. But, she had been told, little black dresses didn't coordinate with her thick cushioned walking shoes.

Earlier in the evening she had circled the room acknowledging her firm's clients and stopping for brief chats with those she knew personally. She and her co-workers had spent some time perusing the silent auction items and she had dropped off a generous donation to the cancer council in the name of Carey, Wiley & Associates.

Now as the evening was winding down she took advantage of a chair on the periphery of the action and slipped off her toe-pinching shoes while she sipped a heavily-olived martini and let her mind go blank while she watched the ice sculpture across the aisle slowly melt into an unrecognizable blob. No shoes, two or three drinks and a host of hors d'oeuvres in her stomach combined with the soft music from the jazz band had all but lulled her to sleep. She likely would have dozed off if it weren't for a vaguely familiar voice that roused her from her haze.

"Is this chair taken?"

A quick dose of reality jarred her back to the present. Greg, the crusty-fish-tire-changing stranger from several months ago was now at eye level.

"Wow," Kennedy mustered. "Who knew we hung out in the same circles? What brings you here tonight?"

"I am the emcee for the evening," he said in a quiet tone she almost had to strain to hear over the band.

"Really? What a great gig!" she blushed, realizing she was shoeless and hadn't checked her lipstick in hours. Not that it mattered. She wasn't here to impress anyone, especially this guy that she hardly knew. But he was strikingly handsome. How had she not noticed that before?

It was hard to gauge his height since he was sitting, and everyone looks better than normal in a tuxedo. However, his eyes were mesmerizing. Perhaps it was the dim light, she reasoned. And his facial features were stunning. Even in the low light she could see his clean-shaven face showed off a strong jaw line and his teeth were whiter than a toothpaste commercial. This was definitely the same man who had changed her tire, but he certainly looked different – a good different - tonight. Perhaps it was the alcohol, she thought.

"Good thing they didn't ask either one of us to cater the event," he chided.

There was that sense of humor she had witnessed on their first meeting. Yep. Same guy. It was a darn good thing he wasn't any closer because if he smelled good, too, it might have made him irresistible. And she didn't need irresistible. The opposite sex complicated life and she was happy with uncomplicated.

"Would you like to dance?" he offered, holding out his hand?

"Only if I don't have to stick my feet back in these shoes," she joked, knowing it would let her off the hook.

"Deal!" he said and almost before she realized it they were waltzing into the middle of the crowd.

And as luck would have it he smelled incredible.

Several songs later Greg returned her to her seat and promised to return with a fresh drink which she definitely didn't need but readily accepted. Greg and Kennedy spent the next hour laughing over the fashion faux pas of several other attendees while they sipped their drinks and enjoyed what was left of the evening.

When at last the band stopped and the musicians faded away for a break, she found both relief and a pang of sadness as he stood to excuse himself.

"That's my cue," he said, as he drifted toward the stage, accepted the microphone from someone and stepped into the spotlight.

Then for a little over an hour, Greg entertained the crowd with his bad jokes, silly puns and hilarious stories. Kennedy's co-workers found her at the table and they laughed together with the rest of the group of business executives who had gathered tonight to raise money and awareness for cancer research.

At last the tone turned serious as Greg reminded those gathered at the cocktail tables why they were assembled and shared a story of his own mother's battle with cancer. The sobering moment was lightened a bit when he shared how humor was the only thing that helped the family survive during her endless hours of treatment and the long path to healing after the loss of a family member left them devastated. He encouraged the audience to give generously and pray earnestly for a cure to the disease that had so affected his life and lives of so many others.

If it was possible after enjoying his light-hearted company, dancing cheek-to-cheek and inhaling his show-stopping cologne, Kennedy was even more enamored with Mr. I-don't-even-know-your-last-name when he stepped off the stage and melted into the crowd.

"He was a great speaker, don't you think, Kennedy?" her friend Paula asked. "I wonder where they found him?"

Before she could answer Greg appeared at her side with her shoes in his hand.

"I think you are going to need these to get home," he smiled.

"You know him?" Paula asked.

"Um, yes. No. Sort of," she mustered.

"I'm Greg," he interjected. "Greg Parker. They found me at Miller & Parker. Do you know it? The accounting firm on west 43rd?"

Did they know it? Yes, they had an excellent accounting team and unfortunately in this particular situation Miller & Parker was their strongest competitor. John Parker, likely Greg's father, was someone she was very familiar with professionally. He was well-respected in the community and had been kind to her on the few occasions when their paths had crossed. Since she couldn't help feeling a tinge of animosity on the rare instances when they lost a client to Miller & Parker, she could understand why Greg's family might not want to be best friends. However, it made this moment beyond awkward.

"Yes, I am vaguely familiar," Paula lied, hoping she had masked her surprise and attempted to avoid eye contact with Kennedy altogether so as not to give away their identity.

"My father has served on the cancer council in this town for years and has given the speech at this event more times than I can count. This time he had to be out of town and they asked me to step in. And you are?"

"Oh please forgive me," Paula stumbled while reaching out to shake his hand. "I am Paula Ferguson and this is Kennedy Andrews."

Greg reached into his breast pocket and offered both women his business card.

"If you ever need anything, anything at all, please don't hesitate to call. We like to pride ourselves on being a small firm who provides a more personal touch than the bigger firms like Carey & Wiley."

So this was what this evening was about? He was trying to recruit her as a client? Disappointing but predictable. Like she always said, men complicated life.

After a pregnant silence Paula was the first to speak.

"I will certainly take that into consideration," she said politely while she accepted his business card. Without reading what she had been handed Paula asked, "Are you an accountant?"

"Oh no, not me. My father is and his father before him was - and his father before him. No, I am just here representing my father tonight. I work in the advertising and public relations arena. We try to protect the smaller family businesses from being run out of town by those bigger conglomerates."

"Bigger conglomerates like Carey & Wiley?" Paula asked, because Kennedy was still speechless.

"Well, yes, as an example," Greg said. "I am sure they are adequate accountants and all, but my father has worked hard to preserve the character of his business."

Surely he wasn't suggesting Carey & Wiley didn't preserve the character of their business. Or was he? Before Kennedy could regain her composure and generate an intelligent sounding response that would allow her and Paula to escape with some dignity, the gorgeous sweet-smelling man who stood before her made that impossible.

"I'm sorry," he said with a half frown. "I have been doing all the talking. We really don't know each other very well. What

do you do?" he asked, looking directly at
Kennedy.

Reaching out to accept her shoes still
dangling from his right hand she said, "I
manage Carey, Wiley & Associates."

Evening over.

Greg

Greg's family had deep roots in Wichita – not only with the family business, but also as leaders in community projects. They were known for their philanthropy and generous devotion of time in their church.

John Parker, Greg's father, had only recently merged the company with his brother-in-law as he knew he should likely retire and enjoy his senior years, especially in light of his wife's passing. Life was short and you never knew which day would be your last.

However, it was also his career that kept him from withering into nothing after the loss of his wife. Sitting at home watching football or worse yet on the bank of a river waiting for fish to bite would not be enough to occupy his mind and keep him from slipping into a depression as he mourned the loss of Greg's mom. John kept busy with community service projects and was always being asked to host or sponsor one event or another so there would likely never be a dull moment, but still retirement scared him and so he continued to work.

Greg's mom had been an elementary teacher. Wichita had over 350,000 residents and Mary Parker had nurtured thousands of them through their primary education years. So she knew their parents, their siblings and their cousins. It was rare that the family could go out to eat or even to a movie without being spotted and someone saying, "Hey, there's Mrs. Parker! She taught me to read!"

As for Greg himself, he had gone to college to be an accountant. But somewhere along the way he had been distracted by women. He had been a stellar student in high school but being out on his own it hadn't taken him long discover college was different. No one took attendance in class at big universities. It would have been impossible in his classes of 300.

He still remembered the culture shock he experienced the first time he walked into his freshman math class and found the theater-style seating, the lighted chalkboard way down at the front of the room and the professor wearing a microphone so he could be heard. This wasn't College Algebra, this was a boredom festival. So he struck up a conversation with the attractive co-ed in the next seat and it wasn't 15 minutes before the two decided to skip the rest of class and grab breakfast instead.

This pattern continued throughout College Algebra and bled into other classes. And if Greg found women more interesting than Algebra, Statistics and Accounting 101 didn't stand a chance. Five years later he was able to muster enough credits to graduate from the University of Texas with a degree in advertising and public relations, although that was only because of a rather serious girlfriend who **was** serious about classes and he attended as well to spend more time with her.

Unfortunately the day before graduation the girlfriend had made a rather public announcement to Greg that she was interested in someone with a little more ambition and at the end of the week she was flying home to get married – to someone else.

And so the long string of girlfriends continued. Greg moved home to Wichita and found a job he truly enjoyed, so he could thank serious girlfriend #1 for that, but he now saw no use for women except for entertainment purposes. He couldn't see himself settling down with anyone, ever. How could you trust any of them, he thought. After all, when you think you know someone so well and she has no problem embarrassing you like that in front of your family and friends, what would stop someone from doing that again? His father had worked hard to assure him he just hadn't found the right one yet and to look to his parents' solid relationship as proof that love could be true and lasting. He wasn't convinced.

God had blessed him with striking good looks and a personality that could charm Godzilla, so there was never any trouble finding someone to grace his arm. However, whenever there was even the most remote chance of things turning serious – like meeting her family or even generic talk about having children someday – Greg would cut bait and run.

Everyone he worked with at his PR company loved him. Greg was the life of the party and made everyone feel welcome and valuable. He was careful not to mix business with pleasure, however. He never dated anyone who worked for him and expected the same of his employees.

Like his parents, he found happiness in giving to others and was generous with his money and time. His favorite charity was Camp Hope - a sprawling campground in Wisconsin where kids with cancer could escape the seriousness of their circumstances for a week at a time. He volunteered there frequently and found his greatest joy when working in the trenches with kids and families who needed extra doses of love in trying times.

He remembered feeling so lonely many, many times as he and his father and sister dealt with the effects of losing someone to cancer. There were countless nights when he craved the opportunity to have someone to talk to - not necessarily about the cancer, but about something, anything that was pleasant. He could see that Camp Hope offered that to children and their families and we wanted to be a part of it.

Greg's extended family was very close knit. He had 11 aunts and uncles and all but one lived within an hour of home. So even though his immediate family was small, he grew up with dozens of cousins and after his mom died when he was a teenager, his aunts stepped in to be surrogate moms - especially Aunt Ashley. Ashley was his mother's sister and she wanted nothing but the best for Greg. Offering him a safe haven in the days, weeks and months that followed her sister's death was a part of her healing process and she had taken Greg his sister Lilly in as two of her own children while John struggled to make his own peace with losing his wife. Ashley attended his ballgames, made sure he had the right clothes for his senior pictures and even helped him apply to colleges.

While he was in high school Ashley's children, Annie and Camille, loved having an instant big brother. Greg often picked them up after school in his convertible and took them for ice cream. They felt special and he felt useful. Between John and Aunt Ashley, Greg had managed to get through the difficult years of high school without a mom. Sending him off to college had been difficult for Ashley, but necessary, and he had turned out to be an upstanding citizen and a successful businessman. Now if she could just find him a wife.

Kennedy

Kennedy had had her share of bad romance. She liked to say her high school sweetheart had caused her the most joy and also the most pain of anyone she knew. Little did she know what lie ahead.

First love was full of those unexpected steamy moments of physical excitement that falsely led you to believe the two of you could never be happy apart. Broad shoulders. Dark hair. Deep voice. Passionate kisses. That was what was important for first love. How many of those relationships did one have to try and fail before you re-evaluated what you were really looking for. For Kennedy, a few. Steve. Ted. J.T.

Then there was college love. Now the priorities changed. Looking for someone with potential wealth characteristics. Of course everyone knows all men who graduates from college will be a doctor or a lawyer and be able to support three children, a huge house, a dog and a white picket fence. Ummm, not. So there were several of those. Randy. Alan. Jay.

And the upward mobility love. This is the type of love you seek when you are developing your independence and you want someone who will support you as you achieve your goals and dreams and value the same things you do. These breakups were perhaps the most disappointing for Kennedy. She was at the don't-say-you-love-me-if-you-don't-really-mean it stage. She didn't have time for that.

And at last there is the forever love. At this point, she had come to realize, there were two choices. Look for someone who was ready to be faithful and satisfied with co-existing for companionship even if your goals might be slightly different or learn to live on your own and be satisfied with it. Gone were the days of seeking tall, dark, handsome and wealthy. Now she would be happy to find a mate with a sense of humor and a job.

Although approaching 50, she was leaning toward being content without love in her life. Love complicated all things and worse than that, breakups were something she could live without for the rest of her life. Days of crying and moping over the loss of a man was just time wasted that could be put to better use.

There were moments when she truly missed having a companion to share dinner with or looked forward to ending her day with an embrace and a kiss from someone she felt connected to. But having those things meant giving up other things – like setting her own schedule, hosting parties for friends at the drop of a hat and spending time alone walking on the beach or working on a project without having to stop to make dinner.

For now she was single and loving it. Her two best companions were her dog, Mattie, and her piano. Life was good.

It was while out walking with Mattie a few months ago that she had happened upon this house by the lake. A cabin, actually. There was nothing NOT to like about the place. The location was remote, the layout was open and spacious, there were boatloads of windows with magnificent views in every direction and perhaps her favorite attribute was the thick carpeting throughout that seemed to massage your feet as you walked across it.

All of her friends had volunteered to help her move and she had accepted. It hadn't take too long. Other than her bed and the piano, everything else had been moved by a car. She would have to invest in some furniture to fill the space and looked forward to decorating the wooden walls with simple furnishings that matched her style. She would begin with a big dining room table surrounded with comfortable chairs in hopes of filling the rooms someday with friends and laughter.

A boyfriend/fiancée/husband was not in the plan. Of course she should have learned by now that the best laid plans were meant to be broken. Enter Greg Parker.

* * *

Kennedy loved weddings. As a musician in high school and college she had been called on to sing at many and like a bride who makes a scrapbook of her own wedding, Kennedy had a scrapbook of sorts with tidbits from all the weddings she had attended. It was a box actually, filled with monogrammed paper napkin momentos, save the date cards, the more ornate and memorable invitations and hundreds of party pics – some formal and posed but many playful.

Over the years Kennedy thought she had seen it all when it came to weddings. The bride got cold feet and the wedding started late was the most common. But she had seen grooms faint more than once and one groom had even vomited just after the vows. They blamed it on too much alcohol at the rehearsal but she had always wondered if that marriage had stood the test of time.

A few months ago she had been asked to sing at a wedding where the parents of the bride and groom got into a verbal altercation at the back of the church after the bridesmaids had already started down the aisle. That was one to write home about but probably couldn't top the time over 200 guests showed up at the reception venue only to find the doors locked up tight as a drum because the groom had not paid the bill. That one gave new meaning to the phrase "All dressed up with nowhere to go."

Tonight, however, she was attending as a guest, not a member of the wedding party. A cousin was tying the knot and throwing a big bash afterward to celebrate with flare. It promised to be a fun evening which she needed. It had been a long week at work as tax season approached and she needed some time to unwind and enjoy a drama free weekend.

Her brother would be attending as well and there was never enough time to spend with him these days. One of his children had come down with the flu so Lane was coming alone while his wife stayed in Maine with the children. Sad as that was she was relishing the down time to catch up with her brother - eat ice cream from the carton while watching old movies or just crack open a bottle of wine, collapse in front of the fireplace and relive old family stories.

As she and Lane sat side by side in the pew at First United Methodist Church about an hour down the road from her home, all indications were that this wedding would go off without a hitch. Allison was a little older than the traditional bride and a florist by trade. She had spared no expense when it came to decorating the church. Roses in pastel colors adorned every flat surface in the 100-year-old building and the multi-tiered candle holders held at least 200 tapers decked with ivy and wide-pastel ribbons. Lane and Kennedy shared a chuckle at the thought it might take longer to light the candles than the service itself.

As tradition would dictate a flower girl preceded the attendants down the long aisle before the music stopped and then swelled with notes of Here Comes the Bride. The congregation stood on cue.

Allison seemed to float down the aisle on the arm of her father and the proceedings began.

Note to self: Not that I am ever going to do this, but if I do, Kennedy thought, spend less on flowers and more on food. In the excitement of picking up Lane from the airport she must have forgotten to eat. Her stomach rumbled and again she and Lane shared a chuckle. This was going to be a great day.

Opening prayer. Check. Blessing of the blending of the families. Check. Unity candle. Check. Soprano sappy love song solo. Check. Vows, rings, kiss, recessional. Check. Another one in the books.

When at last Kennedy and Lane made their way through the receiving line and on to the buffet line, her work stresses were at last forgotten. Cousins, aunts, uncles and long-lost friends dotted all the tables. Children seemed to be coming out of the woodwork. As they ate their dinner Kennedy and Lane tried to name them all. Was that Great Aunt Agnes? No it couldn't be. Hadn't she died years ago? Then who was that lady in the hideous pink frock hovering around the cake table? Her daughter? No. She couldn't be that old yet. Well, maybe she could. She herself was no longer a spring chicken.

The evening continued with thunderous laughter as she and Lane played the identification game from one side of the room. It felt good to laugh. Really good. If she got through this tax season in one piece she would definitely make it a point to spend more time laughing.

Speaking of laughter, one guest must have had a little too much champagne. Her laugh was more like a cross between a cackle and a snort. And she was making a huge spectacle of herself at the moment. This guest definitely wasn't an Andrews relative. That didn't stop her from being amusing to watch. Craning her neck to see more of the action, Kennedy froze.

Standing just upstage of the laughing hyena was her date - none other than Greg Parker.

Kennedy excused herself as quickly as possible, nearly upending the table. She couldn't escape faster if the building was on fire. How in the world could Greg Parker be here, too? Was he stalking her?

From the safety of the bathroom, she gradually began to let logical reasoning take over. After all, there was nothing wrong with the guy. He wasn't scary or evil. But how was it that he could be so incredibly perfect with his charming, funny personality and his powerful good looks and always manage to say the wrong things. And beyond that, why did their paths continue to cross? Actually he didn't *always* say the wrong things. But he had insulted her business that she had worked her fingers to the bone to perfect and that cut deep. Although, he had not made those comments knowingly. Separating logic from emotion, from Greg's perspective it was all about business.

Emerging from the ladies room she was relieved to see Greg appeared to have left the party. Again she questioned herself…why was she so bothered by this guy? He had, after all, changed her tire. He was funny and charming and attractive all rolled into one. And he had no idea what she did for a living when he insulted her business. Anyone could make that mistake. Perhaps it was his choices in women. Both times he had the smarmiest of smarmy dates. And then again why did she care about who or even if he dated? Ridiculous.

Making her way back to the table she had to smile thinking how she could possibly explain this all to Lane. It all sounded so crazy on paper. Absorbed in these amusing thoughts as she meandered through the tables and back to her brother, she was about as far away from the reality of where she was as humanly possible. And so it was not surprising that she did not see it coming when she literally bumped smack into the solid chest muscles of the seemingly ever-present Greg Parker.

There were no words. Greg simply took a step back and looked directly into her eyes with one raised brow as if to say 'You again?'

Trying her best to regain some semblance of composure, Kennedy stumbled to find something intelligent to say. Unfortunately she didn't stumble long enough because what she heard herself say was "Who in the world would send YOU an invitation to this family function?"

Oddly, Greg didn't seem offended by the question in the slightest.

"Ummm, the groom," he mumbled. Could she be related to him? No. Surely not.

"We are, uhhhhh, cousins. So I guess I could ask the same thing. Who in the world would send YOU an invitation to **my** family function?"

"Well I am much relived to know we won't be breaking bread together at any family reunions. I never met the groom until today. I am a cousin of the bride."

"Oh, so we _are_ related, then. Good to see you again, cuz," Greg chuckled.

"Hardly. There is no way I am related to you." She winced at the thought realizing that being related to Greg wouldn't be all that bad. His mother had died of cancer and he and his father – a solid businessman – had spent his life promoting cancer awareness and raising money for research. Those were not exactly qualities to scoff at. He was a great man who kept saying dumb things. Not the first male to fit into that category.

From the corner of her eye she could see Lane was standing now and looking in her direction as if to say 'Is everything good over there?' Kennedy gave him a slight nod and then glanced back to face Greg.

"What's up with your date? He can't function on his own long enough for you to powder your nose?" Greg goaded.

"My date," she started to explain, but then switched gears. "My date? You are being critical of _MY_ date when your date closed down the bar?"

Without missing a beat Greg took that jab in jest.

"True, she had a little too much champagne. I made sure she made it home and came back to celebrate the nuptials. Your date on the other hand…where did you find that guy? You can do better than that. He's so short. And look at that nose? It would block traffic."

This man is incredulous, she thought.

"Well, at least he is sober," she quipped. "And by the way, that short guy with the ugly nose? He's my brother. Enjoy your evening, Mr. Perfect."

Wow. 'How do I do that every time?' Greg thought. Gorgeous girl. Obviously smart. Runs her own business. Kind, polite (except for a few minutes ago and he had that coming), and definitely someone who was hard to forget. And yet he couldn't say the right thing if Emily Post scripted it for him herself.

The wedding reception ended without
further incident. Over the next few days
Kennedy wondered how she could avoid running
into this guy one more time. Short of moving
to Hawaii she couldn't come with a solid
plan. And the way things were going Greg
would probably show up in Honolulu as well.

Greg, on the other hand, couldn't stop
thinking about how he could make this up to
her. He couldn't put his finger on a reason
why it mattered. She was just a girl. Only
she wasn't. She was not like any other girl
he knew. She was pretty, and witty and
sharp. But was it just his pride or his
stupid ego that wanted to prove to her he
wasn't an oaf? Maybe both. But whatever the
reason, he had to fix it and sooner than
later.

In the weeks that followed that crazy
wedding, Kennedy immersed herself back into
her work. She was fortunate that their firm
had weathered the recession with relative
ease and their accounts continued to
flourish. That made for some longer than
normal work days, but she loved her work and
never thought of it as a chore. The only
down side was having to set an alarm.
Mornings were not her friend although only
because she cherished the peace that came
with the dark. She could spend hours at the
piano at night playing and singing with
abandon in her otherwise quiet house on the
lake. Sometimes she would throw a casserole
together and invite her friends from work or
the neighborhood over for a late night of
cards, sharing stories of their lives and

howling with laughter until the wee hours of the morning. Hence, the alarm clock was an evil object of doom.

Tonight was no exception. Although it wasn't much after midnight she refused to go to bed until the table was cleared and the dishes were done. She marveled at the way an evening with friends could completely put you at ease.

Claire, Kari and Kennedy had been friends for what seemed like forever. Odd, really, in that they had almost nothing in common except they were female. Both of her closest friends were married with kids, exceptional cooks and had a passion for exercise. Kennedy, on the other hand, was single with no kids, just a dog. She could barely cook and exercise was her least favorite activity. But the girls did enjoy sharing a bottle of wine and that was enough of a connection. They had been friends for years and all three looked forward to the time they shared together - just escaping from their responsibilities for an hour or so at a time several times a month.

Claire was a science teacher who she had met at a friend's barbecue one summer. She was the center of attention as she detailed stories of her middle school adventures with today's teenagers - omitting their names, of course. She had the group in stitches and it was obvious she loved her job despite the unbridled immaturity of her students.

And she had met Kari years before when working in the news business. They had been copywriters together - both on a mission to move up into the world of big business and big money. But, like Kennedy, Kari had soured to journalism after a number of years stuck in the same place. Kari wasn't able to move from city to city in an effort to advance, however, because she was married to a commercial pilot who was required to be based in Chicago. The two had kept in touch via e-mails and an occasional phone call at the holidays and Kennedy was thrilled when she learned Kari's husband had been transferred to Wichita. Their friendship had picked up right where they left off.

The beginning...

"Hey, girl. Got a minute?" Paula asked as she rounded the corner into Kennedy's office.

"Sure, what's up?" Kennedy asked, putting down her pencil and stretching back in her chair.

"Well, it seems we have been invited out for lunch today."

Kennedy glanced at the clock on her desk. 11:30.

"Really? By who?" She mentally scoured her daily calendar and didn't recall a lunch appointment until Friday.

"Well," Paula winced. "It's a little odd. That PR firm that your good buddy Greg Parker works for called about an hour ago and asked if you had a lunch commitment today. Assuming they had a business goal in mind I checked your calendar and replied there was nothing formally scheduled but that I would have to check with you. I told his receptionist I am your business associate but I do not schedule your appointments. The lady who was calling thanked me, said she would be in touch and then disconnected."

"What? Are you kidding me? It isn't enough that this guy keeps showing up everywhere I go. Now he wants to be the master of my work calendar, too?" Shaking her head, Kennedy felt her shoulders tense.

"It gets a little more complicated I'm afraid," Paula said as she perched on the edge of a chair directly across from Kennedy's big wooden desk. "Just now a messenger arrived and delivered this to me."

She handed Kennedy a large business envelope. Letting the contents drop onto her desk Kennedy hesitantly picked up the hand-written note on Greg's business stationary and began to read out loud:

> Ms. Andrews: Please accept this invitation for lunch today at Antonelli's. I realize one lunch will not make up for all the ridiculously dumb things I have said to you over the last three months, but I hope you will accept this offer as an acknowledgement that I do, in fact, realize I could have handled myself better in your presence – more than once. Please feel free to order whatever you like. I have asked the restaurant to put the bill for your lunch (and Paula's as well) on my tab.

The note was simply signed "Greg." There was also a postscript.

> P.S. I have arranged for a limousine to take you to the restaurant. It should arrive at your office at 11:45. And please do not consider declining because you are worried I will be there. I promise I will stay away because I do not want to risk saying the wrong thing – AGAIN.

"What in the world? This guy is truly crazy!"

"Perhaps," said Paula, "but Antonelli's? At least we know he has good taste."

"True," Kennedy smiled as they both moved to the plate glass window behind her desk to check his claim of sending a limo. Sure, enough, five floors below a sleek black limousine sat waiting accompanied by a tuxedoed driver standing by the front fender.

"You know," Paula mused, "he had this messengered to me instead of to you because he knew you would turn him down flat. Maybe he is sincere."

"That is the truth! I definitely would have," Kennedy half whispered. "This guy is a fruitcake. To assume I would just drop everything and jump in a limo for lunch…really???"

"I say yes, really. Why not?" Paula giggled. "We eat well and some cocky pipsqueak who thinks he runs the world – or at least this city - pays the bill. Can't think of a better way to spend an hour."

He wasn't that bad, Kennedy thought. A tinge of guilt crept into her head as she considered the offer. The limo service alone was more than she would spend on lunch in an entire month.

"Oh Paula, we can't…" she started to say as she turned away from the window. But Paula was already headed back to her office.

"Just let me grab my jacket," Paula was saying as she disappeared from view. Five minutes later, against Kennedy's better judgment, the two emerged from the elevator and onto the street where they were greeted by Alex, the driver who would whisk them to lunch.

Antonelli's was the perfect Italian eatery. The food was exceptional and the atmosphere beyond comparison. Chefs created your custom order right at your table with locally grown and produced products whenever possible. The wine was imported from the best vineyards and the dessert was known to be ordered and shipped all over the country. It was a place you took people you wanted to impress.

Today was no exception on flavor. Kennedy and Paula wondered why they didn't come here more often. As they finished their lunch and pondered over sharing a calorie-indulgent slice of lemon cake infused with brandy their waiter dropped off a complimentary carafe of coffee.

"Thank you. And the meal was fabulous," Kennedy told the waiter. "Could you add a slice of caramel apple cheesecake to my bill, please? And please make that to go."

"Certainly. I would be happy to, ma'am. As for your bill, Mr. Parker has taken care of it."

"I am afraid there has been some misunderstanding," Kennedy told him. "I will take care of the bill with this," she said, holding out her credit card.

"Oh dear, this does present a problem," the waiter said with a wrinkled brow. "Mr. Parker left very explicit directions with the front desk. I'm afraid I can't accept this," he said with worry in his voice and declining to reach for her card.

"I will square things up with Mr. Parker," Kennedy assured him. "Please accept this for payment."

Hesitantly the waiter took her card and exited with haste.

"Are you just trying to tick off the illustrious Mr. Parker?" Paula asked when the waiter had gone.

"You know I can't let him pay for this, Paula. No matter how kind the gesture."

"You're crazy. The guy wants to do something nice and you reject it? To the tune of a bunch of money I might add."

After a brief silence Paula added, "Unless you like the guy. You DON'T actually like the guy do you, Kennedy?"

"No, of course not. Not like that anyway. But just because he made a few well-placed off the mark comments that doesn't entitle me to profit from his checking account. I will thank him for the luxury ride to lunch and call it even."

"And the cheesecake? Is that for Mr. Thoughtful, too?" Paula quipped with sarcasm.

"Listen to you, girl. You are just as bad as he is," Kennedy said, adding a wink so her friend wouldn't think she was mad. "Let's go back to the office before I decide to head home for a nap."

Back at her desk Kennedy took out a piece of personalized stationary and penned a quick note:

> Mr. Parker: Please accept this slice of dessert as a thank you

for your generous offer of lunch at Antonelli's today. While I know from experience the cheesecake from there is divine, it is not an equivalent match for the luxurious ride you provided for Paula and me today. Alex was an excellent escort. However, there really is no need to feel you owe me a meal or anything else for that matter. Consider us even.

She signed it with her scripted initial K, attached the note to the beautiful bow-adorned box of cheesecake Antonelli's had prepared for her and asked her receptionist to drop it off at Greg's office on her way back from dropping off the daily mail. Then she closed her eyes and relaxed in her office chair. That guy was really something. It was such a nice gesture on his part but accepting his kindness entangled her in his life in some way and she did not need that. Men were, as she had often said, a complication. Sometimes a pleasant complication but always a complication nonetheless and her life was rich and full without that complication. Yes, thank you Greg Parker, but I am not interested.

Greg was more than a little amused at his late afternoon delivery. Ever since that awful public break up with Chelsea all those years ago at college graduation, he was a self-proclaimed bachelor who readily accepted that he would probably never understand women. But he had never met a

124

woman who wouldn't accept a monetary gift, especially if he had said or done something stupid. But this girl was bound and determined to make things extra difficult. Perhaps that is when he realized for the first time there was an attraction beyond trying to prove he wasn't an idiot.

He was starting to like this girl and that made him uncomfortable. His dedication to work and subsequent success in business was easy compared to affairs of the heart. He knew he chose women to date who were fun but shallow because he didn't want to fall in love. This thing – or whatever he was feeling for Kennedy – wasn't love, but it was definitely an attraction. Yes, his heart was in trouble.

He intentionally waited until the next afternoon to call her office and was not surprised when the receptionist asked for his name and politely told him to hold the line while she checked to see if Kennedy was available.

"Miss Andrews," Janie chimed over the intercom. "I have a Greg Parker on line 2."

What? You are kidding.

She was trying to compose an excuse to put him off when Janie beeped again. "Shall I put the call through or tell him you are unavailable?" she asked.

"Ummmm, yes I will take the call. Thank you, Janie."

Moments later she felt her spine stiffen and her limbs go limp, both at the same time, when she heard his voice come on the line.

"Ms. Andrews," Greg said with confidence. "I apologize for interrupting you at work but I do not have your home number. I understand from the staff at Antonelli's you are going to make me work a little harder to atone for my repeated offensive remarks. However, thank you for the generous slice of cheesecake. My staff enjoyed it very much."

Long pause.

"Your staff? You don't like cheesecake, Mr. Parker?"

"Oh yes, yes I do. Or at least I thought I did. But unfortunately after just a few bites my throat started to swell. My face turned beet red and I had the most intense allergic reaction. Perhaps it was the caramel? At any rate I spent most of last night in ER."

No.

"Holy cow! I am so sorry! Really? All night?"

Again, a long pause, although this time initiated on his end of the line.

"No, not really. I am just teasing you. It was delicious. I ate every bite and considered sending out for a second piece. Thank you very much but it was not necessary."

Oh, so his charm didn't work. His dashing good looks and no doubt expensive cologne didn't work. And his checkbook hadn't wooed her so he was trying to disarm her with humor. To her disbelief it was working.

"I see. Well, Mr. Parker, your sense of humor is refreshing. I am glad to know I won't be responsible for your medical bills." In spite of herself she noticed she was smiling and suspected he was, too.

"Can we stop with the 'Mr. Parker' stuff? I really do feel awful about insulting you countless times, but I assure you my mouth just got ahead of my brain. I really am a decent human being and I find you to be very pleasant and undeserving of my inane remarks," he finished. He wanted to add 'and you are drop dead gorgeous as well' but wisely thought better of it. After all he was trying to get himself out of trouble, not into more.

"I see. So you would like to be called Greg, then?"

"I would indeed. And also, while I have you on the line, is there any circumstance in which you might consider dining WITH me at Antonelli's? I do enjoy your company."

She needed a second to let that soak in. A date?

"A date?" she alarmingly heard her mouth echo her thoughts.

"I would very much like that, yes," she heard him say. "But if you are uncomfortable with the semantics of the word 'date' I would accept the term 'appointment' or 'business meeting.'"

"I see. And if we were to eat at Antonelli's together you would like to discuss business?" she asked.

"Well, no not really," he answered honestly.

"In that case, I am afraid I can not accept," she teased back. After all, what is fair for one is fair for the other.

"Unless, of course, you promise to be on your best behavior. You do surely have a best behavior gene, do you not, Mr. ...uh, Greg?"

This brought a chuckle through the phone line.

"I do believe I can find my best behavior, yes. Does that mean you will join me for dinner?"

"I would like that, Greg. You seem to be a very kind person and we definitely have gotten off on the wrong foot."

"Excellent. Would dinner tomorrow be too soon?"

"Tomorrow I do have an after hours commitment," she lied, not wanting to sound too eager. "But I can do an early dinner Wednesday if you like. I have choir practice at seven but the church is just around the corner from Antonelli's. That is assuming you still find me worthy of that establishment after I tried to kill you with their dessert."

He was hoping to spend the evening with her, not just an hour, he thought, but he would take what he could get.

"Terrific. Would 5:30 work for you?"

"That would be perfect. Shall I expect a limousine to pick me up at the office?" she teased.

"Hmmmmm, well I believe Wednesday is Alex's day off. I would be happy to pick you up in my slightly smaller personal vehicle if you would be willing to give me your home address. Not near as roomy but it does have leather seats."

"Well, given that Alex has the day off why don't I meet you there? My house is off the beaten path and it would take a powerful GPS to find it. At 5:30 Wednesday?"

Good Lord! What was wrong with her? Had she just told a relative stranger that she lived on a deserted road in the middle of nowhere? What WAS she thinking?

Disappointed but grateful to seemingly be back in her good graces he told her he looked forward to seeing her and then hung up without fanfare.

Immediately after she placed the receiver back on the hook Paula appeared at her office door with a smirk plastered across her face.

"Really?" she questioned. "You are going on a date with him?"

"Yes, really," Kennedy countered. "But the bigger question is really? You were eavesdropping?" she joked with her friend and longtime business associate.

"Well, I didn't intend to. But I dropped some paperwork off at Janie's desk and she told me you were on the phone with Greg Parker. Naturally I thought she had made a mistake but on the way back to my office I heard you on the phone and it sounded like you were flirting."

"Nonsense. I wasn't flirting," Kennedy countered. "But he is funny. What can one dinner date hurt? He will feel better about whatever he has done to offend me and I can stop worrying I will run into him and have another awkward moment. It's not like I am going to date the guy. It's just dinner." Dinner with a handsome, financially independent guy - who smells like heaven and has a great sense of humor - but just dinner. Right? Right.

Surprisingly, Kennedy found Greg to be the perfect dinner companion. She wasn't sure what she had expected but she had carefully planned to keep the date short by pairing it next to another commitment. There would be no need to dress up in fancy clothes or mess with an updo with her hair. Straight from work – wearing slacks and a nice sweater – keeping it light and comfortable. On the way out the door she would add a little lip gloss and probably an extra dose of mascara, but other than that it would be business as usual. There would be no time for a kiss afterwards – just a simple parting of ways. Perfect dinner. Perfect evening. Then off to choir practice.

Still, she was disturbed that she kept watching the clock all afternoon in anticipation. Antonelli's cuisine was top-notch but in her gut she knew it wasn't the pasta that had her stomach in knots.

Greg had arrived at the restaurant early and stood when she approached the table and the waiter pulled out her chair. He was a gentleman it seemed but the true test would be if he could go for an hour without saying something insulting.

Much to her chagrin, he passed with flying colors.

The conversation was light and easy throughout the entire meal. They talked about work for about 30 seconds and then moved on to talk of the weather, baseball, family and music. He told her about his rejection of accounting in college and devotion to pro football, especially the Kansas City Chiefs, but mostly he asked about her and he listened. How was it that she ended up in that silly culinary class? Where did her parents live and expressed sympathy that they were both deceased. He wanted to know about her brother and his family, asked about her music and her dog and even what she liked to eat for breakfast. He told her he regretted never having children and she told him she had never seen the ocean.

She was impressed that he did not get ruffled when the waiter spilled water into his lap and he did not make a scene and send his food back to the kitchen when they brought him soup instead of salad. She noticed, also, that no bill ever came. Undoubtedly he had taken care of it before dinner so there would be no argument over who paid. Damn! She did not want to like him but he was making it hard not to.

After they had both declined dessert he asked if she wanted to take a short walk by the river before she had to go. It was a beautiful spring evening and she had agreed. She was now feeling some regret that she didn't have more time to spend with this new friend – or whatever he was turning out to be.

As they walked they talked about current events and the latest book he had read causing her to ask him more about his interest in public relations. There was, after all, a bit of irony in the fact that he made a living choosing the right words but in her past experience with him he often chose the wrong ones.

As they walked they found a bench along the river and sat down to rest their feet while they laughed about Paula's reaction to his phone call and how he had teased her about his allergy to cheesecake. Dusk had turned to darkness and the path they had walked down was now illuminated by just a few lantern-like lights along the river. Relishing in the warm breeze and the great conversation, choir practice had been forgotten.

"Where's the moon tonight?" he asked as they stood to head back to the main road.

"It seems to be hidden in those clouds." And just as she uttered the word clouds, it began to rain. Not sprinkle. Not drizzle. But rain. And then pour. By the time they had reached the main road they were drenched but laughing like children. What a surprise this night had been – in more ways than one.

"I'm actually kind of glad you didn't have an umbrella," she chided.

"Really? You prefer to be soaked?"

"Well, no. But I was starting to think you were perfect. Now I see you have at least one flaw."

Now she was the one saying stupid things. You don't tell a man he is perfect. Ever. And especially on a first date. That was dating suicide. 'Never be too vulnerable' was her mother's first piece of dating advice. But now it was too late. You couldn't erase words once they were said.

She lowered her eyes and quickly tried to think of something witty to say to sidetrack the conversation. While she was thinking Greg monopolized on the lull in the conversation and pulled her and her wet sweater next to him and his, tipped up her chin and right there in the pouring rain gave her a gentle kiss that alerted her senses – all of them – into paying attention.

And then the short, sweet, intense moment was suddenly punctuated with the loudest clap of thunder she had ever heard. They broke apart in gales of giggles.

"You know," he said, still keeping eye contact in the dimly lit night, "when we made these plans I was pretty sure it would take an act of God for you to let me kiss you. I guess I wasn't wrong."

Then he wrapped her in a tight embrace as she murmured her ascent. When at last he released her she told him it was probably God's way of getting back at her for missing choir practice.

"Come on," he said. "I'll hail a cab to get us back to our cars. If we spend any more time in this rain we will both be sick."

"Wow! First a limo and now a taxi. What next time? A boat?"

"Maybe," he said. "I'll have to keep you guessing."

But his mind had already registered that she said 'next time.' With most of the women he dated he wasn't overly concerned about the 'next time' when the date ended. If there wasn't a next time he would move on to someone else. But with Kennedy he knew he would be crushed if there wasn't a next time. It wasn't too early to tell his heart was in trouble and there was nothing he could do about it.

Thirty minutes later she walked through her door and dropped her wet clothes in the foyer and headed to the bathroom to dry her hair. What a crazy, crazy night. She picked up the phone to check her answering service. Six messages. One from Paula and five from Kelly wondering where she was tonight. Kennedy didn't miss choir practice. Kelly was worried.

Checking the clock on the bedside table she decided it was probably too late to call. 10:30. But Kelly had called five times. With some hesitation she dialed her number and was thankful when it went straight to voice mail. She left a brief message apologizing for calling so late and for worrying her, assured her she was fine and promised to call back tomorrow and explain.

As far as Paula was concerned, she would have to wait until tomorrow to get the juicy details.

Slipping between the sheets she closed her eyes and rolled onto her side prepared to sleep. But, of course, her body wasn't ready for sleep. Obviously she had misjudged Greg Parker. Now she had the difficult task of deciding what to do about it. Men are a complication she kept repeating to herself as she drifted off to a restless sleep. But even as she said it she knew some men were worth it. She had the sneaking suspicion even at this early stage that this one might be one of those.

The following week Kennedy and Greg fell into the habit of meeting at a nearby deli - the Salted Olive - for a bite of dinner before each headed home to their own responsibilities.

He told her about his association with Camp Hope and she entertained him with stories of her nieces and nephew. They talked for hours each night before parting. Oddly, it was as if the relationship went from a budding romance to a solid friendship. In her head it seemed a little backwards. There was no repeat of the tender kiss they had shared in the rain that night. Their deli dinners had, however, become something she would be hard pressed to live without.

The weeks that followed were crazy. Kennedy was scheduled to speak at a conference in Chicago and was away for five days. Then, when she returned late Sunday night, Paula had called to let her know her mother was critically ill and she had to take some time off. It was one of those months when you seemed to take one step forward and slide three steps back. Fortunately Paula's mother would recover quickly so perhaps life could resume to a quasi-normal soon.

She and Greg had spoken over the phone a few times but since she had been home their schedules never seemed to mesh. She was starting to wonder if they could make a relationship work. After all, they barely knew one another. And yet he was mesmerizing. It was hard to imagine she had ever thought he was an imbecile. Thinking back to the black tie event and then her cousin's wedding it was a miracle they were even friends, not to mention the promise of something more.

As she scanned her calendar for the next few weeks she sighed. The only night she didn't have plans in the next two weeks was Saturday and she had tentatively planned to have a few friends over for a casual evening of fellowship. Perhaps she would invite Greg to join them. Over the years she had learned you could tell a great deal about a man's character by observing two things: how he treated his mother, and if he could hold his own with your friends

And the two become one...

Greg arrived at Kennedy's first dinner party at precisely 6:30 (as per the invitation) with a colorful bouquet of fresh cut flowers. It was difficult to believe she ever had ugly thoughts about this guy. He was the perfect gentleman, the kind of guy your parents would want you to marry.

Looking back, the food was unremarkable. It was billed as a dinner party, but the food was secondary to the evening. In retrospect, both Kennedy and Greg recognized this evening as the night they knew they would spend the rest of their lives together. There was no official proclamation to that effect, but there was an unspoken agreement that their two lives would be forever entwined.

Claire and her husband were the first couple to arrive at the cabin. The four of them fell into comfortable conversation in the great room over a glass of wine and a view of lake through the giant window pane. Tonight the weather was perfect for a walk on the beach, balmy and ever so slightly breezy. It was the kind of weather you always hoped for but seldom got. Lately it seemed on those beautiful evenings her schedule was packed with must-do tasks and then when there was time to relax and enjoy a few minutes of down time it was either chilly or drizzly. But no matter. Tonight was perfect and Kennedy rose to open the doors to her walk-out patio.

After the dishes had been cleared and dessert and coffee served, the guests wandered back into the great room and folded themselves comfortably on the soft furniture to relax.

"So," Greg asked no one in particular, "How often do you exercise that beautiful grand piano? Your home is exquisite, Kennedy, and your piano is a gorgeous centerpiece."

"Oh that old thing?" Kennedy offered nonchalantly. "It's just a show piece. One more thing to dust if you know what I mean."

"LIAR!" her two best friends chimed at once.

"Kennedy has been playing the piano since before she was born," Claire said with a smile. "She should have been a composer instead of an accountant. It's a travesty, really."

A light blush graced Kennedy's cheeks and she waved off the compliment with ease. "Not a composer," she said. "Never a composer. My dog writes better music than I do. I find **playing** the piano quite relaxing, however."

"Well, what would I have to do to get a sample?" Greg asked with a raised eyebrow.

"Ah, I do love a challenge," she countered. "Let's see…I play something for you and you…wash my car?"

Greg bellowed with laughter. "Sure, I'll wash your car. I thought you were going to make it difficult on me."

With a lilt in her step Kennedy rose and moved to the piano. She loved their playful banter, even with an audience it was fun to joke with Greg. She lifted the key cover, sat down on the bench and with great exaggeration lifted both hands before lowering them to the keyboard and played a perfect note. One note. A perfectly executed middle C.

"There you go," she said. "I played you a 'little' something. My car keys are on the counter. Be careful with her, I just got new brakes and they are still pretty sensitive."

"You are quite the charmer, Miss Andrews," Greg said with his own brand of orneriness. "Scoot over. Let's try this again."

Scoot over? Was he going to play? Sure enough Greg slid onto the piano bench beside her and launched into an energetic version of Scott Joplin's The Entertainer. Everyone was entranced.

As he played the last note he turned to Kennedy. "So, if I wash your car for one *note*, then I think you owe meeeeeee…" he trailed off with a sly smile. The group of friends howled with laughter. She had met her match with this guy. He could definitely keep up and it was great to see Kennedy excited about something besides crunching numbers.

"When did you learn to play like that?" she asked, still a little shocked.

"Oh that?" he chided. "Well, I remember a few weeks ago you told me you were headed to choir practice so I figured you had some musical talent. I figured if I wanted to stand a chance with you I should take a stab at something – anything – musical. So I signed up for a few lessons. Nothing to the piano really."

"Now who's the liar," she teased. "I am really impressed."

"Well, thanks. I guess it would be fair to say I have taken a few lessons. It was important to my mom. When I play I think of her and since she is no longer with us…well, you know. It seems even more important to honor her wish."

For a moment he lowered his eyes as if offering a silent prayer for his mom. And then a few seconds later he was back on board with the group.

"So there is still that issue of what you owe me," he said with the boyish deviousness returning to his voice.

"Hmmmm…I would have to wash your car for a month of Sundays for a performance like that," she said.

"And as much fun as that would be to watch, how about something else," he offered. "I will let you off the hook on washing my car, but how about you join me for cards with my dad tomorrow night. Since mom died it is our regular Sunday night thing. It gives him something to look forward to. We usually order pizza but I bet I could scare up something a little better if you agree to come along."

"I don't see that I have a choice," Kennedy teased, loving the fact that he had such deep reverence for his parents.

It was hard to imagine the days when she would rather dodge rush hour traffic on foot than see his face. Greg was becoming very difficult to dislike. Aside from the kindness and respect he showed to his parents, he had confidence that lacked even a hint of arrogance. He ran a successful business, believed in giving both time and monetary resources to worthy causes, had a marvelous sense of humor, wasn't afraid to interact with her friends (virtual strangers to him until tonight), could play the piano with a vengeance and was gorgeous. Drop. Dead. Gorgeous. What more could she ask for? She had been single for a long time and had no complaints about enjoying a comfortable unattached life. However, it never hurt to spread your wings a little. Greg might be just what the doctor ordered – a change of pace.

The next few months seemed to fly by in a haze. Despite their many shared interests, there were refreshing differences in their lives as well. Greg taught her to enjoy an occasional art museum and she showed him the finer points of watching professional baseball. What before had been just a tedious drivel of mismatched lines and paint splotches seemed to come alive with Greg's enthusiastic explanations of the canvas. And where Greg previously felt a baseball game was a good excuse for a nine-inning nap, Kennedy showed him how different the game became when you knew the players and predicted the outcome of each pitch before it was thrown.

Together they experienced life with new meaning. The fact that he was petrified of commitment and she had no interest in it whatsoever never came into play. No amount of prodding from his family or hers would remove that invisible barrier that stood between them – marriage

Early in January plans were well underway for a benefit golf tournament in the spring. Greg was the chairman of the Cancer Council of Sedgwick County, a cause that was very close to his heart. For her part, Kennedy was not a golfer, but she certainly would volunteer to help in any way she could and Greg knew he could count on a financial donation from her as well. As much as he had tried to get her to appreciate the game, she told him she just didn't see any joy in hitting a little white ball and then chasing it for miles just to do it again and again. He tried to argue it wasn't much different than the game of tennis that she loved to play, but she just didn't see the thrill. At any rate he was happy to have her by his side in the planning. He also knew as his girlfriend she would stand by him through it all – from the first tee off until the awards ceremony was over and the event venue had been spit shined and polished clean.

"Hey baby," he said one day as they were making a list of distinguished guests to invite with personal invitations. "Does Lane play golf?"

"My brother? Yeah, a little. Why?"

"I just thought maybe he would enjoy coming down for the event. You know, bring the family. We haven't seen them since last Christmas. Your nephew is probably taller than me by now."

Kennedy looked up from addressing her envelopes and considered Greg's idea.

"Sure. I never get to see them enough. Let's give him a call tonight and see if we can convince him to bring everyone out here."

"Tonight?" Greg asked. "Let's call him now. Would he still be in the office?"

Glancing at the clock and mentally doing the time change calculation Kennedy figured there was a good possibility he still would be. "We can't call him now, though. He is probably with a patient."

"Let's see," Greg said. "The worst that can happen is he has to call us back. Tell me his number again. I know it ends in 4443 but you are the numbers girl. I can't keep them all straight."

"It's even easier than all that," she giggled. With this cell phone technology I couldn't even tell you the 4443 part. To me he is just speed dial 1."

"One??? I thought I was one on your speed dial," he said with mock hurt in his voice."

"Sorry buddy. You're seven. I've known Lane longer."

"Seven. Ouch!"

A few minutes later they had Lane on the phone and his voice was coming through the speaker.

"Hey, what's new up north?" Greg asked after the normal pleasantries were exchanged.

"Well, it's mighty cold up here," Lane said. "I guess you guys are feeling it in Kansas, too, but we are plowed under in snow and ice up here. It's awful. Just awful."

"The reason for our call," Greg said, "is we were thinking how nice it would be to

143

see you and Mary Beth – and the kids, of course. Any chance we could get together for a round or two of golf when things thaw out a bit? Bring the family and all."

Lane and Greg talked for a few minutes about the golf tournament and Lane promised to try to clear his schedule for a week and he would get back with Greg and Kennedy as soon as he knew for sure he could work things out. Kennedy chimed in with best wishes to the family and told him to stay warm and be safe and would look forward to hearing from him soon.

"Oh by the way, Lane," Greg said as an afterthought rather than disconnecting the line. "While I have you on the phone and Kennedy here with me in the office, I wonder if I could bother you with just one more thing."

"Sure, Greg, what is it?" she heard her brother ask.

"Well, here's the thing." Greg paused for a minute and looked directly at Kennedy while still holding the phone out between them so they could both hear. "Your sister and I have been dating for almost two years and normally I wouldn't bother you with this, but since your father is deceased I think the responsibility falls to you."

What??? Kennedy's eyebrows knitted with confusion.

"It's just that I really can't do this without your consent," she thought she heard Greg say. "I would very much like to marry your sister but I just can't bring myself to ask her without your permission."

Silence.

The room was suddenly spinning. It was too hot in here. What has happening?

"Um," she heard Lane hesitate over the open line. "Are you sure that is what you want, buddy?" Lane continued with the most serious voice ever.

She wanted to open a window, get some air. But she was certain her legs would not carry her across the room right now so she sat plastered to the chair in shock.

Greg smiled and affirmed "Absolutely, I do."

"Well, you've known her long enough to know her cooking is deplorable. She is stubborn as an old mule and her dog will always be her first priority. But if you can live with all that, then yes, you have my permission to take her off the eligible bachelorette list."

They were joking about this? They had both crossed the line with this one. There were jokes and then there were jokes. This wasn't a funny game. Vaguely Kennedy heard Greg and Lane finish the conversation. Something about the weather and golf and thanks and who knew what else. And then the line went dead.

Finally Kennedy trusted herself to stand.

"What in the world?" she muttered more to herself than anything. And then in the general direction of Greg. "He is a busy man. A professional. You wanted to interrupt what he was doing just to mess with my mind? Some days, Greg Parker, you make me wonder what goes through that thick skull of yours!"

"You're mad." It wasn't a question. It was a statement. Usually a man only got one chance to do this right and he was on thin ice here. He had to make it better and quick.

"Actually," Greg said slowly. "I called Lane yesterday and cleared it with him. We had a long conversation about how much I loved everything about you – even your dog, your stubbornness and yes, even your cooking."

Greg was standing now, too. He slowly closed the gap between them but left plenty of space. Something told him this was not the time for a hug.

"I definitely can't imagine my life without you anymore, Kennedy. I told Lane that yesterday and he agreed that we were right for each other but made me promise to treat you with the utmost respect at every turn and warned me that if I couldn't promise him that then he would not bless our wedding. And of course I could never ask you to marry me without the blessing of your family. You know that. Right?"

Silence.

"Still mad." Greg shifted his weight to the other leg.

"Look. I am doing this very badly. I wanted Lane's blessing before I talked to you. He was expecting me to call with you here today. It has nothing to do with golf or the tournament. I called him back today because I wanted you to know that I respect the wishes of your family. I wanted you to hear him say it is OK."

More silence. He didn't think Kennedy had as much as blinked for the last five minutes.

It was now or never. Greg took a half step closer and dropped to one knee.

Kennedy heard herself gasp. This was real. He was not joking.

"There is no need for a long preamble. I have told you many times what a difference you have made in my life. Growing up without my mom and having such a bad experience in college has made me doubt my ability to commit to anyone for over 25 years. But with you I know beyond a shadow of a doubt that we are meant to be together. There are no secrets between us. I can trust you with my deepest thoughts and feelings. If you feel the same way, too, will you marry me, Kennedy Andrews?"

It wasn't until those last six words that she realized she had been crying. Marriage hadn't crossed her radar screen for a very long time. And yet she knew beyond a shadow of a doubt, too, that she couldn't live the rest of her life without Greg. It was unfathomable to think it.

"Well?" he asked again. "Is that a no?"

She shook her head no but she meant 'no, that is not a no.' Regaining her composure she managed to say yes through the tears and watched his sweet adorable face go from slight fear to welcome relief.

"Um," he managed to say as he stood and she reached out to pull him close. "Um, on the outside chance you would say yes I bought you a ring, too, but it wasn't until I was down on my knee that I realized it was in my jacket pocket back there," he said while motioning to his desk chair several steps away.

"I think I did this all wrong," he finally said as they broke away from their hug and he handed her a Kleenex to dry her tears. "In my head I saw this going way differently. Can I have a do over?"

Finally the tension was released and they both began to relax. Not only did he see her smile for the first time since this serious discussion began but she actually laughed a little.

"So," she said with a big smile, "When you say 'do over,' do you mean you want to propose to someone else?"

Together they laughed and embraced again. Everything was going to be all right. She was going to be Mrs. Gregory Allen Parker.

Suddenly he remembered the ring box and retrieved it from his jacket pocket. Opening the box he held it out to her and met her eyes with an unspoken phrase that seemed to say 'I am yours if you will have me.'

The ring was beyond beautiful. How did guys do this, she wondered. Even under these fluorescent lights it sparkled like the purest crystal imaginable. It was a simple, round solitaire stone with a delicate gold band, but it was the most amazing piece of jewelry she had ever seen. Kennedy allowed him to slip it on her finger and then he sealed it with a deep and tender kiss.

"By the way," Greg said when he released her at last. "Your brother isn't available for the golf tournament week. But he has cleared his schedule for a mid-June wedding. I hope that is OK. The wedding is all up to you – whatever you want. But I had to be sure he could be here. I know how important that is to you."

"Ah, so we are starting this permanent relationship off with a hoard of secrets, huh?" she teased.

"No, no, no secrets," he said. "But sometimes it is OK to have little white lies around Christmas and birthdays. And engagements," he amended.

"Well then, you are forgiven," she said with sincerity.

The only problem was, there was still one secret between them. Actually more like 25 million secrets.

Wedding plans...

Paula was shocked at the news the next day at the office. At least she pretended to be. Kennedy suspected she had known the plan from the beginning. At any rate she and all of the office staff ogled the ring and made all the appropriate remarks of congratulations. Was it possible that 50-year-old work-a-holic Kennedy Andrews was finally going to tie the knot with the handsome public relations guru taking two of the city's most eligible singles out of commission? It seemed it was a fact.

"Oh Paula," Kennedy sighed as she dropped onto the sofa in her office after the others had gone. "How will I ever pull off a wedding in five months? I know next to nothing about all of that. Flowers. Cake. Dinner. It's all a jumble."

"Are you thinking big bash or intimate gathering?" Paula asked.

"Yes," Kennedy responded and they both laughed. "I don't know. I mean all little girls dream of a big wedding with all the trimmings, but I am no longer a little girl. I can't see myself in the big, white 100-pound dress and miles of veil. But neither can I imagine just signing papers at the courthouse. I just don't know, Paula. I haven't thought about this type of thing in I don't know how long."

Paula was quiet but tapped her pencil lightly on her thigh and her mouth twisted into a thoughtful question mark.

"So let's start at the beginning," she offered. "You love the guy so no matter what the day will be a success, right?"

"Absolutely," Kennedy said.

"Then how about you start like this. What is the absolute most important thing to you – other than Greg being there, of course."

"Well, there must be fantastic music," Kennedy said without hesitation. And cake. There must be layers and layers of white cake with that ooey, gooey creamy frosting."

"Perfect," Paula responded. "You take care of the music and leave the cake to me. That's two decisions down. Five hundred more to go. Are you thinking of doing this on the beach or at the church?"

"Oh no, Paula. I have no idea!"

Paula knew Kennedy probably better than anyone and she could sense this was quickly overwhelming her. Kind of ironic really that someone who managed people and money for a living was struggling with how to manage the details of a 30-minute ceremony. On the other hand, people and money were business. The wedding was personal. And yet she knew without reservation that June 14th would be the greatest day of her friend and co-worker's life even if every single detail went south.

In the end she had hired a wedding planner to iron out the specifics. After all, the wedding was a day, but her marriage to Greg would last a lifetime. At least that was the plan. But fate had plans of its own.

Three months later…

As she sat in the iconic restaurant on the quiet side street in an otherwise busy, bustling city, Kennedy let her mind wander while she waited for her catfish sandwich to arrive. Later she would be meeting with Greg and his father at the office to finalize the wedding guest list. She would need to be focused and attentive to detail, but for now it was acceptable to be lost in her thoughts.

In just a month the invitations would need to be addressed, stamped and sent. Today they HAD to finish the guest list at all costs. Although she and Greg hadn't set out to have a small wedding, the list of potential guests seemed to be growing exponentially daily. There were hordes of people they would have to invite, of course, including the closest family members and business associates. Who would have dreamt there were so many? And each time she and Greg sat down to talk there was someone else – or several someone elses – that must be added to the list. They began to wonder if it would be easier just to buy a billboard and post the pertinent information, subsequently inviting the whole town.

Today was the first time in several months she had taken the time just to sit and think. She was over the moon about meeting and drifting deeply in love with this wonderful man. How it had all fallen into place had been a mystery to her. She had not been seeking romance or even companionship. Greg quite literally waltzed into her path and since their first meeting, way back at the cooking class, had become a part of her life.

But there was one problem. And it was a big one.

Kennedy had been keeping a secret from her fiancée and there was no easy way to fix it. Don't tell him until after the nuptials and they would be entering a lifetime commitment with a lie between them. Tell him now and he would hate her for withholding information. After all, his college girlfriend had kept secrets from him and ultimately that was the reason he was still a bachelor at 50. When he discovered she had been less than forthcoming he might possibly consider it a deal breaker and that was something she just couldn't risk. And yet – she had to. She absolutely had to tell him today that she was a millionaire, and a multi-millionaire at that.

Mindlessly staring out the restaurant window she saw a couple casually walking down the sidewalk arm in arm. What was their story, do you think? Were they always as happy as they seemed at this moment? Were there secrets between them? Were they able to thrive and survive?

After all, this secret was something she wanted to share – she truly wanted to share but had protected it for so long because money changed people. Or at least it changed their perceptions of you she thought.

While Kennedy was financially independent, socially confident and had all the outward appearances of being happy with her life's decisions, she had always wanted people to like her for the person she was, not the money she had. To date it had been an easy secret to keep since only her banker knew the total dollar value of her net worth. The last statement had registered at just under twenty-six million dollars and was growing daily thanks to wise investing.

While she hadn't intentionally kept it from Greg out of spite or malice or even to protect it from having to share it with him, she had always wanted to be loved without the attachment of "things" and other material complications. And their relationship had been built on solid trust and an unbelievable friendship. Again she wondered how she had managed to keep it from him from so long, but also why had she not told him already.

As she sat and sipped what was left of her lemon-laced iced tea, she began to devise a plan to tell him. She had to tell him today. Picking up her purse and clearing her table, she knew that he would understand. He had to. Just simply had to.

Walking out onto the fish market patio she noticed the older couple she had seen earlier. They had now slipped into the restaurant and were sharing a sandwich and French fries in a corner booth. This – she thought – this is what she and Greg would be like, too. It might be a little tense up front, but in 24 hours the worst would be over and the secret would be forgotten

The fallout...

Kennedy's smile had always gotten the best of him, Greg thought. He barely remembered the cooking class she credited to their first chance encounter, but he did remember seeing her in the parking lot after the class, staring at a flat tire with frustration. Helping her and following her home for her safety had netted him that first flash of her inner beauty through a smile of appreciation. And even when she wasn't smiling on the outside, he was deeply attracted to the patience and persistence that was evident on her face while she worked. Kennedy had been blessed with the gift of positivity. He could stand and watch her all day.

Even after today's bombshell, he still felt immensely close to her. She was a part of every fiber in his being. So she was a millionaire. According to her well-kept secret she was actually a multi-millionaire. Nothing had changed about her he told himself. Perhaps in a minute way he felt even closer to her because he had seen how incredibly difficult it was for her to share this secret with him.

Now as he lay in his bed just hours after learning he was about to marry into a fortune larger than he could have ever imagined, Greg felt oddly empty. The shock of it had passed. There was no anger. After all she had not lied to him, simply omitted a detail of who she was. A pretty big detail, but the detail itself was not the problem. How could he have fallen for someone AGAIN who wasn't upfront and honest with him? How, in fact, had that happened? He was a reasonably intelligent man and considered himself a solid judge of character. But this was the second time someone he was intimately close to had found it necessary to leave out a big chunk of reality. Was something wrong with him?

Of course, as he predicted, his body wasn't the slightest bit interested in sleep.

Kennedy had told him she hadn't wanted money to be the focal point of her life. So since it had come to her, she had squirreled it away in high interest investment accounts. She didn't need it to sustain her lifestyle and so it sat, waiting, until she could determine the best way to use it to make a difference. For that, he loved her. However, the secrecy of it could very well be a deal breaker.

He felt his feet touch the ground and he mindlessly walked through his dark house into the kitchen then promptly turned around and paced back and forth across his living room with no real sense of direction. So she had created a software program years ago and sold it to a consulting firm back East. They had paid top dollar for it which had even surprised Kennedy herself.

But why the secretiveness? He understood on the ground floor level that she wanted to be known as Kennedy. Not filthy rich Kennedy but just Kennedy. And yet her decision to keep it from him - the person she was the closest to in the entire world - was troublesome to him. Like Kennedy, he had a great deal more money coming in every month than going out, so being the beneficiary of huge sums of cash meant virtually nothing to him. But he would not tolerate dishonesty. Not. Ever. Again.

When he woke he could not remember the last time he'd looked at the clock but he did notice he had six missed calls and two voice mails from his fiancee. But really what else was there to talk about? What else needed to be said? Rubbing his temples to ward off the headache he felt coming on, Greg headed to the shower and tried to put together the agenda for his day. So much to do and no time to deal with precious Kennedy and her unbelievable little surprises.

Greg and Kennedy

Kennedy sat in her office listening to the sounds in the hallway. She was unaware of how long she had been sitting there. The noise was like a dull rumble of senseless sound. She was numb. It was impossible to know how many items she had on the back burner and how long it would be before she could tackle them. All she could do was think.

Across town Greg sat in his office, too, but the scenario was dramatically different. He had thundered into his work and was completing task after task with unbridled energy. His inbox was empty but he kept plunging through work like it was child's play. He didn't want to think.

Minutes turned to hours and at last the sky darkened. She would need to go home. There was no use sitting here wasting time. She would go home and eat. Or read. Or sleep. In the end she wound up at the piano where she was most comfortable.
It wasn't the melodies that soothed her but more the physical activity that busied her hands and the noise of the notes that blocked out her thoughts. She had taken a risk in telling Greg that she was a millionaire but it was a risk she had to take. Marriage was already a ginormous step if all was right in the world. In her mind having a secret between them was not something she wanted to take credit for.

The hours ebbed away and at last she began to let it go. The emotional day had come to an end and it was time to move on.

There was definitely life post- Greg Parker she knew because she had been completely comfortable with her life pre-Greg Parker. At last she let her fingers stop and arched her back. Then slowly rose from the piano and stretched out on top of her bed letting the pillows envelop her tense and tired body.

When Greg finally took time to breathe he scoured his desk top looking for the two bills he knew he needed to pay by the end of the week. No time like the present. But the envelopes seemed to be missing. The normally calm, cool and collected Greg Parker had at last come unglued. All the hours he had spent in this particularly productive afternoon faded away and he felt his blood pressure rise. Never mind the large doses of work he had completed in the last few hours. Where were those bills?

At last he looked at the clock across the room and was stunned to see if was well after 8 p.m. Cursing under his breath he rose from his desk and shut down the office for the night. This is not how I am going to spend this spring evening, he thought. He dashed out the door but ambled slowly to his car.

That's when it hit him. Could it be over between them? He plunked down hard into the leather seat, turned the engine on and cranked the stereo to high letting the music bombard his senses. However it didn't work. Finally allowing himself to check his cell phone he saw he had no missed calls and no messages. That was nothing since Kennedy had tried to call him earlier in the day, leaving several messages. What could he say to her? What SHOULD he say to her?

Finally he rolled down the windows and sped out of the parking lot, an atypical move for him but today was anything but a typical day.

What he couldn't know was he had inadvertently knocked the two bills off his desk and into the trash can. Tomorrow when he returned to work would be too late. The trash would have been emptied and the envelopes would be on their way to the city landfill.

Hours later, after a walk, a shower and more than his share of a bottle of wine, Greg found himself swimming in self-loathing. Nothing, it seemed, could bring him peace. He reached for his phone and made the overdue call.

*****

Kennedy awoke from her unplanned nap in a panic. Someone was hammering on the front door of the cabin. Her location was remote and people almost never ventured out here unless they were specifically coming to see her. It was after 11 p.m. All the lights were out in the house and she briefly contemplated lying still on her bed until whoever was here gave up and disappeared. But then she heard his voice. It was her boyfriend/fiancée/ex-fiancee banging hard on the door and yelling her name. He must be physically hurt, she thought, and raced to the door letting her nurturing side override her panic and anger. For a split second in her heart-racing fright she forgot there might be another reason he was at her door.

"Greg, in the name of all things holy what are you doing here banging and screaming like that?" She reached out and grabbed his shirt, tugging him gently inside the door.

"Me? You are mad at me?" he ranted. "I have been calling you and leaving you messages for hours. Then I drive all the way out here and find the place locked up tight and all the lights out. What are you doing? Trying to scare me to death?"

Kennedy stood back from him and simply stared. Really? Fighting was not normally her style, but something had to be said. She chose her words carefully. Taking about three steps away from him she took in a silent breath and proceeded with caution.

"Well, if you must know, I was at the office from eight this morning until seven tonight. I completed no work. I ate no food. I talked to no one. Then I left the office, drove home, played the piano for several hours and then took a nap."

"Oh."

"You see," she continued, "my fiancée has decided that after a difficult discussion about a topic that is hard for me to talk about he does not have the time or the energy to return my calls. It hurt my feelings and I checked out for a little bit. Oh, and I accidentally left my phone at the office. Thanks for checking on my welfare. Do you need any more information, or can I go back to sleep?"

She realized she had not entirely kept the sarcasm from her voice, but as her words

161

dragged on while he stood cross-armed and angry looking she cared less and less.

"Hmmmmmmmmm," Greg uttered. He wasn't quite ready to apologize and yet everything she said made total sense. And so he paced. As he walked across her great room floor, his back turned to her his mind raced. But when he turned to walk back toward her she was gone. What a jerk he must be, he thought.

He hadn't really taken time to consider her feelings, just his own. He was finally in love, happier than he had ever been in his life when he suddenly discovered she had been keeping something from him. It hurt like hell. But it certainly wasn't grounds to give up all that she meant to him. She had valid reasons for not wanting to tell anyone, not just him. That he did understand and he felt awful for her now. She had bared her deepest secret to him and he had all but spit in her face.

As he approached Kennedy's bedroom he found her curled in a ball facing the window with her back to the door.

"Kennedy," he attempted. No answer. No movement.

He tried again "Kennedy, can I come in?" No answer. No movement.

As he stood in the door frame, knowing better than to walk in without an invitation given the situation, he heard a whimper of a response.

"Why?" she all but whispered. "What do you want from me?"

This was the only invitation he needed.

"I want you to forgive me. I'm sorry. More than sorry, Kennedy. I was just blindsided."

Still she kept her back to him.

"I am thrilled that you told me. You know about my trust issues and in the moment it just felt like a betrayal, you know? Keeping something that big from me." No answer.

"I am not mad about the money. I am not even mad about the secret. I understand. I think. Or I want to. Kennedy please don't shut me out."

At last she sat up and rotated her body toward the door where he was still standing. He was sad to see, even in the darkness of the room that when she pulled her long hair away from her face it was streaked with tears.

She said nothing but made eye contact and he slowly approached her, sat gingerly on the side of the bed and put his hand on her back.

"I love you," he said. "More than that even. You have become a part of me."

"But you don't understand me?" she countered with a question.

"Yes. No. Maybe. I think so."

"Well that is helpful," she said and pulled away so that his hand fell to the comforter and there was no physical contact between them once again.

A minute passed. And then two. It felt like an hour.

She was back to silence.

At last he stood and left her there alone. Pushing the issue by making her talk about something she was so sensitive about was not going to help. As he approached the door he heard her softly weep and knew he couldn't leave. So without turning on any lights or making any sounds, he did all he know how to do. Wait.

It was well after three in the morning when he woke, slouched and crumpled on her sofa. There was no sign of her. He tiptoed into her room and pulled a blanket over her spent body before returning to the sofa. He pulled off his shoes and stretched out to try to rest.

The last thing he remembered thinking as exhaustion overtook him was there was great irony in the fact he was already sleeping on the couch and they weren't even married yet.

Shortly after sunrise Greg woke to the aroma of the automatic coffee maker perking away as if everything in life was normal with nothing out of place. He also discovered his beautiful fiancée sitting on the floor in front of him, sound asleep, with her hand resting peacefully on his chest. Maybe things would get back to normal. That was something.

Wedding plans

As promised, Paula had commissioned an exquisite cake from a bakery just down the street from the office. For her part, Paula thought it might be a nice touch to break from tradition and serve cheesecake from Antonelli's as it had played a big part in the couple's transition from enemy rivals to a perfectly matched bride and groom. But she had promised Kennedy she would take care of the cake and her co-worker was very specific about the countless calories she was expecting in the rich frosting.

The remainder of the wedding details were falling into place as well. The ceremony itself would be in a simple country church about five miles outside the city. The seating would be tight due to the seemingly multiplying guest list, but the architecture both inside and out including a wide intricate entrance archway and a tall stark white steeple made the cozy venue an attractive choice for the blushing bride-to-be and her handsome groom.

Years ago Kennedy would have dreamed of arriving in a horse-drawn carriage or a swanky limo, but at the age of 50 it seemed more practical to simply dress at the church and relish in the beauty of the day rather than focus on the pomp and circumstance of a grand entrance and exit. The wedding, after all, was a day but the marriage would be for a lifetime.

Her wedding planner had suggested a muted color scheme for the wedding party's attire and church decor but added flare with every shape and color of wild flower available. And so it was decided to go with black and white punctuated with fresh cut flowers in bright pinks and yellows highlighted with deep lavender and soft shades of green. The bride herself would carry an elegant bouquet of roses in softer pinks, yellows and lavenders laced with baby's breath. Each of her friends serving as attendants would carry a single pastel rose.

The cost of the glorious occasion seemed to escalate exponentially every day. Kennedy had stopped tallying the receipts long ago. Her goal was to enjoy the day and think about the money later. Calm and serene business accountant Kennedy Andrews almost never spent money like this, but this was not just an ordinary day. It was the day that would mark a change in the rest of her life so if it cost a bit more than normal, so be it.

This afternoon she had taken off work to meet with the dressmaker for the final fitting of her gown and plan perhaps her favorite part of the week's festivities. In less than a week the invitations would be mailed and she wanted to do something special for her some very dear friends from her past that she had hoped would be able to fly in for the celebration and meet her new family and friends.

She and Greg had decided to throw a pre-wedding mini party to reunite with her old friends at a little deli on the edge of town called the Salted Olive. It had been so long since she had heard from some of them since she had shamelessly lost touch over the years.

She had set out to locate addresses for seven of them. She would include two first-class airline tickets and a map of the city with each of their invitations. Kennedy had also pre-paid for their rooms near the country club where they would hold the reception - hopefully insuring they would all be able to attend. Again the price tag seemed a little lofty to the normally thrifty bride, but how could she marry without these seven people who had greatly influenced her life in one way or another?

Father Paul had been her parish priest and had become a close friend and confident during her years at the university, often filling in for the role of her parents since they were no longer living, guiding her and offering her advice, sometimes solicited and sometimes not. She hoped he would be able to share in her special day and would not be upset that she had chosen to marry outside of the Catholic church.

And Jack. Jack had been a wonderful friend to her through high school. They sang in choir together, clowned around in their spare time and creatively found excuses to procrastinate on homework assignments. Like a brother to her, the wedding would be incomplete if he could not be there.

Mary Jane. Brenda. Jeff. All dear friends to her. How she hoped the invitations would find their way into their homes and pull them all together creating the ultimate throw back Thursday before the big day.

Sadie who she had never met but was a special part of her life and was included in her daily prayers. Dear sweet Sadie who had grown up without a mother, much in the same way she had. She hoped with all her heart she would get a chance to tell her how much her mother loved her and yearned for her to be successful.

As far as she knew, none of these special guests knew each other, but with the exception of Sadie they all knew her and she was overanxious for them to meet Greg, her best friend and forever companion.

And then J.T. It was definitely unusual inviting her high school sweetheart to her wedding. However, she and J.T. had shared much together. Had circumstances been slightly different it could have been J.T. that she would be standing at the altar with, side by side, professing their love and lifetime commitments to each other. Years ago her goals were to explore the world, build a name for herself in journalism and follow her dreams across the nation if necessary. His goals had been different. In no way inferior to her own, but different. And so they had parted ways. She hoped he had married well and found happiness in his work. In a matter of six weeks or so she hoped she would know for sure that he was well.

For better or worse

The wedding day inched closer. Invitations were addressed and stamped and all was forgiven between Greg and Kennedy.

Greg settled back into his routine – almost forgetting the big quarrel several weeks ago that had all but separated him from Kennedy permanently. Although somehow the betrayal still had a miniscule spot in his memory. Despite the joy the couple created with their time together and through the mind-numbing but bonding effort to plan such a big event, there was an incredibly tiny bit of doubt that nibbled right at the edge of his mind every single day. He wondered if he could trust this woman he was about to commit to for the rest of his life.

It was ridiculous really. And he knew that. Kennedy was someone who meant the world to him. He had never met another human being like her and knew he never would again. But a multi-millionaire? However, even with that new knowledge she was unique and special. She was not the least bit interested in buying flashy things with the money. She had admitted to being a little extra lavish with a few things for the wedding and reception, but according to Kennedy she had no need for fancy things for herself. The money from the sale of her software program had been a huge surprise to her but not something she just wanted to waste. 'It needs to be for something special' she had said more than once. And 'neither you nor I need the money' she repeated regularly when the subject came up in conversion.

In truth, Greg was a bit jealous although not of the money. He was envious of her ability to think through a powerful solution without getting caught up in the fame of being a rich woman as most people would. Kennedy was right that years of hard work had provided plenty of money for both of them to live extremely comfortably with money left over every month. There was no need to spend it or even really think about it again. She had secured the funds in a very smart way allowing it to multiply several times over and her investments were solid and accounted for. End of story.

Even still. She had lied to him by an act of omission. He had to be able to erase it from his mind in order to move forward. And moving forward was the only option if he was going to marry the love of his life which he fully intended to do in the very near future.

*****

Exactly how much was a million dollars, Kennedy wondered as she tied her left tennis shoe, reached for her keys from the coffee table and headed out the door for an evening jog. Even as an accountant who dealt with millions of other people's funds, the reality of just how much a million meant was a mystery to her. A million, or millions as the case may be, was different on paper than in reality. She imagined great things could be done for others with that kind of spending freedom but she had no idea where or how to put it to use for the greater good. What was clear to her, however, was that she did not need that kind of cash. To her it had become more of a bother than a blessing.

Several years ago Kennedy made the decision to legally make a plan for the money in the event of her death. Should she die before she might someday need the money for her own care, she wanted to be sure the value of her estate would go to care for others. Having no direct descendants there was technically no one for the money to trickle down to. Of course she had made provisions for her bother Lane and his family. The rest she left in a high yield account to gather interest until someone needed it.

Her reasons for keeping the money secret were many but mostly she fiercely believed money could negatively affect relationships. She had witnessed this personally a number of times with others in her life. It became difficult, it seemed to Kennedy, to separate true feelings and emotions once large sums of money were involved. She vowed that would never happen to her. She reasoned that if no one knew about her sudden surge into financial security then the status quo would be maintained. She would make certain that none of her friends, business associates or romantic encounters would be influenced by who she was on paper. Especially her romantic encounters.

It had never been a problem before but now there was Greg. And that was becoming a mammoth problem. She had never intended to be secretive with him, but she never anticipated falling in love with him either.

One never anticipates falling in love she guessed. But now he seemed deeply conflicted about his feelings for her. On a daily basis he oscillated between anger, respect, disbelief, tranquility and then back to anger.

She was done thinking about it for now though. Her decision to tell him could not be undone. A wise friend had said something to her decades ago that stuck in her mind and was as true then as it was today: Sticks and stones may break my bones but spoken words are never dead. Even God can't take back words once they're said.

So Kennedy pulled herself out of her deep and depressing thoughts and began a new task. She needed to plan her pre-wedding party at the Salted Olive. So much to be done and time was quickly slipping through her fingers. She smiled at the thought of the gathering with her long lost friends, pulled out a lined tablet and began to make plans for the long-awaited gathering. The rest of the day was lost in pleasant thoughts.

In and of itself the Salted Olive was just a glorified open space, serving as a home-grown delicatessen on a dead-end street. It was settled on the edge of a row of formerly bustling businesses now mostly lost in the shadow of new restaurants and fancier up-town meeting venues. But the food was outstanding. The now semi-retired owners were more interested in creating a place for people to gather where they could get great tidbits of food and a cold beer than they were in making money. She and Greg had spent hours and hours there relaxing. It was a perfect spot, Kennedy reasoned, for hosting a small gathering such as the one she was planning.

Today she had intentionally parked her car down the street and relished in the late spring weather. She tried to pull her thoughts together into one semi-cohesive jumble rather than the hundreds of details swimming solo. As more and more details were planned for the long wedding weekend, she erroneously thought she would be more settled about the finality of things. It was panning out that the opposite was true. Every day — and sometimes much more than daily — a new idea popped into her head or a detail she hadn't thought of emerged. Did all brides go through this, she wondered. Maybe she should relax more, worry less and accept what her wedding planner her told her on the first day they met. Something will go wrong. Something will be forgotten. Something will not turn out as you plan. But everything will still be perfect because it is all about you and your new husband and not the wedding itself.

"Remember that, remember that, remember that," Kennedy had told herself over and over during the whirlwind of the last few months. Even if everything doesn't go as planned in less than two months she would be Mrs. Gregory Parker. A few days or weeks after the ceremony anything that went wrong would be less than a fragment of a memory. Unfortunately her mind did not work that way. She made her living from being meticulous about details and it was now carrying over into her personal life. So be it. Her unconscious mantra these days was plan for every unexpected detail and then have a backup plan for the backup plan. Uggggg…weddings were supposed to be happy times and she felt as if she were drowning in details.

Now, though, pulling open the heavy wooden door of her favorite little deli, she breathed in the salty aromas of the kitchen and instantly felt more at peace. She ordered a chicken Caesar salad and a Diet Coke with lime, then found a back corner to eat. Pulling out her personal planner she began to write: Thursday, June 12. Plan for 20.

Greg's best friend and his wife would be invited of course. And a few of his business associates would be invited too. All of them lived within 10 miles of one another and were almost guaranteed to come for the pre-wedding shindig. The others were a little tougher to determine. Kennedy had invited seven people and included their spouses if they existed. She had not, however, included an RSVP card for the Thursday ordeal so she was merely guessing at the number of attendees.

There was no need to plan an activity for the gathering. That simplified things somewhat. The group was bound to be small enough she and Greg could circulate among the guests and introduce one another while catching up and sharing laughs. After a brief conversation with the owner the light dinner menu was planned, and she closed her planner with an air of satisfaction. One more detail completed. Life was good and she was amazingly lucky she pondered, as she leisurely walked back to her car. Some people didn't get a chance to be insanely happy with a life mate. Perhaps it was best she had waited as long as she had to make a permanent commitment to a man. She most definitely knew what she was looking for in a forever partner and without hesitation, Greg Parker filled the bill. It had been a rough and rocky start, she remembered, but she was more certain than ever that she had picked the right guy. Absolutely certain.

Love and hate...

Returning from lunch Tuesday, Kennedy noticed an enormous bouquet of flowers on her receptionist's desk. It looked to be just one posy short of a casket spray. Who in the world would send such an exquisite array? No one was sitting at Marcy's desk at the moment so Kennedy splurged, took a moment and inhaled the scent. Fantastic. And she didn't even know Marcy was seeing anyone.

"Oh hey, Kennedy," came a voice from the corner by the copy machine. "Aren't they lovely?" Marcy asked as she returned to her desk with an unopened energy drink.

"I'd say they are," Kennedy replied with genuine admiration for her friend and associate. "So who loves you so much to drop that kind of money on you, Marcy? Have you been holding out on me?" she teased. "What's the story here?"

"Well, my friend," Marcy countered, "I wish I could say they were for me. And I wish they were from a tall, dark and handsome stranger who was wooing me to be his wife and melt my every trouble into oblivion," Marcy added with a chuckle. "But that is just a pipe dream. Romance avoids me like the plague. Look at the card. They are for you. Just delivered about 10 minutes ago."

Me? She mentally ran through her morning and the contacts from the day before. Was there a business transaction that would prompt a client to offer thanks or a sentiment of appreciation such as this? Not really. The week had been very normal with business as usual. It wasn't her birthday and Valentine's Day was months in the past. Hmmmm…

"Oh come on, Kennedy," Marcy said. "You know who sent them. Everyone in town knows he is smitten with you and can't wait to officially be your only suitor. But don't open the card here at my desk. It could be x-rated."

They both laughed at this.

"This is not really Greg's style, though," Kennedy said. "He is more of a cook me dinner and rub my feet kind of guy."

"Count yourself lucky on that account, too," Marcy said only slightly under her breath. "The last time a man did anything that nice for me it was my ex-husband. He only did something nice when he wanted something nice, if you know what I mean. And then a few weeks later I got the florist's bill. Nuts! I guess that is one of the reasons he is my ex, huh?"

"Be patient, Marcy, the right guy is out there for you. Look how long I had to wait for this one. Over 50 years."

With that, Kennedy picked up the beautiful crystal vase and lugged it off to her office. Settling the arrangement on her work table by the window she at last allowed herself to read the card.

It read: K, Just 59 days until you are my wife. Counting the days. With love, G

Fifty-nine days. Wow. Could there be 59 flowers in that vase? Very possibly yes she guessed. In fact, if it was his mission to send her a flower-per-day until their wedding day then the florist gave him a good deal because her estimate was there were far more than 59 flowers floating in that beautiful vase. She could count at least two dozen daisies and infinitely more than that in soft pink, lavender and yellow roses. There were others, too. Assorted unidentifiable blossoms spilled over the sides of the elaborate container.

Her heart melted, yet again, at his generosity. Looking down at her spectacular engagement ring which must have cost at least six months' salary, she took a moment to give thanks. Someone out there in the great big universe had accidentally crossed her path for a reason. Her life had seemed complete before she met him, but knowing someone cared for her at the level she knew he did was something not to be taken for granted. She would spend the rest of her life showing him her gratitude, even if it killed her.

Across town Greg was buried in mountains of paperwork today. It felt as if every time he tackled one thing in his inbox two or three more sprung up that needed his immediate attention. Hours ago his stomach told him it was time for food. Lunch? Dinner? What time was it? He hadn't even had time to look at the clock. What a day.

And so it made sense really that he didn't notice he had a visitor. And wow, a beautiful one at that.

"Kennedy. What a pleasant surprise. What brings you over?" he asked rubbing his temples and crossing the room to embrace her.

"Well," she said with a sexy smile, "I just wondered if you were so busy that you didn't even know I was standing in your doorway, how in the world did you have time to order these beautiful flowers that arrived at my office today?" She placed a soft kiss on his cheek and withdrew a lavender rose from behind her back.

"Mmmmmmmmm...smells nice," he said breathing in the scent. "Almost as nice as you."

"Ahhh, flattery will get you nowhere with me, buddy," Kennedy said in mock anger.

"Really? Well, I bet you will rethink that if I do this," he whispered pulling her tightly into his chest and kissing her tenderly just below her left ear.

A few moments passed before she could speak. She even forgot what day it was for a split second. As he massaged her neck with his mouth it was easy to forget they were standing in her fiancee's agency just seconds away from doing something not meant for the office.

"Ummmm, excuse me sir," Kennedy finally managed to ask, "but is this how you treat all your visitors? If so, I think your girlfriend would be alarmed."

"My girlfriend," he mumbled still dropping warm kisses down her neckline, "is smart enough to know better. Only the visitors who bring me flowers get this kind of 'care.'"

"I see," Kennedy replied smacking him on the forehead playfully with the rose she had plucked from her beautiful arrangement just 30 minutes earlier. Laying the rose on his desk she leisurely strolled back across the room and closed the door, slowly tripping the deadbolt so that it made a loud, dramatic click as it locked them into his office alone together.

"Well, in that case, young man, show me how you treat a lady who brings you flowers."

Sometime after midnight Kennedy woke and untangled herself from Greg's arms. Quietly she pieced herself back together and looked back at her exhausted fiancée still sound asleep on the loveseat in his office apparently unaware that it was long past time to go home for the night.

Searching for her keys and her purse, Kennedy glanced around the office. The rose from last night caught the corner of her eye. Now wilted and frail it still brought a smile to her face. She reached into Greg's desk drawer and easily found a note pad. In the dim light shining in from the window she swiftly jotted a memo and placed it with the rose on his bare chest before she let herself out of the office and jogged to the deserted parking lot, headed for home and a little quality sleep before the sun came up.

Hours later Greg woke and found the message with the lifeless faint purple flower. He read aloud: Now we are down to just 58. Love, K

What time is it anyway, he wondered, vaguely remembering the pleasantly surprising events at the end of his work day. But now Kennedy had disappeared and it was clearly very late – or early depending on how you looked at it. The antique clock on his desk read 3:57. What? How was that possible? He quickly collected his clothes and his briefcase and left a vague message for his assistant on the way out the door saying he would be in late. Don't keep the coffee warm.

Waking up in his own bed hours later Greg sat bolt upright with sweat rolling off his brow. He reached out to the other side of the bed and found it empty. Kennedy rarely stayed here overnight but something about the dream was disarming. He had to find her and know she was OK. No, he was exaggerating it in his mind. He was tired. She was fine or he would have heard from the police by now. Then again it was just after 10 a.m. and nothing else had woken him. Dear God! She had to be OK.

Greg forced himself to pull his achingly exhausted body from bed and stumble to the bathroom sink splashing his face with cold water repeatedly. Tiny fragments of his most recent dream slapped him in the gut with fear. He couldn't remember it all but it was ugly.

Collapsing at last back onto his bed he tried to recall all that he could. It wasn't easy. There was blood. That he knew. And lots of it. He saw her there in front of his left front car tire – mangled and broken. There were colossal parts of the story missing. Where were they? On a dirt road. Remote. Very remote. Nothing but a sandy path flanked by hundred-year-old oak trees on either side. Had he hit her? Please God, why couldn't he remember! Where did she come from? Had he been driving and not seen her? And was she dead? No. No. Not possible. And probably the most nagging question of all –

did he INTENTIONALLY hurt her? Did he KILL her?

Instinctively he reached for his phone and dialed her cell. Voice mail after the first ring. That was good news. It meant she was on another call so she was alive and safe. Or it could mean her phone was off, she was dead and would never answer him again. No. No! Yes?

Without thinking he called her office and tried to quell the panic in his voice when her secretary answered the call. No, Miss Andrews was not in yet today. Could she take a message? No, no message.

Shower. He had to shower and shave and get to work. Twenty minutes later he had all but burned his skin with the hottest water he could stand, swallowed a toasted bagel almost whole and was on his third cup of coffee as he raced out the door. He took the fastest route to work. He had almost convinced himself that the dream was just that. A dream. But a tiny inkling was pounding into his brain and causing his head to throb. So Kennedy was alright, probably in a meeting. But the bigger question was why on earth would he EVER dream something like that. It appeared that he had brutally killed his girlfriend in cold blood and without regrets. He tried to block the gory body scene from his mind. When he did the fact he hadn't even gotten out of his vehicle to try to help her kept coming to the surface. She was dead and in the vision he didn't seem to care.

Of course, he told himself as he pulled into his parking space, I would never do that. I love that woman to death. There it was. "To death." So he had been devastated when he found out she had lied to him. Kind of lied to him – omitted something very important. It would be dishonest to say he wasn't the angriest he had ever been at anyone. Betrayal was hard to take and he had taken it before and vowed never to do it again. But not this. Never this.

Pausing before he hopped out of the car a fleeting thought ran through his mind. He forced himself to recall the images of the dream one last time. It was a rose. Not three feet from her body lay a significantly wilted and thoroughly crushed lavender rose – exactly like the one she had left him with at the office last night. No. No, no, no. That part was real so where did reality collide with fiction?

Greg felt bile rise to his chest. He was sickened by even the thought of his beautiful wife-to-be dying, especially in this cruel and heinous way. And even more haunted by the fact he appeared to be the murderer and seemed to care less. He barely made it to the men's room before he emptied the contents of his stomach into the sink.

Five minutes later he walked into the reception area just a few feet from his office door and was greeted by Anna, one of his secretaries. He realized he was nearly four hours later than normal arriving today and hoped she was busy enough not to notice.

"Good morning, Mr. Parker," he heard her say in a cheerful tone – not at all judgmental about his tardiness. "Rough night last night?" There it was. The unintentional judgment.

Steeling himself to appear normal he didn't glance up when he responded with "You have no idea, Anna, absolutely no idea."

Brenda

The best thing about Monday, Brenda decided, was that it was only four days from Friday. Her life these days seemed to be an endless saga of get up, go to work, come home, eat, sleep and do it over again. And all that for a small pittance of a salary that was barely keeping her in shelter and food. There had to be more to life than this. Where was Prince Charming and his white horse? At this point, she reasoned, she might even settle for Prince Mediocre with no horse as long as he had a few dollars to share.

Walking home she mentally took stock of the contents of her refrigerator. Milk? Maybe. Eggs. Definitely she had a few eggs and the bread on the counter was past its ultimate freshness date, but as long as she toasted it surely it would be palatable. Does everyone live like this, she wondered. And would her life always be this way? She needed a new job, but her skill set was limited. No one was willing to pay big bucks for someone who couldn't type at the speed of light or create business documents out of thin air on a moment's notice to make her boss look like a genius. It was what it was. Work was good and she was destined to be poor, but there had to be more to life than this measly existence. She was bound and determined to find it if it took the rest of her life – and at this rate it just might.

Rounding the corner brought her just a half a block from her duplex. She momentarily stopped short in her tracks when she saw what lie ahead. There was an ambulance and two police cars parked immediately in front of her house and what seemed like hundreds of lights reflected off the pane glass windows of every house in the neighborhood. It had to be Mrs. Wilson, her duplex-mate. Dear God let her be OK she prayed silently as she broke into a jog and landed on her neighbor's doorstep in seconds.

Of course the authorities pushed her back despite her obvious concern for the grandmother she had come to know as a friend and confidant over the years. Where were the children? Brenda panicked and looked across the yard where she found little Teddy and Jane nestled in the arms of another neighbor. They didn't appear to be scared but there was no doubt they were not aware of the gravity of the situation.

Brenda's greatest fear about her neighbor – that she might not make it through the night – had not turned into reality. She had spent it in the hospital, though, and it looked as if she would be alright in the long run. Rubbing her neck and adjusting her legs in the other direction, Brenda noticed the clock in the waiting room read just after 5 a.m.

A few hours ago Mrs. Rose Wilson, or Rosie, as Brenda had come to know her, was moved to a regular room on the fifth floor and was resting comfortably. The duty nurse knew Brenda was not next of kin, but since there was no family present she was willing to keep her in the loop. It seemed Rose had suffered a mild heart attack, lost her balance and fell. Fortunately she was not hurt and the staff was certain she would recover from the heart issue, but she would likely need to find other care for the children and at least for the time being she would probably be moved to a care center.

Over the next few days she had learned that her dear sweet neighbor did, in fact, have an estranged daughter living in Portland. That was at least a thousand miles from here, but she would still need to be notified and arrangements would need to be made for her care. However difficult it might be, Brenda would be the one to make the call.

"Why didn't you tell me your daughter was alive?" Brenda asked when Rosie was feeling up to sitting on the edge of the bed one afternoon a few days later.

"Daughter. Well. I guess she is my daughter but she hasn't claimed me as her mother in years," Rosie said matter of factly as she appeared to stare out the window without seeing a thing.

Brenda struggled over the next few days to understand what could happen between a mother and daughter that would cause such a dramatic split between the two. Clearly her old friend and neighbor did not want to talk about it. When Brenda had been forced, more or less, by the hospital to contact a family member, she was shocked and tremendously disappointed in the daughter's lack of interest in her mother. To the outside observer like Brenda, who had seen nothing of Mrs. Wilson but a kind and generous soul who gave repeatedly of her time and money to care for her two precious grandchildren, it was a mystery beyond comprehension. But the daughter, Brenda learned was named Becky, treated the whole situation as a bother. She would see to the care of her nephew and niece and as for her mother? Her response was simply 'Something will have to be done with the old lady.'

Three days later, when Becky Carlton showed up at the hospital in Rossford, Brenda discovered she liked her even less than she had over the phone. And that was something she had thought would be impossible.

Sitting by her bedside, Brenda was simply talking with her old friend when the repulsive, uptight, ungrateful daughter entered the room, looked Brenda over and dismissed her with harsh words. "I'm here now. You are not needed," the daughter barked.

Leave? How could she leave? And yet what could she do? Brenda herself was just barely making ends meet so there was no way she could take on the care of someone else.

As she paced the hallway outside Rose Wilson's room a million thoughts raced through her head. It started with questions. Obviously Becky thought of her mother as just another obligation, but what did she do back in Portland? She was dressed to the nines, even wearing high heels and fancy diamond earrings just for a visit to the hospital. She must be important wherever she was and whatever she did. Besides the obvious question of why she seemed to despise her own mother, Brenda wanted to know if her dear friend would be alright under the care of the crabby, pretentious Becky.

Even as she walked she knew it was none of her business to know about these things. She had no right to even ask where she was going and who would provide for her. So it should be no shock to her when Becky pranced out of the hospital room without even a glance in her direction. Becky was down the hall and out the door into the parking lot in less than 30 seconds without consulting the front desk, talking to a doctor and certainly not regarding Brenda.

Mrs. Wilson's fate appeared to be sealed. She would likely never see her friend again.

Rose Wilson and the children never returned to the duplex she and her grandchildren shared with Brenda. But a few weeks later she noticed a young couple arrived and left a half an hour later with just three boxes of her neighbor's things. Stepping out on the porch to inquire about Rose's health she learned her friend was recuperating well and a full recovery was expected. The boxes were the clothes of the children who were going to live with a friend of Becky's in Oregon. All of the other things in the duplex – including the furniture - would be sold at auction. What about Mrs. Wilson? Where would she go? The couple exchanged glances and then turned to Brenda and shrugged. Either they didn't know or they were instructed not to tell. Wow. Just wow.

Eventually Brenda learned from another neighbor Rose Wilson had been transferred to an assisted living facility more than 900 miles away on the west coast. It would be impossible to track her down without more information. Not that she had to track her down, the old woman was probably receiving excellent care. It still rubbed her wrong, though, that her daughter had been so cold and calculating. And what was the deal with the children, those precious children that Rose was raising on her own. They weren't her daughter's kids. Becky had referred to them as a niece and nephew. Surely they were alright as well. It was best to leave well enough alone she knew. And she wished she could.

Lately Brenda knew all too well what it was like to lay in bed when sleep would not come. Her mind raced around unanswered questions. Like, why do mosquito bites itch? How old do you have to be for others to consider you mature? Why doesn't lettuce taste like chocolate cake? And most importantly, what in the world has Becky Carlton done with her mother, my friend?

That was the question she had been losing sleep over. Tomorrow she would go to the library and do a little research on Becky Carlton. Hopefully Facebook would be helpful. If not she would use Intelius or privateeye.com. Somehow she was determined to find out the fate of Rose.

***

It hadn't been as difficult to find Becky as she thought it might be but it had taken no less than a hundred phone calls to locate someone named Rose Wilson. Becky, the records showed, was a divorced and remarried woman, 57 years old, no children of her own, worked as a real estate broker in suburban Portland and her hobbies were tennis, golf and wearing designer clothes. There were hundreds of pictures of her at various parties and always with a different handbag and shoes. Brenda reasoned Becky's closet was triple the size of her own apartment.

Narrowing her search for assisted living centers to the Portland area was easy. She called every one of them until she at last found one with a resident registered as Rose Wilson in Sherwood, about 20 minutes from downtown Portland.

Brenda waited a few days before she placed the call to Rose herself. She didn't want to sound invasive and hoped she wasn't being nosy. She was concerned, though. Rose was a friend.

"Hello?" a timid voice came over the line when she at last decided to call.

"Mrs. Wilson?" Brenda asked as a way of validating she had the right number. "It's me. Brenda. Your neighbor. I have been so worried about you. Are you alright?"

There was a pregnant pause before the older lady responded.

"Brenda. Oh yes, dear. I am absolutely fine."

The voice sounded faint, almost like a whisper. Brenda tried again to let her friend know she was missed.

"How's the weather there? Are they feeding you well?" Brenda inquired.

This time, however there was no pause of hesitation. Rose's voice sounded stronger, but not quite 'normal.'

"I am doing well, dear. You mustn't worry."

"I am so glad to know that," Brenda said with sincerity. "We have all been so…"

Brenda paused. She was in disbelief. The line had gone dead.

Jack

The weekend was quickly coming to a close and Jack was checking off his weekend to do list. Both girls' backpacks had been loaded with the necessary books and homework assignments and lunches were prepared and waiting in the refrigerator. Ben had Monday off school for a field trip and he had reminded his son to pack his sunscreen. Mentally taking note of his own tasks to complete Jack was starting to feel accomplished. Everything on the list was done except for one. He needed to make those flight arrangements for Kennedy's wedding. It was just around the corner.

Sighing, he turned on his computer and waited impatiently for it to boot up so he could log on. Money was always tight it seemed. As soon as you got ahead by a few dollars something else came up that was a few more bucks than you had saved. But this was important. He wouldn't miss the wedding for the world and his old friend had sent two first-class tickets with the invitation. He had to be honest, he had never heard of anyone doing that but it certainly made taking his three kids with him do-able. They wouldn't attend the dinner and dance, of course, but he really wanted them to meet Kennedy and this might be the only time that would be possible.

A few minutes in Jack found two relatively inexpensive tickets for Ben and himself. He was anxious for the kids to see where he had grown up. They would have to rent a car for the few days anyway so he hoped to show them the places he had loved so much as a kid. The kids would have to stay in the hotel through much of the planned festivities, but he was sure they would be happy to just "chill" as they said in front of the TV.

As far as the wedding itself was concerned, the girls would love every minute of it. He was sure Ben would find it boring beyond belief. Heck, he probably would too if it wasn't that he knew the key players. He hoped to catch up with her brother Lane, too, while he was back in Kansas and there would likely be many other guests he knew as well. The only thing left was finding a wedding gift for someone you used to consider your best friend but hadn't seen in decades. Oh well, he still had almost three weeks.

Mary Jane

The dinner table was the place where the Mendenhall family shared the news of the day. Unless her husband was traveling it was rare that the six of them didn't gather for the evening meal around their dining room table. The kids, eager to see their father at the end of a busy day were usually the first to share. They talked about everything – the funny joke one had heard at school, the sports scores from the night before, Mike's adventures with this girl or that one. Usually little Maddie chirped in with the adventures of her self-proclaimed stressful life as a kindergarten student. Drama queen, that one.

This was the time Andy announced his out-of-town business trips and promised to bring them all glorious surprise gifts when he returned. On rare occasions Mary Jane even added to the conversation.

So this seemed like the perfect time to drop a bombshell on her naive husband. She started by clearing her throat.

"I am taking a week off in mid-June," she started.

The table fell silent. Even the clatter of the forks, knives and spoons were inaudible. Mary Jane never left home overnight. She continued with fake confidence.

"A dear friend of mine is getting married in Kansas and I will be attending."

More silence. After a few moments the kids commenced eating, but still offered no words.

Andy was the first to speak. His words were not sharp. Heaven forbid the children would find out he treated his wife of 20 years like the family's maid or nanny.

"How will you get there?" he wanted to know. "The car will be needed here to transport the children."

Poppycock. They had three cars and a truck. It was fun in a way to watch him squirm a little.

"I will be flying," Mary Jane continued. "The flight and accommodations have been taken care of," she lied. She had filed the airline tickets in the bottom of a drawer where he would never find them, but she had no idea where she would stay.

Andy continued to chew his pork chop at a snail's pace. She knew he was stalling for time before he found a way to dash her plans and spoil her fun. He just had to be careful in front of the children. She was learning the hard way he was much too proud to let the kids think there was a problem between them. Oh wow, if they only knew their sweet, hard-working, gift-bearing, jet-setting father was not the man they thought they knew. She would probably take his secret to the grave because she, too, loved her kids and couldn't bear to break their hearts. However, she didn't have to like it and she certainly no longer had to play by his rules.

After what seemed like an hour he spoke.

"So, your mother will watch the kids?"

"Well, no," Mary Jane said with a forced smile. "She is going with me. You have plenty of time to make arrangements for the children. It's just a week, dear. Maybe your secretary could even lend a hand." And then without giving him a second glance she rose from the table and began to clear the dishes while he stared at her in shock.

Father Paul

Rain pelted the windows of Paul's comfortable country home. From his reading chair he watched God's extraordinary thunderstorm unfold in waves. Nights like this were made for staying in, but tonight he wandered out onto his porch and let himself become absorbed in the scents and sounds of the downpour. It was exhilarating.

Years ago when he had been a priest he didn't have time to appreciate the beauty of such a storm. As fate would have it, it was almost never a balmy starry night when he was called out to visit the sick and dying. Sometimes there was earth-shattering thunder that kept him awake for hours and hours on a night when he had to rise before dawn to say Mass for special holidays. But tonight the rain was emotionally comforting. As he leaned against the stone front of his home he let the reality sink in – officially he was retired of taking care of other people and it was good. All good.

The next morning Paul found himself outside again. This time in his garden gathering the vegetables that were ready for harvest. The air was still fresh with the scent of last night's storm. The former Father Paul had come to realize this life away from the priesthood may have been his calling all along. He was happy here, perhaps even blissful in the haven of this space.

Just five miles down the road is where he had landed some 20 years ago and the fresh air had served him well. In the beginning his friends from the old church had called faithfully to check on his welfare but those calls had faded over the years and now it was rare if he heard from the old crew at all. It was all natural he supposed after such a time, but if there was one thing he truly missed it was the people.

He had met many *new* people, of course, and knew they would be lifelong friends. Country folks were one of a kind and he loved it. Walking the dog or driving down to get his mail he would visit with those who were now his neighbors. They would be shocked, he was sure, if they knew what he left behind to come to this community. He didn't share his story often, partly because it made him sad and partly because it was his past and he had come to enjoy the relative anonymity of being just a regular guy in regular clothes with a regular job.

There were parts of Paul's old life that would never leave him he supposed. He spent many hours each day in prayer and reading inspirational books. In spite of the way things worked out with his previous career, the Holy Spirit still lived deep in his soul. As Paul mentally prepared for his day, the joys and needs of those around him were foremost on his mind. As he went about his work, quietly completing task after task he would pray for the people who touched his life.

Today he found himself thinking of and wondering about his dear friend Kennedy Andrews - the mystery of her life and how it had unfolded. Her wedding was just a few weeks away now and he was eager to head home and visit with her. Of course she would be busy with all the trimmings of her special day, but she had made arrangements for a special pre-celebration party with some of her old friends. Paul himself could relate to her need to reach out to parts of her past. In this case, however, it was to his benefit as well. He was anxious to reconnect the old with the new.

It was time, he reasoned to make final plans for the travel to Kansas. Kennedy had provided two first-class airlines tickets but there was no one he could think of to share the flight. In fact, normally he would hop in the car and make a week-long trip of it, stopping to take in the beauty of nature and enjoy staying at tiny, cozy inns along the way. Perhaps he would do that any way, he thought. He could cash in the airline tickets and add the money he got from it with his own wedding gift so Kennedy and her new husband would have a little nest egg of cash to start their life together.

Yes, that is what he would do, he thought. He wished he could shake the sense that something was wrong. It did seem odd to him that Kennedy was still single. He tried to put it out of his mind today as he went about his daily routine but it kept coming back to him. It was no mystery, really, he tried to console himself. Many people didn't marry until later in life. In his mind, however, he had already pigeonholed her into the category of happy, healthy and living the American dream in some huge metropolis with a husband, 2.5 kids, a dog and a white picket fence. He was happy for her that she had found someone special to grow old with. He himself might always wonder what that was like.

J.T.

Several hundred miles down the road from Paul Odell, J.T. was finishing his work day. He had made plans to meet friends for dinner and that usually meant cocktails and nightcaps and very little sleep. Fortunately he had the next three days off which would give him some time to relax and regroup.

On his immediate agenda was to spend some time with his nephew. They were headed into the city to take in a baseball game or two. J.T. could hardly wait to get away from the routine of his career for a bit. Although he had grown to love the work, the daily schedule was so much more rigid than when he was traveling and promoting nutritional supplements.

In the old days he would wake up in a new city almost every day, sleep until he felt like getting up, head to the gym for an hour or two and then get ready for an hour or so of work before exploring the night life of wherever he happened to be. Women were plentiful and all his expenses were paid without hesitation. Even though then it seemed his life was enviable, he sometimes longed for stability and structure. Now that he had stability and structure, he missed the ready cash flow that came with being a fitness celebrity. I guess you can't have it all, he reasoned. As for today he was grateful to be leaving the corporate world behind for a long weekend away from the grind of his 9 to 5 desk job.

"J," his nephew asked once they were equipped with hot dogs and sodas while waiting for the national anthem to commence, "why don't you have a girlfriend?"

His nephew Steven had taken to calling him 'J' since he had turned into a teenager and he didn't mind.

"Well, I don't know, Steven. Why don't you?" J.T. countered back.

"Because girls are stupid," his nephew said. "I mean they want you to hang out with them in the dumbest places like the mall or at the Ice Cream Emporium but then they ignore you all night and talk to their girlfriends. I mean, what's the point?"

J.T. stifled a chuckle. It had been many years since he had been a teenager himself but he could definitely remember those days.

"Well, give them time," he said. "Be flattered that they like you enough to drag you along with their friends. Someday they will change their priorities and you will find just the right one."

"Ugggg…that's what Mom says," Steven muttered half under his breath. "I thought you would give it to me straight. Is that the way it really is?"

"I'm afraid so, buddy. There is nothing simple about girls."

"But you are, ahem, older, J, and you still don't have a girlfriend. The right one never came along?"

Now this conversation was turning serious and J.T. wasn't sure he wanted to explain the trouble with women to his nephew so he changed the subject.

"Hey, who is that?" J.T. said turning his head. "Is that Kelly Clarkson? Is she singing the national anthem tonight?"

"Come on, man. Don't wiggle out of this. That is some chick from the rotary club. Not everyone that has blond hair is famous, J. Geez."

His nephew was getting smarter since he turned 14 – not as easy to fool.

"Well, actually the right person did come along for me, Steven," J.T. said with a bit of a sigh. "But it's complicated. I guess I didn't see it at the time and now it is too late. She is marrying someone else in a few weeks."

Silence from his nephew for a bit.

"How do you know?" he asked at last.

"Hmmmm?"

"How do you know she was the right one?" Steven said, cocking his head to avoid the mid-afternoon sun.

"Well, I guess we will never know for sure, Steven. I guess I was too pig-headed to see past my own shadow back then. I wish I had some advice for you, man, but on this topic I am not an expert."

Back home after the game, J.T. fell onto his leather couch and closed his eyes. These last few weeks he had been thinking about the girl that got away way more often than he liked to admit. Kennedy had been beautiful and smart and funny. And probably the best thing about her was she seemed to like him. She wanted the best for him. In the end she had even given up on a relationship with him so he could go out and do his own thing. And look what a mess that had turned out to be.

Maybe he should reconsider going to the wedding. Again was he being selfish in wanting to see her and possibly prove he was still the same high school sweetheart she knew as the romantic and charming J.T.? Surely not. He couldn't be that shallow. Well, for whatever reason he did want to go and he did want to see her and of course he wished the best for her.

He needed to finalize his travel plans and ask his sister if she wanted to tag along. They had been friends all those years ago, too. Maybe it was just what he needed to refresh his tired body and soul.

And maybe, just maybe when he returned he would be able to explain the mystery of women to his nephew.

Not chance he decided at last. There was no answer to the mystery of women.

Sadie

Shuffling through the papers on her dresser Sadie heaved a heavy sigh and fell onto her bed in a heap of frustration. Where was that application? She had meticulously completed it a few days ago and needed to pair it with her updated resume and send it off sooner than later. She absolutely could wait no longer. Money was tight. Actually it was worse than that. She had no money coming in and she knew it was a financial burden for her friend Ami and her husband to have her there although she also knew they would never tell her so.

Sadie longed to have a solid job that would pay the bills. She was going to try her hand at another office job and she had decided she would make herself like it if it was the last thing on earth she did. Back in the days before she had her son, it hadn't been as important to her. Life was easy and carefree. There was always enough food for everyone with some left over. It used to be a matter of deciding which day to make spaghetti and which day to make burgers. These days it was EITHER spaghetti or burgers. And even then there was barely enough money for meat. Things were bound to improve, but how she was simply not sure.

And so Sadie found herself once again rifling through the papers to find the job application. With a disgruntled huff she spilled the contents of her dresser drawer across the tiny desk and at last found what she was looking for. Satisfied she had represented herself to the best of her ability, she placed the two sheets of paper in an envelope and headed out to see if the mailman had already been by. Leaving the mess of papers on the desk, she didn't notice the silky cream envelope that had also resurfaced. The wedding invitation that earlier had been just a fraction of a second from hitting the recycle bin now laid out in the open, still untouched.

A bit of good fortune had finally crossed paths with Sadie Nichols. As of today she was the office manager of Cross & Miller Attorneys at Law. So far she hadn't managed anything, but had answered the phone twice, one of which was a wrong number. Her training so far had been a brief introduction to two of the firm's partners, a 15-second tour of the hallway that led to the seven offices housed in the building and now she was reading through a 600-page procedure manual. As far as she could tell her job was to direct traffic – both when people came into the office and when they called to make or reschedule appointments.

Other than the attorneys themselves, the only other employee appeared to be a receptionist whose job, ironically, was not to answer the phone. Her name was Arabella and she did not seem the least bit interested in Sadie. Since she had been in the office this morning Arabella had been typing incessantly without looking up. It was a huge benefit to Sadie that Arabella could type, because it definitely wasn't in her skill set.

It was probably a miracle she had gotten the job with the few skills she did have, but something about this place felt normal and right. Perhaps this was a new beginning for her. If she only knew how to type maybe it would be an even better new beginning.

Arabella did not roll out the welcome mat for Sadie, but she wasn't unpleasant either. She was interested in completing a full day's work for a full day's pay and walking out the door when the clock struck five - not a minute before or a minute after. Sadie, too, was anxious to get home to her son, but she intended to make this job her last one so she was eager to make a good impression on her bosses. She was determined to leave the office every day at least one minute after the business-like receptionist who shared her office space in the giant lobby of Cross & Miller.

The day Sadie's first paycheck came added a serendipitous moment to her second Friday on the job. There were actually four digits to the left of the decimal point! Plus she hadn't expected to be paid at all until the end of the month. She meticulously checked the pay stub attached to her check and that is when she discovered an even bigger surprise. There was a second check in the envelope - for $750. It was noted as a signing bonus. She might have screamed if it hadn't been for the watchful eyes of Arabella tirelessly clicking her long nails against the computer keys.

Maybe she would go to that ladies' wedding after all. A little extra spending money in her pocket would make it seem more plausible. What did she have to lose?

Seeing through the pain

Jenny faced the unexpected loss of her husband with incredible grace and dignity. Her siblings watched from the sidelines as she not only cared for their five children but moved from person to person comforting all their family and friends. Her sister, especially, knew Jenny was in survival mode for now. She had seen her sister do this before in a crisis situation – sashaying among her friends and family and meeting their needs before she allowed time for herself to heal.

"How you doing there, Jen," Melody asked her.

"Not well," Jenny answered honestly.

"I don't know how you are doing all of this," Melody told her sister. "Most people in your position would have folded under the pressure by now."

"Staying busy helps so much. The nights are the worst so I just have to completely wear myself out so I fall asleep without time to think."

"Have you even allowed yourself time to cry?" Melody wanted to know.

"Oh dear Lord, yes. There have been many, many bouts of tears, but it doesn't help. I just come away from that more tired than before. The only thing that does seem to give me comfort is knowing his children have fond memories of their father. I will do all that I can to be sure those good times are etched in their minds. It is so unfair to them."

"And to you," Melody told her. "What can I do to help?"

"You are such a blessing to me, Mel, just even to ask. Really keeping up with the housework and the cooking are things I need to do myself. The routine of it is all I have to hang on to, but there is just one thing I can't bear to do."

"Name it," Jenny's sister said. She herself was having difficulty coping with the death of her brother-in-law, taken so young in that horrific car accident. It was beyond comprehension how Jenny was surviving.

"It's the mail. The bills. The insurance stuff. Even the sympathy cards. There is just a giant mountain of unopened envelopes I can't make myself touch. It is overwhelming," Jeff's wife told her sister.

"Consider it done," Melody told her touching her arm. "Lead me to this mountain and I will conquer it today."

Together they shared a smile then and a tiny moment of laughter. It did feel good to laugh no matter how brief. Well-meaning friends had told her repeatedly time heals all things. She accepted their words of comfort but had yet to be convinced that even a million years would soften the wound to her heart.

An hour later Melody had sorted all the mail into four stacks – bills to be paid, insurance to be filed, sympathy cards to be saved and lastly anything that needed Jenny's immediate attention. One envelope stood out from the rest. Melody set it aside. It could be a sympathy card, but the return address and name did not look familiar. It was a Kennedy Andrews from Wichita, Kansas. Definitely not family.

"Do you know a Kennedy Andrews?" Melody asked her sister later over coffee.

"Doesn't ring a bell. Why?"

"There is a card here from her. But it looks more like an invitation. Should we open it?"

"Oh my, I hope I didn't miss a graduation or something. Jeff has - err, uh, **had** so many cousins. I couldn't possibly remember them all."

"Don't beat yourself up over it," Melody said as she broke the seal. "Everyone would certainly understand."

What fell out of the envelope surprised them both. I was a wedding invitation for someone Jenny had never met - or even heard of. There was a lovely handwritten note included as well and two first-class airline tickets.

"Dear Jeff," the note began as Melody read out loud.

> As I sit down to write to you I have deep regrets for not keeping in touch over these many years. My intentions are always good but life gets in the way and correspondence with good friends always seems to take a backseat to the "inbox" of reality. At any rate I hope this letter finds you well and your life has been filled with God's love and personal joy.

At long last I have found the man of my dreams and I have agreed to become his wife. I am sure you are as surprised as I was to learn good old Kennedy Andrews is settling down and putting down permanent roots. Those many years we spent together writing papers and cramming for exams so we could go out and tame the world with our career aspirations seem like a page out of a story book now.

While I did not follow the life plan I set for myself back then, I did find my niche as a private consulting accountant and could not have chosen better. Yes, I know, you expected me to be jet setting around the world as an award-winning journalist by now. It's just not how my life story ended. But how grateful I am I found my perfect spot in this life. I hope you have done the same.

I would very much like to introduce you to my husband-to-be and hope you will be able to attend our wedding. It haunts me that we have lost touch and I want to hear all about where you are in your life, my friend.

It was signed "With all God's blessings, Kennedy."

A few moments of silence followed and then it was Jenny who spoke first.

"Kennedy Andrews. A college friend, do you think?"

"It does sound like that," Melody told her. "The wedding is just a little over a week away. This must have arrived shortly after Jeff's accident. What do you want me to do? Send your regrets for having to pass? Explain what has happened over the last month or so? I could even send a gift if you like. Just let me know and I will handle it."

"No," Jenny said as she stood to clear the coffee cups. "I think I will go to Kansas."

"What? Oh Jenny, you can't be serious," Melody told her without even trying to hide her disbelief.

"Will people think I am selfish?" Jenny wanted to know.

"Selfish? No. But why? You don't even know this woman, right?"

"Right. But perhaps it is a way to honor Jeff. I can stand in for him and let his old friend know he lived a full life and lived it well. Does any of this make sense? Please, Melody, tell me if I am wrong."

"I think it is a fabulous idea, Jen. What about the children?"

"Little Abe can go with me. He is so young and would be a handful for someone else. And the others? Well, hundreds of people have offered to help me with the kids. We'll see if they really mean it."

Just like that it was decided. Jenny and infant Abe Moore would be the latest RSVP's to the Andrews-Parker wedding.

To go or not to go

Brenda's head was full of mismatched thoughts tonight. Her good friend Kennedy's wedding was just a little over a week away and she longed to see her friend and watch her get married. But she felt pulled, too, toward her neighbor Mrs. Wilson and the need to be sure she was being cared for.

In truth she could afford neither trip. She really should stay in town and try to pick up some overtime hours. Several weeks ago she had asked to use a week's vacation time so she could attend the wedding. She only had four days so she would have to lose pay for a day. But these opportunities only come around once in a lifetime so she weighed the consequences and opted to head to Kansas to see Kennedy.

Now, however, she was torn. Mrs. Wilson had been a solid friend to her, too. While she had known Kennedy longer, Rose Wilson needed her. If she went to Kansas she would likely have a splendid time but Kennedy would be so busy she might not even notice if she was there or not.

She did feel a pang of guilt for wasting those two first-class airline tickets her friend had sent, but she needed to take care of Mrs. Wilson. Making a mental note to call Kennedy and wish her well she headed out to see how expensive a bus ticket was to Oregon.

Date night

"Do you think we will still go on dates once we are married?" Kennedy asked her fiancée.

"Nope. I will get tired of you within a month," Greg responded without hesitation. This earned him a big punch in the arm which he was certain would have been in the gut if he hadn't been driving.

"That's great information to know up front," Kennedy teased. "All my friends say be sure you really want this whole matrimonial thing. Once you say 'I do' it's the same pair of lips, the same dirty laundry and the same Sunday night football week in and week out. So knowing you will be tired of me in a month makes all that easier to deal with."

"OK, maybe two months," he joked back as he guided his sports car into the parking lot of Antonelli's.

"Keep talking like that and you will be sleeping on the couch before the honeymoon's over, buddy."

Banter like this was commonplace in their relationship and always had been. They rarely had disagreements and when they did they solved them simply and quickly. The only exception being the one big stumbling block – her multi-million dollar nest egg she had kept a secret from him until just a few weeks ago. In the back of her mind she still wasn't sure Greg was completely on board with her reasons for keeping her net worth hush-hush from the world. He, too, was worth millions on paper.

Individually each of them earned far more money than they needed to live a very comfortable lifestyle and together it was ridiculous how much extra cash they would be able to save and/or donate. So his frustration with her couldn't be the money. It was, he said, the secretiveness of the whole thing. But then again she didn't understand because it was no longer a secret. For tonight she had to put it out of her mind, though, because she wanted to enjoy the evening. She was going to have to give this one to God and trust this little relationship stumbling block was in the past.

Greg ordered a bottle of wine and the two of them made quick time in placing their orders. They had eaten here together many times since that first date and definitely had the menu memorized. Today it was chicken Marsala for him and stuffed shells for her.

"I'm feeling pretty hungry tonight. Might need my own piece of cheesecake," Greg told her with a wink. Antonelli's likely could set a world record for most calories squeezed into one of their desserts so they usually shared.

"Not a problem at all," she told him. "No dessert for me tonight. I have to wiggle into that dress in nine days."

"It's wiggling out of it that I am concerned about," he teased.

"Greg! Behave!" she pretended to scold. "We are in public."

"OK, so how's the weather? Do you think it will rain tomorrow?"

"You are impossible. Can we talk about something serious?" she asked.

"Sure. Name it," Greg said.

"What worries you?"

"In general?" he wanted to know. "Or about the wedding?"

"The wedding will go well. Paula has a back up plan for every back up plan. No worries there, but I mean we are older than the average bride and groom. We are established financially and our household is complete. In my eyes that gives us an advantage but do you have concerns about anything before we jump into this big commitment?"

"Running out of dog food? I don't know," he said, meaning it.

"Greg, be serious. Can you?"

"I am. There is nothing that comes to mind. We are older than most people who choose this route. That's true. Nothing we can do about that, but it also makes us more convicted in our decision."

Their food arrived at the table then and it was hard to determine if the smell or the taste would be better.

After thanking the waiter and refilling their wine glasses Greg spoke again.

"Why are you asking me this? Is there something that is troubling you?"

"No, not at all. But we are about to put our feelings for each other in permanent ink and it just dawns on me I don't know your deepest worries or fears."

"Well, then I guess I would say cancer."

"Cancer," she echoed.

"Yes, cancer scares the hell out of me."

That made perfect sense. He had lost his mom to cancer when he was a teenager and had spent a big chunk of his adult life working with children who had been affected by it.

"Wow, that's heavy," she said.

"You did ask. What worries you?" he wanted to know.

"You, I think."

There was a slight pause then while Greg chewed and swallowed before he answered.

"I worry you? That is a little surprising, sweetheart. We are just a little over a week away from getting married. Are you having second thoughts? Please be honest. You know how important that is to me."

"No, no, no worries about that at all. I love you more than I could have ever imagined possible. It's just that I have never been responsible for anyone before," she told him wishing now she hadn't started this serious conversation. "I want to be everything you need me to be and I guess I haven't read the how-to guide on being the perfect Mrs. Gregory Parker."

"Oh," he said with convincing mock seriousness. "If that is all this is about I can give you a quick crash course."

"Please," she said, setting down her fork and wondering if she should order a second bottle of wine.

"It is incredibly easy. There are just three steps."

He was kidding, of course. He had to be.

"First," he said, "You must always press my white shirts. I like to plan on two per day just in case I spill something at lunch. So 10 pressed, starched shirts by 6 p.m. Sunday night."

He better be joking now, she thought, or this marriage was in grave trouble before it began.

"Secondly, there is the whole backseat issue."

"Backseat issue?" she queried with a raised eyebrow.

"Yes, you must ALWAYS take a backseat when it comes to my business dealings and my client list. They always have and always will come first."

Greg watched her sweet, beautiful eyes twist in confusion. He had meant to be funny but she seemed to be taking it all in.

"And lastly," he said quickly so she didn't rebel and run screaming from the restaurant, "you absolutely must forget the first two and just be Kennedy. I just need you to be the smart, witty, compassionate lady I fell in love with."

Now it was her turn to be playful. She threw her napkin at him then nearly landing it on his plate.

"What? Is that too much for you?" He was smiling now and she wondered how he did it. He always had a way of making her feel complete. She hoped she did the same for him. As for being the perfect wife? She would just have to take it one day at a time and hope she was on the right track.

"Can I ask you a question now?" Greg said.

"Yep. What is it?"

"After we're married who pays the bill? Me or you?"

"Well, Mr. Parker, I guess it will have to be NEITHER you or me. It will be WE who pay the bill."

"Now see, that is disturbing," he told her. "Because I have kind of gotten used to writing these tickets off as a business expense. But when my company becomes 50% your company in a few days the paperwork will get a bit more complicated."

"Worth it I hope," she told him.

"Well that depends, Miss Andrews."

"Depends on what?"

"When we are legally wed, will you still let me have cheesecake?"

Pretending to think about it Kennedy made him wait a few seconds for the answer.

"Only if you share," she said.

Life was good. She might even say perfect.

Before Greg and Kennedy left the restaurant they took some time to review final wedding plans. The guest lists had been matched with the RSVP cards weeks ago so there should be no surprise on numbers. Catering and cake preparations were secured and confirmed. Kennedy's final dress fitting was complete and all the fashion accessories were accounted for and ready to be transported to the church. Flowers would be minimal at the service. They had opted for hundreds of candles in different colors and sizes instead. Her bouquet and a single rose for each bridesmaid would be the only floral accents. By design it would be simple but elegant.

"Have you heard from Mike in the last few days?" Kennedy asked as they prepared to settle the bill. "I haven't heard you mention him for a while."

"It has been a few days. He is on a business trip in California but assures me he will get in Thursday afternoon. I would be prepared, though. I think he is taking his best man's toasting responsibility quite seriously. I would expect lots of over the hill hits."

"Ha! Well, we can handle it. We know we're old. I can't wait to meet him," Kennedy said taking his hand in hers.

"You will love the guy," Greg told her. "He has only seen your picture but he tells me every time we talk that I am definitely marrying up."

"Smart guy!"

The conversation carried on for a bit as the two finished the last bite of the rich dessert. Everything seemed to be in order. Her co-workers had told her over and over to expect something to go wrong because it always did, but also to give up on stressing over it because even if everything went wrong at the end of the day she would still be married to her best friend. The perfectionist in her was having a bit of trouble with that but she was trying. So far all things were falling together in perfect harmony. It was difficult to imagine what might go wrong.

Back in the car Greg brought up one last detail.

"Are we all good with the Thursday night plan? I know you are anxious for me to meet your friends, too. Are we still gathering at the deli?" he asked.

"Yes, that is all set. The guys assured me there will be more than enough food set out for everyone and I told them just to run a bar tab. Doesn't that sound like the best way to do it? Oh and they are all coming in from out of state so I paid for some rooms at the Marriott."

"Absolutely. I trust you completely. Are all of them able to make it?" he asked.

"All but one. Well, two actually. Brenda had another commitment already. She was my college roomie freshman year. I was pretty disappointed because it has been years. But things happen. Maybe we can take a long weekend sometime soon and go visit her."

"And where is it she lives?"

"Ohio. A suburb of Toledo I think."

"And the other one?"

"Well, that one is a bit odd," Kennedy told him as they pulled away from the parking lot and onto the side street headed to his house. "It is Jeff. He was my chemistry lab partner. We spent hours and hours studying for that class. We kept asking each other 'When are we ever going to use this stuff?' and we were right. Never. By the time we were done with that class I felt like I knew him better than his family."

"Maybe he is a chemist for some pharmaceutical firm pulling down the big bucks," Greg told her optimistically.

"Nope. Math teacher. Of course accounting wasn't on my radar back then either. I did hear, though, that he was Vermont's Teacher of the Year last year. So maybe all the math in those chemistry labs paid off, huh?"

"I guess so. But he is not coming?"

"Well, I don't know. Paula said the reservation came back for two but it was signed by a Jenny not a Jeffrey."

"You don't think…I mean…is it possible…"

"What?" Kennedy asked him, baffled by his thoughts.

"Is it possible Jeffrey is now a 'Jennifer'?"

"Oh. My. God. Be serious!"

"Just sayin'. You never know," Greg teased her.

"For now I am going to assume it is his wife and she, being the smarter and more responsible of the two, was the one to take care of the correspondence."

"Ouch!" Greg responded. "I felt a little barb in there."

Kennedy gave him another playful arm punch, glad they could spar back and forth like this all the time.

"So who else will I be meeting at that shindig," Greg wanted to know.

Kennedy spent the rest of their drive outlining the group she had invited.

There was Mary Jane, a close family friend growing up who Kennedy used to babysit for. As adults – being just a few years apart in age – they had kept up with each others' lives more than the rest. Mary Jane had married early and had four children, the youngest of which was in kindergarten and apparently thought she was capable of teaching the class. Kennedy had heard a few stories over their brief e-mails this last year but hoped to hear many more and hoped, too, that Mary Jane would bring pictures of all of them.

"Father Paul will be your favorite," she told her fiancée. "He is ornery and full of mischief, just like you!"

"A priest? And he is ornery? That is an oxymoron," he told her.

"You just wait and see. He was a great influence on me. I am so glad he is able to make it. But mark my word, priest and all he will be the life of the party."

Kennedy continued with the list. There was Jack – a high school friend she had spent four years singing with in a competition choir. They had almost lost touch completely, but she was able to get his current address from another friend's mother.

And then there was Sadie. Sadie's story was sad and even as she told Greg about it she felt tears well up in her eyes. She told him about Sadie's mother dying when Sadie was in elementary school and her having asked Kennedy to look after her. An aunt had apparently taken on the day-to-day responsibilities of her care but she had heard Sadie got pregnant as a teenager and was struggling as a single mom. Kennedy regretted not stepping in to help but wasn't sure how Sadie would accept it from someone she didn't know existed. For her part Kennedy had kept her in her thoughts and prayers almost daily. She had promised herself someday she would do something fantastic for Sadie in her mom's honor.

"You mean you haven't even met the girl?" Greg asked.

"I'm afraid not. It's my biggest regret. I was fearful she would reject my offer to meet but she is coming. Hallelujah! We will have to think of something special to do for her, don't you think?"

"For sure. I certainly know what it is like to grow up without a mom," Greg said. "So let's see – Brenda and Jeff/Jenny, that's two."

"Stop!" she chastised him.

Greg took it in stride and kept numbering the guests. "And then the goofy priest, the mother of four. Then Jack and Sadie. That's just six. Didn't you say seven?"

"Oh yeah. And J.T." she said without explanation. "That's seven.

"Who is J.T.?"

"I'm exhausted. Aren't you? All that pasta has made me sleepy."

"Oh no you don't," Greg pressed. "Who is this guy? Old boyfriend or something?"

"Look at the time. I'm beat." she answered.

"Ha ha! Clever. So tell me about the guy."

"Are you jealous, Mr. Parker?"

"Should I be?"

"Not for a second. I will be walking down the aisle to you. He will just be a guest." Then Kennedy decided to have a little fun with it. "However…"

"However?"

"However, he did make his career as a body builder. Maybe you have heard of him. J.T. O'Malley?"

"Holy smokes! You dated J.T. O'Malley?!?!?! He was a fitness icon. His face was plastered on billboards in every city in America!"

"I seem to remember it was more his biceps and his six-pack abs on all those billboards," she told him with a playfully sinister smile.

"Crazy! You are full of secrets. Who else is coming? The president?"

"Don't be silly, dear. The president's schedule is so hectic this time of year."

This sent both of them into fits of giggles. She knew Greg couldn't be seriously jealous of an ex. It had been, after all, more than 30 years since she had seen him. She was sure he had married a beautiful model somewhere along the line and would be bringing her along. Greg was an easy mark when it came to ribbing, though. He was so gullible. It was one of the many things she loved about him and she told him so as they made their way into the house.

"I think I left my laptop here," Kennedy told him as he turned the key and stepped back to let her in. "I have a few things to finish up for an early meeting tomorrow. Would you mind if I just crashed here tonight?"

"As long as you are gone by noon. That's when my other girlfriend shows up. She's a Playboy bunny. Miss September."

"I see," Kennedy responded. "Thanks for the heads up. I will try not to use all the hot water." With a wink she headed into his den to retrieve her computer and get to work.

Detoxing from stress

The next few days were filled with seemingly unsurmountable stress. For Kennedy, who couldn't remember the last time she had taken more than one day off work at a time, preparing to be gone for a three-week honeymoon seemed like scaling Mount Rushmore in flip flops. According to her office staff she was going to have to delegate and trust. Normally she didn't have a problem with delegating or trusting her team, but three weeks was still a long time for her to be away.

Greg, too, had business obligations but he was far more comfortable shelving minor tasks until he got back and asking his dad to attend to anything urgent that surfaced while he was away. His only wedding task was to plan and confirm the honeymoon destination and travel plans which had been done months ago. He was ready to be a married man and the sooner the better.

"Hey babe," he spoke into the phone after Kennedy's secretary had patched him through. "How are you holding up?"

"Ugggg. Maybe we should cancel this whole big party thing and just get hitched at the courthouse."

"That bad, huh? What's wrong? How can I help?"

"Ironically nothing is wrong. I am just having trouble letting someone else be in charge around here. I hope I am not so conceited as to think I am the only one who can operate the system."

"Of course you are the best there is," he told her. "But think of it this way.

There is nothing that can be done that can't be undone. Right? If something goes awry you can fix it when we get back."

"How did you get to be so smart?" Kennedy wanted to know.

"Years and years of expensive education," he said with a muffled laugh.

"Oh yeah? And which class was that? How to delegate 101? Or Basic Rules for Leaving the Office Understaffed?"

"I think it was more at the bar with my fraternity brothers," he said without hesitation. "That is where I learned to put off things I could do today but didn't want to do until tomorrow."

"Hmmmmm…I think I missed that lesson. At any rate, everything is totally under control. I just need a distraction."

"Do you have any ideas? I could probably help you with that if you know what I mean."

"Ha! Yes, I do know what you mean. And as pleasant – no, euphoric – as that sounds at the moment, there will be plenty of time for that later. For now I need to finish up here, then head home early, relax and unwind for a bit and go to bed early. But thank you so much for checking on me. You are a saint and I love you for it."

They disconnected and true to her word Kennedy left work early, bound and determined to relax and enjoy her last five days as a single woman.

Greg, too, left work before five. He opted to skip dinner – at least for a while – and settle into his recliner with a beer. He used the remote to check the news and sports headlines of the day before getting distracted by an infomercial for custom insoles.

A few minutes later the alert sounded for an incoming text and rattled him back to reality. Kennedy.

"I know it's early but I'm headed to bed. Long day. Headache. Love you."

Bed? It wasn't even dark yet. It must have been a tougher day than she let on earlier.

"Good for you. Dream of the beach. Love you, too," he texted back.

Channel surfing had temporarily lost its appeal so Greg wandered into the kitchen and scrambled some eggs while he made toast. A few minutes later he was back in his living room but this time he opted for the stereo instead of the television. He made short order of his makeshift dinner wishing now he had waited on the beer until later. He grabbed another one, though, to chase down his breakfast dinner. He was too lazy at the moment to make coffee so he had a third. No problem. He was in for the night.

Setting his empty plate on the coffee table he realized he did have a few more things to do before the wedding, too. None of it involved things for Saturday, but he and Kennedy had decided they would combine their residences and live at her big cabin-like house on the lake. Rather than sell his house they would use it when they entertained for business. It was in town and would be an easier to find venue for clients. Maybe later they would consider selling his place, but for now it was a great luxury to be able to maintain both homes, each for a different purpose.

That, however, created the challenge of converting this house into more of a restaurant/bar atmosphere rather than a home. The bedrooms could stay in tact for hosting overnight guests and even family members. But this open living space could use some modifications. None of that had to be done before the wedding but the more he got done this week the sooner it could be a usable space after they returned from Tahiti.

The more he sat the less settled he felt. So he stood and he paced. What would be needed? The sofa and love seat could stay but he would need to add more sitting space. Maybe take the coffee table and the recliner out and move them downstairs. That would open up the room more. He could add a colorful area rug and some art on the walls. Maybe a nautical theme?

Too much. Too much to think about today he decided. The food and the alcohol was making him sleepy and unlike Kennedy he wasn't ready to call it a night. He'd go for a drive, he decided. Maybe inspiration would come to him as he drove. Without a second thought about the three beers he'd had in a matter of 30 minutes or so he clicked off the stereo, grabbed his keys and headed out the door. Tonight he would leave the sports car behind and take the SUV. Better stereo for a leisurely ride down the open road to the country.

Second thoughts

Given the fact Greg was about to be married and his whole life as he knew it revamped, he was surprisingly calm. As he guided his Jeep SUV down the highway – windows open, stereo blasting – he felt at ease and more relaxed than he had been in months. His job as a public relations specialist required him to make hundreds of decisions every day but the decision to make Kennedy Andrews his wife was undoubtedly the best decision he had made in his whole life.

She was smart. She was beautiful. She was funny. And most importantly she loved him and for that he would always be grateful. Past relationships had left him jaded and angry as time after time he had been betrayed and lied to by women he loved. People he knew were starting to think he had become a bit of a player since he never stayed with any lady more than a date or two. As soon as things turned remotely serious – even something as simple as meeting someone's family – he would cut bait and run. No, it didn't look like Greg Parker would ever find lasting love. And then he did.

One thing he absolutely could not tolerate in a relationship, though, was dishonesty. Given his past experiences even a surprise birthday party upset him. Secrets. He hated secrets no matter how small. Kennedy knew this, of course. To be a part of his forever life she would have to know this. Maybe that is why it was so hard for her to tell him about the money. The money she had been keeping a secret from him since the day they met.

Relax Greg, he told himself. Don't start thinking about that again. They were past it. She had sheltered it from everyone – not just him – because she didn't want people to think of her as a bank account but rather as a business woman, a friend, a sister and an aunt. He understood that. But the fact remained: If she could keep something as big as almost $30 million a secret from someone she allegedly loved more than anyone else, then what else was she keeping? Or could she be keeping? Probably nothing. He wished it didn't bother him.

Slow down, Greg, he told himself. He realized he was speeding. Alost 90 miles an hour. He had to get a grip on it and give up those feelings of animosity toward her. She was so much more than that one tiny omission. And he had to give her credit. She did tell him. If he had found out some other way it would have been way too much to bear.

Here he was now at the entrance to the lake. Turning left would eventually take him to Kennedy's cabin. But tonight he wasn't out here to see her. She was likely sound asleep by now. He just wanted some time to drive and relax. So he turned right and edged the Jeep slowly around the curves until he could see the water. Pulling over he walked the 20 steps or so to a little fishing dock and sat down intending to stay and watch the sun set.

Alone with his thoughts again he tried to focus on the house remodel. Maybe he could even knock out a wall between the kitchen and dining area. Then he could add an island between the two spaces that would be an ideal gathering area for a small group or to serve a buffet when entertaining larger crowds. Should he change the paint color? Not sure. But he definitely needed a theme. Boats, seashells and lighthouses was his initial thought but now he had time to reconsider. He was not a master at all things home improvement but he could generate some ideas and then hire people to make the actual changes. He didn't want anything flowery, but almost anything else would be up for consideration.

Maybe a sports theme with autographed pictures of famous athletes and an accent wall with a unique sporty wallpaper. A friend of his from home had one room in his house decorated with baseball memorabilia and even had a border around the top of the room made from actual baseball cards. Sounded like a fun way to decorate for him, but Kennedy would probably think it was too casual for the effect they were going for. And she would probably be right. She almost always was.

Kennedy. Damn. There it was again. Those thoughts of betrayal that he just couldn't seem to let go of. Why was he having trouble thinking of the gazillions of great things about her but couldn't let go of that one ugly blemish in their otherwise perfect relationship?

Get a grip on yourself, man. Don't blow something wonderful over one tiny issue. Grow up, Greg, he told himself headed back to his Jeep. Maybe he just needed sleep, too. He could watch the sun set any day.

Music had always been a calming force for Greg. As a child it helped him cope with the earth shattering crisis of losing a parent to cancer. As a teenager it had again helped him cope with the stresses of school and work. Then into adulthood he always found an inner solitude when music was the center of his day. His mother had insisted he learn to play piano and he had suffered through hundreds of lessons even after her passing because he knew it was important to her. In so doing it eventually became important to him, too.

Tonight as he drove around the curves of the lake road he popped in an Eagles CD and waited the few seconds for it to load. First song – Life's Been Good. Joe Walsh. Classic. As he drove he sang along.

> I have a mansion
> Forget the price
> Ain't never been there
> They tell me it's nice.
>
> I live in hotels
> Tear out the walls
> I have accountants
> Pay for it all.

Good Lord! Was that Kennedy? Just up ahead on the path was a jogger – and a dog. It was Kennedy's dog of that he was certain but it couldn't be his girlfriend. He was still a good distance from the runner but it had to be her.

The Eagles continued without him.

            I'm making records
            My fans they can't wait.
            They write me letters
            Tell me I'm great.

    Greg hadn't planned to go that far
around the bend. He was headed home. But if
that was Kennedy she had lied to him AGAIN.
Running with her dog was not going to bed
early with a headache. What reason could she
possibly have to say one thing and do
another? It really didn't matter he told
himself. Maybe she couldn't sleep.
    Hell yes it did matter! Alarmingly he
felt a familiar rage build internally. He
was angry. Angier than he could ever
remember being in the past. He had been
through this before and he wasn't going to
stand for it now or ever. You will NOT lie
to me Kennedy Andrews. No matter how much I
love you I can not, will not forgive you for
that.

            So I got me an office
            Gold records on the wall.
            Leave me a message
            Maybe I'll call.

    Enough! He punched the button to
silence the stereo and sped up. He had
learned over the years there were coping
mechanisms that would help him de-escalate.
However at the moment he didn't want to calm
down. He wanted to confront her, make her
pay for being dishonest.
    "This is not the first time you have
done this to me. I will not TOLERATE this
you little - " he broke off before he could

                                            235

finish. Talking to himself wasn't going to fix it anyway.

If logic had kicked in he would have slowed down, maybe even turned around and let her be. There was an explanation, of course. It wasn't in her nature to be ruthless and disrespect him like this. She was a talented accountant about to get married to the love of her life – him – so there was no reason for her to purposefully spit in his face by saying one thing and doing another. But if he couldn't trust her then it didn't matter. Nothing mattered. Not his life or hers.

He sped up again guiding the SUV directly at her at a dangerously high rate of speed. She must of heard him then as his Jeep approached her rapidly from behind. He saw her face for that split second before it happened. It was a look of surprise that quickly morphed into confusion and lastly fear as the vehicle inched closer and closer to her beautiful lying face. He could have swerved. There was still time. But he didn't.

Thump. Thump. And it was over.

The next few days

He wasn't hungry but he was eating.
Steak. Baked potato. Bread and butter. He
felt the food enter his body and was vaguely
aware he was chewing and swallowing. He was
even able to make pleasant conversation with
the overly attentive waitress. It was
important to act normal as he went about the
task of having dinner at the club,
pretending to study the business notes on
the legal pad he had brought in from the car
as a distraction. He was trying excessively
hard to convince himself and everyone else
in the room that it was just an average
Monday night.

Now as he finished his meal he began to
remember the strategies for ebbing the
anger. Deep breaths, clenching and
unclenching his hands, rubbing his temples.
Only now it was too late. He had let his
unfounded anger get the best of him and now
it would destroy him. Too little, too late.

Oddly he noticed as he left the club
determined to head home, his cell phone had
not jingled in his pocket. It had been
almost two hours. No one had found her yet.
He wasn't sure how long he could go on
acting normal but he didn't have a choice.
He pulled the Jeep into the driveway and
went inside to wait. It was useless to go to
bed because sleep would not find him
tonight. What in the world had he done? He
would have to pay. It was just a matter of
time.

His father was the first to call.
"Greg? My God. Where are you? At work?"

"Yeah, Dad. What's wrong? You sound upset. Panicked almost."

"Aren't you? Haven't you seen the news?"

He hadn't. But he could imagine.

"It's Kennedy, son. There's been an accident. They aren't releasing much information because they have to contact her next of kin. Greg, she was hit by a car."

Damn it. Where were the police? Why hadn't they questioned him? He needed to get through that interrogation and then he could grieve. His mind was a mess of disbelief and regret. Last night he had acted in a fit of indignation and this morning he was no longer angry only that no longer mattered because you can't un-kill someone. Greg, Greg, what were you thinking, he asked himself. The only answer was he hadn't been thinking.

"Dad, no," he remotely heard himself say over the phone. "You must be wrong. It's just not possible. She was going home and going to bed. She had a headache. She couldn't possibly have been out."

That's when he heard the knock on the door. The police had at last arrived to tell him what he already knew. He would not be getting married on Saturday.

In truth the police visit wasn't as terrible as he had imagined it could be. They weren't accusatory in the slightest. Of course he knew his guilty conscience was working overtime and he was certain the officers would be able to read his face which in his mind clearly said:

I did it. It was me. I am guilty. BUT SHE LIED TO ME.

Neither policeman seemed to see that. In fact they appeared to be a consoling committee. First of all, did he know? Then was there anything they could do? How awful this must be for him. Was there anyone they could call?

After giving him sketchy details and leaving out the gory parts about her mangled body left in a heap on the side of the road they finally let themselves out. There appeared to be no witnesses at this point and they had no leads but they promised him they would do everything they could to find the person who killed his fiancee.

His reaction had been deadpan. Completely stoic as a matter of fact. He was in shock although not for the reasons the Sedgwick County Sheriff Department thought. He was in shock because he had let his ugly temper rule him yet again – and this time it had fatal consequences.

Trying to describe what he felt was impossible. He was numb. It had been just a little over 12 hours but it felt like just minutes ago he had snapped. A good woman was dead because of his stupid insecurities and he would have to live with that for the rest of his life. Nothing was clear to him. Why? Why was he able to manage and control a large corporation and all the miniscule details and problems associated with that and yet his personal life was a shambles. Kennedy and her family did not deserve what he had done. And now he would likely spend the rest of his life behind bars. No music would be able to console him there. He, too, would be better off dead.

Fortunately the media hadn't gotten ahold of the details and converged on him yet. His father did arrive, though, and then neighbor after neighbor and friend after friend came to the house, many with a casserole or a cake. No one seemed to know what to say but it was just as well because he didn't want to hear it. They were all well-intentioned but he didn't want food. He didn't want company. He just wanted this to go away.

Tuesday and Wednesday came and went while his family and his office handled the calls. Yes, Mr. Parker was going to be fine. He was resting and asked not to be disturbed. All the wedding vendors had been cancelled and his family had handled the funeral arrangements for him. He knew her plans were to be cremated and with her brother's approval the family decided to wait until later to plan a service. It was all too much for him right now. He was in hibernation survival mode and those close to him accepted that and left him to mourn alone in his room.

There was one detail he must deal with personally, however. Kennedy's friends from out of state would be in Kansas tomorrow and so far due to the incomplete details media coverage of the alleged murder had been light. It was very possible none of them knew. Somehow he had to find the strength to pull himself together and get to the Salted

Olive tomorrow night and give them the news himself.

"Why don't you let me handle that for you," his father had told him. "Although there is no doubt it would do you some good to shower and get out of the house for an hour or so, I am not sure I could do it if I were in your position."

"I don't know, Dad. I want to go. I feel like I should be the one to tell them. But…"

"No one would blame you if you begged off on this one, Greg."

One part of him wanted to come completely clean with his father. John Parker had been his rock for more than 50 years and he knew he would hold him up now, too, both literally and figuratively. But he had already lost so many people who meant so much to him. On that outside chance his father wouldn't understand he couldn't take the risk. Without his support he could not go on.

"What if," Greg started as the two of them sat on the edge of his bed. "What if I get there and can't do it? What then?"

"I don't know. I have no idea what to tell you," his father said while his sister looked in on them. "We can wait until tomorrow and see how you feel. Things usually look clearer in the morning. You need some sleep."

At the moment there were no truer words. He hadn't slept more than five minutes at a time since Monday evening. It had been just a little less than 48 hours since he had mowed down his girlfriend in cold blood.

Closing in

Jack was the first to arrive at the classic deli in the quaint Valleyview neighborhood. The room was dark and he had to give his eyes time to adjust. There were a few others at tables sharing an early dinner but he didn't see Kennedy. He knew he was about 20 minutes early but was a little disappointed. The mood was more like that of a deserted after hours bar feel than a celebration. Again he reminded himself he was early and found a seat on the edge of the all but empty room where he settled with his kids waiting for someone else to arrive.

Mary Jane was next. Jack noticed she was looking around in the same way he had and he stood to introduce himself. As Mary Jane shook his hand she seemed grateful to not be the first one here. With an admonishment to his children to order what they liked but be on their best behavior, he and Mary Jane wandered to the center of the room and found a table for eight where they settled to chat while they waited for Kennedy.

Paul was next and made the proper assumption Jack and Mary Jane were part of the guest list. They were both surprised he had taken the time to drive in and quickly struck up a conversation about the mild summer weather and scenery between here and Arkansas. It was difficult to explain to Jack and Mary Jane how he knew Kennedy without explaining he had been a priest. If they were shocked they politely didn't show it and the three of them continued to talk like they had known each other for years.

Jenny and Sadie walked in together, apparently meeting in the parking lot and easily found the group they were looking for. The last to enter was J.T. who joined them and also looked bewildered Kennedy wasn't here yet.

The group of six didn't have to wait too long to discover the reason. A seventh person joined them then. He looked uncomfortable and more than a little out of place in this relaxed atmosphere. The man was wearing a business suit, jacket and all, on this warm June afternoon. He carried with him a briefcase and held a thick cream-colored folder in his left hand. The six exchanged glances. Could this be the groom?

"Welcome," the stranger said. "My name is Ed. Edward Luginbill and I am Kennedy's attorney."

There would be no wedding Jack, Mary Jane, Paul, Jenny, Sadie and J.T. learned simultaneously. And although Greg wanted to be here he didn't feel he was ready to make a public statement. The lawyer told them Greg sent his regrets and wanted Mr. Luginbill to assure them rooms had been secured at the Marriott on Ridgewood Road and they were welcome to stay as long as they wished. All of their expenses would be taken care of.

Wow. Just wow.

The large, open, dark room at the deli was suddenly alive with questions.

"When did it happen?"

"Has there already been a service?"

"Do they know who is responsible?"

"What can we do for Greg?"

"Has a memorial been established?"

"Does the family need anything?"

How sad. Yes, it was a travesty.

For nearly an hour Mr. Luginbill attempted to answer their questions although he admitted he knew very little. Just that Mr. Parker was still in shock and grief had overtaken him to the point he couldn't make solid plans for the future.

At last the questions diminished and a hush fell over the newly acquainted.

"There is one more thing, however," the attorney told them. "While there was no way to know it would happen this way, in the event of her death Miss Andrews' intentions were for each of you to receive a piece of her estate."

If it was possible to be more surprised than they already were, the six guests were stunned into silence. Then one by one the attorney called their names and handed each a sealed envelope which he asked them not to open just yet.

"Sadie Nichols. Paul Odell. Brenda Davis. J.T. O'Malley. Mary Jane Mendenhall. Jeff Moore. Jack Redman."

It was quickly determined that Brenda was not here today and Jenny was Jeff's wife and then Mr. Luginbill stood and continued.

"I need to read what is written here to all of you. It may come as quite a shock but please let me finish before you open your individual letters."

The group of six, already stunned with the news of Kennedy's death remained silent and all eyes were on Mr. Luginbill who cleared his throat and continued.

"She has provided for her brother and his family both monetarily and with the personal effects of her estate. However, she would like to gift each of you with something special."

The group again remained mute but exchanged random glances around the table trying to imagine what trinket their friend might have left each of them, especially since most of them had not seen her in many years.

"My dear friends," the lawyer read from the file in his hands, "I want you all to know beyond a shadow of a doubt that each in your own special way have earned a place in my heart. Over the years in one way or another you have touched me in a way I can not explain. I have been fortunate to be a part of your lives – Brenda, Mary Jane, Father Paul, Jeff, Jack, Sadie and J.T – and so in the event of my death I have asked my attorney to distribute a letter to each of you."

Ed Luginbill paused here to be sure everyone was listening. He knew the bombshell he was about to drop on each of them but they did not. After a brief pause he went on.

"Life has been good to me and my career has offered me far more treasure than I could ever spend. For the last 20 years I have put this money away hoping I could find the ultimate way to use it for the good of humanity. Many projects have come to mind but I was never able to decide on the perfect way to use this money for good. So please forgive me for passing that responsibility on to you."

Forgive her? Jack was deeply pensive as he listened. Apparently Kennedy had left each of them a small cash gift and she was asking for forgiveness? He was having trouble processing all that had been said already. And apparently there was more.

"The money is yours to spend as you wish. There are no strings attached," Ed continued to read. "My hope is you will find a way to use it for the betterment of your families and your communities. My grandmother always told me 'Money can't buy happiness, but it is a great start.' I trust that each and every one of you will find a way to make a difference in ways that I could not even have imagined."

When the attorney finished he sat and waited. He knew there would be questions. There were none immediately but then it was J.T. who spoke first.

"So you are saying there is a check in here," he said waving his envelope "that is written out to me. As in I am one of the heirs in her will?"

"The envelope itself contains a personal hand-written letter to each of you. My office will issue the checks to you individually. They are prepared and ready to distribute but I will need each of you to stop by my office before you return home so that I can verify your identity. I will make contact with Ms. Davis since she is not with us today. Mrs. Moore since you are Jeff's next of kin we can proceed with the payment to you after you provide a death certificate for your husband."

"I am completely stymied," Mary Jane told the group. "I thought I was coming to Kansas to meet her family and wish her well. This is all so surreal."

"I do understand," Mr. Luginbill told them. "In an ideal situation we would not be dividing the assets of someone who was barely 50 years old. I know the circumstances are grim as you all thought you were assembling for a wedding. However, these were her wishes. Together we wrote and notarized the will over 10 years ago. I personally can assure you she selected each of you as an heir with careful consideration."

"What about Greg?" Jenny asked.

"As I am sure you are aware there are privacy laws that will not permit me to give out personal information," he told them.

"So he is not a part of this?" Jenny clarified. "I mean if the will was written before she met him and she died unexpectedly it seems the money should revert to him. Maybe she just didn't have time to change the beneficiaries with all the details of the wedding."

"I do understand your concern but I can assure you I spoke to Miss Andrews just last Thursday regarding some other legal issues and she was quite clear she did not wish to make changes with regard to how her estate was distributed," the lawyer told them.

"She left everything to us?" Jenny asked, once again seeking clarity to this highly unusual situation.

"Her brother and his family, of course, will receive a large portion," Mr. Luginbill said. "Everything else will be left to you – just the seven of you."

It was unthinkable. Truly. Sadie, the youngest among them was the next to speak.

"Is it appropriate to ask how much we have been gifted? I did not even know this woman."

"Yes, Miss Nichols, she told me it was her biggest regret that the two of you had never met but she wanted to honor a promise made to your mother many, many years ago and to that end you have been included. The details of her wishes are spelled out in your individual letters."

The silence was deafening, no one wanting to be the first to break the seal of the letter.

"Oh yes," the attorney added. "The amount you will receive – after the taxes and fees have been accounted for – is just a little over $1.4 million."

"No," Paul said. "That is impossible. That would be almost a quarter of a million dollars for each of us."

The others nodded assent. It was hard to imagine.

"Oh no, you have misunderstood" Mr. Luginbill told them all. "Miss Andrews left you roughly $1.4 million apiece."

The attorney excused himself and left the deli after reiterating the details of how to find his office. He wished them well and told them the legal part of it all would just take a few minutes. There would be no need to make an appointment. Any time would be fine.

Left alone then the six new millionaires didn't know what to do next. They hardly knew each other so there was nothing to talk about and yet they were thrown together by a chance and a common thread so perhaps it was time to get acquainted. There would be time to deal with their new financial status later.

Jack invited Ben and his twins over to the table then to meet his new friends and the mood was instantly lightened while the group got to know his children. For a moment it felt extraordinary to talk about something – anything – other than what had just been dumped in their laps.

Father Paul, as the group knew him, struck up a conversation with the girls immediately about school. He wanted to know their interests and what types of courses they planned to take in high school. J.T. and Ben began to discuss sports, tennis in particular, and then moved on to baseball. Jenny took Sadie under her wing. Sadie wanted to know how long it had been since she lost her husband and the two ladies began to bond over having lost a loved one too soon.

That only left Jack and Mary Jane. Raking his hand through his hair and exhaling deeply he found himself at the bar. He was tempted to order a stiff drink but since he was here with his children opted for a Dr. Pepper instead. Mary Jane was close behind him but decided it was never too early for a glass of wine. And certainly in these circumstances maybe a bottle of wine would be more appropriate. Taking their drinks back to the group, Jack and Mary Jane chose to sit at a table nearby since the others were already absorbed in conversation.

"Join me here?" Jack asked her.

"Sure. How are you holding up?" she wanted to know.

"It sure isn't what I expected. I mean just learning Kennedy is gone. And that she was murdered. At least it sounds like they are investigating it as a homicide, right?" Jack asked her.

"Yeah, and who would want to murder Kennedy? Of all people," Mary Jane told him. "She was the picture of kindness and compassion. Even to the end. I mean she divided her money among her friends so she could take care of others even after her death."

The two continued to marvel over the gravity of what they had just learned but they also began to get to know each other. Between them they had seven children so there was plenty to discuss. There was almost an hour of small talk before it turned more personal.

"What? Your husband has all of that and he has rejected you for a roll in the hay?" Jack asked.

It was hard to believe, even as she spoke the words out loud, that she had shared her family's deep, dark secret with someone she barely knew. At the same time it felt wonderful to be able to say it to someone. Maybe the fact that she didn't know Jack at all and after this week would probably never see him again made it easier for her to open up. She had not been able to do so to anyone she knew back home.

"He is not all bad. He is excellent with the children," Mary Jane heard herself say feeling an odd need to defend Andy. "When he is home," she added.

Jack was flabbergasted at what she was telling him. Here was a beautiful, smart woman - trained as a registered nurse - who stayed at home to raise four children and drop whatever she was doing to entertain her two-timing husband's business clients at the drop of a hat. She had dedicated her life to taking care of him and he repaid her by enjoying the naked company of his secretary and a number of other women as he saw fit. Men like Andy Mendenhall should be castrated and put out to pasture, Jack thought. He stopped short of telling her so, however, because at the moment Andy was still her husband. Telling her what an idiot he was probably wouldn't make her feel better. She already knew.

"So what is your story, Jack?" she asked him. "I am so sorry I just dumped all of that on you. Please forgive me."

"Wow, well, compared to you my life is all roses," Jack told her. "Being a single dad isn't always easy but it is my life and I love it. My ex-wife is 100% non-existent in their lives. That breaks my heart for the children, but certainly makes my job easier."

For the next hour and a half they entertained each other with funny stories about their kids. For both of them it felt good to laugh. At last the group decided to disperse but Paul suggested they meet for lunch the next day. Since they had been thrown together in such an unconventional way he would like to exchange contact information with them all. Everyone was in agreement and since no one was familiar with the area they agreed to meet right back here at the Salted Olive tomorrow at noon. After briefly saying their goodbyes on the sidewalk the group slowly faded into the crowd of others going about their business on a Thursday evening, oblivious to what life-changing events had happened to six unsuspecting people several hours before.

Media frenzy

By the following morning the silent spell of the last few days had been broken. Every news station in the state was airing pictures of Kennedy Andrews, the manager of Carey, Wiley & Associates accounting firm, who had been the victim of a fatal hit and run accident while jogging with her dog near her home in rural Wichita. According to the reports, her fiancee, Greg Parker, was overwhelmed with grief but the family would issue a statement through their attorney later in the day.

Sadie flipped through the channels on her hotel room TV and saw the exact same reports on every channel. Greg's family had offered a sizable reward for anyone with information leading to the arrest of the guilty party. So far there were no witnesses to the crime and the police had no credible leads.

Sadie also noticed as she watched one news report after another there was no mention of Kennedy's excessive fortune and how it had been divided. Obviously her family had chosen to sweep that under the carpet. It wasn't too surprising, though, because she had learned from the attorney yesterday Kennedy had kept her millions a secret from everyone citing the fact that money changes people's opinions of you and she wanted to remain Kennedy. Just Kennedy. Not embarrassingly rich and famous Kennedy.

Today she wished more than ever that she had known this friend of her mother's. Apparently it was not meant to be. Now it would be her responsibility to honor Kennedy with the way she chose to spend the money rather than Kennedy honoring her mother by caring for Sadie. There was a pound of irony there.

While she dressed to join the others for lunch, Sadie considered turning off the TV, but just as she was about to a picture surfaced of Greg Parker. It was just a file photo - like a headshot used for his business promotion. He was strikingly handsome.

A fleeting thought crossed her mind as the news anchor gave a brief bio of Kennedy's boyfriend. If the money Kennedy left to them was a secret and Kennedy didn't want anyone to know she was wealthy, did Greg know? Could it be that he killed her for her money? No. No, no, no. The reporters were displaying him as a prominent business man and philanthropist who gave tirelessly of both his time and his money to help others, specifically those with cancer and those affected by it. What they were saying painted him as a saint who was robbed of his fiancee and his future. Although she didn't know the guy at all it seemed there might be a chink in his armor. Two plus two was not adding up to four in her mind.

At last she slipped into her shoes and grabbed her purse trying to dismiss these thoughts. Greg Parker had lost his girlfriend and his future would be forever marred. To think of him as a murderer was unfounded and unfair. However, it was hard to imagine how he would feel or how anyone would feel if their fiancee was a multi-millionaire and divided her net worth between seven people he had never even met.

She clicked off the television, pulled he door shut behind her and rushed to hotel lobby to hail a taxi back to the Salted Olive.

*****

John Parker knew it would just be a matter of hours before the press was hounding them for an interview. He had been with his son since an hour after he had heard of the accident and so far had been able to keep them at bay. Greg had checked in with his office and asked them to respond with "no comment" and then turned off his personal phone so he would not be disturbed. John had taken a few calls from friends and of course family but for the most part had been the one to run interference.

Now it was starting to get harder. He peered through the sheer curtains in the main living space of Greg's house and could see news outlet trucks converging across the street. One reporter was even preparing to broadcast live with Greg's house as the backdrop. He had called in his attorney a few hours ago and the two of them were busy preparing a statement to be issued when it became absolutely necessary.

He left Brett Alvord at the kitchen table to craft the perfect statement and went to check on his son. He was at a loss for how to help him. John, too, had lost the love of his life when Greg's mother had died of cancer all those years ago. But it was different. They had had time in advance to grieve and to say their goodbyes. It was some of the worst days he had ever lived through. Now Greg was having to live through it again – only this time there had been no advance notice, no chance to say goodbye. Maybe if he could get him to eat something.

John found his son in his den reading a book. Reading a book?

"Hungry?" he asked.

"Not too. You?" Greg asked moving the open book to his lap.

"I think you probably should eat something, don't you?"

"How long will it take, Dad?"

"How long?"

"Yeah, how long will it take before this all goes away? I can't stay hidden away in my house forever."

John was at a loss. He had never experienced anything quite like this before but he imagined it would never really completely go away. He was a bit surprised by Greg's comments but what is normal when you go through something as devastating as this?

"Have you seen the news?" his father asked.

"No, what are they saying?"

John gave him the basics and then told him Brett was ready to give a statement to the press emphasizing the family's request for privacy and asking for the help in finding the killer. Did he want to speak to the press, his father asked him.

"Yes, yes I think I am ready for that," Greg said.

You could have knocked his father over with a feather.

*****

This time Jack left his kids at the hotel and headed over to the deli on his own. He found Paul, Jenny and Sadie already seated and quietly discussing the menu. Mary Jane and J.T. joined them shortly thereafter. It was odd to him how six people who knew nothing of each other yesterday had almost become friends overnight. Not that he was complaining. All of their personalities and life situations were so different even though they had the common thread of a mutual friend. He was a bit dazed by the events of the last 24 hours but he was sure they were too.

Twenty minutes later all their sandwiches had been delivered and the group visited quietly while they ate. No one was at a loss for words but neither was anyone brave enough to bring up the subject of money. Or weddings. Or murder.

The Salted Olive was loaded with big screen televisions and J.T. was the first to notice the breaking news as it popped up on one of the screens. He nudged Paul and Jack and soon they all stopped talking to watch.

"We are on standby at this hour as we wait to hear from Gregory Parker regarding the death of his fiancee. We are told he will make an appearance from his office within the hour," they all heard the reporter say.

"What we know at this time," the newscast continued, "is Kennedy Andrews, the manager of a large accounting firm in the city, was found dead by the side of the road near her house Monday evening. A neighbor discovered the body just after 8:30 p.m. and alerted authorities. According to police records she appeared to be the victim of a hit and run automobile accident. She was scheduled to marry Greg Parker, CEO of the city's largest advertising and public relations conglomerate, on Saturday. Again we are standing by as we wait to hear from a representative for the Parker family. As the story develops we will bring you more information."

J.T. and the others as well as the other deli patrons and employees waited a few seconds to see if the press conference would be immediate or there would be a delay. At the moment it appeared there was nothing more to report and so the screen showed the front of Greg's office building while pictures of Greg and Kennedy, both separate and together, flashed on the right side of the screen in slide show fashion.

For all of the wedding guests it was their first glimpse at their friend's boyfriend. As Sadie surveyed the group in the room while they all waited she wondered if any of them questioned Greg's authenticity like she had. It was impossible to tell.

"We now have word that Mr. Parker is making his way to the microphone," the reporter broke in again. "Please stand by."

There was some shuffling off camera and then three men came into view and stood shoulder to shoulder. A makeshift briefing table had been set up and there were at least a dozen microphones centered at shoulder height on the table. One of the three men, clearly Greg Parker from the pictures they had just seen, stepped slightly forward and addressed the crowd that could not be seen on the TV screen.

"I want to keep this brief," he told everyone. "As I am sure you all know this is an extremely difficult time for me and for Kennedy's family."

As the small gathering took in his words they also watched Greg's gestures and his demeanor. He looked tired and somewhat pale, but he spoke clearly and with confidence. Jenny, who had just recently lost a loved one, could relate to the stoic outside appearance one felt they had to paste on for the public while their inner thoughts were in turmoil and pain. Tears welled in her eyes as she subconsciously related to what Greg must be going through while trying to make his best effort at a public appearance.

"Her brother Lane and his family have all been in contact and together with the Parker family we are diligently seeking information on how this happened. We ask for the public's support and that if you have any information at all, no matter how insignificant it may seem we ask you to call the Sedgwick County Sherriff Department at the number listed on your screen."

For a split second it appeared Greg's voice was going to crack but he steeled himself and continued with a final statement.

"Lastly I ask that you give us time to grieve privately. Neither my office or Kennedy's will be accepting calls for the time being."

That was it. He was done. Greg stepped backwards and lowered his eyes to the floor.

It was difficult to tell if there were tears but it was clear there was a definite seriousness to his words and the way he carried himself. He was professional to the tee.

"Mr. Parker, do you have any idea who might have done this?" shouted an off-camera telecaster.

"Did she have any enemies?" another person yelled.

"When did you last see her?" from still another.

To try to quiet the group one of the other two men stepped up to the table and introduced himself as Mr. Parker's attorney. He simply told the cameras there would be no further questions and asked the group to respect Greg's wishes for privacy at this difficult time. With that, Greg and his attorney and the third man who looked like he could be Greg's father quickly walked away and out of view. The reporter returned and told the audience they would break into regular programming if there was any new information throughout the day.

It was hard for Mary Jane and the others to resume normal conversation after that. Seeing an image of Kennedy's fiancee and then remembering tomorrow would have been their wedding day made everything they knew – and even what they didn't know – seem more real than it had been the day before.

A deeper investigation

Greg had anticipated Saturday would be tough for him. He thought maybe he would spend it at the office. With none of his regular office staff in the building he could get caught up on the work he needed to do. It would be better than sitting around at home staring at all the food and flowers well-meaning people felt obligated to bring or send.

To his surprise, though, after the press conference was over he felt strangely at ease. The worst was behind him. No one suspected he was the last one to see her alive. He had played the innocent grieving boyfriend well. It would not do to just sit and wallow in the pain they all thought he should be experiencing. He would just have to act mellow for a few weeks so people wouldn't be suspicious and then he could get on with life as normal. Well, normal without a girlfriend that is. He could probably do without one of those for a while.

Several weeks passed and Greg maintained a low profile. He still went into the office, conducted business as usual and made social appearances when he absolutely had to. Those around him tiptoed with care hoping to support him without smothering him. It seemed to be working with stellar precision. In his mind it was almost as if the incident hadn't happened. Family and friends had suggested he seek counseling but he didn't need it. An awful thing had happened and yes, he was responsible for it. But as long as no one knew that the world would right itself again soon and it would just be a distant memory.

He did find that he missed Kennedy to some degree. She had become a part of his client dinners recently and jumped right in to help with fund raising causes. Their lives and their careers meshed well together and had it not been for her little lies everything would still be great today. Unfortunately dishonesty was not something he would tolerate and he would not be embarrassed by a public break up.

If he were to say these things out loud a trained professional would tell him there were other options for dealing with relationship issues rather than murder. There were hundreds of coping strategies to manage anger. And, of course, there could have been an absolutely plausible explanation for why his girlfriend had gone out for a jog that night rather than going to bed early.

Still, it didn't matter now. What was done was done and he couldn't erase it. Thank God no one had seen his car on the road Monday night. And the community had embraced him as the distraught, grieving boyfriend instead of a cold-hearted murderer. He still regretted that he had snapped but since he couldn't change that it was time to move forward.

That is why he was so surprised when two police detectives arrived at his office just as he was headed to the elevator at the end of the day.

"Mr. Parker," the taller of the two said. "I'm Detective James Bowersox with the Sedgwick County Sherriff's Department. This is Detective Rhonda Billings. Can we have a moment of your time?"

Greg's heart stopped for a moment and his hands turned to ice. He just hoped they couldn't read all of that in his face. But after all he knew they had no evidence so here was no reason to fear their questions.

"Of course," he told them. "Let's go back to my office. Is there any news?"

"No, I'm afraid not," Officer Bowersox told him. "We are still in a holding pattern without evidence but the chief is pressing us for answers. Miss Andrews' family is obviously serious about getting to the bottom of this."

"I do understand," Greg told them. "However, there is nothing I can tell you that you don't already know. I didn't see Kennedy at all that day."

Be careful, Greg, he warned himself. They are not accusing you of anything. Don't give yourself away.

"What can you tell us about her friends?" Officer Billings asked. "Do you think someone could have been with her that night?"

"No one was with her," Greg answered, probably a little too quickly.

"But you didn't see her?"

"No, I didn't see her with anyone," Greg said, modifying the statement to try and reflect the truth. It was just the dog. But they already knew that.

"What about her neighbors? Surely you must have spent a significant amount of time at her house over these last few months. Was there anything out of the ordinary there? A disgruntled co-worker maybe? Anything you can tell us would help."

Greg scratched his chin, pretending to think. "No one. Nothing at all that I can think of. You know everyone in this community loved her. I think it had to have just been a mistake."

"With all due respect, Mr. Parker," Officer Bowersox said, "it was a pretty big 'mistake.' I have been doing this for a long time and when there is an accident with this consequence most people don't run unless they have something to hide."

Were they on to him? He wasn't ready to accept that yet.

"So true. I just wish we had an answer – for Lane and the kids, you know?" Greg said trying to divert the conversation away from their potential accusations.

"We are working on it," the female detective told him then as she extended her business card to him. "This is my private number in case you think of anything that could help us put this case to rest. I hope to hear from you and thank you for your time."

Then they were gone.

Greg waited a bit to head back to the elevator. He wondered how long this whole investigation would take to run its course before it went cold. They would find nothing to implicate him. It just wasn't possible but he was going to have to spend a lot more time playing the injured party than he planned. Whatever it took he would do it because there was no way he would go to prison for this. Compared to all the other bad things in the world this was barely a blip on the radar screen. Surely his local department had bigger things to worry about than one little homicide.

Sleep had finally been easier for Greg over the last few days. He drifted into an easy, dreamless rest. However, he always woke with the same overwhelming feeling of dread. What if today they discover what really happened? There was no way to squelch the emotional anxiety but a steamy shower and several cups of coffee later and he was usually able to block it from his brain long enough to go about the daily routine of running his business.

He knew the mini panic attacks were based on guilt. He had trained his mind to compartmentalize the good from the bad and the ugly and then write off the bad and ugly as mistakes with the equivalency of a speeding ticket. Greg Parker was a kind, generous, decent human being. He routinely gave of his time and his money and no one who knew him would profile his as a killer.

Unfortunately, though, he did have something inside him that was broken. He had a short fuse on rare occasions. That temper had cost him his first marriage and ultimately his second one, too.

Over the years he had learned to tame the anger with music – playing the piano, singing in the church choir and even getting absorbed in classical music on the stereo. Music was his only consoler. It didn't – it couldn't – stop him from making bad decisions in the heat of the moment, though.

He seemed to be pre-programmed to hurt those he loved the most. Often he had thought it wasn't worth it to go on living. But do what? End his life? He couldn't do that to his family. So he did the best he could to cope with his actions. In this case that meant rationalizing his actions, making himself believe Kennedy deserved what he did to her.

She didn't, of course. No one deserved to die. Especially because she tried to cure insomnia by exercising with her dog.

Damage control

"Hey boss," Greg's business manager greeted him at the door to his office.

To date the whole staff had avoided mentioning anything to do with the alleged murder and his foiled wedding. They tried to support him by keeping things as routine as possible for him knowing if he wanted to talk about it he would. Today was a bit different, though, because the daily headlines were creating new ripples of bad publicity for his business which ironically earned their pay from making other people look good.

"Good morning, Steve. How are you? Hey, by the way, do you have that Anderson/Stevens file? I thought I left it on my desk last night. Did you file it?"

"Well, no. I can check with Cindy on the file. But we have bigger problems. Have you seen today's newspaper?" Steve asked him while dropping the morning issue of the Wichita Eagle on his desk.

"I'm not in the mood for problems, Steve. My patience is frazzled today. Can you deal with it? Whatever it is?"

"Probably not," Steve told him seriously. "This is bigger than you and I."

The headline was larger than normal font:

KENNEDY ANDREWS: LEAVES MILLIONS TO FRIENDS, STIFFS FIANCEE

Wow.

"Did you know about this?" Steve asked. "I mean, your girlfriend was a millionaire? Maybe a billionaire."

"Yes, I knew," Greg said. "There is no shame in making good investments. You knew her. She was smart."

"No question. But…it's the post-comma part that worries me," Steve told his boss and friend. "All of the sudden a woman dies and leaves you, the man she was about to marry, completely out of her will. It gives the cops a huge motive, Greg. You look guilty as hell!"

"Well, thanks for the vote of confidence, my friend. I don't need Kennedy's money. You think I killed her to get to a few bucks?"

"No, I am not saying that at all. I could never think that. No one who knows you would think so. But the jury of public opinion will. We have to deal with this sooner than later or this could get ugly."

"And by WE you mean ME," Greg said while he started to pace in front of his desk.

"If I were you I would be proactive on this one, Greg. The media is already raising suspicions."

The press was a dominant force. This he knew from his experience as a public relations expert. He had used the media to promote his causes many times over. Now this new wrinkle of settling Kennedy's estate was something that could throw him into the limelight, the very thing he was trying so hard to avoid. If he wasn't careful he would be front page fodder for every paper in the nation.

He understood completely why she had left her fortune to her brother and her friends. Greg's financial empire was far-reaching and as a married couple they didn't need her millions to lead a wonderful life. He wasn't bothered in the slightest by who she left her money to, or even that it wasn't him. His only issue was that she had fostered a secret from him for their whole courtship. If she could do that once she could do it again and again. That simply was not acceptable.

He would prove to the world Kennedy's money was not an issue between them. It was time to fight fire with fire. Two days later the Wichita Eagle boasted this headline:

MEDIA MOGUL GREG PARKER DONATES $2 MILLION TO ANIMAL RESCUE MISSION IN HONOR OF SLAIN FIANCEE

True to Steve's word, Greg was back in the good graces of the public. At least to everyone except the Sedgwick County Sherriff's Department.

To him it was starting to feel like harassment. Almost daily there was a phone call or a visit from the local department just wanting to ask one more question or clarify a statement he had made earlier. Under normal circumstances he would have deflected to his legal team but in this case thought it might make him look even guiltier. You typically don't hire legal counsel unless you have done something wrong.

He could get angry and refuse to take their calls. But that could look like he was covering up for something he had done. Their questions, while polite and well-stated were starting to carry the tiniest bit of accusation and for the first time since that fateful Monday night he was starting to feel uncomfortable.

The only way to avoid the police completely would be to leave town. That, too, could raise questions. Unless he left town and didn't come back. Ever.

Three months later

Brenda had been stunned when she had received the certified letter a few weeks after Kennedy's wedding. Her college roommate had named her as an heir in her will. The letter outlined the process for claiming her check and included a written transcript of what Ed Luginbill had read to the others that day at the deli and of, course, her personal letter from Kennedy. It was hard to fathom her 50-year-old friend was dead and even harder to imagine she, Brenda Davis, was an overnight millionaire.

Daily Brenda worried about how to best use the money. It had arrived last week and for now it sat in her bank waiting for a decision from her on how to use it best. Having made the decision not to attend the wedding seemed right at the time, but now she just felt a deep loss. Money should make you happy. It always had before. Even finding a $5 bill in a jacket pocket or getting an unexpected $20 birthday gift from her aunt in a belated birthday card had brought her joy in the past. Somehow carrying the burden of being a million-dollar recipient made her feel blah.

She had no idea where to start so she unfolded the attorney's letter and reread what Kennedy had written:

> The money is yours to spend as you wish. There are no strings attached. My hope is you will find a way to use it for the betterment of your families and your communities. I trust that each and every one of you will find a way

to make a difference in ways that
I could not even have imagined.

Stretched out across her bed she laid the letter down and closed her eyes. She wondered who the "each and every one of you" were and what they had decided to do for the betterment of their families and communities.

It was tempting to quit her job, take a vacation, buy a mansion and just go crazy. While that sounded great in the moment she was pretty sure that was not her friend's intention. Many times Brenda and her friends had joked about what they would do if they hit it big in the lottery. It was fun to dream about it, not so fun to be saddled with it.

She could just flat give the money away and be done with it. Homeless shelter. Food pantry. Some church. Some school. Some library. In the end she had decided all of those options were far too impersonal so the money sat in her bank account earning interest and waiting for the perfect plan to fall into her lap. It wouldn't be today. It wouldn't be next week. Maybe next month or next year she would think of something grandiose to invest in to honor her friend.

For now she just needed a nap to stave off the mild depression she had slipped into because she was wealthy but couldn't the money

*****

A side benefit of learning you had more money to spend than you knew what to do with was meeting a set of new friends, more specifically Jack. Mary Jane had found a confidant in the Nebraska letter carrier and they had begun a solid friendship since her return to Tennessee - entirely through text messages.

What she had come to value in Jack had nothing to do with what her husband valued in the neighbor Cyndi Henderson nor his secretary nor any of a number of others he was sharing a bed with. What she had with Jack was a one of a kind friendship based on the joys and perils of raising children. She had met his kids while they were in Kansas and Jack had told her he felt like he knew hers from the stories she told. Their conversations were light and funny and extremely platonic.

"How is first grade treating Maddie?" Jack texted her one evening.

"She loves it. Except for the whole reading thing."

"Ha! Isn't that a big chunk of first grade?" Jack asked.

"She says it's boring."

"What? Nothing like a good book."

"Maybe she will have to be our age to appreciate it," Mary Jane texted back.

"If you don't like to read you just haven't found the right book," Jack said.

"Her vocabulary is still a little limited. Cat, dog, is, the and very."

"Those were the days," Jack sent back. "When life was as simple as a dog, a cat and a book."

"True. She does like writing, though. She makes up these wild fun stories. Her spelling needs some help, though."

"Maybe she needs a pen pal," Jack suggested.

"A pen pal?" Mary Jane questioned.

"I bet Bea would write her a letter to read. Then Maddie could write back."

"Excellent idea. Kind of like you and I only without the technology," Mary Jane teased him.

"I'll put a bug in her ear," Jack said. "That girl needs something productive to fill her time."

"I won't hold my breath since you are the only mailman in the country who can never find a stamp."

There was more than an ounce of truth to that.

"Never should have told you that," he texted back but added a smiley emoji.

"Gotta go. Dinner's ready," she texted and slipped her phone into her pocket before putting ice in glasses.

She was a good lady, Jack thought. Too bad her husband was such an idiot.

*****

J.T. wasted no time quitting his job. From the moment he left the fitness industry he had only found marginal happiness at work. If he had done the math right he could draw a $60,000 a year salary from his surprise fortune for the next 23 years and still have money left over just from the principal. He would be well into his seventies by then so why work. Even if he took a $100,000 salary every year he would be past retirement age when the well ran dry. And there would be interest, lots of interest since most of the money would be multiplying while he spent relatively small segments a time. While he was relaxing on a beach somewhere every day with a Bloody Mary in his hand he would have plenty of time to figure out how to donate the extra to some well deserving cause.

The beach. The ink was barely dry on the check and he had already booked his first vacation. He started with Aruba. Even though his previous job had afforded him many perks, J.T. had never taken an entire month-long vacation before. It felt extravagant and made him feel powerful and in control again rather than crippled and ugly. He could almost feel the sand between his toes as the airplane sailed over the ocean and prepared to drop him off for 30 days of fun in the sun with zero responsibilities.

That first week was beyond comprehension. The accommodations were exquisite and he spent nearly every waking moment on the beach. Just like in the old days it was easy to wine and dine any woman he wanted and then whisk her off to his bed. At home that was a bit more difficult. A woman was a little more territorial after she had spent a night or two in your arms. She wanted to call you and expected you to call her. She was offended and made you feel guilty if you didn't want to spend every Friday and Saturday night with her. Here, though, it was unlikely that after a couple of days you would ever see the woman again.

It was true J.T. thought he had left behind his days as a jet setting playboy. After his whirlwind marriage and subsequent wicked divorce he had grown accustomed to being single. But it was so easy to get swept up in the beauty of a slightly younger woman in a bikini, the feel of her warm naked skin on yours and the passionate kisses that led to all other things blissful.

Having unlimited cash flow allowed him the freedom to feel attractive again. He still had a muscular body, a full head of dark, wavy hair and after dinner and a few glasses of wine he hadn't met even one lady who seemed to notice he walked with a limp and had a number of scars on his legs and his back.

Week two of his vacation also glided by with warp speed.

Going into the second half of his trip he couldn't say he was bored exactly, but the days did seem to feel pretty repetitive. It was a great routine, though. It was hard to argue with having to choose between parasailing or scuba diving.

Waking up one morning to the sound of his phone ringing J.T. was surprised to see it was a call from the States. Paul Odell. Kennedy's friend who had been a priest all those years ago when she was in college. Now he was a farmer or something like that. Heck of a nice guy but the details were fuzzy. Was he a teacher? He didn't get to know anyone very well in that short time they were all together but he did remember the guy. He seemed very driven. By what he wasn't sure.

Glancing toward the bathroom he could still hear the shower running. Melanie was out of earshot. Or was it Megan? Maybe she would stick around and they could order room service. That would be something different and he was suddenly famished. Hoping it wouldn't be a long conversation, J.T. picked up on the third ring.

"Paul? How are you doing?"

"I'm great, my friend," he heard Paul say from across the ocean. "Just checking in with you to see how you have been. Work treating you well?"

Would Paul judge him for going on a semi-permanent leave of absence? Hard to tell but it would do no good to lie.

"Actually Paul, I am out of the country right now."

"Really? How exciting! Where has your business taken you?" Paul wanted to know.

Hmmmmmmm…how should he answer?

"Ummmmm, it's not exactly like that. I am on vacation right now. Aruba, actually. It is beyond beautiful here."

"No kidding? How great for you."

J.T. was now aware the water was no longer running and his roommate of sorts would soon be resurfacing. Whatever Paul wanted he wished he would make it quick.

"What can I help you with, Paul?"

"Oh, well, I am not sure I should bother you with this while you are off relaxing and all. Do you want to call me in a few days when you are back home?"

"Is everything alright? I mean, is there word about the accident? Do we know what happened yet?" J.T. asked, thinking maybe there had been news about the murder. He had been off the grid for a few weeks.

"I wish I knew," Paul told him sincerely. "I am afraid we may never find out. It breaks my heart for her family and her fiancee as well. But, no nothing like that. I just had an idea I wanted to run past you."

An idea. What could that possibly entail? So much for a short conversation. He glanced up to see Melanie or Megan, whoever she was, pick up her bag and let herself out of the room with a little two-finger wave to him as she closed the door behind her. Damn. An opportunity lost.

"Shoot. What it is it?" J.T. said, leaning back against the pillows and reconciling himself to a slow-starting morning.

"Well, I have been doing some real soul searching these last few months with regard to this money that has fallen into my lap. There are so many places short on resources. Where do you start, you know?"

J.T. probably would know if he thought about it long enough. The truth was all the money he had spent so far was on himself.

"You are so right, Paul," was his honest response, still not willing to admit he was now unemployed and planned to be for a very long time if not forever. The longer Paul talked the more J.T. started to listen to his conscience which so far had been relatively silent.

"May I ask if you have tackled your thoughts on how to spend it? Maybe that is too personal and I have no right to ask, but when we met back in April I was so moved by how you help others. It is inspiring to me. I try to do the same."

"How I help others? You mean at work?" J.T. asked.

"Well, yes. You give them skills to be great in sales and then you motivate them to be better. You do good work, J.T."

Now Paul was really laying the guilt on thick. J.T. was sure it was unintentional but it was still working.

"I guess I see what you mean…"

"I thought maybe you and I could work together and channel our ideas," Paul interrupted. "Maybe you could come out this way or I could come to you. We could outline a plan to give people who are struggling a bit of a financial lift and then pair that with teaching them to use their wealth to help more people."

It **was** a terrific idea. In a way it would be doing what Kennedy had done for the seven of them. Together they would have almost three million dollars to invest in people who could then invest in others.

"Oh I don't know, Paul. I'm not sure I have it in me to do all that. I was thinking more along the lines of…" J.T. trailed off because he didn't think it sounded good to say 'I was thinking more of selling my house and buying a yacht.'

"I know it sounds mighty lofty but to he who much has been given much is expected. Kennedy has given us great power to do marvelous things. In the short time we have known each other I get the sense you and I are like minded. Give it some thought, won't you? I'll be in touch."

Just before he disconnected J.T. promised he would give it some thought but was almost certain he wouldn't. He was able to help his employees become financially independent. It had been easy for him because business was second nature to him. That was work, though, and as of two weeks ago he was no longer working. He was lounging and he was pretty positive he could get good at that, too.

The catalyst
for change

Kennedy Andrews had been a blessing for Mary Jane Mendenhall in more ways than one. As she suspected the other six were feeling, she had no idea on earth how she would spend the money and honor her friend. What she did know was Jack Redman was a first-class friend. She was able to tell him things she couldn't tell anyone else.

The relative anonymity of their lives gave her the freedom to share her deepest frustrations about Andy. Venting locally would be a risk. After all, who knew who was on his booty call list? She feared she could trust no one. She still didn't have an escape plan but as the days wore on she was having more and more trouble pretending she was a happy, supportive wife and playing house with a man who didn't play by the rules.

"I think you need a change of venue," Jack texted her one night after the kids were in bed and Andy was who knows where with who knows who.

"You mean a vacation?" Mary Jane texted in return.

"No. I mean I think it is time you follow his example."

"Oh no, I would never stoop to his level."

"I don't mean that at all. Of course you wouldn't. I mean leave him."

"Don't be silly, Jack. That is not possible."

"Why?"

"How in the world would I support myself? And the kids? I don't even have a job!"

"So get one," Jack told her.

"Is the post office hiring?" she teased, assuming he was joking. It was sometimes hard to tell in a text.

"Ha! Possibly, but you are a nurse."

She could go back to work and earn the money to support the kids on her own. But Andy would never allow it.

"Plus," Jack said, "you are a millionaire."

"Yeah, but that money isn't for me. It is for a worthy cause."

"You are a worthy cause, Mary Jane. Use some of the money to establish yourself somewhere else. You should not have to put up with that for even one day more."

"I can't even imagine. This is all I have known for 20 years."

Jack was right, of course. She didn't deserve to be treated like a servant and a babysitter. It had been years since she and Andy had had a real marriage.

"Andy wouldn't stand for it."

"This isn't about Andy," Jack told her. "You deserve so much more and frankly so do your children."

She thought about his words for 15 minutes before typing back.

"I want to, Jack. I really do, but I don't know how."

"After you are back on your feet you can replace what you spent of the inheritance and then you will be in a better place to donate it to others."

"I can't," she told him.

"Why?" he asked.

"I'm scared."

"I know."

Now Jack paused. After he typed his next message he wasn't sure if he should hit send.

"I'll help you," was the text that he decided to send.

Silence.

"I mean it, Mary Jane. I don't know how I am going to spend the money either. Come to Nebraska. We'll find a place for you and your kids to live. Then we can figure this whole money thing out together."

"Oh Jack, you are silly. What's in it for you?"

"A friend," was the immediate reply.

It would be weeks before they would speak about it again but the conversation never left her mind.

Media meltdown

Tonight's menu was fried cheese with a side of steamed asparagus. It was easy enough to make and relatively healthy. And Sadie's son Ronnie would even eat it which was always a plus.

"I don't know why you like that," her friend Ami said while she watched her make dinner. "It's just a bunch of empty calories all wadded up in a ball."

"Don't knock it until you've tried it," Sadie told her.

Before this week it had been years since she had let herself indulge in the crispy snack, and it really wasn't too unhealthy. Once she tasted it again it became something she couldn't stop craving. Sadie simply laid a slice of American cheese in a super hot non-stick skillet and waited for it to bubble. She flipped it quickly and waited a few seconds for maximum melting watching it carefully so it wouldn't burn. Then she quickly slid it onto a plate and waited a few minutes for it to solidify. The result was an ooey gooey piece of warm cheese with a crispy crusty exterior. It was heaven on a plate.

Sadie could remember watching her mother melt cheese like this on the stovetop. Her mom would steam broccoli, asparagus or even brussel sprouts and heap them on their plates before laying the crispy cheese on top. To Sadie that seemed like a waste of time because the cheese melted again and lost its crunch. To keep it healthy she still served it with the steamed veggies, just not on top. If she was being completely honest with herself she would prefer to totally skip the vegetables and just power through the cheese. Tonight she added a dollop of spicy, brown mustard to her plate for dipping and headed into the living room to watch the news.

Ami joined her but skipped the snack.

"Wow, that is the guy who was going to marry your mom's friend?" Ami asked when one picture after another of Greg was flashed across the screen. "He is gorgeous!"

"Yeah, I guess," Sadie said. "We never met him. When I was in Kansas it had just been a few days since she died and the boyfriend was really messed up. Understandable. It was quite a blow."

They watched a few minutes more before Ami spoke again.

"It looks like they think he did it," she said.

"Do you think he could have?" Sadie asked her friend. "I mean could you?"

"Could I kill my fiancee? No way! I mean I think I couldn't," Ami said, eyes still glued to the TV. "There must be more to the story than we know."

"I think it is probably routine to investigate the boyfriend when something like this happens. After all he was the closest to her. There could have been all kinds of issues between them. I really don't want to believe that, though."

"Maybe he is guilty," Ami told her, "but if that guy is a killer I am a swimsuit model."

They both laughed at that and then listened a little more to what the news anchor was reporting. She was giving the basic biographical information about Kennedy for the umpteenth time and then told her listeners about the financial side of the unfortunate situation. Kennedy was single, it was reported, but slated to marry PR expert Greg Parker in just a few days. In the wake of the investigation KWCH-TV in Wichita had learned the deceased had left a sizable fortune to seven of her friends and left her fiancee in the cold. They stopped just short of accusing Greg of killing for the money but left it to the viewer to draw their own conclusion.

"It seems plausible," Ami said after the reporter moved on to her next story. "Money is a strong motive. You see it all the time on those crime shows."

"Yeah, but this is a little different," Sadie said. "The guy was worth as much as she was – maybe more. He didn't need her money. It does look a little fishy and I can't tell you I haven't wondered about it. But would you really kill the person you loved for a little cash?"

"It's more than a little cash, Sadie," Ami told her. "Speaking of that, what are you going to do with your part?"

"I wish I knew. I'd love to buy a big house complete with servants and a swimming pool. I'd quit my job and have crazy parties every night."

"But?"

"But, that is not what Kennedy had in mind," Sadie said. "She wanted to make a difference in the world. Since she never got around to it she wants us to do it for her."

"Buying a castle with a pool and servants would definitely make a difference in your life," Ami said.

"True. I could even buy you a house to make up for all these months you guys have put up with me sponging off you."

"Don't be silly. We love having you here. However, if you do get that big new place you better invite me to your parties."

Again the two girls laughed. Sadie was the first to speak, this time, much more seriously.

"It would be nice if I didn't have to work, though. I have gone through more jobs than I care to think about."

"You have seen your share," Ami agreed. "But you love your job now, don't you?"

"For the most part, yes. The attorneys are fabulous. The work is easy and almost fun. But that nutty Arabella who just sits there and types all day I could do without."

Closing in again

Greg had been avoiding the newspapers like the plague but thought he had seen every newscast on every network. Each time he turned on the television they were talking about Kennedy. At home he couldn't even watch a baseball game without a news ticker running across the bottom of the screen reporting how business aficionado Greg Parker had been slighted from his girlfriend's will and lost millions. It was always the same thing – no witnesses, no leads - followed by a plea for the public's help and the offer of a reward for any information leading to an arrest.

Even at work his own staff was talking about what the news was saying and most were outraged the police hadn't gotten any closer to solving the case. They never talked about it when he was in the room, of course, but he would pick up bits and pieces of their conversations as he walked down the hallway or entered a room. Why couldn't people just leave this alone? Even if someone did miraculously discover what happened it wouldn't bring Kennedy back. Let it go, people, he wanted to shout. Common sense kept him from it. He slipped back into his office, took two aspirin and chased it with a shot of quality whiskey.

Later at home over warmed up spaghetti and meatballs, Greg did his best to avoid the television. Popping open his laptop he intended to recharge his energy level by catching up on his personal e-mails. Unfortunately even cyberspace seemed out to get him. The search engine default page now sported his face. There he was in a file photo from several years ago. There was another one – a candid shot from the last wedding he attended. And still another of him with his family.

Since he hadn't granted any news interviews after the initial press conference all they were reporting was speculation. Did Greg know about her net worth? Was he upset she didn't leave her fortune to him? Had he maintained contact with her family? Why were there no plans for a local service?

He was in disbelief. Can people just say anything they want on TV or the radio these days? Are there no regulations for the newspapers or even the internet? He snapped his computer shut and reached for his phone to call his lawyer just as the doorbell rang. He shuffled to the door hoping it was his dad. Even his talkative sister would be a welcome distraction right now. Grateful there were no TV trucks camped out on his front lawn he opened the door. The police.

He wrongly jumped to the conclusion they were here with good news and let them in.

Ninety minutes later Greg felt like he had been flattened by a beer truck. The two officers had asked to search his home. Although they didn't have a warrant Greg felt he had nothing to hide and let them in. He wasn't prepared for them to rifle through his underwear drawer, look through his refrigerator and even take his pictures off the wall.

"I am sure you can understand why we feel compelled to leave no stone unturned," one of the officers told him. "There is a bunch of pressure from the community to find out who did this."

He guessed he did understand. Had it been any other situation he would want to know, too. He could live with a little invasion of privacy if it meant this would all go away very soon.

"Are you guys saying you think I had something to do with this?" Greg asked.

"You have told us you didn't," was the response. "If we don't find anything here it will be so much simpler to tell the public we are looking in the wrong spot."

"Look, I have given you guys a statement," Greg said politely but firmly. "There are people who saw me eating at the club at the time you say this happened. What else can I do? I am starting to feel like you are accusing me of something."

Both officers assured him this search was just a precautionary measure to rule out foul play. Between the total disarray they were imposing on his personal belongings and the constant updates with no new information from the press Greg was beginning to feel his anger rise again. He would wait for them to leave and then he would make a new plan – a plan that likely involved leaving Wichita for good.

The Andrews' camp

Paula and the others who had worked for and with Kennedy were all in a jumble. They, too, had seen the bad press on Greg. Kennedy's boyfriend had been nothing but a perfect gentleman in their eyes. It was unthinkable that he might have been involved in her death in any way. Her office staff had been equally surprised by the reports about her inheritance. Certainly their friend, co-worker and boss was entitled to spend her money as she saw fit. That didn't erase the shock of learning someone they thought they knew well did have some secrets.

Being her business partner, Paula had taken it upon herself to organize a private memorial service. Her wishes were to be cremated and her brother Lane had taken care of the legal requirements. Now, though, he was back in Maine. It had been months since the horrible incident and because the circumstances surrounding her death were still incomplete, no official funeral arrangements had been set.

Try as she might, planning a ceremony of any kind to commemorate Kennedy was harder than she thought. Her only family was her brother, then there were all the people here in the office, her friends who had come to the wedding and – of course – Greg Parker. What do you do with that? She hadn't spoken to Greg since the week before the wedding. As much as she had wanted to reach out to him and knowing he had to be racked with grief, the time never seemed right. Perhaps that is why she still had not put something together.

At last she decided to plan a dinner at their church and hoped all who knew her would share a special memory. She would arrange for a videographer so she could share the event with all those who could not attend.

Satisfied it would be the right thing to do, she cleared her afternoon schedule and prepared to put a letter of invitation out to those who knew her best. She was only about 10 minutes in to the task when she had to take a break and wipe the tears from her eyes, then start once again with a clean sheet of paper.

*****

A celebration of life has been planned for Kennedy Andrews. Please join us this Saturday at 6 p.m. at First United Methodist Church, Valleyview. We ask that you bring a picture or a memory to share with the group who gather to honor the life of a daughter, sister, aunt, co-worker and friend who was taken too soon. Dinner will be served at 6:30.

Greg's invitation arrived in his mailbox on a Tuesday evening. Internally he groaned with dread. This was one more thing he would be judged for in the court of public opinion. If he went, the feelings of guilt and sadness would likely resurface. He was working so hard to push them aside. He did feel guilty and immensely sad. Kennedy had not deserved what he had done to her. No one deserved that and especially Kennedy who was a life-changing positive influence in his life.

The flip side was he could ignore the invitation and be a no show. People would react to that in one of two ways. Either they would understand his need to stay out of the spotlight or they would forever hold him accountable for being a jerk and not offering his support to others who had loved her to.

He couldn't win either way so he would forget about it for now. He had 11 days to decide.

The first...

Mary Jane was the first to spend a portion of the money. It really was just a tiny fragment of what she had been gifted, but she had taken her new friend Jack's advice and made plans to leave her philandering husband behind. Several states behind in fact.

Divorce, she learned, was a long and drawn out process that could also become quite expensive. All those years ago when she had stood at the altar and professed to love, honor and obey in sickness and in health and for richer or for poorer she would have never dreamt this day would come. It had, however, and she would get through it one day at a time.

In hindsight she probably should have told Andy before she had him served with the papers. She felt some shame for blindsiding him even though that is exactly what he had done to her. Maybe a part of her thought he would be relieved to be released from his wedding vows. She had been dead wrong about that.

From what she could tell he was not as mad as he was embarrassed. It was incomprehensible to her that it was her actions embarrassing him after all the things he had done to dishonor her. His spiteful words to her all centered around what others would think of him. His partners at work. The guys at the club. His friends at the bank. He had done so much for her over the years he told her. 'And you have done so much *to* me, too,' Mary Jane thought but didn't dare say.

Since this was only the second fight in their entire courtship and marriage she had very little experience with it and wasn't sure what to expect. Last time she had been so taken aback that she had cowered and silently wallowed in her self-pity. This time was radically different because this time she had a plan.

By the time Andy knew what was happening she had already found a new place to live and had all of the essentials she needed to survive packed up and shipped to her new address. She even had a job as a medication aide at a hospital in her new town. She would have to take a few courses to renew her nursing license but that plan was in her immediate future. Life as she known it for the past year was changing for the better.

As for the children there was no humane way to tell them the truth about what was happening. Together with Jack she had decided to tell them she was taking a new job in a new town. This was certainly not a lie. It was just leaving out some vital information like your father is a lying jerk, your father is having sex with half of Tennessee and your father treats your mother like a piece of trash.

She strategically waited for just the right moment to tell her the kids hoping they would be excited to move on to a new adventure even if it meant leaving their dad behind. Maddie and Max, the two youngest were brimming with glee. Mark wasn't overly excited at first but she could tell the idea was growing on him. But Mike was a tough sell. She had told him he was old enough to make his own decision since he was just getting ready for his senior year. In the end even Mike decided to join them in Nebraska. It would be an interesting summer for all of them.

"What about dad, though?" Max wanted to know. "Can he come, too?"

Mary Jane was only semi-prepared for this one. She knew they would ask but wasn't sure exactly how deep to delve into an explanation. She carefully explained Andy's work was here in Tennessee. It would be almost impossible for him to come along. She did assure them there would be plenty of trips back and forth and she would never stop them from seeing their dad. This seemed to satisfy them all. She stopped just short of sharing life as they knew it would never be the same. She hoped it would be better. And she hoped little Maddie would be able to meet her pen pal in person.

Andy, for his part, outwardly handled the kids' joy about moving with tremendous restraint and finesse. Watching their interaction from the sidelines she was amazed at how he masqueraded his feelings for them. Although it was obvious he had become quite the master of lies. He was dishing them out in huge doses. All the while Mary Jane knew he would take it out on her later. It was a darn good thing there were only four days left until they were set to leave.

A few hours later Mary Jane was shocked when her soon-to-be-ex husband came into their bedroom and slipped into bed beside her. Sleeping together – literally sleeping in the same bed – was a charade he had given up immediately after she had made it clear their marriage was over. They hadn't been intimate in over a year but they did share sheets and a blanket on the nights he was in town. That is until she had made it abundantly clear with a legal document she was leaving and taking his children with her. All further correspondence could be handled by their attorneys she had told him coolly after dinner.

It had taken a bit of finagling to safeguard her million-dollar windfall but legally it was now protected. Without it this move would not have been possible. She was certain he would discover it in the drawn-out proceedings but her lawyer had assured her the circumstances of Kennedy's intent would protect him from garnering half. She had taken that item off her list of worries.

This is when things got weird.

"Mary Jane?" Andy asked. "Are you asleep."

"Yes," she answered without hesitation and moved a few inches closer to the edge of the bed.

"Come on, honey, talk to me," he said.

"Andy, you haven't talked to me since you slept with your secretary."

"Now that's not fair," he said in a voice so soft she almost couldn't hear him.

"Isn't it true?" she asked even though she could care less what he answered. She knew it was true. No need for him to confirm or deny it.

Her husband's body slid closer to her in their bed and she felt his arm move over her side and rest on her belly.

"Really, Andy, I think we are past those days, don't you?" she asked, again not needing an answer. Then she reached for his arm and lifted it off her body.

"Is this how you want to end things? We have been through so much together."

That was certainly an understatement.

"Good night, Andy."

Hours later when she woke to make coffee and start breakfast he was gone. She never saw him again.

Another day, another island

After wrapping up his time in Aruba J.T. found himself booking another vacation without even returning home in between. It was amazing what money could buy. A part of him, a very tiny part of him, felt guilty for spending it on himself given how it came to be in his possession. However, there was so much of it. A little here and a little there wouldn't make a dent in the $1.4 million. Maybe as some form of justification he told himself he would spend not a penny more than the $400,000 leaving the million untouched.

On the plane he picked up the SkyMall magazine and began to thumb through it. Normally he gave the outlandishly expensive unusual gift items found on the magazine's pages little more than a glance. Today he had plenty of time to kill as the plane floated through the clouds on its way to Jamaica. And he could afford to buy anything he wanted. So what exactly did he want? What would make him happy?

He laughed at the battery-operated heated sleeping bag for $450. That kind of defeated the purpose of camping. You might as well stay in a hotel. On the next page was a coffee table sculpted in the shape of a hand holding up a circular piece of glass – roughly like a waiter holding a tray of hors d'oeuvres. It would definitely be a conversation starter but he didn't really need a $2,500 coffee table not to mention the expense of having it shipped to him.

Fortunately J.T. had a window seat on this trip so there was plenty of time to enjoy the view and daydream about what truly would make him happy. In the past it would have been liquor and sex and hours at the gym, not necessarily in that order. Travel had always been pretty close to the top of the list, too. So minus the gym time he was living the good life. If it hadn't been for Paul Odell's phone call the other day he might have just kept on enjoying those things in large doses. Nevertheless, that conversation wouldn't leave his mind despite every effort on J.T.'s part to thwart it.

Paul had told J.T. he was inspired by him. That was something he hadn't heard in a long time. To J.T. work felt like work. Just work. He hadn't really thought of it any deeper than that. He just needed an income to pay the bills and for his occasional nights out on the town with his friends. Work seemed like a means to an end. A job rather than a career. Perhaps that was why it was so easy to leave it.

And what was it Paul did? He wished he could remember. It had something to do with farming or something similar. Did he breed cattle? Was it something to do with horses? Or was it crops? Wheat? Soybeans maybe. Calling him back to find out would not do, though. Paul was onto something glorious to do with his part of the inheritance. He should be flattered some guy who barely knew him wanted to partner with him to make something great even better. He was flattered but without Paul he could just go on enjoying life at a breakneck pace. With

Paul he would need to find his responsible gene again.

He had to find a way to block Paul's well-meaning conversation from his mind, at least for a couple of weeks or this trip truly would be a waste of good money. He was here to escape from responsibility, not create it. The airplane magazine wasn't helping. So he did what he knew best. He reclined in his seat and focused on the pretty young stewardess's legs. What fun it would be to help her explore all Jamaica had to offer for a few days. It probably wouldn't happen but thinking about it made him smile and definitely diverted his energy away from the noble, virtuous ideas of the former Father Paul Odell.

Leaving Kansas

Anyone who knew Greg at all could not blame him for needing an escape plan for all that had unfolded over the last six months. Losing his fiancée was bad enough but watching the police and the media convene at his office and at his home had been almost more than he could stand. Greg had always been one to reach out and help others. Now in his time of need he was having great difficulty accepting help from those around him.

One of those he trusted most at work had been a good friend of his family as well. It was Brad Jackson who had suggested it first.

"You need some down time, man," he had told Greg over lunch one afternoon.

"And you suggest?" Greg asked. "I mean how do I do that? Yes, it has been tremendously stressful. Do I just pick up and leave? And no matter where I go the issues will not go away."

"You are so right, my friend," Brad told him. "I wish I could say a few weeks away from the office would completely change what happened."

Greg could second that. If he had it do over again he would definitely choose a different route.

Brad took another swig of his drink and continued offering his unsolicited advice.

"What it might do, though, is give you a chance to recharge your batteries. You could get away from all the people who know you and take time to rethink your priorities. Maybe come back and semi-retire if you want. You know, work a few less hours and do some things you have always wanted to do but there has never been time for."

"Are you talking about taking up fishing, because I don't know, Brad…"

"If that's your thing, then yeah. You could find a new hobby or just hone one you already have. For example, you work with those camps to help people who have lost families to cancer. Why not start a new camp here in Wichita? Build it from the ground up if you have to. You have the knowledge and the resources to do great things. You could kind of re-create yourself."

Greg scratched his head and then rubbed his temples.

"I'm not sure I am strong enough to reach out to others right now," he answered honestly.

"Maybe helping others is just what you need," Brad said. "Dealing with other people's problems could help you minimize your own. Look, I'm no expert, but I can tell you are struggling. We all can see it. You go through the motions and get the work done but inside you are crumbling."

Brad was so right. He was almost positive the police – or anyone else for that matter – would never discover he was a murderer. Every day that passes he felt better about that part of it. However, there was always an outside chance the next knock on his door would involve a set of handcuffs. There was no way he could go to prison. He would rather die first.

The rest of the afternoon Greg busied himself with mundane chores in his office but found himself distracted more than once. Maybe if he did leave town, or Kansas altogether, the great mystery of the century would fade into the woodwork and the mention of his potential wrongdoing would be a passing fancy. The stress was getting to him. He could see it in his eyes when we washed his face in the morning and it was getting harder and harder to motivate himself to get out of bed.

There was always that one chance someone would discover his evil deed and come looking for him. The further away he moved the better his chances of staying off the radar became. So he spent the remainder of the afternoon researching places he might go to rest and recharge. He would tell everyone it was just temporary but he knew he would never come back. He would force himself to go to Kennedy's memorial dinner Paula was planning and then would leave the next day. Good bye, Kansas.

*****

Since he had made the decision to leave the state the morning after Kennedy's service, Greg had changed his mind at least 100 times. In the end he found himself slowly driving to the church but he waited on the periphery of the parking lot before going in. If he had been counting he would guess at least 200 people found their way inside. He followed and stood at the back for a few minutes before he was recognized.

It was her neighbor, Santos Hernandez, who spotted him first.

"Greg! So glad you are here. All of us have been praying for you since day one."

He didn't need anyone's prayers. What he needed was to get through the next two hours and then leave this place far behind.

"Thank you, Santos," Greg heard himself say. "It has been very rough but I am powering through."

Next there was her friend Sue from one of the foundations she supported. Then two ladies from her office and even her dog groomer. They all smothered him in hugs and wanted him to sit at their table. What he thought might be unbearable was turning out to be comforting. These people were hurting over the loss of their friend. He was so grateful they didn't know it was his fault this dinner gathering was even necessary.

One at a time those assembled stood and shared their association with his now ex-girlfriend. Some cried. Some even laughed. Most of the memories they shared he knew of. There were a few surprises. Overall it was a healing experience and he was glad he had come. At last the food was served and everyone ate their fill. Then plates were cleared and the crowd began to thin. Just as he was contemplating sneaking out Paula caught his arm, acknowledging him for the first time tonight.

"She loved you so much, Greg. There was nothing she wouldn't have done for you," Paula told him while reaching around to extend a one-armed hug.

There it was. A brutal stab to the heart. Could she know? Was she calling him out or offering genuine sympathy? Whatever it was it gave him goosebumps. For the first

time since the accident tears began to flow.
And flow and flow.

Paul's Mission

There it was again. Another missed call. If you could say nothing else for this guy, Paul was persistent. To be fair J.T. was sure Paul thought he was already back home. He probably couldn't keep ignoring him forever. Tomorrow he would call him, J.T. told himself. Or maybe he should call him back tonight and just get it over with. If he could think of a stellar reason to turn him down it would be quicker not to mention easier return his call. So far he couldn't think of anything he could say that wouldn't sound selfish.

"Paul?" J.T. asked when he older man answered. "Paul, it's J.T. I'm sorry I haven't called you back sooner. My…errrr…vacation turned into something more complex than I first planned."

"Not a problem at all, my friend. I am just glad to hear from you," Paul told him and sounded sincere. "I hope all is well."

There was a pause there and J.T. expected Paul was giving him an opening to explain. He didn't want to. So he didn't, just letting open air fill the space.

"Have you given any more thought to combining our resources? I really think together we can multiply the good we can do exponentially," Paul told him enthusiastically.

"Well, about that…" J.T. started. "I was thinking…"

"I was, too," Paul said. "I have been doing little else but thinking about it. When can we meet? I can come to you. I won't be a bother, of course. My dog and I love to get away on a little road trip. Kansas City, is it?"

"Yes, I will be back in the city next week."

"If you can text me your address I will look for lodging close by. I am anxious to pick your brain so we can get started on something wonderful – something to honor Kennedy."

There it was. This was more than about his selfish desires. This was for Kennedy. He owed her that much, probably more. Before he knew what was happening he had extended the invitation for this near-stranger Paul and his mangy mutt to stay at his home.

After he hung up he wondered if he should have his head examined. He should have never quit his job, signed the $1.4 million check over to some charity, any charity, and gone about his business as normal. Kennedy was right. Money changed you.

Paul Odell was anything but what J.T. had expected. On the surface he looked like a kind, aging, grandfatherly type. His hair was starting to give way to a gentle bald spot, his eyes were surrounded by wrinkles and he used a walking stick if he was moving very far at a time. The crazy part was he looked old and decrepit but his heart and his words were chuck full of youthful energy and powerful ideas. And his dog was not a filthy, shaggy mutt at all. Rather he was a quiet, well-mannered basset hound who rarely left Paul's side.

The first night he was in town J.T. wanted to reflect the image of a perfect host so he loaded Paul into his fancy car and drove him to his favorite barbecue spot on the edge of his suburb. Fortunately there was a booth available where they could visit quietly and get to know one another. Before they could start working on Paul's grand idea it would help to break the ice by talking about old times.

The waitress was someone J.T. knew – actually he knew them all – but Janie knew he was a usual here and brought him a tall beer in a frosted mug. To his surprise, Paul ordered the same. Adding an appetizer of loaded potato skins, the two men set out to get acquainted.

J.T. learned about how and why Paul left the priesthood and Paul discovered he had heard all kinds of stories about J.T. Kennedy talked non-stop about her high school sweetheart when they had first met, he just didn't know his name.

"Oh my goodness," Paul told him. "You have no idea how much you meant to her."

"She told you that?" J.T. wanted to know.

"Yes, yes. She thought the world of you. Said you were both headed in different directions after high school, though, and she wanted you to pursue your dreams and not feel pressured to go to college just so the two of you could stay together."

Wow! J.T. knew that is what she had said all those years ago, but to have another human recant that same story was eerie.

Paul went on.

"The more I got to know Kennedy the more she asked me to pray for you and your future. She desperately wanted you to be happy even if that meant the two of you had to travel different paths.

J.T. was speechless. Their appetizer came and the two men ordered another beer and continued to share stories. She prayed for me?

"Tell me more about Kennedy in college," J.T. said to his new friend.

Paul went on to explain how she had been active in the folk choir at the small Catholic student center on campus. She became interested in the ministry of serving communion to shut-ins and frequently donated her time to tutoring students, especially in math. Sometimes there was a whole flock of kids in there studying with her, Paul told him.

"What path did you take after high school," Paul asked.

"Nothing that noble, I'm afraid," J.T. said.

"Don't sell yourself short, J.T. Everyone has a talent to offer the world. Tell me more about you."

J.T. told him he initially worked in the fitness industry. He was married briefly and quickly divorced. Then there was the skiing accident that left his body badly marred and his career a shambles. Since then he had been floundering to find himself. He had taken a job in sales and found it somewhat fulfilling but he longed for the days when he could spend hours on the tennis court or run a 5K or even spend time with his nephew on the golf course. It didn't take Paul long to understand there was a sadness in J.T. that hadn't yet been able to escape.

After they finished their potato skins and spent a few minutes contemplating what to order for dinner, Paul changed directions in their conversation.

"Your story reminds me of a favorite quote of mine."

"Something from the Bible?" J.T. asked with a raised brow.

"Well, the good book has a great deal to say about using your talents to serve others, but this is from another source. You must know a man who dubbed himself Dr. Seuss."

"Really? My messed up life reminds you of a silly children's poem?" J.T. asked Paul.

"Not exactly that, no. But nevertheless that particular children's author is credited as saying 'Don't cry because it's over. Smile because it happened.' Your life is a gift from God, J.T. Every experience you have, every deed you do is of benefit to someone. You have people skills and business capabilities far greater than mine. Now together you and I – and the others we met in Wichita – have a great opportunity to make an even greater impact on the world than we could before. What do you say?"

"Ummmmm, I say, I don't know."

Now it was Paul's turn to furrow his brows.

"What's holding you back?" the older man asked.

"Wouldn't it just be easier to sign the money over to some wonderful organization and let them do with it as they see fit? What do I know about making a difference?"

"Oh J.T." was all Paul said. He let that soak in for a few seconds. "I hope I have not wasted your time. I was just hoping we could join forces."

Damn it. Paul was right. Three million dollars was a whole bunch of money. The guy across the table from him seemed to see something in him that he hadn't seen in himself for a very long time. If he could help someone else – or many someone elses – why not do it? Why not start today?

"Let's do this, Paul," J.T. told him. "I'm in."

Finding Mrs. Wilson

Today more than ever Brenda wished she had traveled to Kansas all those months ago. Then maybe she would have someone to share her feelings with. She used to be able to talk to her neighbor Rose Wilson about anything. Over the years they had shared opposite sides of the duplex where she lived and Mrs. Wilson, or Rosie, had become somewhat of a surrogate mother to her. Then after her fall and subsequent move to a nursing home half a nation away, Brenda had come to realize just how much she cherished her former neighbor and their visits.

In the dark of the night when she simply couldn't sleep, Brenda would toss and turn worrying about Rosie's welfare since the daughter who had come to "rescue" her seemed to be more like a repulsive cockroach than a caring daughter. Mrs. Wilson was mute about the reasons for the cold war that existed in her family so Brenda had come to accept that. As far as she could tell the older woman was being provided for and not just left to die. It really wasn't her place to intervene.

Sleep still evaded her.

The money her friend had left her as an unexpected inheritance would allow Brenda to take a short leave of absence from work and travel west to visit. Maybe that is what she should do. While she was out there she could do something nice for her friend. Perhaps even step in and help with her care for a little while to give the family a break. Making a mental note to follow through with arrangements, she fell into a peaceful,

dreamless sleep that carried over
uninterrupted until her alarm woke her in
the morning.

Jack and Mary Jane

Sunny Springs, Nebraska, was just a hop and a skip off the interstate. Mary Jane's children would soon be enrolled in school there. While they had not yet met Jack's children, the four Mendenhall kids were enjoying many things about their new temporary home. At least they believed it was temporary. The city swimming pool was just down the street from the house she had rented and the boys enjoyed the skateboard park a few blocks away. Little Maddie spent much of her free time trying to teach herself to knit, so far unsuccessfully.

The divorce had gone through the rudimentary steps quite quickly as Mary Jane did not ask for any money – only custody. Through Andy's lawyers she learned he was willing to give her a large lump sum of cash if the children could live with him six months of the year. Since she did not need or even want his money she stood firm explaining this would be detrimental to the children and their schooling but conceded Andy could visit in Nebraska any time he liked and she would see to it the children arrived in Tennessee four times a year for a week at a time. Andy was not at all happy but put up very little resistance. Mary Jane found it incredibly sad their marriage vows had to be broken for her to survive yet grateful to be out from under the stifling iron hand that had ruled her life for so many years.

"How are you holding up?" Jack texted her about two weeks after the big move. Even though he lived less than five miles away, most of their conversations were still limited to late night texts when the children were all asleep.

"I'm good," she typed back. "Having the kids on my own is no different than back home, but going to work every day is kicking my butt."

It was shocking how fast an hour went when they were chatting. Before they fell asleep for the night they quickly made plans to meet for lunch on Jack's day off next week. Despite their relative proximity now they hadn't seen each other in person since they had met in Wichita all those months ago.

With the move and divorce mostly behind her and getting used to working outside the home once again, Mary Jane was ready to give some serious thought to how she could use Kennedy's money to make an impact. She knew enough about Jack Redman to know he was thinking about it, too. She could hardly wait to bounce ideas around with him.

Sherwood

Fall weather in Oregon was among the best she had ever seen. A gentle breeze fell over the small town of Sherwood and the autumn temperatures begged you to bring along a sweater.

Brenda had contemplated calling ahead to let Mrs. Wilson know she was headed her way but thought better of it. Surely her old friend would welcome her visit. If she didn't then so be it. Brenda would stay a few days and then head back home to her daily routine. As for her goal for the trip, Brenda wasn't sure. She wanted to confirm Rose was doing well and a bigger part of her wanted to be sure the daughter who brought her to the west coast was treating her like a human instead of chopped liver. Their first encounter had not been a pleasant one.

Rounding the corner toward the address she had been given, Brenda turned the rental car into a majestic circle drive. This place looked much more like a mansion on steroids than an assisted living center. Her expectations had been low given the demeanor of her daughter Becky who arrived to take her away months ago after her fall. The daughter appeared to be a self-centered monster with almost no regard for humanity. Brenda didn't know what she expected but it certainly wasn't this. Even as she thought that a man dressed up to look like a bellman in a swanky hotel appeared and offered to park her car. What was this place?

Before getting out Brenda checked her contact information: Sloping Meadows Manor and Assisted Living Center. Double checking the sign she knew she was in the right place.

"Can I help you, Miss?" another finely dressed man asked her as he appeared from nowhere.

"I am here to see Rose Wilson," Brenda told him. "Can you show me the way?"

"I see. Ms. Wilson is not accepting visitors at this time," he told here without even consulting the front desk. This place was huge. There was no way he could remember every resident. She tried again.

"Rose Wilson was my neighbor in Toledo," Brenda told him politely. I have come a great distance to see her today."

"I do understand, Miss, Miss?"

"Miss Davis. My name is Brenda Davis. Can you at least tell me if she is OK?"

The gentleman was not easily swayed.

"I can confirm Mrs. Rose Wilson is a resident here, but she does not accept visitors."

"Fine," Brenda told him as politely as she was able. "I will come back in the morning."

"As you wish, Miss Davis," the man told her while the other man appeared at her other side holding out the keys to her car that he had not parked after all. "However, the answer will be the same. We have explicit instructions."

This was highly unusual, Brenda thought as she wound her way back through the maze of buildings associated with the manor and found her way back to a main street. This was a beautiful estate. Surely her friend was getting great care inside those walls. Still, something was suspicious. She would have to figure it out in the morning. For now she needed to find a comfortable place to stay for a few days and maybe a bite to eat.

Rather than Google hotels, Brenda rolled down the windows of the Toyota Camry and explored the small town of Sherwood, a pleasant little bedroom community to Portland, Oregon. She passed a trio of beautifully sculpted baseball fields, several different clusters of residential housing and eventually found a strip of businesses properties along the town's east side. There was a small grocery store, a liquor store, two gas stations and a free-standing ATM. Surely there was a bit more to Sherwood than this. Slowing, she turned into the Fred's Food Mart parking lot and waited until a native Sherwood resident walked by her window.

"Excuse me, sir," Brenda said to an elderly gentleman carrying a case of beer to his car. "I am just passing through and looking for a place to stay. Can you point me in the right direction?"

"Ain't nowhere but Mamma Molly's. You seen it already?"

"No, I don't believe I have," Brenda told him wondering what kind of hotel called itself Mamma Molly's.

"Great little place out by the highway. Just has five rooms but sure is comfy. Molly'll make ya breakfast, too. Her husband's a little cuckoo if ya ask me, but she is a good woman. Tell her Jud sent ya."

OK then. Maybe she should drive on up to Portland for the night. She thanked the man – Jud – and headed in the general direction he motioned, fully intending to hit the highway and get to a bigger city before dark. However, Mamma Molly's found her first.

It looked like a spacious home sitting all alone on a mini cul-de-sac. The yard was well-maintained and dotted with blooming flowers in all colors. A small sign close to the front door identified the inn as "Mamma Molly's – Bed and Breakfast." A fairly young man, maybe in his early forties sat on the porch rocking slowly back and forth while he listened to country music on a transistor radio.

Tired and hungry, Brenda cut the engine and walked up to the house. The man on the porch stared blankly ahead and made no motion of greeting so she walked by and rang the bell. Seconds later she was met by the bubbly personality of Molly Mullins, the keeper of the non-traditional inn.

"Jud sent me," Brenda said with a wide smile when Molly opened the screen and invited her in.

"That Jud is a character," she said. "I suppose he told you I make a mean breakfast."

"That he did," Brenda told her. "Do you have a room for the night? Actually, I am in town to see an old friend. I might plan to stay three nights, maybe four. Can you accommodate that?"

"Absolutely. Right now I only have one room rented and she is leaving in the morning. Let me give you a tour and then you can pick your spot."

Jud seemed to be right about this place. Molly and her inn were just what she needed today. At least there was one friendly face in Sherwood.

Brenda fell in love with every one of the beautiful rooms in the redecorated home the instant she saw them. While the outside of house-turned-hotel looked like a normal rectangular ranch-style single family dwelling, the inside was a different story. Through the main entrance was a hallway that led into a circular gathering room. There were comfortable chairs, sofas and loveseats neatly arranged in clusters with end tables and lamps to accompany each small grouping. Along one rounded wall was what seemed to be a coffee bar and Brenda noticed a tray of peanut butter cookies set out as well.

Six doorways led out of the spacious center room – five were to individual bedrooms with a private bath – and the sixth door led to the back of the house which was home to the kitchen, a laundry room and eventually the owner's living quarters.

"Wow," Brenda said without even realizing it. "This is an amazing place."

"We like it," Molly told her. "My husband and I bought the place about 15 years ago. It had been gutted by a fire so we got it for a song. Lots of blood, sweat and tears went into the renovation. It has been worth every penny we spent on it, though. It's out the way of the bigger city so it has that small town charm. And the best part is we can meet new people from all over the world or just close down and lock everything up if we want to go away on vacation for a spell."

"I am so glad I ran into Jud, then," Brenda said. "And that you are open for business this week."

The tour continued of the four unoccupied rooms, each one more lush than the last. Brenda settled on the middle room since it had just one queen-sized bed. That was really more than she needed. The color scheme was several shades of peach with off-white lace curtains. On closer inspection she found the room opened onto a small patio deck overlooking Molly's backyard where at the moment a small dog was chasing a butterfly.

The bathroom was equipped with a long counter and mirror, a shower and a deep whirlpool bathtub. For a moment she hesitated knowing his was far too nice to match her budget. She was prepared to turn and tell Molly she wouldn't be able to afford it and then remembered her budget was a little more padded at the moment that it had been in the past.

"This is perfect," she said. Do I pay you now?"

"Oh no, dear. Just wait until you are ready to check out. We just ask for $50 a night which includes your breakfast and we do ask that there is no smoking on the property. Do you have a pet with you?"

She couldn't believe her luck. The only hotel in town, it happened to be a lovely bed and breakfast and was only $50 a night. There had to be a catch. Maybe the place was haunted.

"No, it's just me," Brenda told Mrs. Molly Mullins.

"That is just as well. Small dogs are fine, but our own mutt Jackson is not a fan of cats."

With that Molly handed her a key and reminded her breakfast would be served at 7:45.

Brenda probably could have laid across the cushiony comforter and slept until morning. However, she did find she was a little hungry and she wanted to take care of a few things before morning.

Back in the car she took out her phone and dialed the number of the nursing home, Sloping Meadows. A pleasant young woman's voice – perhaps a teenager – answered on the second ring.

"Yes, I am calling about a Rose Wilson," Brenda told the receptionist. "I am in town from Ohio and would like to make an appointment to see her tomorrow."

There was a brief pause before the response.

"Thank you for calling, ma'am, but Mrs. Wilson does not accept visitors."

What? This couldn't be happening. Brenda tried again.

"I am an old friend – in fact Rose and I used to share a duplex when she lived in Ohio. We became great friends. I am certain she would like to see me."

"I am afraid that won't be possible, ma'am," the young voice told her. "Thank you for your call."

The line disconnected. She would straighten this out tomorrow come hell or high water. As for tonight? She was hungry.

Less than a mile down the road Brenda's Toyota pulled into to an almost empty parking lot of what she guessed to be a coffee shop. The lights were on and the "open" sign was still in the window. If she was lucky there would still be time to grab a quick sandwich and then she could head back to Molly's and sleep off this frustrating beginning to her trip.

"Can I help you, Miss?" a gentleman said as she approached the counter. "Our special today is the roast beef on rye but I am out of rye and the roast beef I have left is a little sketchy. Maybe a tuna salad on sour dough?"

Brenda laughed before she answered.

"You are a pretty good salesman," she told the man. "How about a bowl of soup and a muffin?"

"The soup is a no go," the man told her. "I wouldn't even serve the bottom of the pan to my dog. But if you come back tomorrow I will make you a bowl of the best tomato and rice soup you have ever tasted."

She appreciated the barista's sense of humor. She desperately needed some light conversation at the moment.

"As tempting as that sounds, I am hungry tonight."

"Well that does present a problem. I can do a grilled ham and cheese. Double pickles on the side. Or I can put together a salad for you."

Again Brenda laughed.

"Let's go with the grilled ham and cheese."

"Pumpernickel or wheat?"

"Surprise me," Brenda told him. "And tea would be great. No sweetener, extra ice."

Brenda slid into an available booth and took in the atmosphere of the roomy venue. There were two other tables occupied in the coffee shop that seemed more like a restaurant that served coffee. At one table a couple was studying the newspaper – maybe the want ads – and at the other table a group of lively middle-aged women appeared to be discussing a book they had read.

The art on the walls of Eddie's Coffee Emporium was composed primarily of photographs. They were probably local people and places. There were only a few windows but they were large and let in lots of light, even now when it was closing in on 8 p.m.

With impressive speed the gentleman prepared her sandwich and delivered it with a hefty glass of black tea.

"Are you closing soon?" Brenda wanted to know. "I can take this to go."

"Nope. We are open another hour or so. And I never kick anyone out. You are not from here are you?"

"No, but I wish I was. This town is a lovely place just to be."

"Oh yeah? What have you seen so far?"

The man who had waited on her was wearing a name badge identifying him as Shane.

"Well," Brenda said, motioning for him to join her at her table, "I met a kindly old gentleman at the grocery store when I first got here."

"Oh, so you've met Jud," Shane told her.

"Everyone knows Jud?" Brenda wanted to know.

"It's a pretty small town. How about the bait shop? You haven't lived until you have tried Old Mac's homemade ice cream."

"Yuck! A guy makes ice cream in a place that sells worms?"

"Don't knock it 'til you've tried it," Shane told her. "What brings you to town?"

Brenda took a bite of her sandwich before answering and gave Shane the thumbs up for its taste.

"I have an old friend staying at Sloping Meadows," she told him then.

Shane let out a whistle.

"Ooooooooohhhhh laaaaa laaaaa! That is a nice place out there. Your friend is living in style. I heard they serve caviar for breakfast."

"Wow! Well I haven't actually been inside yet. They gave me a bit of a run around I'm afraid."

Now Shane furrowed his brows and looked confused.

"That is unusual," he said. "Good people run that place. Friends of mine," he lied. "If you have any more trouble you let me know. Seriously."

Brenda certainly hoped it didn't come to that – having to ask a stranger to intercede just to make a courtesy call on a friend. Although this stranger did make a killer grilled sandwich.

Just then the bell rang on the door indicating a new customer was coming in.

"Hey, Marcy," Shane called out as he slid from the booth. "Do you want the usual tonight? I wouldn't bank of the special. I'm out of rye."

With that Shane was back at the counter taking Marcy's order but not before reminding her to stop in tomorrow for his tomato and rice soup.

When Brenda found her way back to Molly's the gentleman from the porch earlier was nowhere in sight. The front door was open so she let herself in and easily found her room. The bed had been turned back and on her pillow was a tiny box of Russell Stover's chocolates. A girl could get used to this place, she decided. Within a few minutes she was sound asleep and didn't stir until the aroma of Molly's bacon woke her in the morning.

The next day was Saturday. Brenda thought she might have more luck with the weekend staff at Sloping Meadows. Unfortunately, no. This time she asked a few more questions. Was Rose OK? Had family been by to see her? Was there a reason she wasn't accepting visitors? And finally she asked if the receptionist would just call into Rose's room and ask her if she would receive Brenda Davis as a guest.

No such luck. Every answer came back the same. No entrance. No visit. No exceptions.

At a loss, and more angry than concerned, Brenda took a seat on the ledge of a beautiful fountain near the edge of the rambling assisted living estate. She thought about her options for a long time and eventually gave up and got back in her car. She could try a bribe. Or disguise herself as a florist making a delivery. A doctor who needed to see a patient? She didn't have it in her to be dishonest. She would just wear them down with her persistence. Not knowing what to do next, she headed out of the parking lot and followed the road over to Eddie's Coffee Emporium. It was time to try the soup.

Brenda found it hard to believe she was a little disappointed when Shane wasn't working. True to his word, however, the chalkboard menu board was featuring tomato and rice soup as well as the daily special sandwich which was turkey with an avocado cream cheese pasta salad. That was different, she thought, but she decided to go with the soup and then splurged on an iced mocha just for fun.

Today the tables at Eddie's were almost all full. Even though everyone was talking at once the noise level was minimal and she noticed soft, instrumental music was coming from somewhere. A quick scan of the room led her eyes to a beautiful grand piano in one corner and even though his back was to her, it was easy to tell the musician was none other than her server-sandwich maker-soup promoter from yesterday, Shane.

While she ate she listened and was amazed at how easy Shane made it look. There was no sheet music visible so he had memorized his work and he played one song after another, nodding to guests as they came and went from the busy lunch spot.

"Do you have other talents you are hiding?" she asked as she stood to leave, timing it perfectly as he finished a piece. She hadn't meant it to sound flirtatious but realized it did. Once you say something you can't take it back so she was silent and waited for his answer.

"Many," Shane told her, standing. His smile and wink told her he knew she was teasing and he appreciated the compliment. "Would you like to know what they are?"

Brenda blushed and hoped he didn't notice.

"Well I know you make a mean sandwich, you can sell soup to strangers and now I am just learning you are on loan from Carnegie Hall."

"Ha! You are too kind. Did you come back for the soup?"

"I'm afraid I did. And it was terrific. Are you guys the only restaurant in town or your food is just that good?"

"Oh no I can't give away ALL of my secrets, Miss, Miss…?"

"Davis. Brenda Davis."

The name sounded familiar but he couldn't place her. There were lots of people named Davis. If she wasn't from here he wouldn't know her anyway.

"So Brenda, do you play the piano?"

"Heavens, no. But I do sing on occasion."

"Is that so?" Shane asked. "We do have an open mic night here several times a month. You could come in and sing. It always draws a big crowd."

Brenda reminded Shane she was just passing through and would be gone in a few days. They shared a few more minutes of small talk before he asked her another question.

"So have you made it to Mac's for the ice cream yet?"

"Uh, well no. I can't even imagine."

"It's just down the street," Shane told her. "Want to join me? We can walk."

It seemed harmless. She couldn't imagine eating anything else at the moment, but if she was only going to be here a few days and the place was that good it would be a shame to miss it.

To her surprise the bait shop was more like a shopping mall. It had everything from camping gear and fish bait to towels and dishes. It was impeccably clean and every employee she saw was wearing a starched blue uniform with "Mac's" embroidered on the left breast pocket. It was impressive and she told him so.

"You doubted me?" he asked with a smile.

"A bit."

Shane ordered their ice cream special which today was strawberry cheesecake and brought it to a little picnic style table in the back of the store. It was delicious. He had been spot on with his assessment.

"So you know I like to cook every now and again. You have heard me play the piano. Tell me a little bit about you."

Brenda enjoyed their light conversation. She left out the part about being a recent millionaire and didn't want to talk about the frustration with Sloping Meadows so she played it safe and told him she worked in retail, spent a great deal of her time reading good mysteries and occasionally enjoyed eating strawberry ice cream.

The more they talked the more she liked him. Shane was funny and interesting. If he lived in Ohio she was certain they would be friends.

"So tell me about Eddie," Brenda said.

"Eddie?"

"Yeah, Eddie of Eddie's Coffee Emporium. You know? Your boss."

"Oh about that," Shane told her with a laugh. "You might be disappointed to learn there is no Eddie."

A twist of her head told him she wasn't sure what he was saying. So he continued.

"I guess you could say I am Eddie."

"I thought you were Shane," she told him, obvious confusion in her voice.

"Well, there used to be an Eddie. I bought the business from the guy some time ago. He was long past retirement age so his wife talked him into moving to the ocean. The community knows the place as Eddie's, though. So I just left it that way."

Wow! He was full of surprises.

"That explains why you cook, wait tables, promote your daily specials and even entertain the guests with your music."

"Well, don't make me out to be super human or anything. I have lots of help. The people of Sherwood are incredible. Serving others is a great way to make a living. If I get to enjoy cooking and playing at the same time? Well then, all the better."

A few minutes later they bussed their own table and headed back down the street to her car. Brenda promised to check back in before she left town for good and thanked him for his hospitality. A brief hug later and he was back inside leaving her standing in the parking lot.

As Brenda drove back to Molly's house her head was full of questions. There were the obvious ones, like why Rose Wilson was not accepting visitors. And if her daughter was such an ogre why did she put her mother in a first class assisted living center? And then there were the less obvious ones, like why had she never wandered too far from Toledo and discovered lovely little places like Sherwood, Oregon.

Maybe it was because she was deep in thought that she nearly bumped into a woman leaving the house as she was coming up the steps. Mumbling an apology, she looked up just in time to see the woman's face and it was none other than Becky Carlton, the daughter of her dear friend Rose Wilson. As for Becky, she was true to her personality, greeting Brenda with an evil grimace of agitation before sidestepping and continuing on down the sidewalk without a backward glance. Clearly she did not recognize her.

What was she doing here at Molly's? Brenda was determined to find out. Passing the same gentleman who was on the porch the day before, she hustled in to the gorgeous stone inn hoping to find Molly in the kitchen. Instead she found her in the garden just off the back of the house.

"Well hello, dear," Molly greeted her. "How is your stay coming along?"

"Everything here is perfect," Brenda told her. "You have built a lovely space, so welcoming and relaxing."

"Thank you, you are so kind. It's home," Molly replied.

"I wonder, though, if you can help me decipher a few things," Brenda asked.

"Oh? Like?"

"Like what can you tell me about Becky Carlton?"

This brought Molly's head up from the vegetables she was picking and loading into her apron.

"You know Becky Carlton?" Molly wanted to know.

"Not very well I'm afraid, but she is most of the reason I am here in Oregon."

Molly asked Brenda to help her bring in the bowl of berries she had picked earlier and then followed her back into the kitchen.

"If you can sit with me while I chop I will tell you what I know," Molly told her. "I'm afraid I don't know her too well myself."

Brenda poured them each a glass of lemonade while Molly got a knife and cutting board for each of them and together they made short order of cutting tomatoes, cucumbers, radishes and bell peppers into bite-sized pieces.

"Becky is a high end real estate broker in the city," Molly started. "She has been married more times than I can count. Her life seems all glamorous and full of energy, but she never seems very happy."

"That is for sure," Brenda said.

"It seems her mother is living here in Sherwood so she comes down once a month or so to attend to her needs. I don't know much more than that. She doesn't have kids of her own but there is a niece and nephew she watches out for as well. Her mother, though, is a wonderful lady."

"Wait! You know Rose Wilson?" Brenda asked in shock.

"Oh my yes. I am a hairdresser," Molly told her. "Rose is staying out at the Manor and I do her hair every week. That lady is feisty and funny and just a ball of joy. It is so hard for me to believe cranky old Becky Carlton is a member of her family – not to mention a daughter."

Her luck was looking up. This may have been the connection she was looking for. Over the next 15 minutes or so Brenda told her the story of how Becky showed up in Toledo after Rose's heart attack and the ugly incident in the hospital that followed just before Rose was moved to the coast and the children – Rose's grandchildren – were moved to live with some friend of Becky's.

"Well Rose will never speak ill of her daughter, but there is definitely more to the story."

"Becky is staying here, too?" Brenda asked. "Because I bumped into her on the way in. She didn't seem like she remembered me but I have to tell you, she is not my biggest fan."

"She does stay here when she comes into town. This is such a small town and there are no other hotels," Molly told her. "But she just checked out right before you came back."

"Is Rose well?" Brenda had to ask.

"I think so. She walks with a cane but I think that is just a safety precaution for her balance. She walks down that hallway faster than I do," Molly said. "Like I told you, she is a feisty little old lady. I just love her personality."

"I wish I knew the rest of the story," Brenda said, putting down her knife and scooping the vegetables she had chopped into the large bowl beside her.

"Well, I don't know this from Becky and Rose would certainly never reveal anything negative about anyone, but like I said this is a small town."

Molly stopped talking as if she wasn't sure it was right to spread gossip. She kept working, though, now moving on to cleaning and slicing the strawberries.

Brenda decided to pry just a little bit.

"Rose was my neighbor before all of this. I just want to be sure she is alright. I just get bad feelings about Becky."

Molly was still a little hesitant to share.

"I am a little leery about her, too, but Rose seems to be adapting well out at Sloping Meadows. It is an outstanding care center. Haven't you been out to see her yet?"

"They won't let me in," Brenda told her with a frown. "They say Rose is not accepting visitors and won't even tell Rose I am there."

"Wow. That has Becky stamped all over it. Just like everything else she does she seems to want to be in charge. I hate to talk bad about people, really I do," Molly continued. "But that lady has a huge chip on her shoulder."

Brenda helped put the vegetables away then and refreshed their lemonades. Molly, grateful for the help, suggested they move into the living room area and then she began to share the story of sweet Rosie Wilson and her mean-spirited daughter.

It seems there was a terrible accident about five years ago. Rose's son and his wife were instantly killed leaving her grandchildren, little Teddy and Jane, orphans. Becky, who at the time was on the fast track to be a partner in her real estate firm, was crushed at the loss of her brother but had no interest in raising the children. She apparently wrongly blamed her mother for the accident and despised her for suggesting she put her life on hold for a bit to help raise the children. That is how they came to live with Rose. As sad as that whole saga was, after getting to know Becky better she felt the children were in far better hands living with their grandmother.

"Wow! I bet Mrs. Wilson hasn't even seen those children since she moved here," Brenda said.

"You are probably right," Molly told her. "It's a travesty. Listen, why don't you come out with me to the Manor. If you are staying on for a few more days you could come along when I do her hair on Thursday. The staff won't question a thing if you are with me."

"Really? You would do that?" Brenda asked.

"Of course, dear. I have no doubt Rose would love to see you and we will beat that cantankerous old Becky at her own game. For now would you like to stay for lunch?"

Brenda wished she would have been able to capture the look on her old friend's face when she walked into the Sloping Meadows beauty salon with Molly Mullins. Priceless.

The three women talked like teenagers for ages, a wash and set hairstyle the last thing from any of their minds. Rose wanted to know how – and why – she had found her. How were things going back in Ohio? How did she know Molly? How long could she stay? It was unmistakably evident she had no idea there was a "no visitors" list.

It wasn't until Brenda volunteered to walk her back to her room that the happy spirit of the afternoon morphed into something darker. Rose was skeptical and almost seemed nervous. Was she hiding something? At last she agreed to let the women walk with her back to her room but her demeanor was significantly stilted.

Together the three of them walked down a lengthy hallway flanked with large windows on both sides revealing lush gardens and fountains as well as extraordinary views of the countryside that separated the villa from the mainstream town of Sherwood. Mrs. Wilson easily kept pace with them as they walked and eventually made it to a recreation room of sorts. There was a pool table, a big screen TV and several clusters of people gathered to play cards and dominoes. Right in the middle there was even a tiny mini bar where the residents could get snacks. Too bad Brenda wasn't old enough to live here, she thought.

The furniture here looked more expensive than the lobby of the Ritz Carlton. She was so grateful since her friend had needed to move to assisted living that she had landed here. Rose spoke to a few people as they moved through and several raised a hand to wave to her.

As they moved through the large rec room Rose guided them toward another hallway that had resident rooms on either side. Glancing from left to right as they moved down the hall it was evident the residents here lived in style. Each room they saw was expansive and looked very much like a small apartment rather than the hospital rooms she would have expected. No beds were visible as they passed by. It just looked like a big living room/kitchen/dining room combo. Obviously these people had to sleep so these must be suites with a bedroom attached. Holy moly it was a nice place.

Plus the facility was huge. Brenda was starting to worry a bit about how far her friend would have to walk every day just to get "home." It didn't seem to bother Rose, though. This corridor ended with a T formation and Rose led them to the left.

"Really girls, you can just leave me here," she told Molly and Brenda. "I can make it on my own."

Since they had already come at least a half a mile they might as well see it through. Both women insisted they continue and they followed her down another long hallway. This time most of the doors were closed and the few that were open were either empty or scantily furnished. It wasn't until they had made yet another turn and passed another 10-12 rooms that they at last came to a door labeled simply "4905."

"Here we are," Rose announced with no effort to open the door and let them in. "Brenda it was so good of you to come. You have made my day."

There was no need to tell her she had been trying to see her for almost a week.

"I brought you a little something," Brenda told her then. "Can we come in just for a second?"

Again there was hesitation but finally Rose did open the door and step inside. What they saw was scandalous.

Inside room 4905 was a bed. There was one well-used recliner and a hard backed chair. A small dresser was on one side of the bed and a mismatched end table on the other. That was it. There was a small window with no curtains and a door that presumably led to a bathroom. The difference between the other rooms they had seen was beyond comparison.

That little witch. Becky had found a lovely estate for her mother's end of life home that by all accounts was top of the line to all who knew it by name and reputation. Anyone who asked would be told her mother was staying at Sloping Meadows and she would be able to collect all the "oohs" and "aahs" from her friends and co-workers while her mother lived out her days in a bland corner of the grounds in a room without a single personal effect.

Brenda fought to find words that wouldn't come out spikey and rude while they settled themselves on the chairs and Rose sat on the edge of the bed.

"I brought you these," Brenda said.

From her purse she pulled out a good-sized box of chocolate-covered cherries, something she knew her former neighbor loved.

"Bless you my dear Brenda," Rose said and her smile returned to her face. "I will cherish these like they are gold."

They all laughed a tiny bit that at this and then Brenda changed the subject to keep from spitting venom about Rose's daughter and what she had done to her mom.

"So how is the food here?" she wanted to know.

"Most of the time it is really great. They always have a salad bar so if you don't like the meat choice you will never go hungry. We have a lot of chicken."

"Maybe you should step into the kitchen and show them a thing or two," Brenda told her. "I have tasted your lasagna. It would set this place on its ear."

"Ha ha! Well I haven't had lasagna for a very long time. Once in awhile they do have spaghetti, though."

Uggg. This was getting worse by the minute. And more and more difficult not to let her emotions show.

"Oh and I brought you something else," Brenda suddenly remembered.

She pulled another box out from her purse and handed it to her friend. This one was neatly wrapped in lavender paper accented by a fluffy bow. Brenda and Molly watched while she carefully unwrapped the picture frame and turned it over in her hands to see the image of Rose with her two grandchildren - Jane hugging her grandma's neck and Teddy leaning in from the side showing off his toothless grin. After a quick glance, Rose clutched it to her chest and held it tightly in her arms.

The next few days passed uneventfully. With the help of Molly Mullins she spent as much time as she could with her old friend Rose. They walked the grounds together, sat in the gardens and visited for hours and Brenda was even brave enough to eat with her in the center's cafeteria. If she didn't know better in her heart, Brenda would have thought everything was perfectly normal and nothing had changed in the life of her old friend.

**

Ever present these last few days in Oregon was her recent friend addition, the owner of Eddie's coffee shop who she simply knew as Shane. Brenda found Shane to be incredibly witty and full of life. Sherwood was fortunate to have him as a business entrepreneur and a community leader. More than a little of herself wished he lived in Toledo. Hopefully they would be able to exchange contact information when she headed back home to her drastically more mundane life and the job she loathed but needed to pay the rent and support her ice cream and pizza addictions. The at least once daily visits to Shane's restaurant were something she truly would miss.

"I wonder," Shane told her one lazy afternoon as they shared more of Mac's daily ice cream specials, "if you would consider having dinner with me."

Shocked at the implication of a date, Brenda took a moment to formulate an answer.

"Well, normally I am not in the habit of accepting dinner reservations with men I only know by a first name."

"Walker," he told her. "I am Shane Walker."

"Well then, Mr. Walker, I would be honored to be your dinner companion."

After a brief discussion about dates and times Shane agreed to pick her up at Mamma Molly's at 6 p.m. the following evening. Brenda found she was excited, apprehensive and flustered all at the same time.

True to his word Shane arrived promptly at 5:59, rang the bell and when she came to the door offered the small floral bouquet he had brought to the surprised but delighted Molly.

"That was beyond sweet of you to bring flowers for Mrs. Mullins," Brenda told him after he opened her car door and let her in to his black sporty Mustang.

"Well, if you must know," Shane told her, "I bought those flowers for you. But there she was just standing there and it seemed appropriate to offer them to her."

"I am sure it made her day. To see the look on her face I don't think she has had a man bring her flowers in years," Brenda said.

"That may be a fact. Have you met her husband?"

"No. Someone told me the guy was a little out there, if you will, but I have been at the inn almost two weeks and I have never been formally introduced to him."

"Oh I am sure you have," Shane said. "He is the older gentleman who always sits on the front porch, rocking his life away and listening to the radio."

"That guy? No. I just figured he was a guest there."

Shane went on to tell her the sad saga of Molly's husband Steve. Apparently he had been drinking a little too much at the pub downtown one night, drove away and was involved in an accident. The victim was a child who ran into the street while chasing a ball. She didn't die, but has no use of her legs. Steve is tortured by his part in it all and just sits and stares into space almost 24 hours a day.

"Poor, poor Molly," Brenda said as they continued to drive through town. "Have they tried counseling?"

"I think they have tried just about everything. The parents of the little girl are friends with the Mullins' family and they have discounted it as simply a horrific accident and forgiven him tenfold, but Steve just can't forgive himself. It is so hard on everyone who knew Steve before. I wasn't a Sherwood resident yet, but apparently he was a top-notch carpenter and marketed his products all over the world before that happened."

"Wow! It makes you feel lucky for what you have, doesn't it?" Brenda asked him not really needing an answer.

"Yeah. Sure does. In the blink of an eye your life can be altered forever. And good-hearted Molly does all she can to make him happy and encourage him. Tough, tough deal. On a brighter note, how do you feel about Chinese food?"

"Love it!"

The restaurant Shane chose was not at all crowded. In fact there were just a handful of guests sitting at tables in a bar area when they entered. The hostess recognized Shane and they were escorted to a table immediately. After taking their drink order the hostess disappeared and never returned. However, a portable grill and a personal chef arrived a few minutes later with their wine.

For almost an hour the chef entertained them by flipping shrimp onto the top of his toque, making a fire-filled volcano out of onion rings and singing them a silly song about cows while he cooked their steaks on the grill just inches from them at their table. Brenda hadn't laughed like that in a long time and knew her sides would hurt in the morning.

At last they were left alone with an almond apple tart and fresh coffee. Brenda couldn't remember ever being on such a fun date, not to mention a first date. Her apprehension was long gone.

"So tell me," Shane began when they had time to visit again, "did you ever get to see your friend at Sloping Meadows?"

"Oh yes, didn't I tell you that earlier? I am not sure how that slipped my mind."

Brenda told him then how she had creeped in with Molly and that Rosie was completely unaware she wasn't accepting visitors. Without meaning to she went on a long rant about Becky and the way she had basically just dropped off her mother in this fancy home to die. She expressed her anger at the way it looked on paper. By all appearances she had sent her mom to a state-of-the-art nursing center by anyone's standards. The reality was she had unloaded her in the tiniest of rooms with not one single perk except three meals a day and call button in case of an emergency. Brenda pulled no punches in telling Shane just exactly how she felt.

"Wow. What are you going to do about it?" Shane asked.

"What can I do? I am not her next of kin and Becky and I have only met once or twice. She hates me. I brought her a picture of her grandkids. I think that's my limit."

"You have done far more than that," Shane told her. "You have brought yourself to visit her. She will never forget that act of kindness."

Brenda wasn't sure. It seemed there should be more ways she could support Rose but she was certainly at a loss.

When the bill came Shane immediately took care of it and then stood and motioned for Brenda to lead the way back to the parking lot. No, they certainly did not make men like this in Ohio.

The evening ended when Shane walked her to the door and gave her a polite kiss on the cheek before heading back to his car. It was just as well it ended there since she would be leaving tomorrow afternoon.

No need to get romantically entangled. She knew if he wanted to stay in touch he could get her contact information from Molly and if she absolutely needed to reach him for some reason she could Google Eddie's Coffee Emporium to get his business number. Her time in Oregon had exceeded her expectations and now it was time to return to her normal life once again.

Christmas for nine

It had been a little over a year since Mary Jane and her four children had moved to Sunny Springs – and about 18 months since she and Jack had first met back in Kansas. Both of them had erroneously thought they were there for Kennedy's wedding only to learn they were each million-dollar heirs. Neither of them had finalized their thoughts on how they could best utilize the money to honor their mutual friend even though it had been the topic of discussion at least a hundred times.

Jack and Mary Jane had become the best of friends. They discovered that other than children they had almost nothing in common. He liked coffee. She liked tea. He loved exercise. She loved reading. He wanted to retire. She loved her job. All of that being said, they were still inseparable. The text messages they used to send had now turned into long phone calls and Skype sessions.

As for the children, Jack's son Ben went to high school with Mary Jane's two older sons. All three of them loved participating in sports and got along like brothers. Jack's twin girls were about Max's age, went to the same school and tolerated each other. There were no issues between them, they just had different interests. But Maddy idolized Jack's Bea and Betsy. In turn they spoiled her rotten – more rotten. As a whole the troupe of nine enjoyed getting to know one another and spent hours hanging out together and attending each other's activities.

One evening as Mary Jane and Jack sat side by side on the bleachers watching Bea play volleyball Jack asked her if she had plans for Christmas.

"Other than spending hours wrapping packages just to have them ripped open in minutes, you mean?"

Jack laughed but continued.

"Yeah, I mean wouldn't it be fun to do something special this year? You know, in honor of our new friendship and all?"

"The children – my children – will be in Tennessee with Andy for the holiday," she reminded him.

"Then we can do it early, before they go. I was thinking of something fun – like a party," Jack said.

"A party. Tell me more," was her reply.

"No idea. That's all I've got. But my house hasn't seen anything terribly festive in years. We always put up the same old fake tree and sometimes we make cookies but we almost always eat them before any get frosted."

Mary Jane really didn't need time to think about it at all. It sounded like a great idea. To her Christmas was the most romantic holiday ever. With its almost certain snowy weather, singing around the fireplace, stringing popcorn and the glitz and glamour of the big city Christmas lights there was no denying Christmas had a feel of love.

Not that there was anything romantic between her and Jack. Not in the slightest. But still it was a time to celebrate the people you loved and she did love the guy. He had saved her from a mere existence and a feeling of desolation she hadn't been able to escape until he unexpectedly dropped into her life.

"Let's do it!" she said.

As the holiday season approached the weather did its November and December thing delivering insanely cold days and nights for weeks at a time. Most of Jack's work days were spent outside so when he came home all he wanted to do was bond with the fireplace. However, they had made a commitment to throw a big Christmas bash on Saturday night before Mary Jane's children flew back to Tennessee a few days later. There wasn't much time to waste.

So far there was not a guest list. Initial plans were to make it a special celebration for just the Redman and Mendenhall families. Jack wanted to invite a few neighbors as well and perhaps even let each one of the children invite a friend or two. The bigger the better was his idea. There would be plenty of food and he hoped if he dug his guitar out of the closet the group would get lost in singing carols and drinking hot chocolate.

Maddie and Max had taken the lead on the tree. It was the first time in years Jack's dining room had been graced with a real tree. The two older boys and Ben had gone with Jack to cut one down and there were gales of laughter when the four of them realized they had overestimated the girth of the tree compared to the size of the space they were squeezing it into. Once it was in the house and safely balanced in its stand,

Max and Maddie went to work almost immediately stringing popcorn garland.

Jack drove Maddie and Max back home while the whole Redman kid clan embraced the ornament hunt digging through several boxes of archived baubles until they found the best. Several hours later it was hard to believe what stood in the corner of his dining room was the same awkward jumble of evergreen branches they struggled to fit in the room earlier. Jack had to admit the tree almost looked like it belonged there.

He had promised to let the Mendenhall kids help with the tinsel and the other finishing touches so he shooed his kids off to their rooms to finish homework, then snapped a picture of the tree-in-progress and texted it to Mary Jane.

"Nice, but…" she started a few minutes later when she called him.

"But? I think they did a great job," Jack told her, obviously disappointed in her initial assessment.

"Oh they did. It looks very festive, but…"

"But what?"

Mary Jane almost didn't want to tell him.

"I think they have created a one-of-a-kind Christmas special. Maybe the first one of its kind. You forgot to put on the lights."

Whirling around to re-assess Jack was appalled. How could he have forgotten the lights? This might be his first real tree in ages but he couldn't remember any year of his life without a tree and the lights ALWAYS go on first.

"Uh oh," Jack mumbled into the phone.

Mary Jane was silent. Unusual. This worried him. He hoped she wasn't going to tell him to start over.

"No worries," she finally said. "We will have the first light-less Christmas tree Nebraska has ever seen. People will come from miles around to see the great, dark tree of 2016."

This brought a laugh from Jack and he changed the subject.

"What about the food?" he asked her. "A buffet? Or should we serve family style?"

"Having everyone gather around one table is always best, I think, but there will be so many of us. Can we do that?"

Together they counted the number of potential guests and came up with close to 30.

"If we do buffet style everyone can sit around the room and visit more. I know we can find 30 seats. Wouldn't the girls have fun making place cards, though, and elegant place settings?" Mary Jane asked by way of a suggestion.

"I wouldn't recognize an elegant place setting if it hit me in the face," Jack told her honestly, "but I trust you completely and it would be good for the twins to learn to set a beautiful table."

Mary Jane accepted the challenge and made a note to sell the concept to the girls later in the afternoon.

Other party plans came together throughout the month. It seemed like every day someone had a new idea and the plans were changed again. And again. At times the stress of bringing both families together combined with friends and neighbors didn't seem worth the pain and expense. Jack had naturally taken on the leadership role and keeping and updating the master "to do" list.

The only disappointment, really, was the Christmas tree. While elegantly decorated its lack of lights detracted from making it the center of attention.

One evening as they gathered at Jack's for an informal spaghetti dinner and to finalize the party plans it was the youngest child among them who discovered a solution to their light-less tree problem.

"Mommy, what if we make the star on top shine all over the tree," she said after a few minutes of consideration.

"How would we do that, sweetheart?" Mary Jane asked. She knew the tree was the center of the celebration but the party would go on regardless of the darkened tree. It was still elegant and special due to the combined efforts of all nine of them.

"Well, most lights go AROUND the tree but the angels sent the wise men to find Jesus using a star, right?"

"That they did," Mary Jane agreed.

"So what if we make our lights go DOWN the tree. Then we can all pretend it is Jesus' star spreading light all over the top of our decorations."

She was a genius at seven years old. Work began immediately with Jack and the boys attaching strings of lights to their star with fishing line. They silently agreed less was more - quite possibly because it was tedious work. At any rate, after the frustration of weaving everything together it was ready at last to plug in. No words were spoken but everyone was worried it wouldn't light. There wasn't one among them who wanted to dull the excitement of Madeline Mendenhall.

Jack was the first to speak.

"Maddie? Want to plug it in?" he asked handing her the cord.

She didn't say a word but her smile spoke volumes. She stepped up and accepted the responsibility while the rest of them stood in a loose circle around the tree, held their breath and waited.

It flickered and then it lit. Exquisite. The room broke out in spontaneous applause. Mary Jane was amazed that what the rest of them saw as a major obstacle little Maddie saw as a challenge. Then she solved it. There was no denying it looked far better than the traditional approach. What a happy accident.

Bea leaned down and picked up her friend Maddie, hugging the breath out of her.

"Don't thank me," Maddie told the group when she could breathe again. "Jack is the one who made it all work out!"

Wow! Humble, too, Mary Jane thought to herself. While the others resumed conversation and fell into light chatter Jack and Mary Jane shared a smile over their heads. Crisis averted.

"Maybe we should do it this way every year," Jack told her.

Mary Jane agreed and told him so by reaching out to squeeze his hand.

Handwritten invitations were created by the girls. Mary Jane helped with the wording, but each of the seven children joined in the making of the folded cardstock homemade invitations. Even though they were ecstatic it was happening, both Jack and Mary Jane were more than a bit surprised at how easily everyone – even the high school aged boys - chipped in to help plan and carry out such a big event.

Please join the Redman and Mendenhall families
for a Christmas celebration

What: Food and fellowship
When: Saturday, December 17, 6 p.m.
Where: Redman home, 8311 W. Deer Ridge Road

Please bring a favorite Christmas memory to share.

Betsy was so artistic. The cards she made almost looked like they had been pre-printed by Hallmark. She added tiny embellishments of holly and greenery at the corners and along the borders. Bea was less interested in making hers pretty. She just got the basic words down and then decorated hers with stickers. Her talent came in helping young Maddie space and center the words, offering her praise and encouragement, and pretending not to notice when one – or two – words were misspelled.

Jack's responsibility was to gather the addresses and address the envelopes while Mary Jane made sugar cookies to frost after the cards were done and ready to mail. It was fun to have them all together even though it was a bit crowded. It would be even more crowded the night of the party, of course, but surely no one would complain if there was plenty of food, music and laughter.

Finally, with just one week remaining until the guests arrived, the team of nine had figured a way to seat 30 people by pushing back living room furniture, combining card tables and borrowing folding chairs from the church. It was a trial and error process with lots and lots of errors. And at first it was pretty rough. Once the red tablecloths they had purchased and the frosted pine cones the younger children had made and arranged in clusters with sprigs of holly to make centerpieces the room was transformed.

Ben and his twin sisters grumbled often when they had to step over and around Christmas décor in the weeks leading up to the big event. However, Jack's mention that Santa was watching usually held off the complaining – not that they didn't offer an eye roll or two.

"What about presents?" Bea asked her dad over breakfast. "Will we open presents at the party?"

That was a good question. It hadn't been discussed.

"What if we draw names? I mean, there are so many of us," Bea said.

"Oh I don't know," Jack told her. Many of the people don't know each other. Plus I hate to ask someone to be a guest at your house and then buy a present, too.

"No, Dad. I mean what if Mary Jane and her kids and Ben and you and Betsy and I all drew names. Then we would just buy something really special for one person. We could open them after the party."

Great idea.

"It would be like a party after the party," Betsy said with a smile. "What do you think, Dad?"

Jack would run it by Mary Jane but he was all in.

All the children had contributed to decorating the Redman household, both inside and out. Mike, the only one bringing a girlfriend to the party, was insistent there was mistletoe hanging from more than one doorway. Ben and Mark still thought girls had cooties and vowed to avoid the mistletoe at all costs.

All that was left was the final food preparations. It would be a significant amount of work for sure. Jack and Ben were tackling the meat, both a turkey and their famous Coca-Cola ham. His girls would shred 15 pounds of potatoes for their family's favorite cheesy hash brown casserole and the Mendenhalls would take care of the rest. They had planned and shopped together for several vegetable side dish recipes and a large relish tray. Dessert was still undecided.

Perhaps the best part of this holiday party was not the party at all, but the time the two families had spent together engaging in all the traditions of the season. Even if the party was suddenly and unexpectedly cancelled, the months of November and December had been a success. Of course, Mary

Jane hoped that didn't happen or they would be eating leftovers in June.

One by one the children had wrapped their presents for the after party and added them to the pile under the tree with the other gifts at Jack's house. All of them had agreed to keep mute about whose name they had drawn. The only thing they knew for sure was no one was allowed to spend over $10.

One present, tagged for Ben was so small there could be nothing inside bigger than a thimble. And the one marked for Max was roughly the size of a station wagon and wrapped entirely in newspaper. It was hard for the grownups to decide which would be more special – the monster celebration with their friends and neighbors or the private gift exchange they would have after the table was at last cleared and the dishes were done.

"I think we have lost our minds," Mary Jane told Jack the night before the big bash. "This fun party idea of yours has grown to mammoth proportions."

"That it has," he agreed. "I wouldn't change a thing, though, would you?"

"Honestly? I am thinking we hire a sitter and just you and I go out to a movie," she told him.

"You are such a liar," he teased back. "You have loved every minute of planning things. I mean did you even imagine three high school boys would join forces to cook a meal and frost cookies for people they don't even know?"

"That is true," she conceded. "Plus the tree. Normally I can't get my four all to stay in the room long enough to get that task done. This year we had nine on it and not one argument among them."

"True that," he said. "I only see one problem with the whole thing."

"Just one? Do tell," Mary Jane said switching her cell phone to speaker status so she could pour herself a glass of wine while they talked.

"How in the world will we top this next year?"

"Jack Redman, shut your mouth!" she pretended to scold him. I don't want to think about next year until – well – next year."

Their light conversation continued for a few minutes and then turned to wrapping up the details of what still needed to be done. Most of the responsibilities were already accounted for. They would just need to get the Mendenhall food from her house to his.

There was still the issue of dessert but after the mountains of Christmas cookies they had already consumed she couldn't imagine anyone of them would find sugar appealing. They had decided on making huge balls of peppermint ice cream and freezing them in clear plastic bowls. When it was time to serve they would set out trays with the ice cream and an assortment of toppings for everyone to enhance their own.

Every detail was set. It had been almost as extravagant as planning a wedding although not nearly as expensive. Now all that was left was to wait.

Their conversation was interrupted by Ben crashing through the door yelling for his dad to come quickly. Fearing the worst he told Mary Jane he would call her back and followed his son outside praying incessantly his girls were alright.

*****

The house was a total loss. Fire had consumed the wooden structure at the end of the street on the cul-de-sac. It was likely not savable even before fire units arrived. Fortunately his neighbors had not been home, but everything they owned including their Christmas presents were a loss. They were still waiting on word if the pets were safe. For Jack and his children the blow was hard. Faulty wiring was suspected but no one was sure.

Jack and his children had rushed to the scene but there was nothing they could do to help. They were pushed back by the fire department staff and watched with horror as the smoke billowed out in every direction. The temperature was barely over freezing yet they couldn't pull themselves away. Side by side the Redman family stood thinking of their friends and neighbors whose Christmas would be lost.

The next morning a pall of disbelief still filled the air. The scent of burnt wood surrounded the whole neighborhood letting no one forget how fragile each day was. To the Redmans it was difficult to imagine having a celebration in their home tonight. No one felt there was anything to celebrate.

Twelve hours later guests began to arrive. One by one the children's friends were dropped off and invited in. Everyone was offered kid-friendly eggnog or warm apple cider. Standing off to the side while Ben, Bea, Betsy, Mike, Mark, Max and Maddie welcomed their friends Jack and Mary Jane silently marveled at how the children were acting as impeccable hosts to this party they had all planned and prepared together. Everything was falling together perfectly. And to top it off it was beginning to snow. Mary Jane noticed first and nodded to Jack. Had it not been for the fire last night, this evening would be flawless.

Bea and Betsy circulated among the guests and invited them to find their places at the table so dinner could be served. The plan would be to share Christmas memories during dinner and then finish the evening with caroling around the fireplace. Slowly the guests found their places. They all looked stunning in their party clothes and the house surrounded them with Christmas joy. The ham, turkey and potatoes filled the room with an incredible aroma. It was time to eat.

Jack had asked Ben in advance if he would say grace before the meal. There was a long hesitation but with much prodding he had finally agreed. So when all were seated and the chatting quieted, Jack nodded to his son who bowed his head to begin.

"Dear Heavenly Father, thank you for this time we have tonight with our family and friends," Ben began, but then stopped momentarily. He opened his eyes and looked across the table at the four empty chairs where his neighbors, the Miller family, should be sitting. Frank, the father, his wife Maria and their two young boys Billy and Braden were obviously missing.

Ben cleared his throat and continued.

"Father we ask you to bless the food we are about to eat this evening to nourish our bodies. We thank you for Mary Jane and her family who have joined with us to prepare this celebration for this special holiday and for each and every one of the people gathered here with us tonight…"

"Wait just a minute," Maddie Mendenhall interrupted. She stood up as others opened their eyes and looked at her small frame standing tall, arms crossed over her chest and voice just a pinch short of angry.

"We can't have this party. We can't thank God for all this stuff either."

Mary Jane rushed to kneel by her daughter's side, trying to soothe and quiet her at the same time. There was no telling what might come out of her mouth next.

"Maddie, it's alright, let Ben finish," she whispered.

"No, it's just not right," Maddie told them. "Where are Billy and Braden tonight? Where are Frank and Maria? Christmas is about love and people. I can't eat mommy's sweet potatoes if the Millers don't have food."

"Honey," Mary Jane tried to console, "we didn't expect the Millers to come tonight. I am sure they are…"

"Where are they mom? Do they have food? They can't have food because they don't even have a house. And all of their Christmas presents are burned up."

"Maddie's right," Max said turning the group's attention to him. "It will be pretty hard to enjoy all of this without them."

One at a time the children and their friends began quiet conversation while Mary Jane and Jack exchanged glances completely unsure what to do next.

"Let's find them," Maddie said, louder than before. "They need all this more than we do."

"Yeah, let's find them," her friend Katie echoed.

Jack knew the family was staying at the church where the Red Cross had set up cots and were trying to make them as comfortable as possible. Of course they had shelter and some food would be provided as the community banded together over the next few days and weeks to help them rebuild their home and their spirits.

Little Maddie Mendenhall had a sixth sense about fixing things, though. In the short time he had known her Jack knew she was a little girl with a plan and it was best not to stand in her way. And it didn't take much coaxing for everyone else in the room to get on board.

"I'll warm up the truck," Jack told the room. "Boys help me load this food into the vehicles. Ladies can you help Mary Jane gather plates and silverware?"

They were on the move.

"Oh and Ben?" Maddie said looking up to her much taller friend. "Sorry about your prayer and stuff. You were doing real good."

Ben reached down to tousle her hair with a grin. Even in this somber situation, Maddie Mendenhall was the life of the party and everyone's life was richer for knowing her.

*****

Frank and Maria were overwhelmed with gratitude as person after person traipsed through the snow each carrying a large container of food. The girls made short order of finding tables and setting up plates in the parlor while the adults arranged the food along the wall so they could keep the meat and potatoes warm. Mike and Mark found Billy and Braden, both under the age of three, and scooped them up in a tight embrace. Somehow they would find a way to make them the guests of honor tonight.

Everyone ate and ate and ate. Still there was plenty of food to leave behind for the Millers. If only they had presents. It was still a week until Christmas so there was still time.

"Hey Dad," Ben said when dinner was over, "you forgot this."

He was walking through the door with Jack's guitar.

"What did you do, son? Go back home?"

"Yeah, it's just a few blocks. I wanted to get the ice cream and then I remembered. There is no fireplace but if we go to the sanctuary we can all sing around the tree. Will the pastor think it's alright?"

"The pastor will be the first one in line," they heard the minister say from somewhere in the middle of the group.

Assembled in a room lit only by the lights on the church's enormous tree, the group sang song after song. They held hands, they laughed, they cried and they loved their time together. This Christmas party was far different than what they planned. In an honest assessment it was better than they planned.

"Hey buddy," Jack asked a few hours later, "where did you put that ice cream?"

Ben's face went slack and he admitted that with the excitement of the change of plans he had left it in the seat of his father's truck.

"No worries, I don't think there is a chance in the world it has melted on a night like this."

Snow was really coming down now. The sidewalk was invisible. No one seemed to mind, though, as they helped bring in dessert. Billy and Braden, it appeared, were huge ice cream fans and there was more than enough for them to have seconds.

"I wish we had presents for you," Maddie told the Miller family when there was a break in the conversation.

Tears filled Maria's eyes and she wasn't able to keep them from falling. She pulled little Maddie into her arms but was unable to formulate words.

"Ummmm, we kinda do," Max said.

What? There were no presents. Max was easily the most soft-spoken of the seven children so when he did have something to say the room easily fell silent.

"It's not much," he said. "It's not anything like what you lost under your tree."

Then he pulled a small flat package out from under his hoodie and handed it to Braden.

"I grabbed this from under our tree before we left."

Braden didn't waste time on formalities. Even at the age of two he knew what to do with wrapping paper. He pulled and tugged until at last it broke free and the whole room was able to see what was inside. It was a tablet of paper. From a distance, it looked like every page was a different neon color. Max stepped up and gently took the tablet from Braden. He pulled it apart into two pieces then handed one half back to Braden and the other to little Billy.

"I'm sure they have some crayons around here somewhere," he said with an almost unnoticeable smile.

To his surprise the room broke out in applause. Max blushed and quickly blended back into the crowd. Mike had already found a crate of crayons and was situating the two boys at a table to color. As the others gathered around the happy little Miller boys to watch they noticed the colored paper wasn't just a normal tablet.

At the top of each page were the pre-printed words "Jack Redman."

"Sorry, man," Max told Jack over his shoulder. "It's all I had to give on short notice. I drew your name. I'll have to get you something else."

Now it was Jack's turn for tears.

"Don't worry about it, Max. You have given me the best present imaginable."

Three days later the Mendenhall children were on a plane back to Tennessee to celebrate Christmas with Andy and his new wife. Jack had invited the Millers to stay with them through the holidays and both Jack and Mary Jane had returned to their regular work schedules. After their thwarted Christmas party everything was beginning to go back to normal although nothing would ever be quite the same.

Lost and found

Getting away from the city had been just what Greg needed. He had never been an official suspect in Kennedy's murder. Never even considered a person of interest but the police certainly did enjoy badgering him with questions. He was tired of seeing his picture on every major news station and newspaper. The community had painted him as the grieving boyfriend. He knew that was better than them turning on him and pointing fingers. He also knew in time other stories would surface and the case would lose its public interest factor. It did seem like it was taking forever, though, for people to move on so it was best that he find a new place to live until that happened.

He told his staff and his family he needed some space for the time being and would be in touch. He was careful about how much money he took with him knowing he could access his accounts remotely from anywhere. Cleaning out his apartment and taking all his money with him would raise suspicions. For now he would just take it one day at a time. He didn't mind relocating – more than once if he had to – but he would not go to prison.

That's how he found himself in Las Vegas. Intending to stay for just a few weeks, a month at the most, he settled into a comfortable suite off the main strip. At the airport he had picked up several books without even taking note of their titles. It had been ages since he had taken time to read something other than technical documents for work. It sounded like euphoria to hole up in his room, sleep, read and take advantage of room service. Maybe he would even take a dip in the pool. No one knew him here and that suited him fine.

The down side was Greg Parker was not used to being a beach bum. Less than 48 hours into his plan and he was bored. One could only sleep, read and eat so much before you were crawling out of your skin. He wasn't ready to socialize so hanging out in the bar or even on the casino floor held little appeal. So stage two of his plan was hatched. Exercise.

As a public relations officer and manager of a fairly decent sized firm, Greg had many responsibilities that kept him busy but it was still reasonable to say his career was primarily an office job. He was fairly good about healthy eating and he was not afraid of taking the stairs over the elevator. His doctor would say he was in good shape, but muscular? Not so much. Since he had nothing else to do while he waited for the public to forget about him, Greg found a gym and embraced twice daily workouts with passion. It wasn't so much he needed it. He was bored.

In a week he had lost 10 pounds. The second week he had gained it back, but it was all muscle. Lifting weights in the past had not interested him. Now it was his life. There was something about the challenge of always trying to lift more weight or do more reps than the day before. Lifting weights fit his personality type. And once he had his headphones in and his music cranked he lost track of time.

In the evenings he did his cardio which was either a long, brisk walk down the Las Vegas strip or running the stairs in the hotel when the weather was bad. He savored his mornings to sleep in – something he rarely got to do when he was absorbed in the corporate life.

One particular morning as he was enjoying a cup of strong black coffee he scanned the newspaper. He spun through the sports section and the editorials before tackling the comics and occasionally he took time to work on the Sudoku. This morning something caught his eye on the folded page with the puzzle. It was a string of investment properties – several high-end condominiums at what he considered a very reasonable price. He could buy and sell them to turn a quick profit or perhaps rent them and collect a monthly profit. He certainly didn't need the income. What he did need was something to do. So he circled the info for easy reference later and headed out for the gym.

*****

Texas was the next stop on Greg's whirlwind trip to forget his past. He was far more fond of big cities than rural suburbs so he sought out and rented an apartment in downtown Houston. For a little bit he toyed with the idea of getting a job. He really didn't want to work for someone else at this point in his life, but he could do something related to financial planning or even commercial budget consulting. All he would have had to do was place an ad on digital media somewhere. No office space was needed. He could use the apartment to work from home or meet people at their offices. Many business transactions took place in restaurants even. There was also the music industry. People were always looking for a keyboard player. The practice hours would keep him busy but he didn't have access to a piano and owning a keyboard would become a hassle to transport each time he decided to move on.

For now he would just ride the wave, he decided. There would be plenty of time to work later should he choose to. For the moment he kept contact with his family telling them he was doing fine. Even though he had been away over a month he wasn't ready to come back quite yet. They told him things were starting to settle down about the case. The police were no closer to solving it and other headlines had forced his story to page three and then eventually out of the press all together. They told him they loved him and to take his time coming back but please to keep in touch.

He wished that was possible but he knew eventually it wouldn't be. It would be safer for him to just fade away.

***

Greg had become a floater. Most of his personal belongings were still in his Kansas apartment. He bought what he needed and rented the rest. Moving from state to state was a more of a vacation now than an escape. He had been in contact with his assistant at the Wichita office and told him he was considering a more permanent leave of absence. His co-worker and friend was more than capable of overseeing daily operations and was happy to stand in. His friend did tell him he was a bit surprised Greg wasn't a little more eager to get back given how hard he had worked to build the business from the ground up. At any rate, everything was in good hands. Greg felt another milestone in his healing process could be checked off his list. It was time to buy something else. A movie theater perhaps? A strip mall? Construction company? Baseball team? Money was fun.

Last week he had moved out of Houston. It was just too hot. He was looking for warm. Texas had moved beyond warm and was just plain scorching. Now he was starting to think about putting down some semi-permanent roots mostly because he missed having a dog. California might be a great fit, something on the coast. The cost of living was atrocious there but at the moment his business mergers and acquisitions were bringing him far more money than he had going out. Why **not** California?

Finding a cottage on the beach had been easy. Oceanfront property was much more abundant than he anticipated. He looked at half a dozen or so before deciding and then picked one with a nice-sized deck and just one large bedroom. He didn't need much room to live, just a little room to breathe.

Greg had sold his car months ago and found his way around using public transportation. This place was a bit more remote, however, so after he picked out his new home he made short order of buying a motorcycle, too. If he decided this wasn't his final destination he could just ship his belongings to his new place. A motorcycle wasn't conducive to moving. For now that didn't matter. He already loved California.

Epilogue

Jenny

It had been almost three years since Jenny Moore's husband Jeff had died in a horrific car accident, just days away from being back home with his family after a year of traveling for his work. So much had happened since then. If she hadn't been keeping a journal she couldn't be sure she would remember it all.

Jenny had gone to college to work in the youth ministry field and while there she followed her father's advice and got that "back up plan" teaching degree. While she had never used it up to this point in her life, she realized she hadn't pursued a career in youth ministry either. She and Jeff had married shortly after they both finished school and shortly after started building their family which not included five children. It had been an excellent ride. Like everything in life, time changes things. It was time to leave the stay-at-home mom role behind.

All of the children would be in school in the fall except for little Abe. Jeff's insurance was more than enough to cover funeral expenses and pay off the mortgage. Of course the children would receive social security benefits. Taking on a full-time job was less about financial necessity and more about making a contribution to the community. The money Jeff's former neighbor and friend had left to their family had been a testament to the spirit of giving back.

Her only regret was she never got a chance to meet Kennedy Andrews. She would forever carry the woman's legacy with her as she carefully decided how to best spend the $1.4 million dollars Kennedy had gifted to Jeff. Plus she had made a number of new friends as a result of her trip to Kansas. Maybe someday she would even get a chance to meet Brenda.

In a few months Jenny Moore would be the new second grade teacher at Willow Wood Elementary School in West Newburg, Vermont. Her oldest, Abigail, would be starting middle school and promised to help her grade papers. Angie and Ava, 10 and 8 respectively, pledged support with the cooking and cleaning and first grader Adalyn was thrilled to have her mom in the same school and just down the hall. Jenny's sister had recommended a friend of hers to care for Abe, the baby. Actually the "baby" was four now. It was all going to be fine.

The recipient of Jeff's inheritance from his friend Kennedy had gone to the church camp back in Kansas where Jenny and Jeff had met all those years ago. The same camp where Jeff had literally saved her life and then the two of them had fallen in love would now be able to afford new cabins, electrical upgrades and an expansion allowing the camp to serve almost twice as many campers. Frank and Ellie Jacobson, the older couple who managed the Bible camp, had been more than grateful to receive the unexpected windfall.

Shortly after the money had allowed the upgrades to begin, Jenny received a call from Ellie Jacobson. The expansion had led them to offer retreats for adults now. She and her husband would be hosting these events during the winter months when the children were not on campus. However, she and her husband were getting a little older she explained and she wanted to know if Jenny would consider coming down each summer and managing the summer part of their program.

Jenny promised to give it some serious consideration and get back with her in the next few days.

From watching the press cover the death of her husband's friend and the outpouring of money that had been dispersed because of it, Jenny had learned Kennedy kept her net worth a secret from all who knew her – including Greg Parker through their courtship – because she believed money changed people. Kennedy didn't want people to see her as an asset because of what she owned but rather because of who she was.

While it was difficult to know how anyone else would handle being a multi-millionaire Jenny knew there must be at least a morsel of truth to what Kennedy felt. At least in her situation, money did change things. It changed her family for the better. A family of seven – suddenly a family of six – had been given an opportunity to serve God in a way that otherwise would not have been possible.

Yes, Jenny Moore would become the new summer camp director at the quaint church camp back in Kansas. A few years later she would leave her job and her home in Vermont, permanently moving her family back to Kansas where they would take over for the retiring Jacobsons. The six of them would live at the camp year round and she hoped Abigail, Angie, Ava, Adalyn and little Abe would someday find the loves of their lives there, too. Then God's divine plan for them would have truly come full circle.

For now she would settle for camp counselors from her two oldest girls, kitchen assistants from Ava and Adalyn and she had to be sure to teach little Abe to swim.

Sadie

Sadie had once again found love at the office. It had happened so many times it was hard for her to think back to a boyfriend she hadn't met at work. Fortunately for all parties involved, this man was single.

Thomas Michael Showalter III, or Tommy as Sadie called him, was a fourth generation businessman. He was relatively young to have a corner office and bring home an almost six-figure income like he did. He had told Sadie on their first date the only downside to all the perks of this job – one most people would die for - was he hated it. He was more of a hunter/fisherman/athletic type of guy he had said. The suits and ties were driving him crazy. His family, however, was insistent he learn the trade and appreciate the benefits. So right now he was appreciating the benefit of having a beautiful secretary named Sadie Nichols.

She wasn't sure why but Sadie always felt more content with her life when there was man in it. She was smart enough to know that usually came with complications, though. Tommy was a little different than most men she had dated and that was refreshing. He was funny, he was intelligent and he was responsible. Even though he didn't really care for the mundane chores of an office job, he worked through the details of it and made the most of his hours spent in the office. And then at 5:00? He was out the door and on to something fun and exciting. Lately he had included her in those plans almost every night. She wasn't complaining.

Most of the time when she had a new love interest she held back on introducing the guy to her son Ronnie. Tommy was a little different in this category, too, because he loved the same things her son did. They fished together. They hiked in the mountains together. Once Tommy and Ronnie even went on an overnight canoe trip together. Over the last year Tommy had truly become a blessing in her life.

Tonight was Friday and Ronnie had plans to see a movie and have a sleepover at his friend's house so Tommy and Sadie spent the evening alone. He had insisted on stopping by with Chinese takeout and she didn't argue. Not having to cook meant one less mess to clean up.

"Hey, you know what?" he asked her while passing her the chopsticks.

"No. What?" she asked back, digging into the bag looking for the rice.

"I never closed the account on Marshall Tedders. I bet I left the file right there on my desk."

"No you didn't," Sadie told him.

"No? Are you sure?"

"Yep. It was the last thing I did before I left today. I saw your note so I shredded it like you asked me to."

"Tedders? Are you sure? I asked you to file Tedders and shred the Keller file."

"No you didn't!" Sadie told him with a jab to the ribs. "You used to be able to pull that stuff on me but I am on to you now, buddy."

Tommy smiled. She was right. When she first stepped into the position she seemed a little flighty – or nervous or something. He had enjoyed teasing her and playing off of her gullibility. In fact it was their playful bantering that drew them together.

He shot her a wink and stabbed at his noodles.

"Do you really want to talk about work?" she asked him then and reached for the stereo remote.

"No, not really."

"Me either," she said. "I mean really. That Arabella is driving me nuts."

"Oh look who's talking about work now," he joked with her. "What has she done now, though? You can't leave me hanging."

"Same song, second verse. She never speaks. She never looks up. It's just click, click, click with those acrylic fingernails. Eight hours a day. I don't even think she gets up to go to the bathroom."

"Are you jealous of her fingernails?"

"Good Lord, no. But it does grate on my nerves."

"Maybe your sweet, gentle personality grates on hers," Tommy countered.

"Wouldn't that be something. Doubt it. I don't even think she would notice if I wasn't in the room," Sadie finished standing up to clear the table.

"I would notice," he said, following her and dropping a soft kiss at the base of her neck while she put their napkins and paper plates into the trash bin.

"Mr. Showalter, if I didn't know better I would say you are trying to sweet talk me to get something you want from me," she said, pretending to be mad.

"Is it working?" he asked, adding a second kiss for a little insurance.

"Absolutely."

Several hours later Sadie stirred and snuggled deeper under the covers next to Tommy who was likely out for the night. She knew she could close her eyes and drift right back into peaceful sleep. And she should. Something about their earlier conversation kept floating through her mind. Now in the absolute silence of the darkened room it didn't want to let go.

Unlike her boyfriend, Sadie really did like her job. The tasks were varied enough so it was rarely mundane. The hours were great and let her spend evenings and weekends with her son. It was kind of nice have the charming, well-dressed, sexy Thomas Michael Showalter III walk through your personal space multiple times a day, too. More than that, though, she felt useful and productive at Seachrest & Waverly. It was just Arabella. She really didn't do anything wrong, she just was like a pesky gnat that wouldn't go away. Maybe one day she would get promoted and could take her noisy fingernails to someone else's office.

The next time Sadie woke it would be to the smell of bacon and eggs. It was difficult to dislike this guy.

"Hey sleepyhead," was his greeting.

"Uggggg," was hers.

"I take it you didn't sleep well?"

"No, I did," she said. "The sleep was great. It was getting up that was the bummer. Plus I think I was dreaming about the office."

Tommy poured her a glass of juice, refilled his own and they sat down to eat.

"Are you really that bothered by Arabella?" he asked her. "I thought you were just playing around last night."

"Do I hate her? No. Do I wish she would get a job somewhere else? Yes."

"Wow, I had no idea."

"Work is never perfect," she told him before taking the last bite of her eggs. "I can deal with her. If I was going to start making changes at the office she would be the least of my worries."

"Really," he said with genuine surprise. "Go on."

"Oh I don't know. Doesn't matter. Can't change things," she said.

"Sure you can. If you have enough money you can change anything."

Money. She did have lots of money these days. Actually it was fascinating how quickly interest accumulates on that kind of money, too. In her own savings account it took years to earn a dime. Kennedy's money was not meant to be spent frivolously, though, for minute changes at work. It needed to be earmarked for a purpose. So far she hadn't figured out what that could be.

"Ha, yeah, money can change the world," she teased him, knowing he had no idea she had enough money to change a small corner of the world.

"What would you change?" he asked her. "I mean if you could. I'm curious."

"First off, I would give everyone Mondays off," she said without hesitation.

"Wow! That would be a novel idea," he said. "Four day work weeks would make a lot of people happy – until they got their paycheck."

"Oh I don't mean we would work less. I just think it would be great if people could spend an extra day with their families. Just giving people an extra day off wouldn't mean there would be less work to do. Employees could choose to take the day off and just get paid for 32 hours, but each person could choose to come in early or leave late Tuesday through Friday if they wanted to."

"You have really thought about this, haven't you?"

"A little I guess. In my experience with Ronnie – especially when he was little – I had to take off work when he had a doctor's appointment or something for school. Those were lost wages and being a single mom is already hard. Having an extra work day off would let me make those appointments and not have to miss work."

"You are on to something there," Tommy told her. "What if people could choose to work three full days of 10 hours each and then two five-hour days? They could have a morning off and later in the week an afternoon off."

"See? Or what about people who like to get up early? We could make it flexible so they could come in at 6 and work until 3. Or those who hate mornings like me could come in at 10 and work until 7. Everyone would be happier because they were still doing 40 hours worth of work, but I think they would feel like the company valued their needs not just as employees but as humans with families."

Tommy and Sadie talked for hours about what could be done to make the office - any office - a more desirable place to be. Some of their ideas were practical like an on-site day care center and others were silly like milk and homemade cookies every day at 3. As long as they were dreaming, anything was possible.

Monday morning came too soon for Sadie. She had truly enjoyed the weekend with Tommy and Ronnie. Once she was up, had taken a hot shower and swallowed a large glass of tea she was ready for the day. She even smiled at the ever-irritating Arabella when she came in that morning. The keys to her computer were already clicking away while Sadie turned on her own computer and waited for it to boot up.

While she waited she tried to imagine what Arabella's life was like outside of this place. Sadie had no idea if she had children, if she was married, if she like sports or even if she could cook. She opened her mouth to ask and then promptly thought better of it and went about the business of starting her day. One thing was different today, though. Arabella didn't return from lunch.

"Hey sport," Sadie said, popping her head into Tommy's office. "Arabella never came back from lunch. Have you heard from her?"

"Oh yeah. I fired her this morning," Tommy said just as calmly as if they were talking about the weather.

"You WHAT?"

"I fired her. You said she was driving you nuts. So I fired her."

A red flag just went up. This guy she thought she knew just fired someone without just cause based off one person's opinion.

"Tommy, she didn't do anything wrong. She worked like a demon around here. How could you fire her?"

"It's just a job, Sadie," he told her. "Don't be mad. She will find another one. I mean, look how many jobs you've had. People like her will find something."

'People like her'? Did he really just say that? Another red flag. It was becoming clear Tommy didn't understand what it was like to live from paycheck to paycheck. She was glad for him that he didn't have to, but she would not stand by and watch while he treated people like they were Monopoly properties that could be bought and sold at will. Too angry to respond Sadie turned and left. Left Tommy's office. Left her office. Left THE office. She would make up the time later – if she decided to come back.

Decisions like this were what had gotten Sadie in trouble in the past. This job had been good to her. Quitting on impulse was not a good idea. Not a good idea. Not a good idea. She kept telling herself that all the way home. She wished there was a way she could fix the Arabella situation and get her job back for her. That is just what she told her friend Ami when she showed up at her house unexpectedly in the middle of the afternoon.

"I mean he fired her!" she told Ami, her voice a little louder than she meant for it to be. "If I were the boss I would NEVER do that."

"It sounds like he was trying to do something nice for you," Ami said. "Right?"

"Yes, but not at the expense of someone else. What if someone in the office doesn't like me? Will I be next? Will he come to me and say 'I am sorry Sadie but you are fired because Larry hates it when you put your lunch bag on the top shelf instead of the bottom one.' I really like him, Ami, but he doesn't value the employees. He says he does, but he doesn't show it."

"Hmmmmmm," Ami said. "I think you might be being a little too hard on him. He treats you great."

"That is true. He does. I am starting to think that is because I offer him some after hours 'services' that he enjoys. Oh Ami, how do I always get myself in these messes."

Ami refilled her friend's coffee and nodded in agreement.

"You do pick some winners for bosses," she told her friend. "What you need is to BE the boss."

"Ha ha! Wouldn't that be a pleasant change."

"Why not, Sadie?"

"Why not what?" Sadie asked.

"Why not be the boss? Buy the building. Buy the company. You can afford it. Then you make the decisions."

"Yeah, but what do I know about running an accounting firm?" Sadie asked her friend.

"You don't have to run it," Ami said. "You can hire someone for that. Or you can just buy the building if you want and start over with new clients."

Once again Sadie knew nothing about business but her friend was right, with enough money you could hire someone to do anything. Every day people hired others to wash their windows, pedicure their feet, cook their food and even wash their cars.

"I could lease part of the space to an in-house day care so single moms would have an easier time of it," Sadie said starting to feel a little more energized with every sentence. One thought led to another one and another one.

"Yes, and you could put in that healthy snack area you are always talking about. Do away with the vending machines and offer fresh fruit and vegetable choices at affordable prices so your employees don't have to leave work to get a healthy lunch."

"Oh Ami, this is craziness."

"It does sound like it, Sadie, but this is a way you could honor that lady who gave you the money. Kami, right?"

"Kennedy," Sadie corrected. "How would buying the building honor Kennedy?"

"Well, her idea behind leaving the seven of you that gift was to enrich your life and make your community a better place to be. Think about how much easier life would have been for you over these last 10 years or so if Ronnie could go to work with you. Other single mothers will be in the same boat. You can create a work space that is employee-friendly."

"Yeah, you know this is funny because whenever we have talked about these ideas before you act like I'm crazy," Sadie said.

"That's because they were great ideas but they took money – money that you didn't have. Now you do. You can buy the building and then rent the office space out but only to people you choose. Put in a fitness center. A yogurt bar. Maybe a same day care center. You could even contract with a taxi or limo service to help those with less than reliable vehicles. All those places could rent space from you, you have created jobs for those businesses and then all the others who work there can benefit from the healthy conveniences your other tenants provide."

It was hard to tell who was more excited – Sadie or Ami.

Sadie knew this would be a way to initiate her flexible hour idea, too. If she did it right her business would be to help others who struggled in the traditional work setting because of small children, lack of transportation, difficulty getting their families to doctor's appointments without getting docked pay. Making these things more accessible and manageable could get more people in the work force. It sounded like a win-win situation.

It would be a lot of work. It would take a lot of time. There would be a significant investment to get it started. Hopefully it would be profitable and the money she made beyond the money she and her son would need to live on she could invest and use the interest to help those like herself who had struggled. She knew there were people who wanted to work rather than accept government assistance but child care costs were greater than their paycheck. If she could help offset child care and transportation costs for people AND make them more readily available at the work place she would have done a good thing.

There would be an added benefit, too. How fun would it be to deliver the eviction notice to one Mr. Thomas Showalter indicating 'people like you' shouldn't have a problem finding a new office. For now she would just spend less and less time with him but someday soon his corner office would be hers.

Two and a half years later, Spaces for All Faces opened its doors for the first time with eight businesses plus a day care center, a mini gym, a no-carb snack bar, a dental office, a branch banking location and two health friendly restaurants.

Oh Kennedy, Sadie thought to herself as the Chamber of Commerce was setting up for the traditional ceremonial ribbon cutting. I hope you and Mom are proud of me because I am exhausted. Good things come to those who wait, though, and her company was providing ample opportunities and affordable leased spaces for many in her community who would otherwise be unemployed.

Paul

Even though he had almost no responsibilities in Arkansas except taking care of his dog who was with him on the trip to Kansas City, Paul still had not intended on staying so long in Kansas to meet with J.T. Looking back on that first meeting it was hard to believe he had had to work so hard to convince J.T. to partner with him. Now J.T. had become one of his best friends and together they were making a difference.

In the beginning their project started small. Deciding they wanted to remain anonymous the two of them each took $5,000 in $100 bills and sat down with a phone book, a stack of envelopes and 100 stamps. Starting with the As they meticulously marked every 50th name and sent that resident a crisp $100 bill with this note:

> You are a blessing from God. You can be a blessing to someone else, too. Please pass this on to someone in need.

For a short time the anonymous gifters made the news. People were both excited and a little uncomfortable getting unexpected letters. Paul discovered he was a little uncomfortable, too. He didn't want any recognition. He didn't need to know how they chose to regift their money, or even if they did. What did seem broken in their early system of sharing their wealth was it felt a little **too** random. It was kind of a shot in the dark hit and miss type of thing.

Many phone calls later and a visit from J.T. to his Arkansas home resulted in hours of brainstorming. What if they sent the money out $1,000 at a time? Maybe people would think through their choices for using it better if it was a bigger investment. It took J.T. to remind him they didn't want to be judgmental either. No matter how the recipients spent the money it would benefit someone in one way or another.

"You were right," Paul told J.T. one day. "Donating it to one big cause would certainly be easier."

"Easy isn't always best," J.T. told him mirroring his words from months ago.

It would take months of planning and legal consultations to set up the foundation they had mutually decided to call the Kennedy Caper. It was based on developing families of poverty. Classes on parenting skills, budgeting and learning to be self-sufficient were offered weekly. The only requirement was families had to attend together. Paul and J.T. had worked tirelessly to seek out volunteer opportunities for the families to engage in together hoping to model good citizenship skills for the families – especially the children. Each family in turn earned a monthly stipend as long as they agreed to find steady work and come to classes regularly.

To Paul it still sounded a little judgmental but J.T. had convinced him it was a way to insure Kennedy's lofty gift was not spent with frivolity. Together they were building a program to help low- or no-income families develop skills and grow productive young citizens. Based in Kansas City for now it was a work in progress with opportunities to expand to other cities one step at a time.

J.T.

It had been five years since the inception of the Kennedy Caper project when J.T. got the news his friend Paul Odell had died peacefully in his sleep. He was 79.

It was hard to believe the depth of the hole he felt in his heart over someone he had known for such a short time. Paul's attorney had called with the news on a cold and blustery January afternoon. Paul had left plans for his assets to be sold with the funds to be placed into the corporation he and J.T. had created with Kennedy's money. There was just the matter of his dog, the lawyer said. Would he be willing to care for him?

Paul had been so right. A person's self-worth has nothing to do with the way that you look. It is all about the way that you feel. His body was no longer the stuff that made women drool. His athletic talents were no longer top quality. His financial portfolio was no longer something others envied. What was true, however, was he was able to make a difference in other people's lives by just being himself - regular old J.T. O'Malley.

Traveling to Arkansas one last time to pay his respects was bittersweet. At his request Paul was cremated and a small graveside service was held as a final tribute to his life. The attorney had made all of the arrangements with the exception of one thing. J.T. had asked if he could add an epitaph to the headstone. He would, of course, pay for it.

As a community of mourners huddled together to keep warm the final blessings and prayers were offered under a makeshift shelter – a portable canopy set up to keep the giant snowflakes off those gathered to say goodbye to their friend and neighbor. One by one the people pulled their coats tighter to ward off the frigid icy weather and headed back to their cars. J.T. was he last to leave.

"I'll try to make you proud, my friend. Rest in peace."

Then pulling his own coat tighter to shield his neck and ears he bent down to pick up Paul's beloved dog Spice who had been obediently waiting at the other end of his leash. J.T. turned back one last time. Even though he knew his friend was not literally there in the cemetery it was difficult for him to leave him behind. He did take small comfort from what was etched into the stone.

Paul Odell

January 8, 1940 – January 29, 2019
"Don't cry because it's over. Smile because it happened."

-Dr. Seuss

Mary Jane

Even if she could see into the future, five years ago Mary Jane would have never believed she would be living in Nebraska, raising her kids on her own and working as a surgical nurse. Her life before meeting Jack and his children was something that was almost hard to imagine. Andy had predictably moved on with his life. If he was upset about losing his wife and children he didn't show it.

The children loved the schools here – all four of them. They had made friends and found activities both in and out of school that they loved. Mike was enrolled in college studying architecture and Mark was working full-time at a home improvement store learning a trade. Max was just beginning to drive and Maddie? Well Maddie was just Maddie. As a mom she was bursting with pride over all of their successes.

Jack's twin girls had become somewhat of an extension to her family as well. Now about to graduate from high school, Bea and Betsy had adopted her daughter as a sister and watched over little Maddie at every turn. Jack's son Ben had gone to the University of Kansas on a tennis scholarship and kept promising to get them basketball tickets. So far that hadn't happened. The important thing was he was happy and loving college in his yet-to-be determined major.

Together the nine of them were a solid team. The seven children had come to think of each other almost like cousins even though, of course, there was no blood relation. As they started to grow up, leave home and spread out across the country they always came back together for the holidays and a special Christmas party not unlike the first one they planned together years ago.

Mary Jane knew she could have never planned her life and had it work out this well. God had provided for them and walked with them every step of the way through this mid-life transition.

As for her friend Jack? She couldn't have found a better companion if she had planned it herself. When their paths accidentally crossed and Kennedy had unknowingly set the stage for them to become friends, her life had forever been changed for the better.

Together Mary Jane and Jack had kept in contact with the others from that fateful failed wedding day – although mostly Jenny and Paul. The whole Mendenhall-Redman family had been to visit Jenny at the Kansas Bible camp and made her promise to come visit them in Nebraska when her life settled down. And Paul. It was difficult to hear of his passing but inspiring to learn of his joint venture with J.T. and to know J.T. would continue on with the wonderful work they had started together.

"Do you think we should do something together?" Jack had asked her one day as they enjoyed a lazy Saturday at the pool.

"Together? Nope. I can't stand hanging out with you," she told him without even cracking a smile. Sarcasm had become her coping mechanism over the years. With Jack, though, it was just fun to be silly.

"Good to know," he told her with an equally serious tone. "I guess you can call a cab to get home then."

This earned him an unexpected splash of water in the face and the war was on. Jack wasted no time pulling her legs down into the pool and pressing her head under water. Getting her hair wet was the impetus for Mary Jane to leap forward and tackle him until he, too, was under water. Like two crazy teenagers they sparred back for and forth for a few minutes until they both popped back to the surface laughing and gasping for breath.

"You are such a smartass," she told him, crawling back out of the pool and perching once again on the edge.

"Me? Me a smartass? You started it," he said.

"Hmmmmmmm...oh yeah." With this came a sly grin. He loved that smile.

"Before you almost drowned me a few minutes ago I was asking if you thought we could do something together. I meant something big. Bigger than the two of us," he told her, turning serious. "Something with the money Kennedy left us. Something like J.T. and Paul."

"You may be on to something there," she said. "It has just been sitting in the bank, waiting for just the right project. You know, I kind of feel like once I spend it Kennedy's memory won't be alive any more. Does that make any sense at all?"

"Kind of," he said. "We are just holding the money for now waiting for the perfect mission to come along."

"If we wait too much longer we will have to leave a plan for it when WE die," she said. She was joking but there was some truth to it.

Thirty minutes and a little more sunscreen later they still weren't any closer to a solid strategy for getting the unforeseen windfall to a worthy cause.

"What do you think ever happened to her fiancée?" Mary Jane asked.

"The last I heard he had sold his company and moved out of town," Jack told her. "Can you even imagine how difficult all that would have been? First her death and so close to their wedding. Plus I don't think they ever figured out what really happened."

Mary Jane couldn't imagine. She couldn't even imagine life without Jack but she stopped short of telling him so.

"Tell me again how you knew her back then," Mary Jane asked.

"We sang together in a show choir. She was so full of energy and was so musically talented. Everyone knew she would make the cut long before the audition."

"I kind of remember that, too," Mary Jane said. "When she would babysit my little sisters and me she was always making up silly songs. We would dress up and act out the words. It was great fun."

"Maybe we could donate the money to things she loved. Music? Accounting? What else?"

"Great idea, Mary Jane," he told her. "But how do you effectively donate money to music? Maybe music education?"

"What about a scholarship?" Mary Jane said with a sudden panacea.

"A three-million dollar scholarship?" he asked with a hint of that smartass snarkiness she had accused him of earlier.

"Sure. Why not?" she returned once again pushing him into the water. That guy.

It had taken some time to work out the details. Neither of them knew the first thing about how to set up a scholarship program. There were so many details and questions. Would the scholarships just go to Kansas residents? Did they have to be music or math majors to apply? How would people know about the scholarships? How would the funds be administered? Who would administer the account?

After consulting several experts they had made some tough decisions. The plan was to use only the annual interest. They would start with 30 scholarships of $10,000 each and if the recipients maintained a 3.0 or better GPA they would automatically earn $10,000 for the next year. For a nominal fee they were able to hire a firm to manage the details. It sounded like a solid plan and the Kennedy Andrews Memorial Scholarship program was hatched.

Only one detail remained. In the event Mary Jane would die first, Jack would be the executor of the trust. Should Jack die first Mary Jane would become the soul executor. In the highly unlikely event they would die simultaneously it was recommended they

select a contingent beneficiary to fulfill
the role. Being the youngest among them and
undoubtedly the one to live the longest it
was decided: Miss Madeline Marcella
Mendenhall. Lord help us all!

Jack

Jack Redman had it all. His children were grown now and had been blessed with spouses and children of their own. Being a grandpa, he had been told, was an even greater gift than having children. He couldn't remember who had told him that but certainly it was true. He couldn't remember a lot of things these days. Getting old was not for the feeble.

As with most rites of passage in life, his retirement from the post office was something he both dreaded and anticipated. Oh to have the luxury of not setting an alarm. And oh how frightening to have 24 hours of daily free time. It had been ages since there had been nothing to do. There was always something.

He supposed he would take a few golf lessons. There would be time for that later, though, as he and his wife were planning to spend a few weeks in Hawaii before they settled into their new unemployed lifestyle. Both were still in good health and they wanted to see parts of the world they hadn't yet explored before their bodies started to give out and they needed to spend vacation money on knee and hip replacements.

Daily he counted his blessings and Kennedy Andrews was at the top of his list. Yes, she had left him a million dollars and some change, but that was not the reason. Through her connections and a chance meeting after her death he had met five new lifelong friends – Jenny Moore, Sadie Nichols, J.T. O'Malley, the late Paul Odell and the love of his life, Mary Jane Mendenhall-Redman.

Shane – and Brenda

To his surprise Shane found he missed Brenda when she returned to Ohio. He hadn't been on a date in years and it was nice to be in the presence of a woman even if it was just for a few hours. Aside from their oriental adventure that night, there had been the short walks to Mac's for ice cream. What he missed most, he discovered, was wondering if the next guest through the coffee house door would be her. He so hated it when a woman got under his skin.

Not prone to wallow in "what could have beens" he put those thoughts aside and returned to the kitchen to experiment with a new pasta sauce. He was looking for something between a marinara and an alfredo. Cream and tomato sauce were an obvious beginning. Basil, oregano and rosemary were the usual players. He added, stirred and tasted. A touch more cream and then some parmesan cheese – a lot of cheese – and one more taste. It needed salt and something else. Heat? He tossed in a few more herbs and a chopped jalapeno then left it to simmer while he answered the phone in his office.

"Eddie's. How can I help you?" he asked.

"Hey Bobby Flay!" was the response on the other end of the line. Brenda?

"It's me. Brenda. What's the soup of the day?" she wanted to know, as if it mattered half a country away.

Shane wasn't sure what to say. Could she read his mind and know he had been thinking about her? Surely she wasn't still in town. Or back in town.

"Soup's a little overrated today. Leftover chicken and something. Noodles maybe? Can't tell. Dumplings? I would suggest the Pasta a la Brenda. It's extremely sweet and a little spicy."

"You don't say," she told him. Funny guy.

"Are you back in Oregon? Didn't you just leave a few days ago? Can't get enough of good old Sherwood, huh?" he teased.

"Oh no, nothing like that," she said with a noticeable sigh. "I am definitely back in Toledo. I was wondering, though, if you could do me a favor."

"No can do," Shane said. "I only do favors on the 32nd of every month. Today is just the 9th."

"Well, OK then. Thanks anyway," she said pretending to end the call.

"Wait! Errrr, I mean hang on. Of course I can do you a favor. What do you need?" If it meant he might see her again he would take advantage of helping her out.

"Well, I was just wondering. How is your lasagna?"

Lasagna wasn't on his menu.

"It's damn good. Who's asking?" he said.

"You know my friend Rose Wilson that I talked about while I was there?"

He did.

"Yes, sure. Is she planning an Italian party out there at the Meadows?"

Brenda went on to explain what Rose had said about the food selection at the manor. How they always gave them entrée choices but they leaned a little toward the bland and boring side. The closest they got to Italian was a haphazard meatball-less spaghetti.

"I was just wondering if you could whip up a little tray of lasagna and deliver to her out there. It would so make her day. I know it is a lot to ask and I would pay you for your time and all that. You just name the price."

How about a second date with me? You could stay over and I'd cook you breakfast in the morning. Of course that is not what came out of his mouth, but it was a very pleasant thought.

"I can do that," is what he did say. "Lasagna is not on the menu so I would need to pick up a few things. Do you want it out there today?"

"Oh heavens no. Any time would be just fine. It would be a lovely surprise for her I think. There is so little I can do from here and she has always been there for me – kind of like a grandmother."

"Consider it done," he told her. Shane's mind was still processing the fact that he now inadvertently had her phone number.

"How much should I send you?" Brenda wanted to know. "Will a check be OK or do you want a credit card number?"

"A check is fine. Let's say about $500. Will that work?" he asked putting as much business-like tone in his voice as possible hoping she would appreciate his sense of humor.

"That is fine. For that price, though, you better include a salad and a bottle of wine. No, a case of wine," she told him seeing right through his funny façade.

"How 'bout we settle for installment payments? The next time you are in Sherwood you see a movie with me. Then we go bowling. Then a day at the beach. After about 10 dates your bill should be paid in full."

"Aren't you funny," Brenda told him and laughed. "How about you send me a bill?"

Grateful they had had a nice conversation, he agreed to send her a bill, even though he knew he never would. They hung up with the promise of talking soon.

Back in the kitchen he poured a ladle of his new sauce onto a heap of linguini and walked the plate out into the dining room to give it a try. Yikes! Way too spicy! He needed to rethink that sauce. For now, though, there wasn't time. He needed to research lasagna recipes.

*****

Mrs. Wilson never got to taste his award-winning lasagna. Shane made the delivery himself the next afternoon – just five days after Brenda Davis had left town. Brenda Davis. There was something so familiar about that name but he couldn't place it.

"I'm sorry, Shane," the receptionist told him when he told her he had a delivery. "Rose Wilson is dead."

****

Oddly enough Rose's death wasn't the most surprising thing he found out that day.

It seems a lady named Brenda Davis, the office staff at the manor told him, had set up a fund to upgrade Rose Wilson's level of care. She was to be moved to a first-class suite with all the amenities the very next morning.

Shane learned the check she wrote was enough to cover her costs for the next 20 years. Since it was likely she would not outlive the money, the remaining balance was to be gifted to Shane Walker, owner of Eddie's Coffee Emporium, to be used as he saw fit.

"We haven't had to use a penny of it, though," the staff director told him. "She passed away before we could move her. You might want to sit down for this next part, though," he said.

"How much?" Shane asked.

"$1.4 million."

The lasagna hit the floor.

Greg

Greg Parker had changed his name just before he bought the first condo in Las Vegas. He had truly wanted to just disappear and remain anonymous. He was a good guy that had done some really dumb things. While it broke his heart to sever his relationships with his family – especially his dad and sister who had been a rock for him growing up – he knew it was the only way to be sure he wouldn't be charged for the murder of Kennedy Andrews. He was guilty but couldn't – wouldn't – go to prison.

A few business connections later and he had a new identity. A new life. First in Las Vegas, then in Houston he had transformed himself into someone different. He had a new name, a new muscular body and had let his hair grow longer, down to his collar, and didn't try to tame the natural dark wavy curls that disappeared when he kept it cut short. In California he had thrown out his contact lenses opting for dark-rimmed glasses instead and by the time he landed in Sherwood, Oregon, and bought Eddie's Coffee Emporium, he was a totally different man – both physically in appearance and legally by name.

Brenda Davis was the seventh friend of his murdered fiancée Kennedy Andrews. The one who never made it to the wedding. The one who unknowingly just gave him $1.4 million dollars of the secret that made Greg Parker turned Shane Walker angry enough to kill.